SHATTER

Also by C. S. Doraga

RISE OF THE EMPRESS
Defy

SHATTER

Book Two in the Rise of the Empress Series

C. S. Doraga

Dragon's Nest Books

Content/Trigger Warning

This book contains physical violence, moments of peril, and images that may be disturbing to some readers. It also contains depictions of PTSD/PTSI, panic attacks, and thoughts and discussions of suicide. There are also discussions of genocide. Please, read with care and make sure it is safe for you to do so before embarking on this journey.

To all the readers who ensure that there are book twos.
I promise this ends well.

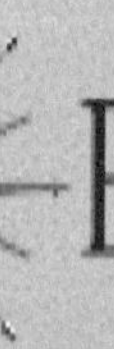

The Mount
Imperial Capital
Hidden Gems
Toryin Village
Agicae Mountains
ERIDIAN EMPIRE

Degeraturi Mountains
Esuni Desert
Legend
Mountains
Dormant Volcano
Active Volcano
Plateau
Hills
Desert
Canyonlands
Lake
Water
Forest
Moderately Dense Forest
Thick Forest
Evergreen Forest
Plains
Marshland
River
Coral Reef/Keys

Pronunciation Guide

Cast:

Redrinna:	REH-dree-nah
Xandrin:	ZAN-drin
Brion:	BREE-awn
Reyna:	RAY-nah
Timothon:	ti-MUH-thawn
Osiris:	oh-SY-ris
Tak:	tahk
Amaris:	ah-MAH-ris
Kyvo:	KEE-voh
Mika:	MEE-kah
Shappa:	SHAH-pah
Astra:	A-shtrah
Takota:	dah-KOH-dah
Chumani:	choo-MAH-nee
Chatan:	chah-DAHN
Wicasa:	wee-CHAH-shah
Ohanzi:	oh-GHAHN-zee

Talutah: duh-LOO-dah

Kangee: KAHN-ghay

Hanska: HAHN-shkah

Ehawee: ay-HAH-wee

Macha: MAH-chah

Mato: mah-DOH

Ioana: ai-oh-AH-nah

Mistra: MIS-trah

Renoan: reh-NOH-un

Matte: MUH-tay

Places:

Oriana: oh-REE-ah-nah

Agicae: A-ji-kay

Eridia: e-RI-dee-uh

Degeraturi: deh-JAIR-ah-too-ri

Manon: MAN-ahn

Other:

Avarian: ah-VAHR-ee-an

Torijin: TOH-ree-jin

Wotitakuye: woh-dee-dah-koo-yea

Hikarijin: hee-KAH-ree-jin

Sorajin: soh-RAH-jin

Umijin: oo-MEE-jin

Shinrinjin: sheen-REEN-jin

Hamajin: hah-MAH-jin

Dohbutsujin: doh-BOO-tsoo-jin

Sunajin:	soo-NAH-jin
Korijin:	koh-REE-jin
Kaenjin:	kah-EHN-jin
Kinzokujin:	keen-ZOH-koo-jin
Torijin:	toh-REE-jin
Kokorojin:	koh-KOH-roh-jin

The Story Thus Far...

After her parents tossed her in a cave and left her to die, Imperial Princess Redrinna took advantage of the situation to flee the confines of imperial life, but a creature named the Dragon Slayer hunted her and her new friend, a dragon named Xandrin, claiming that it had come to take her to 'Father.'

They were rescued by the ghost of Timothon, her uncle and a past member of the Dragon Kin—a group of humans and dragons sworn to protect the continent—who told her the shocking truth about the previous Dragon Kin and the creation of the Eridian Empire. She was horrified but decided, with Xandrin's encouragement, to fight to get stronger and find the lost Dragon Gems.

She succeeded, even managing to find someone else who'd been marked by a gem—a young man named Tak—but her gem didn't bond to her. For one month, she desperately fought to prove her worth but to no avail. In a final attempt to prove herself, Redrinna and Xandrin returned to the Imperial City to steal much-needed information from her father.

Instead, she learned her best friend, Lady Cel Tradat, was actually Reyna, an ally of the Dragon Kin's enemy: Osiris. Then, she was dragged before Osiris himself, where he offered to take her kingdom in exchange for one thing: herself.

When she rejected him, he let her go on the condition that if she failed to escape, she would belong to him. Xandrin and her gem ensured that she evaded his grasp.

The gem finally bonded to her, and she looked to the future with her head high, determined to put an end to Osiris...

Chapter One

Today was the day Redrinna was going to use her fire magic without almost blowing herself up. She was determined to do it this time. Closing her eyes against the tug of the wind, she raised both hands—palms down—to waist height, holding them perpendicular to her body. She snuck a glance at the book she'd been studying, adjusting her stance a smidge to be more in line with the one in the picture. Then she took a deep breath, preparing for the next steps.

For the last week, she'd been practicing this set of stances, something she'd uncovered while scouring the library for help mastering her magic. The techniques in question hailed from various regions on the Oriana continent (according to the book, at least), and if the book was right, they were some of the best when it came to magical combat.

And after what had happened in the Imperial City, and with Xandrin nearly dying to protect her not quite a month ago, learning to protect herself was one of her top priorities.

Redrinna took a steadying breath, redirecting her focus to what she was going to attempt. So far, she could get through the entire set if she went slow and only did the stances. The second she tried adding magic, it blew up in her face. Literally. She'd almost set her hair on fire once, and from then on, she'd begun wrestling it back into a decent ponytail before practicing. She wasn't anywhere near being good at that, especially when she painstakingly remembered the care her old guardian—Captain Brion—had taken when he'd done her hair almost every day while she'd lived in the palace. Compared to him, her skills were practically non-existent, but she was improving.

Squeezing her eyes shut, she shook her head hard enough she hit herself in the face with the end of her ponytail. Right now, she needed to focus more on the pulse of the earth's spirit beneath her feet and less on mundane things like whether she could do her own hair.

Stepping forward, Redrinna moved into the first stance, fire crackling to life between her palms. A shudder swept up her back. The memory of the fight on the mountainside, of her using fire magic—throwing it, making it explode out of the ground—flashed through her mind. If things had been different, if she hadn't been in a war with people's lives on the line, there was absolutely no way she would ever, *ever,* use her magic. She hated it.

All at once, the fire between her hands went out. Blinking a couple times, she stared at them for a moment before sighing and straightening. Not for the first time, she'd hesitated too long between stances and broken the flow of energy, subsequently putting out her fire. Rapping her knuckles against the side of her head, she returned to the resting stance.

All she had to do was stay focused. It wasn't that difficult.

Closing her eyes, Redrinna took a calming breath before shifting back into the first stance. Fire sizzled to life between her palms right before she dipped into the next. As she moved her hand to her other side, the fire whipped around her. Then she hit the third stance before moving to the fourth, the fire growing stronger, roaring louder with each movement. She braced herself for the fifth stance, the one where she was supposed to release the fire and shoot it out in front of her.

All at once, Reyna's face flashed through her mind like a lightning bolt, dark eyes vivid enough to nearly stop her heart. Until the day Redrinna had returned to the city, they'd been friends. Then—the scene etched itself in front of her eyes for the thousandth time—she'd pushed her used-to-be friend off a cliff, abandoning her in a second for Xandrin.

In a heartbeat, she'd not only ended a friendship, Redrinna had snuffed out a life.

The scene melted like wax at the mercy of hot flame, vanishing almost as quickly as it had appeared, but she'd hesitated between the stances yet again. Realizing her mistake, she rushed into the final stance. The flames blasted out in a ball instead of a stream. Not again! Throwing her arms up in front of her face, she winced at the heat as it threw her back, sending her rolling in a couple painful somersaults before she managed to catch herself on her knees.

Once the shock had passed, Redrinna glanced herself over, relieved to find nothing more than a few scrapes. Still, everything stung.

Sighing, she sat back, wincing as her stomach clenched, a reminder she hadn't eaten breakfast yet that morning. She massaged it until it quieted down, thinking through the stances and mentally kicking herself for hesitating yet again. She'd been so close; it was the closest she'd ever gotten to doing it right. It'd be much easier if the past would stay in the past.

That was a lot closer than before. You'll have it before much longer.

"I did get close," she admitted, glancing down at the large, red Dragon Gem hanging from her neck. It hadn't been very long since it'd hung cold and dormant, making her desperate enough to do something completely insane. Redrinna wasn't mad at the gem for the way things had played out, but she was terrified of what she'd been willing to do and how much she'd been willing to sacrifice in order to prove herself to be something she wasn't sure she actually was.

The gem's ever-present light pulsed a little stronger as it spoke again. *Please don't beat yourself up. Considering the material you're studying, and the fact you have to study it by yourself, your progress is remarkable. Clearly you have a talent for it. Don't take that for granted.*

Redrinna almost sighed again, but managed to hold it in. Despite the gem's encouragement, she couldn't help but feel she should be able to do it already. This was the most basic set of stances. It shouldn't be this difficult.

A bird zipped past her head, its wingbeats thrumming in her ears. She glanced after it, grimacing as she realized the sun had already crested the mountain peaks. It was late enough that if she stayed out here any longer, the others would notice she wasn't there and wonder why. Despite that, she found herself pausing to enjoy the view, admiring the green forests draping the steep slopes like a cloak, and the thin, glittering trickles of streams weaving in and out of sight.

Since she was training with fire magic, Redrinna had elected to find a high cliff on the Mount, one rocky and barren of life where just breathing the air made her shiver. The sun had risen enough that its rays were peeling away the thick layers of mist that cloaked the Agicae Mountains every morning, warming the air and chasing away the morning chill. A few lilting strains of birdsong still floated on the breeze, and for a moment, Redrinna could forget all the worries and burdens clinging to her skin like leeches, threatening to suck the very life out of her.

Then, that moment ended, and the sigh she'd been restraining passed through her lips. If she didn't hurry back inside, Timothon would start asking questions she'd rather not have to answer. If he knew how often she bolted awake from nightmares she couldn't remember and then forced the panic away by scaling the mountain and practicing with her magic so hard, sometimes she threw up, he'd try to stop her.

However, after what had happened—after what she'd done—it was best if she fought through this on her own.

After all, if Redrinna hadn't been so negligent, the people of the Imperial City might not have had to die, or at least, not the way they had. If she'd been stronger, she might've been able to do more than cower and flee when she'd come face to face with Osiris himself. If she'd been able to actually fight, her friend wouldn't have been almost killed trying to help her escape.

So, in that sense, the sleepless nights and near constant exhaustion were fitting. She'd messed up big, so the consequence she deserved had to be just as huge.

Redrinna started to push herself up before her ankle seized with pain, nearly dumping her back on the ground. Wincing, she hopped off the ankle in question, scowling at the nasty cut running across her skin, the garish purple of a bruise already manifesting around it. She must've smacked a rock or something when the fireball had knocked her back. Fortunately, it didn't seem too serious, so she would just have to wrap it once she made it back inside the Mount.

Limping now, she retrieved her boots and brushed pebbles and dirt off her feet before slipping them on. Then she grabbed her book and headed down the Mount at a much slower pace than she liked. With luck, no one else was awake quite yet, or, at the very least, they hadn't been awake long enough to worry about her.

⁂

Tak was almost out of fingers. He glanced over his digits, noting the little cuts on the tips of nearly all of them. Hopefully, he and Redrinna would soon be finished with this experiment of hers, otherwise he was going to have no unmarred fingers left.

After a moment longer, he left his room, heading straight for the library. When he arrived, he peeked in, not entering until he spied Redrinna sitting cross-legged on a table she'd dragged from the corner, framed by the wall of windows behind her as she frowned at one of her hands. Dark mountain peaks blocked out most of the early morning sky framed in those windows, but what little he could see of it was a soft blue. Some sunlight slanted through the glass, throwing long shadows across the room, leaving most of the shelves and books in deep shade, but a few streams of the morning light touched Redrinna's hair, almost making it seem like she wore a crown of flame.

The unnatural shade of her hair made him recall his own, peculiar shade, and he had to forcibly stop himself from touching it. His aunt had told him it'd been a dark, earthy brown when he'd been born, but it'd changed to this foresty, black-ish green around the time he turned five. At the time, people in his village had said he'd been cursed by spirits or demons, like one of his ancestors had, but he knew now that he and his ancestor had both simply been marked by one of the Dragon Gems.

Even though it'd been a couple months since he'd lived there, a shudder shook him at the memory of that place. Quickly, he shoved it away before unwanted memories could settle on his shoulders like crows perching on iron gates.

Redrinna glanced up then, almost smiling when she saw him, but his gaze immediately flicked away in embarrassment. Hopefully she hadn't noticed him staring.

"Good morning," she said, her partial smile fading as her attention returned to her hands.

"Morning," Tak said, stopping a short distance away, realizing a second later he was partially in the shadow of a bookshelf. "How's your experiment going?"

"Fascinatingly," she said, dropping her hands so she could write something on the piece of paper next to her. "Look."

He stepped closer as she extended her hands. Aside from a few calluses, there wasn't much to see.

"Once again, the cut from two days ago is gone." She leaned forward and snatched his hands, the intensity with which she studied them making him a little uncomfortable. "But your first cut from five days ago? Mostly gone, but still healing. Isn't that strange?"

"Your cuts have all healed faster than mine." He shrugged, hiding his hands once she'd released him. Perhaps Redrinna's dad had been telling the truth about how her enormous fall couldn't have killed her. If that was the case, then it confirmed in his mind that her parents hadn't actually been trying to murder her.

Frowning, Redrinna hopped off the table, grabbing a loaf of bread Tak hadn't noticed. The crust crackled as she tore it in half, the sound reminding him he hadn't eaten yet. Eagerly, he took the half she held out to him, uttering a quiet 'thank you.' All the food he'd been given here had tasted better than anything he'd had in a long time, better than anything he'd been able to make for himself ever since... Never mind.

"I guess my dad was right after all," Redrinna said, leaning against the table. "According to all the research we've done, small cuts like these would take anywhere from three to seven days to heal completely, and yours fall well into that average so far. None of mine have though."

Tak didn't know what to say, so he kept quiet.

"However, none of that seems to explain what's going on. Am I just weird?" she muttered. Then, abruptly, "Let's go ask Timothon. He's met more people than us, so maybe he'd have a better idea of what's happening."

He nodded when she glanced at him, and she pushed off the table, heading for the exit. After a moment's hesitation, he followed, noting that today, all of the sudden, she walked with a faint limp. However, she'd probably just get mad if he said anything, so he kept it to himself.

As he trailed after her, Tak couldn't shake the nagging feeling that he didn't belong here, doing this. He shouldn't have been with the Imperial Princess, talking to her like they were friends or eating at the same table. A gem shouldn't be sending him dreams, asking for him, over and over again—not after the life he'd lived.

Regardless, that didn't stop him from wanting all those things.

They arrived in the kitchen a minute or so later, and as expected, Timothon was there, beating lumpy dough into submission. Tak was convinced this was the man's favorite place.

"What are you two up to now?" the man asked as they trotted in, making Tak feel five again.

It'd been a long, long time since he'd felt like a kid.

"I wanted to ask you something," Redrinna said as she sat on one of the stools at the table where the red-haired man worked. Tak hesitantly sat on the stool next to her.

"Do you now? What makes you think I have answers?" The man pushed his dough to the side as he cocked his head.

"You've seen more of the world than me," she said, propping her elbows on the table and resting her chin in her hands. "And you've met more people. Tak and I can only get so far with our experiment with the resources we have."

"Experiment? Is that what you've been doing with my bread?"

"Not exactly. We've been testing the rate at which small cuts heal, and we try to eat about the same amount of food so we get the same amount of energy. So the test is more accurate."

"You're what?" Timothon's brow furrowed, a concerned look creeping onto his face.

After a moment, Redrinna held up her hands. Tak did the same since there wasn't much to see on her hands.

"You've...been cutting your fingers? Do I need to point out the questionable nature of this experiment?"

Tak glanced at Redrinna as she hesitated. Now that he thought about it, he guessed it was a bit...unusual what they were doing.

"It's not with the intent to harm. Just science."

Timothon sighed, shaking his head. "What was it you wanted to ask me?"

"Have you ever met someone whose injuries heal faster than normal? Like a tiny cut healing in about a day instead of a week, faster than normal?"

The man frowned, his thinking expression similar to Redrinna's,

Tak noted. "Not that I know of. Are you saying yours do?"

She nodded, grabbing Tak's hand again. "See? This cut here? It should be fairly similar to this one on my hand, but they're not, even though they were made at the same time."

The man studied both their hands for a long minute. "I see... But are you making sure you take every factor into account?"

"Every factor?"

"Like, is there a difference between the rate of time at which men heal versus women? Or how your diet as a child affects your body's ability to heal as you get older? You also said you guys are trying to eat the same amount of food, but men do tend to need more food than women do, you know. Because they tend to be a bit bigger and all that."

Redrinna frowned at her hand again while reaching up and catching hold of her mother's necklace.

"On top of that, Tak wasn't very healthy when he first came here," Timothon continued, a frown on his face. "But now that he is, he's been growing."

Tak's gaze fell to the table as he frowned. Had he?

"But you haven't, and that might be affecting things." Timothon shrugged in an almost apologetic way. "I'd love to be of some help, but I don't know the answers to any of those questions, and it's hard to give you a definitive answer without them. Sorry."

Redrinna tapped her fingers against her chin and didn't speak. After nearly an entire minute, she rose and left without a word.

Even though she hadn't said anything, Tak was pretty sure she was going to find Xandrin. For a moment, he debated following, but something about seeing her and the dragon together always made him...he didn't know...sad? Or maybe it was jealous? Whatever the emotion was, it wasn't one he enjoyed or was comfortable having inside him.

"You aren't going to follow?" Timothon asked, pausing in his dough kneading to flick his vibrant red hair out of his eyes. The errant strands flopped right back where they'd been before, but he didn't seem to notice.

"N-no," Tak said quietly, focusing his gaze on the dough instead of the man's face.

"Ah, I see." Timothon paused, giving his dough a pinch and staring at it for a long minute.

As he did so, Tak noticed he and Redrinna had similarly shaped noses, both with a narrow bridge and a wide base, except Redrinna's was a bit longer. The way their bangs rested on their foreheads was similar, the shape of their eyes was similar, even the faces they made were often near mirror images. They were similar in such small ways—tiny ways—that, for some reason, left him feeling out of place. Estranged, almost.

"It's kind of nice to see Redrinna interested in something for a change, isn't it?" Timothon suddenly asked, startling him.

Tak agreed, though he wasn't sure 'interested' was the word he'd use to describe her right now. He still remembered how, when he'd first come here, she'd been while trying to wake her Dragon Gem. She'd always shut herself away. The few times he'd seen her, she'd barely spoken, and her eyes had always been red and swollen. Her current sullen, withdrawn mood didn't seem much different.

"Hey, Tak," Timothon said, pulling him from his thoughts once again. "Are you ready to go get your gem? Xandrin's almost healed enough to take you."

A chill seeped into his gut. No, he wasn't ready. He didn't think he'd ever be ready, but what he said was, "Y-yeah, I'm...ready."

Timothon stopped, mouth pressed in a line as he studied Tak with those unnerving red eyes. "That's not the most convincing answer you could have given. It's okay if you're not ready. Just be sure, all right?"

Tak's voice fled, so he settled for a nod instead. He wanted to be ready, but at the same time, there was still that nagging sensation—

almost like a little voice in his head—whispering that he didn't belong here. What right did someone like him have trying to join a group like the Dragon Kin, defiers of evil, when he was...?

A tiny sigh escaped him. That was part of the reason he had a hard time being around Timothon. Somehow, the guy had a knack for asking pointed questions that made him uncomfortable. It was almost like the man could tell something was off. It was unsettling to imagine that if Timothon prodded long enough, he'd eventually jab the wounds Tak held tight to his heart. Would getting the gem change that and make those feelings disappear? Or would it make them worse?

Chapter Two

Redrinna glanced up from her papers in time to watch a drop of semi-opaque wax slip off the top of her candle and race down its side like a raindrop on glass. It was easier to study the map when she had the light of the sun, but she didn't want to waste a single second of the day, sun or no, and as soon as she could pinpoint the location of the nearest dragon, she'd be less stressed about Tak. Maybe she hadn't been paying enough attention before (which she completely believed), but while they'd been stuck in the Mount waiting for Xandrin to recover, she noticed how often Tak put his barriers up. He was always nearby but never close. It was like he wanted to be friends but didn't at the same time. So, maybe if he could make friends with a dragon, develop a bond similar to what she and Xandrin had, he would be able to settle in more. Then again, maybe it wouldn't help at all.

Shaking her head, Redrinna turned her attention back to the map in front of her. With one finger, she pointed to where she estimated them to be, buried deep in the winding trail of dark, jagged slashes that represented the Agicae Mountains. Then she glanced at the slim sheaf of creased, wrinkled papers, their corners yellowing with age—the information her father had given her the last time they'd seen each other—resting an arm's length away, partially within the halo of light from her candle.

Her heart wrenched into a tight, confusing spiral of love and pain at the memory, so she shook those thoughts away, pulled the papers closer, and forced herself to focus on the words written on the pages instead of the paper itself.

A list of dragons ran down one side, and their locations were listed parallel to them down the other side, all in her father's scratchy but almost calligraphic handwriting. Redrinna had put a small check beside the dragon she'd figured to be Xandrin and a circle beside the one she was hoping to find for Tak.

It lived close to where she'd found the gems, thus making it the nearest dragon to them. Once Xandrin was strong enough to fly with them again, they'd be going and getting a gem for Tak, so finding that dragon was the most logical next step. It was strange to think Redrinna had been so close to another dragon all this time and had never even had a clue, but then again, she'd lived near Xandrin her entire life, and no one had ever seen him.

"Why aren't you sleeping again?" Timothon asked so unexpectedly, Redrinna jumped and smacked her injured ankle against her chair.

Before she could stop it, a little cry escaped her.

The following silence was nearly suffocating.

Redrinna kept her head lowered as her uncle sighed. He approached, bending down and grabbing her ankle before propping it on the chair next to her. The next moment, he placed ice wrapped in a towel on it, making sure she was holding it before he let go.

"When you get an injury, you should take care of it."

Ignoring that, she squinted at the little chunk of ice wrapped in the towel. "Where did you get this?"

"That's for me to know, and you to not unless you're going to be honest with me." He propped a fist against his hip. "Why didn't you take care of your ankle?"

"I did." She glanced at him before hurriedly turning away.

"Mmm," was all he said in response. "Back to the first question then. It's a little late, don't you think?"

"I want to find Tak a dragon as soon as possible, and I'm not tired yet, so..."

Timothon tilted his head to the side, a few locks of his hair shifting across his forehead. "Okay, I'd be more inclined to believe that if you were even trying to get some sleep. Don't think I didn't notice you staying up late and getting up abysmally early. You know you don't have to put in all these crazy hours, don't you? It's not like Xandrin's strong enough to fly with anyone on his back just yet, and if charting a course is all you intend to do until then, you can afford to get more sleep."

The thought of sleep almost coaxed a yawn out of her, but she kept it in check. "I'm really not tired." Before she could stop herself, she muttered, "It's not like I'd be able to sleep anyway."

Timothon's eyes narrowed, making her heart skip a beat. He hesitated for a minute more before taking the seat across from her, his eyes glowing like embers in the candlelight. "You can't sleep?"

Curse her stupid mouth. Refusing to respond, Redrinna focused on her map instead. After everything that had happened, she'd been shaken and devastated, but at the end of the day, she'd truly believed she'd been fine. Or, at least, after some time, she would be. Then the nightmares had set in and—

A shudder swept through her. It was like time was marching forward, dragging her along behind it without giving her a chance to find her footing. Losing so much in one go was just... Redrinna felt hollow, like a loaf of bread someone had holed out, leaving nothing but the crust.

"Do you want to talk?" her uncle asked, pulling her back to reality. "I don't know if there's anything I can do to help you if I don't know what you're feeling right now."

"I'm fine," she said as she touched her thumb to where she guessed they were on the map. Then she slid her pinky to where she'd found the gem. The papers from her father said the dragon in question lived at a waterfall in a forest near the west coast. However, there was lots and lots of forest near the coast, and the map didn't have any waterfalls marked on it, not even any of the famous ones like Azure Falls or Crescent Fire Falls. How was she supposed to figure out where the dragon was if there weren't any—

"Hey, would you pay attention to me for a minute? I'm trying to talk with you." Timothon caught hold of her hand, lifting it from the map. "Pretending nothing is wrong isn't going to make the pain go away; it's going to make it worse. You're not going to heal if you close your eyes and make believe that what's hurting you doesn't exist. These things take—"

"How many times do I have to tell you I'm fine? I'm fine, I'm fine, I'm fine!" Redrinna snapped, jerking her hand away. "Just shut up!"

His mouth popped open.

Immediately, shame blossomed in her chest, and she returned her hand to the ice on her ankle. "I-I'm sorry. I didn't mean that."

"Redrinna," Timothon began slowly, cautiously, "I don't want to overstep, but you're scaring me. I get that you're determined to do what you feel you need to but—"

"It's important," she said quickly, unable to meet his eye.

"And so are you," he said, voice gentle. "Just...try not to get so lost in yourself that you forget the rest of us exist, all right? I know you're miserable; trust me, I've been there. But just—" He interrupted himself with a sigh before he smiled one of those sad smiles she was starting to dislike on his face. "Don't forget, okay?"

Redrinna didn't know what to say, so she stared at her hands on her ankle. The hands that had pushed a friend-turned-foe to her death. The hands that trembled at the mere memory of her enemies. The hands that had miraculously saved Xandrin but couldn't perform a simple set of magic stances. She shuddered again, resting her head against her knee, and pushed those thoughts far away.

Timothon stayed quiet now, but he didn't leave. So, after a minute more, Redrinna continued with her project.

Maybe they should just go in the general direction of the dragon and see what they could find. It'd be more productive than sitting here and making guesses based on information she didn't have. Though, if she was honest with herself, she wasn't sure she wanted to go. A month ago, she would've gone in a heartbeat, but now...the idea of leaving the Mount again, of risking being out there and at Osiris's mercy filled her with unspeakable terror, with a fear so vivid it felt like it would devour her. However, letting the others go out there and face who-knew-what without her filled her with a dread so intense, it made her chest clench and burn like she was drowning.

Shaking her head, Redrinna decided she needed to move on to something else, otherwise she'd get lost in these thoughts bobbing in her mind like boats on the edge of a whirlpool. Entertaining them was flirting with disaster. She'd already experienced that more than once in the last month.

Timothon silently watched as she stacked all her papers together and set them aside. "Is it bedtime now? Please?"

She shook her head, forcing her tumultuous thoughts away with a smile. "There's a book on magic I found yesterday that I want to check. I don't like using weapons—and all I have is this little knife anyway—but magic is okay." Kind of.

A sigh escaped him as she set the half-melted ice aside, left the table, and headed towards what she'd realized must be the magic section of the library. She was slowly figuring out the organization of this place. Hopefully, she'd have it down soon so she could find things faster.

Redrinna heaved the book she wanted off the shelf, having to use both arms to lug it back to the table. She hadn't realized how huge it was, but hopefully, its size was because the book was stuffed full of knowledge rather than fluff.

When Redrinna returned to the table, Timothon wasn't there,

making a flicker of relief flit through her chest. If he wasn't here, then she couldn't yell at him again. She understood where he was coming from, but the truth was she didn't know what to say to him or how to answer his questions. How could she explain feelings she didn't understand or the ones she did feel but didn't want to?

Frankly, she wished he would let it be and stop worrying about her. She didn't want anybody trying to protect or watch out for her anymore. Being alone wasn't an attractive alternative, but she didn't want anybody to be hurt in her place ever again, even if that meant she ended up having to stand completely on her own. That was why studying magic, something she was half good at, was something she had to do. Then, whenever her friends were in danger, she'd actually be able to protect them.

Maybe then she could get some sleep again.

Redrinna had just cracked her book open when Timothon returned, setting down a loaf of bread, a knife, and butter. He then tossed a big blanket onto the far end of the table before retaking his seat. She shot him a questioning look before returning her attention to the book.

"If you're going to pull an all-nighter, then I'm going to sit up with you. It's not like I need to sleep anyway."

She eyed the bread he'd brought, her stomach almost twinging with hunger, but at the same time, the sight of the golden-brown crust and its accompanying, warm aroma couldn't entice her to even want to eat. Instead, staring at it made nausea creep into her gut.

"Don't scowl at it like that," her uncle said, resting his chin in his hands. "I worked very hard on it, you know."

"I'm not...scowling." Redrinna dropped her gaze back to the book.

"Sure. Besides, you might get peckish later. Or I might."

She didn't even get the chance to make it through one sentence before looking back up at him. "You...might get peckish?"

He shrugged. "I still like food from time to time even if I'm dead and don't need it. But more importantly, let's study this book of yours. I can help you."

"But you said you didn't study magic because it was hard and took too long."

"Which is true!" He nodded emphatically, but a hint of a smirk twisted his mouth. "That doesn't mean I'm completely clueless either. I might know some things."

She didn't respond right away. "Fine. Just...stay quiet though."

"Quiet. Got it. I can do that. No prob—"

Her brow lowered as a scowl threatened to creep onto her face. Flashing a brilliant grin, he shut his mouth.

⚬⚬

Morning light coaxed Redrinna awake, startling her a little. When had she fallen asleep? Her shoulders were unbearably heavy, so she didn't think she'd slept for long. The usual, as of late.

She shifted and paper crinkled as she did, making her sigh as she carefully smoothed it back out. Once again, she'd fallen asleep while reading.

Pushing herself up, she stretched, working out the stiffness in her neck when the weight abruptly vanished from her shoulders. And it was suddenly much colder.

Glancing down, she found herself half-wrapped in a blanket. So this was why Timothon had brought it last night. Her gaze traveled over the table, and she noted the food he'd brought with him was gone, as was he.

Fighting back a yawn, she wondered what time it was. A quick glance out the window didn't help since the surrounding mountains blocked out most of the sky, but the slim smear she did see was a pale, watery blue. It was probably early in the morning, which didn't surprise her much.

Stretching again, Redrinna lifted the blanket off and stood, pushing her chair back with her legs. A loud thunk rang out and pages fluttered. Jumping, she swiftly righted the candlestick she'd knocked over with the blanket. It was fortunate that had been out for a while, otherwise her papers would've been ruined.

She turned to leave, but nearly jumped out of her skin when she ran right into Timothon.

He grinned. "Good morning. Did you sleep well?"

"Where did you come from?" She took a step back, bumping into the chair.

He pointed over his shoulder at the library's entrance.

Redrinna did not appreciate his humor. "Is Xandrin awake?"

"I haven't seen him, but that doesn't mean anything. I've been baking bread." As he stepped to one side, she dropped the blanket into her chair and led the way out of the library. "Hey, don't you want to eat breakfast?"

"I'm not hungry yet," she said, trying to walk faster than him, but his legs were longer than hers so he kept pace with her anyway. "Besides, I had some bread last night, remember?"

"Yeah, one slice. Without any butter on it. The butter is the best part."

Taking a deep breath to avoid sighing, she ignored him and focused her thoughts on what she'd read last night. It was all a bit hazy. A lot of last night's reading had gone over her head, especially when Timothon had tried to 'help' by explaining it to her. Maybe she would've gotten farther on her own—as it turned out, her uncle barely knew a thing about magic, though he'd tried hard to be helpful.

Shaking her head, Redrinna pushed that thought to the back of her mind where she'd examine it later. For now, she wanted to check on Xandrin, just in case she'd forgotten to yesterday. She thought she had, but all the magic facts buzzing in her brain made it difficult to remember, and at the very least, she knew for a fact she hadn't checked on him the day before. Today, she'd make sure to spend time with him.

"Where are you off to now?" Timothon said. Redrinna didn't hear his footsteps behind her any longer.

"Xandrin," she called over her shoulder as she entered the main room of the Mount. Their conversation from last night flitted through her mind, but it was successfully chased out when she touched one of the two necklaces hanging from her throat, the one with the two intertwining hearts. She understood where her uncle was coming from, but her neglect had cost hundreds of people their lives and almost Xandrin's too. Her mother had been murdered because of her. If running herself into the ground ensured nothing like that ever happened again, then she wouldn't voice a single complaint.

When Redrinna arrived at Xandrin's door, she shook those thoughts away. It was dark, like usual in the dragon's room, so she paused, listening for the dragon's breathing. Deep and heavy. She almost smiled. Typical Xandrin, sleeping like always.

Quietly, she approached and scrambled onto the dragon's shoulders, carefully lying down. Normally, she would wake him up, but her chest ached at the thought of depriving him of the rest he needed to recover, especially since the only reason he needed it was because he'd been hurt protecting her.

Lightly, Redrinna traced a finger along the edge of one of his deeper wounds, the faded grey of the scarring a stark contrast to the vibrant red and smoky black sheen of his scales. It was a miracle he hadn't died that night.

Fortunately, Xandrin had recovered enough to take short, solo flights. After some more days of building his strength, Timothon had said the dragon would be recovered enough to take her and Tak on short trips. The knowledge that Xandrin would soon be well enough for them to continue their journey assuaged the guilt that nagged at her every time she looked at him or the scales of the shirt he'd made for her, the one she now wore. Even though Xandrin had gone to great lengths to make her this shirt, a part of her hated wearing it.

Every time she saw his scales, they were just another reminder of her mistakes and stupidity.

While she didn't actually sleep, Redrinna caught herself dozing as she waited for him to wake up. Eventually he shifted, pulling her out of her sleepy haze enough to lift her head and find him staring at her.

"Good morning," she said before stretching.

He yawned, ear frills fanning out as he did so. "Have you been here long?"

She shook her head. "Even if I had, I don't mind waiting for you." After sliding off his back, she watched him climb to his feet, waiting for any glimpse of pain. There was a grimace here or there, but he didn't hesitate once in the motion. That was an improvement.

They headed to the dining hall together, where Redrinna forced down a couple slices of bread—making sure Timothon was watching as she spread butter on them. At the very least, it made them slide down her throat easier.

After Xandrin had eaten his fill, she followed him outside, standing a few paces back until he'd launched himself into the air. From the ledge of the Mount, she watched him fly in large, slow circles before he dove and threw himself high in the air. Even if he was merely doing exercises to get his strength back, watching him fly was captivating. Her chest ached at the thought of what had almost happened to him once more.

As long as she drew breath, Redrinna never wanted to watch someone she cared about go through something like this again. If she was strong enough to protect herself, no one would have to put their life on the line for her. Nobody would have to risk dying for her.

It's cold, the gem around her neck whispered. *You should've grabbed your cloak before coming out here.*

"It doesn't bother me," Redrinna said, folding her arms as a slight, chill breeze blew over. The palace had been about this cold, so she was used to it. Besides, spring was coming to the mountains now; there was an undercurrent of warmth in the cold wind and faint strains of bird song traveling through the air.

If she'd still been at the palace, spring would've fully taken root by now. Or, at least, it would've felt like it. There would've been a lot less snow crouching in the shadows at any rate.

The palace was one of the last places she wanted to think about right now, though. For the time being, even if it could only be for a short while, she simply wanted to be Redrinna, a member of the Dragon Kin, and nothing more. That was enough of a task to focus on for now.

"He's certainly getting better, isn't he?" Timothon said from right beside her, getting her to look his way. "You know, the next few days are going to pass quickly. Are you sure you aren't going to miss me while you're gone?"

Frowning, she raised an eyebrow at him. What was he on about?

"Don't scowl at me," he said with a frown of his own. "You should smile. I'm saying in a few days Xandrin will, for sure—unless something weird happens—be strong enough for you guys to make a short trip, so you'll be free to go if you want."

"Go?"

"Last time you left, something bad happened, so you should go out there and have a better time. That's all. Well, and I've always found hard stuff easier to work through when I've got something to do. Finding a dragon will probably keep you pretty busy, don't you think?"

He might have had a point there. It wasn't easy to get swept up in a whirlpool of negative thoughts when Redrinna had something to do.

"There's something special I want you to take with you. Meet me in the Hall of the Dragon Kin, okay?" The sternness of his gaze reminded her of the time he'd told her about the Dragon Kin, something that seemed like it had happened forever ago now. It almost made a chill race down her spine.

She nodded, and he went back inside the Mount. Xandrin finished his exercises a few minutes later and went to his room when Redrinna told him where she was going. Taking a deep breath, she turned and headed up the tunnel.

Chapter Three

The walk to the Hall was still long and tiring, but Redrinna didn't mind the exercise. It distracted her from the anxiety gnawing on her nerves with each step she took. Timothon had been frighteningly serious out on the ledge, and she wasn't sure she was genuinely ready for whatever he wanted to give her. The last time he'd been that serious, he'd been about to explain how the Empire had come to be and how Osiris—

Her thoughts stopped, and so did she. The mere thought of him dumped floods of fear into her chest, making Redrinna want to run, hide, and never come back out. She hated remembering the way he'd lounged on her father's throne with that disturbing grin, the way he'd discussed killing innocent people so nonchalantly, or the way he'd confessed to murdering her siblings like he'd been proud of it. He alone made her terrified of the idea of leaving the Mount ever again.

Worse than that was the recollection of Osiris saying he was letting her go, implying that to him, her freedom was his to grant or take away. His words lingered in her nightmares, lurked in the shadows of Redrinna's every thought. Was there a point in even trying to oppose him?

Whatever his plan was, he was confident enough in its success to let her run around trying to stop it, but what happened when he decided she'd run around enough and it was time for her to come back? Already, he'd almost had her racing back to his side to save Xandrin, so when he truly wanted her back, how far would he go? What else would he delight in ripping away from her in order to get his way? Who else would he try to take?

No. Redrinna couldn't let herself think like that or let those thoughts linger. She couldn't quit this race she'd agreed to run. If she stopped moving, if she just rolled over and died, Osiris would be there waiting.

Shaking those thoughts away, she forced herself to keep walking.

A few minutes later, Redrinna arrived in the hall, pausing to take in the kaleidoscopic sunlight streaming through the stained-glass windows, throwing fractured rainbows against the stone and the nine statues towering over the room. Timothon stood in the center of it all, at the heart of the platform in the middle of the room, his back to her.

"What did we come here for?" Redrinna asked, stopping a short distance away.

"Because I want you to understand how serious this is." Timothon turned, a sheathed sword in his hands.

Her heart wilted at the sight of it.

He approached but didn't hand over the weapon. "This belonged to me when I was alive but don't ask how it got here. My guess is the gems had something to do with it. Either way, the sword was a gift to me from one of the other human tribes, and it's pretty special. I managed to set it on fire once."

He slid it out of the sheath a little, letting the slender, jet-black blade peek out. Redrinna blinked in surprise. She'd never seen a sword with a blade quite like this before.

"See? Not a normal sword given the color of its blade and all, right? I believe the magic that's in it did that, but I'm not the right person to ask." He slid it back into its sheath, the weapon letting out a menacing hiss as it went. "Regardless of any of that, no matter how pretty or cool it is, this is a weapon."

"I know," she whispered, her hands trembling. For most of her life, Redrinna had been convinced she could get by without ever having to touch a weapon, but now she knew that line of thinking was naïve so long as they were in war. Regardless, that didn't change the fact she hated this sword—this instrument of pain and death—and the weight it brought with it.

"Swords have their uses, but they aren't the best weapons when it comes down to it. And I know you told me you'd rather use your magic than a weapon. It's smart to take out an enemy before they can get close, but in case someone does manage to do that, I want you to take this. Only use it if you must. Promise me."

She met Timothon's pained expression with one of her own before nodding. "I promise."

Repressing yet another shudder, Redrinna reached out and took the sword, wincing as its cold weight came to rest in her palms. She wanted to throw it back at him, but instead, she pulled it to her chest. In order to protect herself and those she cared for, she'd do what she had to. Even accepting this.

Timothon smiled then, but it was one of the ones that didn't reach his eyes. "Be careful out there, okay?"

ॐ ॐ

Tak jerked awake, panting and drenched in a cold sweat. For a long moment, he couldn't figure out what was happening, but then it came to him: the dream. Not again. Suppressing a groan, he laid back down before swiping at the tears. Then he hid his eyes beneath his arms. He didn't know why when the gem sent him its dream, tears and sleeplessness came with it, but it happened every time.

Soon though, it would all be over. In the morning, they'd be leaving and not coming back until they had his gem. Timothon had said as much, and Redrinna hadn't denied it. They'd go find a drag-on, then get his gem. Then, according to Timothon, the dreams would end, Tak would be able to sleep, and he'd officially be a part of the Dragon Kin.

After all these years, Tak would have a place to call his own that no one could try bullying him out of. Even if they got tired of him or realized they didn't like him, they wouldn't be able to say he didn't belong. Perhaps then, for the first time in his life, he'd be able to breathe easy. He couldn't even begin to imagine what that would be like. Yet, even if no one could chase him away, that didn't mean he'd have a home or a place to belong. Even with a gem around his neck, he'd probably always be an outsider and a burden.

Sighing, Tak lowered his arms a little, staring up at the dark grey stone above him. Thin rays of moonlight painted silver beams across the stone, making bars on the ceiling. While they'd been stuck in the Mount, the gem had left him alone somewhat, but maybe it sensed he was on his way now and that was why the dream was back.

A reminder had been neither wanted nor necessary.

Unexpectedly, a memory of his aunt surfaced in his mind, remi-niscent of a night similar to this one. He'd spent many nights like this, lying awake in the dark while sleep evaded him—long before the issue had been exacerbated by the gem. His aunt had had some sort of sixth sense for his sleeplessness, Tak supposed, since when he'd had these nights, she'd often come to find him. She'd taught him lullabies, songs from an age past cocooned in the forgotten language of Avarian. It may have been illegal to utter it, but that hadn't stopped her from teaching him enough to understand the songs.

A deep ache blossomed in his chest like a thorn-laden rose, making Tak squeeze his eyes shut as the bittersweet memories dug into him with the intensity of knife-like thorns. He didn't want to remember any of those times with his aunt; not the times she'd taught him how to bake nor the times they'd gone into the woods to find berries—not a single second of their time together. It stung, calling up other memories he didn't want to think about, memories that were even more painful than losing the last of the only family he'd ever had.

A long sigh rushed out of him as he pushed the memory away. He would've given anything to spend a minute with her—just one—but he didn't have that kind of power. The magic he did have was worthless, only able to bring pain and suffering. Never, in all the rest of his days, would he touch that power again.

Rolling over, almost as though he could turn his back on all the thoughts nagging at him, he shut his eyes. However, the sweet escape of sleep never came.

⚬⚭ ⚭⚬

Redrinna released a deep breath before lifting her palms in front of her, concentrating hard. A minute ball of fire sprang to life with a soft crackle, and after a moment of watching the little flames, she passed it back and forth between her hands, forcing herself to take it slow. The books she'd been reading about magic had stressed practicing control and having a solid mastery of the basics above all else.

She should've been sleeping, but since she wasn't tired—and if she left her room, she'd have to deal with Timothon—she'd chosen to practice her magic in solitude. The last thing she wanted was to be in a position where she would have to use her new sword, so she desperately wanted to have near perfect control over her magic. Otherwise, she would end up having to rely on that weapon.

For a few minutes, the only sound in the room was the faint sizzle of the tiny fire as it leisurely bobbed from one hand to the next. There was almost something soothing about this, watching the tiny ball of flickering flame bounce back and forth, its soft light dancing on and off the wood furniture and the stone walls.

Not tired again? her gem asked.

Redrinna jumped, the fire vanishing with a hiss and a curl of smoke.

Sorry.

"It's okay," she said, holding in a sigh. "And no, I'm not tired. So I'd figured I'd practice until I am." She restarted the fire between her hands.

You won't 'forget' to sleep again, will you?

"That only happened once."

The gem returned to being silent, but, once she'd put the fire out a while later, it spoke again. *You should rest now. You'll be leaving in the morning, and you'll need all your strength.*

Redrinna hesitated with her hands still in the air. Leaving. To-morrow, she would have to depart from the safety of the Mount and exchange it for the danger and uneasiness of the unknown, and since Timothon had already told the other two, it was impossible to pro-long or avoid it. She couldn't put it off until these feelings and the sleeplessness went away, and she couldn't justify staying here either. Except...what if something happened out there? What if it ended up the same way the last time had? What would she do if she couldn't save her friends this time?

Is everything okay?

She flinched away from the gem's voice. Because it was awake, it couldn't miraculously save her this time. It may have been a powerful relic, but Redrinna didn't have a clue how it worked, and when she'd asked, it'd given her a cryptic: 'every bond with a gem is unique, so I don't know how ours will work' kind of answer.

Either way, how was she supposed to protect her friends if she was barely any stronger than she'd been before?

Redrinna?

"I'm sorry. I'm fine," she said, setting her hands in her lap.

Then please, try and get some rest, okay?

With a resigned sigh, Redrinna climbed into bed. The moment she did, the light in her room dimmed before going out. The dark-ness settled over her like a heavy blanket, both comforting and suffo-cating at the same time. In an effort to stem the usual tide of relentless, heavy thoughts before they could start, Redrinna stared at her gem, watching its soft light slowly pulse, its unhurried, steady rhythm almost like a heartbeat.

It seemed like she stared at it for hours before her eyelids finally grew heavy and closed. Her sleep was shallow; she drifted in and out, only seeming to doze. She wasn't sure if she'd actually slept or not, but when the sun's rays first began brightening the sky, it didn't feel like she'd gotten an ounce of rest.

Redrinna sat up, fighting off the weight of the exhaustion plaguing her. Even if she deserved it, it stunk. For the first time, it occurred to her that if she was this tired, there was a chance she could convince the others to go without her. Granted, if she gave in to the exhaustion, gave in to her fear and hid, she would have to tell them something was wrong.

You don't have to get up. It's early yet.

"I'm fine." Even though she was exhausted, there'd be no more rest for her; she already knew it, so there was no point lying here and waiting for rest that wasn't going to come.

Redrinna rose and, a few minutes later, left her room before coming to a stop. What now? There was always the option of scaling the mountain and practicing, but after her recent failure, she had no motivation to take another crack at it. The only other person awake right now was probably Timothon, and she didn't want to see him either.

After a minute more, Redrinna turned and headed to the Hall of the Dragon Kin. The early morning quiet of the Mount was pleasant, but as she stepped into the hall again, unease took root in her chest. The hall was as beautiful as ever, but today, standing in the enormous shadows of the people who'd come before her, it was more intimidating than awe-inspiring. The people who'd comprised the last Dragon Kin probably never would've considered leaving their friends to fend for themselves because of something as pathetic as fear.

Redrinna's gaze stayed fixed on the ground as she came to a stop in the center of the room. A chill trickled down her spine at the memory of Timothon gifting her his old sword, swiftly being followed by the memory of the night she'd spent in here, waiting for an answer that had never come, and then when Timothon had first told her about the Dragon Kin. She had yet to form a memory in this room that was truly a happy one despite the kind of place it was.

All at once, a footstep rang out behind her. Spinning around, Redrinna was startled to find Tak standing in the doorway. He appeared just as alarmed, though, and swiftly looked away.

"What are you doing?" she asked.

"I've never been up here, so I was wondering why you keep coming here," he said, his quiet voice hard to hear with the distance between them. "What...is this place?"

"Timothon calls it the Hall of the Dragon Kin. I'm not sure how it all works, but these statues are the rest of the old Dragon Kin."

Tak nodded, hesitantly joining her on the platform, his gaze slowly taking in the room. For a long moment, he seemed to pause on a woman with curly green hair. Then, almost like he was embarrassed or something, he looked away.

"I come here to think sometimes," Redrinna said once he seemed to have his fill of looking around. "It's quiet."

He nodded again.

An awkward silence settled between them, and Redrinna found herself thinking back to the night on the Mount's ledge when they'd been able to talk like friends. How had they done that? Why did most of their conversations end up like this now?

A quiet sigh slipped out of her. It wasn't Tak, she supposed. It was her. Again.

"Well this is new," Timothon said from behind them, making both of them jump. "Normally, I find only one of you here."

"Oh," Tak began, his voice getting quieter until he was mumbling. "I...just wanted to see what was up here."

Redrinna couldn't think of anything to say, so she shrugged. She still hadn't figured out what had brought her here, but if it was peace and solitude, she didn't think she was going to find it anymore.

"The two of you make quite a pair of sour faces," Timothon said after a long moment of silence Redrinna hadn't noticed. "You'd think I was punishing you by letting you leave."

Despite herself, Redrinna peeked at him.

He stared at her and Tak in turn, a slight frown on his face.

"Sorry," she offered after a long minute. "I was just...thinking."

"Mmm," was all he said. He stepped forward, staring up at the statues.

Redrinna found herself exchanging a look with Tak.

"Oh, I get it now," he continued, getting both of them to turn back to him. "Are you worried about what'll happen out there?" Timothon stared pointedly at her with those piercing red eyes of his as he spoke.

Hurriedly, Redrinna looked elsewhere. How did he always manage to figure these things out?

"I understand," her uncle continued, his gaze coming to rest on the stained-glass window hanging behind where his statue would have been, the one depicting his dragon. Amaris, if Redrinna remembered correctly. "The world out there is unforgiving, even if you don't have enemies trying to make it harder. And sometimes...the worst enemy is the one you have to take everywhere with you."

Redrinna kept her gaze lowered. If she looked up, he'd know for sure. Granted, she had a feeling whether she met his gaze or not, he'd know, but she refused to look anyway, just to be safe.

"Before I let you both go, I have something important to tell you." Timothon stepped over to the two of them and took one of each of their hands. "Regardless of whether you encounter trouble out there or not, you take care of each other. Protect each other. You work as a team, you guys and Xandrin. You are the Dragon Kin. You're a group; none of you have to be alone. Don't forget that."

"Shouldn't you tell this to Xandrin too?" Redrinna asked, unable to keep a glum tone out of her voice.

"He already knows." Timothon's red eyes were serious, almost stern. He stayed quiet for a minute before he spoke again. "And one last thing for both of you to think on: there are things about ourselves we cannot change, that's true. However, if you don't like the face staring back at you in the mirror, you still have two choices: one, you can change the face you see, or two, shatter the mirror and get a better one."

Redrinna's gaze drifted to the floor like a discarded leaf. If only solving her problems were so simple, but she supposed she appreciated the thought.

After a moment longer, Timothon released their hands. "Now, unless the two of you have some more business in here, you should both go eat breakfast and get ready to leave. After all, who knows what you'll find out there? It's best to be prepared for anything, and make sure you come back safe, all right?"

Redrinna hesitated before nodding. Without saying a word, she turned to follow the others out of the room. She didn't want to leave, but she was going to go anyway. No matter what it cost her, she would protect her friends and keep either of them from getting hurt.

Yet, after only a few steps, she stopped and glanced back, studying the statues and the windows, not entirely sure what she hoped to see, but unable to find it anyway. Even still, Redrinna lifted her eyes to the statues. "Help me, please."

A deep shame flooded her in response, making her hunch her shoulders and turn away. What was she thinking, asking statues—ghosts of the past—for help? It wasn't like there was anything they could do, even if they'd wanted to.

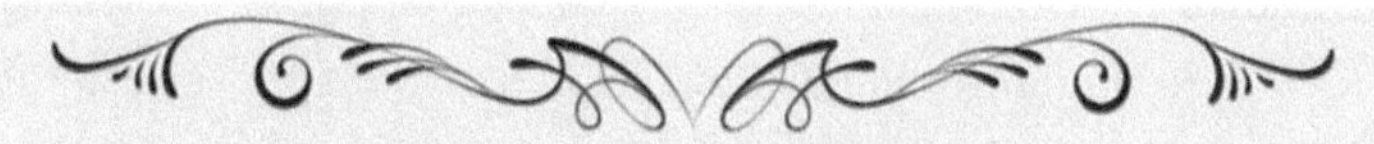

Chapter Four

Tak had forgotten that riding on the back of a dragon meant having the wind rip through his hair despite the fact he was sitting behind Redrinna, and she was getting the brunt of it. At least, mercifully, her hair was pulled back and not hitting him in the face, but that didn't help his hair at all. All he could picture was that once their dragon ride was done, his hair would be all over the place and standing on end like he'd been struck by lightning.

Redrinna and Xandrin sometimes talked to each other, but Tak remained silent for the duration of their flight. It was too hard to talk over the rush of the wind, and it wasn't like he had anything worth saying anyway. It wouldn't make time go by any faster, and already, they'd almost made it over the mountains and to the forest where Redrinna believed the dragon they were searching for was. They'd only had to stop once for Xandrin to take a break, so they were making good progress.

Regardless, Tak's nerves felt frayed like he'd been gnawing on them in agitation. They were going to find a dragon. To work with him. Then, he'd be getting a gem, and he'd be safe. He'd have a place to call his own, and even if the others learned the truth about him and his past, they couldn't throw him out. Even still, that thought didn't bring any semblance of comfort with it.

A short time later, they descended into the cool shade of a forest similar to the one Tak had grown up in but different enough to make him uneasy. While it was warmer here than it had been at the Mount, he didn't want to linger in the woods longer than they had to. Hopefully, they would find the dragon quickly and it would be willing to go with them, making this part of their journey short and unmemorable.

"Where should we start?" Xandrin asked, bumping against a few branches as he stretched in a cat-like fashion between the trees.

"According to my father's notes, the dragon in question lives at a waterfall. Unfortunately, I don't know where to find one off the top of my head and the maps back at the Mount didn't show where any waterfalls are." Redrinna set her hands on her hips, spinning in a slow circle with a frown on her face. After a minute, she closed her eyes.

Tak discreetly tried to copy what he thought she was doing and listen for the sound of water, but the rush of the wind in the trees sounded almost the same as a river, so he left it to her.

After a short while, Redrinna turned and began walking. Xandrin was right beside her and Tak trailed on the dragon's heels, warily eyeing the swish of his long tail.

As they walked, the sound of rushing water became more distinct. The first waterfall they found was thin and tall, tumbling off a high cliff and throwing spray high in the air. Tak wrinkled his nose as the frigid water misted his face. He enjoyed swimming, but not when the water was still this cold.

After a while, Redrinna decided it wasn't the waterfall they were searching for and led them on.

He hurried and caught up with her. "Why don't you think it's that waterfall?"

"There's nowhere big enough for a dragon to hide near it," she said.

Frowning, Tak glanced at Xandrin. The dragon shrugged, ear frills held out wide like sails, almost like he was attempting to catch hold of every sound in the forest, which was something Tak could imagine him trying to do. A sigh almost escaped him, but he held it in check, wrapping his arms around his waist.

His gaze drifted over the trees as they walked, the smells of the woods and the ocean dredging up old memories. Hours spent with his aunt and uncle beneath the protective branches of the massive oaks with their frilled leaves and with the slender silhouettes of the hazel trees, sunlight piercing their green leaves and making them seem to glow, flooded his mind. At that time in his life, the forest had seemed enchanted, bursting with secrets and mysteries.

Now, it lay empty. Hollow, almost. Like a graveyard.

To their right, Tak occasionally caught glimpses of the grey ocean, its familiar, salty tang making his nose wrinkle. A chill wind moaned as it passed between the hollows in the tree branches, the young leaves rattling like bones.

All at once, a stunted little leaf with brown encrusting its edges dropped through the air without a sound, spinning in slow arcs until it fell on the grass. It went still, resigning itself to its fate of shriveling and being forgotten.

Grimacing at the image, Tak wrapped his arms tighter around himself and kept his gaze fixed on his feet.

After a long while, they came across another small waterfall, but this one seemed as unlikely as the first. Redrinna studied it for only a minute before she moved on.

It was nearly an hour before they found another waterfall, and the second Tak saw it, a shiver raced down his spine.

He knew this place. He remembered this waterfall, taller than any human he'd ever seen, but also slow-moving and squat. Willow trees ringed most of the perimeter of its deep pool, their thin, leafy limbs trailing lifelessly in the water like tired stuffies after they'd been dragged around by children.

"Maybe this one," Redrinna murmured, crossing her arms.

Behind them, Xandrin flopped onto the ground with a massive

sigh. "How much longer will this take?"

She turned back, a pained look twisting her features. "As helpful as my father's notes are, they didn't come with a map. So, this might take us a few days."

He groaned, resting his head on the ground and hiding his face beneath his claws.

Tak simply kept quiet, hoping they could leave this waterfall as soon as possible. This was the last place he wanted to be.

"Wait," Redrinna said, turning to him. "I don't know why I didn't think about this sooner, but you lived near here before we met. Did you ever see anything or hear someone talk about a dragon at all?"

He froze, unsure what to say. The truth was his first instinct, but with that truth came a memory he desperately wished would go away, one of blood and an awful sickness that had left him bedridden for almost a week. He couldn't stare that in the face, not now. That was the one part of himself he absolutely couldn't accept or let anyone know existed, but he couldn't lie either. Finding this dragon was Redrinna's top priority. Hiding that he'd seen it, that he knew it—or at least, he had once—seemed wrong, but if the dragon she wanted to find was the one he was thinking of, then he didn't want to be here.

Yet, he had nowhere else to go nor did he want to leave.

"It's okay if you didn't," she said, turning back to the waterfall. "It just might've been helpful."

Tak's mind still chewed on him to say something, but his heart clamped his mouth shut. He didn't resist and stayed quiet.

Redrinna stared at the water for a minute longer before glancing back at Xandrin. "We've been out here for the better part of the day. It's a bit early still, but we should probably let him rest."

He nodded, though he didn't think his opinion mattered much.

"Xandrin," she called to the dragon, getting him to open one, dark eye. "Let's call it for today. We'll continue searching tomorrow."

"Oh good," Xandrin said, pushing himself to his feet, wincing slightly as he did so.

Tak turned to follow, but all at once, the sensation he was being watched slithered up his spine. Whipping around, he scanned the waterfall before he saw it. Standing at the head of the waterfall, water gushing around its legs, stood a painfully familiar dragon, green scales glittering in varying shades—from dark forest greens to bright greens that almost seemed gold in the light of the sun—making it nearly impossible to pick out from the surrounding greens of the forest. Truthfully, if it hadn't been for its eyes, black as shadows in winter, Tak might not have seen it at all.

His chest constricted as their gazes met, but he forced himself to turn away and follow the other two. Squeezing his eyes shut, he fought against the tumult of heavy, dark emotions pressing on him. That dragon... Tak couldn't handle that dragon. Even still, he got the foreboding feeling it was the one they were here for. So what did he do?

They struck camp in a small, almost meadow-like clearing near the base of the mountains where there was enough room for Xandrin to sprawl out without getting caught in any trees.

Tak hung back on the fringes of the space, distinctly feeling like he would be intruding on Xandrin and Redrinna if he stepped into the clearing. Desperately, he wished he could even pretend he fit in here for a moment. Just that would be enough.

After a minute, Redrinna glanced back at him, beckoning him over. "It's still too early for dinner, but it's not far off. Do you want to find some firewood while I—?"

"We don't need firewood," Xandrin piped up, lifting his head. "I can cook whatever you want."

She shook her head. "We're in a forest, Xandrin. If we're not careful with our fires, the entire place will burn down."

He blinked, pulling his head back slightly. "That would be bad. But we might find the dragon faster."

The corner of Redrinna's mouth turned up, but she said, "How about we don't do that? Tak will get wood so we can build a cooking fire, and I'll go find something for us to eat. If you want to help, you could always clear a spot for a fire."

Xandrin scowled, ear frills lowering. "That sounds boring."

Redrinna smiled, but it seemed forced. However, before either of them could say anything more, she turned and vanished amongst the trees.

Tak remained where he was for a moment before stifling a sigh and heading off as well. As he went, he recalled Timothon telling them to watch out for and protect each other. They were a team. They were *the* Dragon Kin. However, as he bent and retrieved his first stick, he couldn't help thinking they weren't much of a team. They were more like...people—plus a dragon—who'd been forced together like different types of dough. Granted, he'd never been on a team before, but he wasn't sure if it was supposed to be like this; this mismatched, disjointedness that seeped between them like mist.

It took Tak longer than he'd expected to gather enough sticks, but once he had, he turned to head back to their camp. All at once, the brush behind him rustled, making him freeze. There wasn't a breeze of any kind. Slowly, he glanced back, nearly leaping out of his skin.

Standing nearby, almost blending in with the surrounding trees was the dragon from earlier. She stood just out of reach, her diamond-shaped head held high and frilled neck arched. She wasn't as large as Xandrin, but there was a ferocity seeping from her wiry frame, from her reptilian face with a few of her fangs protruding from her closed mouth, that set Tak on edge. Her claws, gleaming dully, dug into the earth when he noticed her.

"Hello again," she whispered, her voice much higher than Xandrin's, like a star to the ocean higher. "Do you not remember me?"

He fixed his gaze on the sticks in his arms and said nothing.

"Well, I guess we met a long time ago, so maybe you did forget." The dragon sat, pulling her wings close to her sides. "It's okay. I'm not mad or anything."

"I...didn't forget," Tak said. He'd wanted to, though. Unfortunately, it seemed like everything he wanted to forget, he couldn't.

"Then why did you ignore me earlier? Am I frightening now?"

He shook his head. A dragon was far from the scariest thing he'd ever encountered.

"Oh," she said, shifting her feet. "Then why... I guess we barely met before, and it's not like we're friends or anything. Actually, I almost didn't recognize you with all that green hair you have now. It suits you though."

His brow furrowed. She'd meant it as a compliment, he knew, but her words still burrowed into him like a tick.

After a moment of hesitation, she quietly said, "You know, what you did for me that day? I never got the chance to say thank you."

"Don't, please," Tak said, glancing in her direction for a second. "I-I don't want to talk about it."

She didn't say anything.

Seizing his chance, he took a couple steps back. "Just...leave me alone. Please."

As Tak hurried away, dodging a couple low branches, his heart pounded so hard and fast it felt like it might explode. He felt rude, but at the same time, he didn't want her to follow him.

Shuddering, Tak pressed through the brush, determined to put as much space as possible between him and the dragon. So far, he regretted leaving the Mount and wished he hadn't come.

After a few minutes of hurried walking, Tak stopped at the edge of a river so slender, he had half a mind to call it a stream. He panted slightly from the exertion of his hurried pace, so he paused, trying to get himself back together before he turned to return to the others.

All at once, he got the feeling he wasn't alone. Thinking the dragon had followed him, he spun on his heel, his meager bundle of sticks tight to his chest. After a moment of panic, he spied Redrinna a little way upstream, staring into the water that glistened in the light of the few sunbeams managing to work their way through the thick canopy. She said she'd search for food for them, hadn't she? So what was she doing here? He doubted they'd find any fish here with so little water, and she didn't even like fish anyway.

Tak considered getting her attention or saying something, but his throat closed like a window shut against a storm. The longer he stood there, the less he could think of something to say that wouldn't make it weird or awkward, and beyond that, there was something different about Redrinna at that moment, as she stood there, then there had been before. Here, in the thin rays of sunlight filtering through the trees, the expression on her face was so hollow, it almost seemed like she was made of glass and the light was passing right through her.

'Take care of each other,' Timothon had said. Tak sighed, glancing away. How? How could he, of all people, be of any help?

"Tak?" Redrinna said a second later.

He looked back, eyes wide. She stared at him with a hint of surprise on her face, making his cheeks burn. Oops. A strained smile appeared on her face, definitely a sign that he'd intruded on a moment not meant for his eyes.

"Despite my intentions," she said, her voice a bit empty, "it has occurred to me that there's no way I can find enough food for you, me, and Xandrin." The strained smile vanished, and she looked away.

Tak eyed her knife and sword, and he knew Redrinna was getting quite skilled with her magic. On top of that, she was clever and had fast reflexes—he'd experienced all of those, plus her strength, firsthand the few times Timothon had had them train against each other. If she wanted to, she could've caught them enough food.

Why do you think so little of yourself? he found himself thinking. However, he pulled that thought tight to himself. It wasn't like he had any room to talk.

"I figured I'd wander around for a while before going back and admitting defeat. I suppose that'll make Xandrin happy." A quiet, barely audible sigh slipped out of Redrinna as she stared at the hushed river in front of them. "Hey, Tak?"

He braved a few steps closer. "What?"

"You...your home is near here, right?" Slowly, she turned to him, some of the light from the water reflecting off her red eyes. "I took you away without so much as a thought for any of that. No one's...missing you right now...are they?"

Tak hesitated for a second before shaking his head. "No. I never met either of my parents. My aunt and uncle raised me, but they've both passed away."

She didn't respond right away, but he noticed her fingering her mother's necklace. "I'm sorry."

"For what?"

"That you didn't have anyone to miss you."

Shame crept into his chest and Tak looked away. He was acutely aware of the fact there had been no one left to miss him before he'd met Redrinna. If she hadn't found him that day, then... He shook that thought away. That wasn't a time in his life he wanted to re-member, not even in its smallest measurement.

All at once, Redrinna said, "Can you tell me something?"

Staying quiet, Tak met her gaze.

"What if there was something about yourself, whether it was something you'd done or just a part of your...personality or whatever, you couldn't stand? An inherent piece of yourself you couldn't get rid of, no matter how much you wanted to?"

Instantly, the blood-stained memory of him and the dragon sprang to mind, followed by a few other memories Tak wished would disappear.

"Do you think what Timothon said is possible? Do you think you could change yourself into something you like better?"

"I...I don't know." Tak wished he knew the answer.

"Or 'shattering the mirror?' What did he even mean?" She let out a huff, like she was trying not to sigh again. As Redrinna went quiet, that hollowness from earlier crept onto her face for a second before being forced away by a smile that didn't reach her eyes. "Who knows, huh?"

"Yeah," he said slowly, unsure what to say. His gaze fell to the water. He, too, desperately wished to understand what Timothon had meant, but he did not. Even if he did, Tak wasn't sure it would help. How could you fix a piece of you that had always been a broken, jagged piece of glass that tore at anything and everything and didn't fit with the rest of you?

"I suppose we'd better head back," Redrinna said, turning away from the water.

Tak didn't speak, instead waiting for her to go before following after. He caught a glimpse of something out of the corner of his eye, and a quick glance over his shoulder to investigate told him the dragon was back, haunting his footsteps. Scowling, he fixed his gaze ahead.

Chapter Five

As night settled in, its deep darkness creeping between the trees like mist, Redrinna found herself as awake as ever, though she hadn't expected anything different. So, with nothing more than the sounds of Xandrin's slow, rumbling snores, Tak's faster but softer breathing, and a cool breeze gently stirring the leaves in the treetops echoing in her ears, she stared up at the stars glistening far away.

Once, she'd thought of them as mocking, having fun at her expense from up on their inky black thrones. Sometime afterwards, she'd seen them as beautiful. Now, as she stared at the vast expanse dusting the darkness above her, Redrinna felt nothing. They simply existed in a separate, distant place.

Can't sleep again? her gem asked in its quiet voice.

Redrinna wasn't up to responding.

Maybe if you got a little exercise, you'd be able to get some rest.

That might work, she supposed. It did sometimes. So, pushing herself to her feet and ignoring her body's protests, Redrinna walked a short distance from her friends—just close enough she could still see Xandrin's shadowy outline, but far enough away to avoid waking them.

For a moment, she debated practicing that set of magic stances again, but she didn't want to. The thought of her last attempt alone made frustration pound through her veins, and besides, using her magic here could be disastrous.

Instead, Redrinna drew the sword Timothon had given her. Cold slivers of pale moonlight shone on the long, black blade, making it gleam like the smooth, glassy surface of a lake. She was used to the heft of the wooden training swords, and this was about the same, but it still felt different in her hand. The chance of her killing someone with a training sword was slim; it would be quite difficult. But this...

Lightly, she touched her thumb against the edge of the blade. The sharp metal effortlessly sliced her skin, but she hadn't pressed hard enough to make herself bleed. Rather, a tiny bit of skin curled back on itself like a withered leaf. With this, taking a life wouldn't be hard; it would be easy.

That scared her to her soul.

Closing her eyes, Redrinna took a deep breath and pushed those thoughts from her mind as best she could. She focused solely on working through the newest set of stances Timothon had taught her and adjusting to the feel of the new weapon. When Timothon had given it to her, he'd told her to use it only if she had to, but she couldn't shake the feeling that using the sword wouldn't be a matter of if.

It was a matter of when.

Night pressed in deeper as she swung and swung her sword, her arms burning with such intensity, they shook like dead leaves in the wind whenever she lifted them. Regardless, she kept pushing herself, unable to convince herself to stop and not wanting to either, no matter how much it hurt. Maybe she could burn away the pain inside her if she kept going long enough.

You need to stop, her gem said in the sternest voice she'd ever heard from it. *You've been at this nearly all night.*

Redrinna turned eastward, towards the mountains towering above them. It was faint, but the eastern sky was brightening at the edges, framing the mountains with a thin line of pale light. She'd been at this for that long?!

"Sorry," she said, slipping her sword back into its sheath, having its weight back around her waist almost throwing her off balance. Even still, despite training all night, she didn't feel tired enough to sleep at all. Why couldn't she go to sleep for once? She was so stinking tired, she wanted to scream.

You can't keep doing this to yourself. You need rest, not—

"I know, I know! I said I was sorry, okay?!" she snapped. "Leave me alone already. You're not my mother!"

I know I'm not your mother. However, I am your friend, and I'm worried about you. I'm sorry for making you upset.

Not again. Redrinna hid her face in her hands, fighting off the urge to cry. "I'm sorry. I didn't mean it, I promise."

I'm not upset. Instead of worrying, try and rest as much as you can.

Nodding, she demurely returned to the sleeping forms of her friends. Settling down in Xandrin's shadow, she closed her eyes and hoped rest would come.

Redrinna wasn't sure how well she slept, but she did fall into a kind of doze for a while. All too soon, though, the sun peeked its fiery head over the mountaintops, and Xandrin nosed her awake. Well, some sleep was better than no sleep, she supposed.

The second she sat up, blearily attempting to rub the exhaustion out of her eyes, Xandrin bolted to his feet, thrusting his face inches from her own.

"You look more tired than I feel," he said, hitting her full-on with his morning meat breath.

She pushed his snout back a couple inches. "I did just wake up, you know."

He leaned forward, staring at her with his dark, unblinking eyes. "You don't look like you slept at all."

"I'm fine, Xandrin," she said, glancing Tak's way. The young man silently watched the two of them, appearing quite tired himself.

"Besides, we should focus on getting some food and finding that dragon."

Xandrin stared at her before scowling. "Oh, I get it. I'll go." Turning—Redrinna had to quickly duck beneath his tail—he romped off through the forest.

Tak almost drew even with her—keeping himself a step behind her like always, she noted—and said, "We should be careful. I-it looks like it's going to start raining soon."

She glanced up, noting the grey clouds potentially hiding a storm. There was a good chance he was right.

Folding her arms and closing her eyes to keep any trace of frustration at bay, Redrinna tried to keep her focus on how they should approach today's search. Depending on how big of a storm hit them, they might not be able to search at all, so they would have to work hard in the time they did have. The last waterfall they'd come across yesterday had been almost identical to the one described in her father's notes, but she'd seen no signs of a dragon living there. Even still, she had a nagging feeling to check again, just in case—

Her eyes snapped open. Something or someone was watching her, making her skin crawl. Whatever it was didn't seem friendly; malice was in its gaze.

Keeping her head still, Redrinna scanned the surrounding trees.

A moment later, she spotted the culprit. Her heart almost stopped. It wasn't a something, but a someone—someone she knew bitterly well, someone her mind insisted couldn't be real.

Standing nearly a Xandrin-length away, shadowed by a towering oak and cluster of ash trees, was Reyna.

It was impossible. Yet when she blinked, the woman didn't go away. Frantic, Redrinna dropped her gaze, hesitating for a second before working up the courage to look again. When she did, the woman was gone.

Her rapid pulse thrummed in her ears, blocking out every other sound.

Had that been real or a hallucination? If it had just been her mind playing tricks on her, then that was the most vivid hallucination she'd had yet. Never, ever had she actually seen something before. Usually, they were corner of the eye flashes that gave her the creeps. So why had that one been so real?

Or maybe Reyna really had been standing there.

"Redrinna?" Tak asked, almost scaring her out of her skin.

Wide-eyed, she stared at him.

He paled and went wide-eyed in return. "A-are you okay?"

"I—" Despite herself, her gaze flicked to the place where Reyna had been. It stood empty still. "I...I'm fine."

She hoped.

Tak watched her for a minute longer before hesitantly nodding and looking away.

⋅⊙⋅ ⊙⋅

They only managed to search for a couple hours before the rain broke loose, dumping water on them with such fury they were left with no choice but to get out of it. Redrinna hoped it would ease off or clear up soon, but the storm raged for hours, the rain pounding the leaves like it was intent on ripping them to shreds.

Eventually, the rain let up, and Redrinna crawled out from beneath Xandrin's wing. The sky was still grey, but some sunlight was breaking through, its meager light catching on the water clinging to the trees and brush. They'd spent most of the day here, she realized with frustration, held up by the storm. Now, instead of heading out, they should focus on finding something to eat.

Striving to shove her irritation down deep, she and Tak did their best to make camp comfortable despite how soaked the forest was while Xandrin hunted for dinner. Neither Redrinna nor Tak seemed to have anything to say and spent the entire time in silence. Redrinna kept her gaze on the trees around them, half-afraid her mind would conjure up Reyna yet again.

Fortunately, she didn't see the woman, and eventually, they settled down to sleep after their long and unproductive day. Redrinna glared at the sky which was clear enough now that thousands of stars had come out, the irritation churning inside her burning a little stronger. For a moment, she debated continuing the search during the night to make up for it, without the others, but she quickly turned the idea away. Not because it wasn't tempting, but because she didn't know how far she'd have to walk to find another waterfall or what she might encounter on the way. Plus, after seeing such a vivid image of Reyna earlier, a great unease had settled in her chest at the idea of what might happen if she went off alone.

Eventually, Redrinna's mind quieted, her eyes closed, and she fell into a restless sleep. She didn't dream—or at least, she didn't think she did—but all at once, she bolted upright, completely out-of-breath and heart racing, fear raging in her chest. Her hands scrambled in the grass, ripping through it as she fought to breathe—to orient her mind enough to figure out what was going on.

Slowly, the world came into focus around her: Xandrin and Tak were both sleeping nearby with the moon resting high in the sky, its cool light brushing over the trees. A light breeze blew, stirring the shadows, making them shift and move. Gradually, she calmed, leaving her utterly exhausted.

She dragged her hair out of her face, clenching her fists with the strands still caught between her fingers. "I just want to sleep. Why is that so much to ask?" she whispered, tears biting at her eyes. She forced them away.

All at once, a crunch rang out from the nearby brush. A chill raced over her skin. What was—

She looked up and recoiled.

Reyna, again. Leaning against the nearest tree. Was Redrinna hallucinating or not? She was so tired, she couldn't tell. Almost defiantly, Redrinna stared at the woman, willing her to prove whether she was a hallucination or real.

The woman just stood there, staring back at her.

Several minutes passed with them staring at each other. No matter how many times Redrinna blinked, Reyna remained unchanged. Her gem warmed the chain, almost in warning. Was...was the woman really standing there?

All at once, Reyna lifted a hand, her skin gleaming coldly in the moonlight. She lifted two fingers and beckoned her.

Redrinna's heart stuttered, but she held still. If this was a hallucination, she wasn't going to feed it. And if Reyna was real—if she really was standing that close to her—then there was absolutely no way she was going anywhere with her. Never again. No matter how much her heart wanted her to.

Every second that passed drove anxious agony deeper into her chest. The woman stared at her in silence, hand still raised. Redrinna wasn't sure if she was breathing.

After what seemed like ages, Reyna smirked and vanished in a rush of black mist. A shudder swept up and down Redrinna's spine, making her realize she was shivering—not from the cold, but from the fear pounding through her veins.

If that'd been a hallucination, then that had been the wildest one yet. There'd never *ever* been one like it before. Was she losing it or was Reyna actually here? Her mind said no; Redrinna vividly remembered taking her life. Yet, all at once, it occurred to her that if Reyna was in league with Osiris, then the odds of her being like the Dragon Slayer and her father were highly likely. Which meant—

Wild fear gripped her heart, and before Redrinna fully registered it, she shot to Xandrin's head, pressing herself to the back of his jaw, right behind his ear frill.

Reyna was alive. It hadn't been some bizarre trick of her mind, but the woman had been standing right there, taunting her, trying to trick her into the woods in the dead of night.

Or maybe, if she had any luck left, this was only a nightmare, and when she woke up in the morning, she'd realize that. She closed her eyes, but sleep didn't return until dawn.

⁓◌ᑫ ᑐ◌⁓

The rain continued the next morning, but to Redrinna's relief, it was light. If it stayed like this all day, it wouldn't hamper their ability to search too much.

Perhaps while they were searching, she'd even be able to forget Reyna entirely.

They ate breakfast in silence since nobody seemed awake enough or in the mood for talking, but Redrinna didn't mind. If the others did try talking to her, she wasn't sure she'd be able to keep her mouth shut, which she needed to do until she was sure whether Reyna was real. Until she could figure it out, she had to keep it to herself. If Reyna was here, she didn't want anyone going after her— just to be safe— and if she wasn't, she didn't want to needlessly freak anyone out.

Once they were finished, Xandrin stood and stretched. "Should we get going?"

Redrinna glanced at him, opening her mouth to speak when she spied something in the corner of her vision. Her heart skipped a beat, and it took her a minute to work up the courage to glance over. The air rushed out of her lungs. Again?

Reyna stood in the shadow of a massive oak, smirking at her. This...couldn't just be some kind of illusion anymore, could it?

"Um, Redrinna? Are we gonna go?" Xandrin asked, but she kept her gaze fixed on Reyna.

All at once, the woman dipped her head and walked away. She didn't vanish, but walked away, calm as the sea on a windless day.

Redrinna stared after her, barely breathing. She couldn't take this anymore; she had to know for sure whether or not Reyna was alive. No more of this.

Her feet were moving before she'd even finished the thought.

Tak stepped after her. "Wh-where are you—"

55

"Stay here," she cut in, not looking back.

There Reyna was again, moving rapidly through the trees ahead, black hair sporadically catching the sun, gleaming like obsidian. The woman glanced back and smirked again.

Redrinna, don't run off on your own!

"Wait!" Xandrin called as she burst into a run.

Redrinna wasn't waiting. If this truly was Reyna—if it wasn't some bizarre trick of her mind—then the last thing she wanted was to risk either Tak or Xandrin getting seriously injured. She was one thing, but they were another. There was no way she was going to risk their lives.

Reyna dipped in and out of sight, and every time Redrinna was ready to give up on finding her, she'd reappear, just ahead, taunting her forward again.

As they rounded a clump of trees, the landscape in front of her unexpectedly jutted upwards. Redrinna skidded to a halt, managing to stop before running into a boulder. Gasping for air, she stared at the mountains towering over her. She...was back at the base of the mountains? And Reyna was—

Gone. Redrinna furiously glanced around, scanning the forest. Really gone. There was no one but her now.

Dropping her hands onto her knees, it hit her all at once that her legs were on fire, and she was so out of breath, her lungs ached. How long had she been running?

Had...her mind just been playing tricks on her the last couple days? Was Reyna actually alive or— No. The reality of the situation was that Reyna probably was alive, even if she wasn't here in the forest, but whether or not Redrinna had, in fact, seen her—that she didn't know, nor did she know how to tell anyone without getting her friends involved.

"Redrinna, what is wrong with you?" Xandrin snapped seconds before landing nearby.

A concerned-looking Tak slipped off his neck, nervously watching the dragon as he stomped over to her.

"What are you running off for? Do you understand how much you freaked us out?"

A couple angry retorts jumped to the tip of her tongue, but Redrinna held them in as she straightened. She didn't want to snap at anyone. "Sorry, I...I thought I saw something, but it ended up being nothing."

Xandrin grimaced. "What did you see?"

She shook her head. "It was nothing. I promise."

Xandrin's brow lowered, but before he could say a word, something barreled into her back, knocking her to the ground. Panic tore at her throat for a solid second before a fuzzy, white head with strangely calming blue markings around its eyes popped into her field of vision. Large ears stood out on either side of its head, both angled at her. What?

Hold on. This was—

"It's you!" She pushed herself up, and the creature hopped off her back. Now that she'd gotten a good look at it, she recognized the fox-like creature. They'd met back in the woods when she'd been taking her test, and while she'd hoped for it, she hadn't imagined they'd ever meet again.

"I finally found you!" it said in a high, squeaky voice. "I've been looking for forever."

Redrinna stared at it, completely speechless.

"Who's this?" Xandrin asked, cocking his head at the creature.

That spurred Redrinna into action. "I met him while I was taking my test in the forest." Then, turning to the creature, she managed to say, "You can talk?"

He nodded. "Yep! I figured it out shortly after you left. I didn't know I could, but ta-da!"

She was smiling before she realized it.

"After you left, I got super bored, so I started searching for you. Oh! I think I have a name now too."

"Oh?"

"Yeah. This guy who saw me called me: 'Kitsune.' So I'm pretty sure that's it." He wagged his long, but still very floofy tail.

Kitsune? She'd heard of those before, but if she remembered right, the species was only found on the Oriana Continent, so how had this little guy ended up here?

"I'm not sure kitsune's your name. I think it's what you are," she said slowly. "But I guess you can keep it as one if you like."

His tail wagging stopped.

Tak hesitantly approached, studying the kitsune with a curious light in his eyes. Xandrin peeked over Redrinna's shoulder, but neither of them said anything.

Redrinna frowned. "Do you remember anything from before we met?"

He sat, curling his tail over his paws and cocking his head to one side, then the other. "Not really, why?"

"I was just curious," she said. "Anyway, you can keep your name if you want, but if you'd prefer, we could always try coming up with a new one."

Leaping back onto all four feet, the creature wagged his tail so hard, it looked like it was going in circles. "Really? I'd love to have a name from you!"

Redrinna smiled a little more, then thunder cracked above them. She jumped, glancing up right as the rain changed from a drizzle to a full-blown storm. This wasn't good.

"Again?" Xandrin fanned out his wings, trying to block the rain.

"We should find shelter before it gets worse," the kitsune said. "Oh! I found a cave nearby that'll fit all of us. Let's go!" Without warning, he took off.

Redrinna followed with Tak and Xandrin hot on her heels. Within a few minutes, the little kitsune led them into a cave at the base of the mountain right as the rain began falling in sheets so thick, she almost couldn't see the trees.

Redrinna stopped in the entrance, just enough to be out of the rain. Tak stopped nearby, but Xandrin stayed outside. The entrance wasn't big enough for him.

The kitsune blinked at him. "Oh, sorry. I guess it wasn't as big as I thought."

Xandrin blinked in return. "I'm fine."

Redrinna almost smiled before taking a seat on a nearby rock, hoping today's storm wouldn't last anywhere near as long as yesterday's. Her kitsune friend plopped himself right at her feet as Tak sat on the ground. Nearby, but not close, she couldn't help noting again.

Gazing at her with his gorgeous brown eyes, the kitsune said, "Have you thought of a name for me yet?"

She sat back a little, trying to get her mind working. What would be a good name? One immediately came to mind, but at first, she shoved it aside. There was a part of her that didn't want to use it. After all, it had been intended for someone else. Yet, at the same time, it would be nice for it to be used, wouldn't it?

After a minute more, she relented.

"How about Kyvo?"

He twitched an ear, murmuring the name a couple times, his tail wagging harder every time he did. Leaping to his feet, he cried, "It's perfect! From now on, I will be known as Kyvo!" He paraded around her, swishing his tail back and forth like a banner.

She found herself smiling a little again, despite the slight sting it brought. Kyvo had belonged to one of her younger brothers, the one who'd been born soon after her. He would've been sixteen now if life had been different.

Kyvo, the kitsune, however, pounced at a pebble on the ground, chanting his new name quietly to himself. At least he seemed to like it, she supposed.

"Oh wait," Kyvo said, straightening and peering at the three of them. "I don't know any of your names."

"I'm Redrinna," she said before introducing the other two. Then she turned her attention back to the storm outside, irritation flicker-ing in her chest as the downpour continued.

Kyvo bounded into her lap without warning, nearly pitching her over. "It's nice to meet you, Redrinna. Officially." He grinned, one ear twitching towards the rain. "And now—what's that?" His gaze focused on something in the cave behind them.

Redrinna turned. Her eyes went wide.

Instantly, she was on her feet, accidentally sending Kyvo tum-bling. Behind them, far enough back it was difficult to see, lay anoth-er blood circle, just like the one back in the Imperial City.

Chapter Six

Tak's blood ran cold at the sight of the vivid red circle painted across the back of the cave. He didn't have a clue what it was, but staring at it made his flesh crawl like ants were scurrying under his skin. A glance at Redrinna and Xandrin simply made him more anxious. Both of them had gone ashen.

"We need to go," Redrinna said, taking quick steps out of the cave and into the rain. "Now."

Tak swiftly obeyed, taking shelter from the rain under the wing Xandrin offered. None of them spoke, a heavy silence pressing on them. A chill raced down Tak's spine, but he kept quiet. His mind went back to what they'd seen in the cave, to the red circle with intersecting lines and strange symbols drawn around the edges. What did it mean and why was there one in a random cave of all places?

For some reason, when he'd overheard Redrinna talking about the one in the Imperial City, the idea of it hadn't been much of a shock to him. Perhaps, he'd simply figured it was Osiris's mark or something along those lines and had consequently not given it any more thought. Or maybe it was because he hadn't seen it with his own eyes. However, for one to be all the way out here in the middle of nowhere?

That made him unable to stop thinking about it.

After a while, they found a thick stand of trees far enough away from the cave that Tak no longer felt as though something were wriggling through his organs. The trees were large enough even Xandrin could take some shelter beneath the enormous oaks, so they quickly took refuge.

The storm lasted most of the day, not petering out until evening. Then the clouds broke apart, creating a sunset that painted the sky with bright streaks of gold and pink. Despite the beauty above, there was a sour air over the group, and while Tak wanted to believe it was the result of two unsuccessful days in a row, he wasn't completely sure. Redrinna hadn't said a word since they'd left the cave.

Almost as though he had read Tak's thoughts, Kyvo plopped himself at Redrinna's feet. "What was that thing in the cave?" he asked, his brown eyes shining with innocence.

Tak shot a worried glance at Redrinna, who, fortunately, remained oblivious.

"I don't know what it was," she said, fists clenching. "But I think it's dangerous, whatever it is. That's why I figured we shouldn't stay near it."

Xandrin nodded, his color just starting to come back. "We've only found one other one, but we got attacked by a weird creature last time. If we'd stayed, maybe we would've been attacked again."

"Why is it here?" Tak asked, unable to raise his voice above a whisper.

With a shrug, Redrinna said, "I don't know. I don't know what they mean." She didn't say it, but he could tell from the way she hunched her shoulders she was worried. It was how she'd often been when she'd been trying to wake her gem.

"Let's not worry about it right now," Xandrin cut in. "There's nothing we can do, so fretting won't help. Instead, we should try and find something to eat before we sleep."

Redrinna didn't respond.

Xandrin left to find them some food, and after a minute, Tak said, "I'll go try and find some dry wood."

She still made no response, so he turned and left. Hopefully, she wouldn't vanish while they were gone.

Those thoughts were driven from his mind, however, when Kyvo came trotting through the wet underbrush after him. The appearance of the creature had startled him, but it seemed nice, at least. Even still, Tak hadn't expected it to follow him.

"Heya!" Kyvo chirped. "Redrinna asked me to come help you out, so here I am!"

Once again, Tak worried she wouldn't be there when they got back, but he was more than a little sure Kyvo would obey her requests over his, so he didn't object. He just nodded and kept walking, picking up any sticks that looked promising and not too wet. The kitsune bounded through the underbrush, dragging back any sticks he found while waving his tail like a flag.

Before much time had passed, they had plenty to cook with. Gathering his courage, Tak said, "Th-this...is all we need. We can go back now."

"Oh, okay." Kyvo tossed his latest find back into the brush before trotting alongside him again. They stayed quiet for a minute before the little creature said, "When did you meet Redrinna? I don't remember you being with her last time. Or the big red guy, for that matter."

"Oh," Tak began, not sure why the kitsune talking to him had caught him so off-guard. "The dragon wasn't with her when she took her test but they knew each other, and she found me after she'd met you, so..."

"Oh, I get it. At least she wasn't lonely this whole time."

Tak grimaced. Even though she'd had them around, he wasn't sure Redrinna hadn't been lonely. On the contrary, there were quite a few times where he was sure she'd felt completely isolated, like she was the only human being left on the entire earth. He knew how that felt. He knew it very well.

"Hey...you don't have to tell me if you don't want to, but...is she okay?" Kyvo paused in his tracks, glancing up at him with big, concerned eyes. "Something about her seems...off, you know?"

Tak lowered his gaze. "Since she met you, something...something terrible happened to her. She's never been the same since, but she doesn't like talking about it either."

"Oh that's okay. I can pretend I don't know." Kyvo resumed walking, his tail held high. "I'm sure everything will be okay eventually. She's pretty strong, you know."

Hesitantly, Tak nodded, except the kitsune didn't see it. Redrinna was strong; he already knew that. But whether she'd be able to conquer this? That he didn't know. Stuff like what had happened to her didn't leave you unscathed. He knew that firsthand.

They didn't speak again the rest of the way back to camp, and to Tak's immense relief, Redrinna hadn't moved from her seat on a stump since they'd left. Her current position wasn't encouraging, but at least she hadn't raced off again.

The fact that Redrinna didn't even watch as he and Kyvo arranged the wood gave him next to no confidence in the idea that she was as fine as she kept claiming. Neither did the fact Tak had to call her name three times before he could get her attention. Even then, she stared at him blankly until he stammered through asking her to light a fire for them.

"Oh, right," she said, brow furrowing. A moment later, a fire sprang to life, eagerly eating at the wood.

An awkward silence poked at Tak while they waited for Xandrin to return, almost making him wish they'd gathered more firewood instead of coming back to their makeshift camp so soon. However, he had to admit he'd been more than a little concerned Redrinna would've vanished if they'd been gone too long. Regardless, that didn't make the uncomfortable silence jabbing at him any easier to bear.

Relief washed over Tak as Xandrin came back with a deer in his mouth. Quickly, they got dinner prepared, and the silence became less uncomfortable as they ate—though Tak couldn't help wondering if the slow, almost methodical way Redrinna chewed was because she was enjoying it or if she was just eating to fill a hole and her mind was occupied by other thoughts.

By the time they were all finished eating, the sun had almost vanished beneath the horizon, retracting its golden beams as the sky turned an inky blue. What was left of their little fire crackled happily while thin tendrils of smoke rose in the air and sparks skipped upwards before winking out. Tak watched the sparks, rubbing out any of the ones not completely extinguished by the time they hit the forest floor. They probably weren't hot enough to set anything on fire, but it gave him something to do, something to distract him from the fractured feeling skulking between everyone.

Kyvo seemed to sense it too, but instead of rubbing out errant sparks like Tak, he trotted over to Redrinna and sat next to her. "You know what I saw one time while I was looking for you?"

"What?" she asked, her voice a bit flat.

"I saw these kids sitting around a fire like this, and they were telling each other stories. It sounded really fun and cool." He turned his big, pleading eyes to her. "Can we try it? Please?"

Xandrin glanced at the sky. "Well, we still have some daylight left, so it might help us pass the time. Does anyone have any stories?"

Tak thought of a couple, but they brought back the time in his life when he'd been with his aunt, which wasn't a time he wanted to reflect on. So he stayed quiet.

"Please?" Kyvo begged, wagging his tail a bit. "You can make up a story if you don't have one."

Frowning, Redrinna stared into the depths of the fire for a long minute before a quiet sigh escaped her. "Okay, okay. I have something like a story."

Kyvo scooted closer, his tail brushing over the tips of the grass. For a brief second, a ghost of a smile touched her mouth before it faded like mist at the mercy of the sun.

"If you want, I could always tell you the priestess' legend," she said, mostly staring at Kyvo, but she glanced at Xandrin and Tak as well. "It's...pretty much the only story I know from memory."

"I don't mind. Any story is fine." Kyvo stared at her with rapt attention.

She stared back for a moment before turning to the fire, the flickering light from the flames dancing in her eyes. "A long time ago, in the age of myth, man and spirit walked the world together. It was an age of prosperity and peace, and all the human races lived in harmony."

"Then, I'm going to guess something bad happened," Xandrin cut in, resting his head on his claws.

Kyvo's ears flattened against his skull. "Hey, don't spoil it."

The dragon had the decency to look a little sheepish.

Redrinna glanced back and forth between the two of them before continuing. "Well, Xandrin's right. That time did come to an end. A faction of the human race sought the power of the spirits. When it proved impossible to obtain, they turned to dark, corrupting magic to slake their thirst. That power belonged to an ancient demon, a being said to be older than time itself, crowned with shadow and wreathed in flames, and those humans eventually managed to find it. They did everything the beast asked in order to set it free, all deluded, convinced that one day, they would become the possessors of its power.

"However, when their promised day came, on a day when darkness blotted out the sun, they released the beast, and instead of granting them power, it took their lives for itself before turning its gaze on the rest of the world.

"It swept nations before it; kingdoms fell to ruin at its touch; parents turned their blades on their children—all vying in vain for the beast's favor. It wasn't long before the entire continent was dragged beneath the weight of the demon's heel. The human race was subjected to its greed, bent to its desires, and made slaves to its will."

Despite the fact Tak was familiar with the legend, he found himself leaning in, gaze fixed on Redrinna. Chills crept down his arms. Something drew him into the story tonight, something he couldn't explain.

"The spirits that had walked the land were powerless against the combined might of the beast and its slaves. Grieving, they resolved to withdraw from the affairs of men, but before they did, they poured their power into one of the last uncorrupted souls."

"The priestess!" Kyvo said, his ears pointed right at Redrinna.

She nodded. "That's right. She was only a young girl at the time, not yet of age, but she was gifted the power of the spirits and a quest: to purge the world of the demon's power or die trying to set mankind free. She trekked the continent, uniting what remnants of the human race she could find: people of the sea and sky, people of ice and wood, humans clothed in feathers and fins—she sought them all. With the aid of the remaining human races, she raised an army in defiance of the demon.

"The two forces clashed in the heart of the continent, demon against human, shadow against light. Despite the army with the priestess, in the end, she ended up facing the demon alone. It's said that while none of her friends stood by her side, they burned in her heart, and with their power and the spirits' gift in her veins, she faced the demon completely and utterly alone. She defied him, and she defeated him, banishing him back to the prison where he was bound."

Kyvo bounced in a tight circle, but Tak's gaze fell to the fire. The story wasn't finished, and he'd never much cared for the ending.

"Yet, the priestess, while endowed with the love of her friends and people, was not left unscathed. Despite her victory, her life was cut short, diminished by the power that had dwelled inside her. She took her place as the country's ruler, beginning a new phase of her life, but she was physically weak. It was considered a miracle she was able to bear two children, a set of twins. Her last act was to pass the responsibility of caring for the land to them."

"She died?" Kyvo's ears drooped. "That's not a nice story."

A smile almost touched Redrinna's mouth. "You know, Kyvo, some people say she didn't die."

His ears perked back up. Tak sat up straight too. He hadn't heard anything like that.

"Some people say that when they saw she would soon leave this world, the spirits took her with them, and instead of tasting death, she became a spirit, unshackled from the scars of her battles and free to watch over the land she loved for the rest of time."

Kyvo flicked an ear. "I like that much better!" Without warning, he dashed off to Xandrin, the two of them quickly falling into acting out parts of the legend.

Tak blinked. Children back in his village had done that. He'd never joined in.

Glancing at Redrinna, he was surprised to find her expression a mix of sorrow and thoughtfulness.

After a minute, she noticed his gaze. For some reason, she appeared abashed. "I hope you don't mind me skipping some parts."

He blinked. In truth, he hadn't even noticed. Though, now that he thought about it, there was one part in particular she'd left out, one he'd never been able to understand why people loved. "You mean the part about the knight?"

She lowered her head. "I used to think he was an amazing person for sacrificing himself in order to save the priestess's life—and I still do—but at the same time, I can't help but wonder how the priestess felt afterwards. They were best friends."

The knight's story also left him conflicted. Caring about someone that much was admirable, but at the same time, he, at least, never could understand how dying for someone proved how much you cared. Granted, in the moment, that probably hadn't been what had run through the knight's head, but even still, Tak, for one, had never understood the necessity of glamorizing an event that had devastated so many people. It almost made it seem...arbitrary, in a way, almost like people were glossing over the pain the knight's friends and loved ones had all endured to try and paint it as something it wasn't: glorious.

Then again, Tak's aunt had always said he didn't have the right mindset for a knight or anything of the like, so maybe he just didn't get it.

However, he was sure it was different for Redrinna since she'd almost been on the other side of that sacrifice, the side of the one who got left behind. He was sure that would change anyone's perspective on that part of the legend.

The sun disappeared completely a short while later, and they all settled down to sleep. Tak kept himself a bit apart from the others, still unable to help feeling that if he got any closer, he'd be intruding. Despite how much he wanted to believe otherwise, he wasn't sure getting a gem would make that go away, but he wanted to cling to the hope it might.

Sleep avoided him for a long time, and Tak seemed to lay beneath the dark sky, watching the moon make its way across, for hours. The forest gradually quieted around him, almost like it had given up on trying to lull him to sleep.

He rolled onto his side, trying to get comfortable. A blade of grass tickled his ear, and he rolled the other way in an attempt to avoid it. Something moved amongst the trees, making him freeze.

His heart skipped a beat as he realized it was the dragon again. She was still following him around? What did she want from him exactly? She'd already said thank you and all that stuff, so what more could there possibly be to say?

He closed his eyes, determined to convince her that he was asleep in hopes it would deter her from coming any closer. He heard nothing from her, which slowly put him at ease. So long as she stayed there, everything would be fine. He would be fine.

However, as Tak kept thinking she was nearby, potentially getting closer while his eyes were closed, his mind kept turning back to the first time they'd ever met. No matter how hard he tried to distract himself, he was wading through the memory before he even realized it.

The memory had dulled with time, but he still remembered those creeps harassing her and the blood. There'd been so much blood. He remembered running until each breath had stung, and finally, finding the dragon in the woods. She'd been hurt so bad, in his memories, he saw her as a red-scaled dragon instead of green.

The events after were fuzzy, difficult to pick apart or make sense of. What little he did remember he forced away, curling himself into a ball like that would keep them at bay. It worked to some extent, holding the memories back until he finally drifted off. However, they returned in his dreams.

Chapter Seven

Redrinna did her best to hold in a frustrated sigh as rain poured from the sky for the third day in a row. It was the end of spring, nearing summer—not yet monsoon season. Was this some kind of weird wet spell, or did this have something to do with Osiris?

A shudder swept down her spine, so she hastily threw that thought away.

Xandrin huffed. "This is a lot more boring than I imagined."

She agreed but kept quiet.

"I don't know," Kyvo chirped after giving himself a shake, which made Tak wince as extra water hit his face. "This has already been way more fun than wandering in the woods alone."

Xandrin acquired a thoughtful frown. "I guess that's true. This is more fun than when I was living alone in the cave."

For half a second, Redrinna wanted to say this was better than living practically alone in a big, empty palace, but she wasn't sure. At least, when she'd been alone, no one had attacked anyone trying to get at her. Her friends couldn't almost die protecting her if she didn't have any.

In truth, she wasn't sure which way was better or which she preferred. She just wanted this to be over so they could go back to the Mount, and she could focus on forgetting the misery that had latched onto her mind like an anchor. At the same time, a part of her didn't want to go back yet. She was certain Timothon would figure out that sending her off hadn't helped in the slightest, and who knew what he'd do to try and help her then. Just imagining that was exhausting.

"Okay, I'll go try and find us something to eat now," Xandrin said. "Be good or I'll sit on you."

Redrinna didn't respond, and a minute later, the dragon romped off through the trees. She was far more worried something would happen to him than something happening to them.

"Hey." Kyvo popped his paws onto her knee. "Do you wanna play a game while we wait?"

"Not really. Sorry," she said, resting her jaw in her hand.

He blinked. "You seem kind of tired. Oh, it's probably because of the rain, isn't it?" He glanced at the sky. "Unfortunately, I can't control the weather." Hopping off her knee, he trotted over to some nearby bushes, sniffing at them for a minute. He raised his nose in the air, still sniffing. "Do you smell that?"

She inhaled, but all she got was the sweet, wet scent of the forest in the rain. "No."

"It smells like an animal of some kind." He trotted closer to the bushes, tail starting to wag. "Oooh, what do you think it is?"

"Don't go after it. You don't know what it is," Redrinna said, sitting up straight. "What if it attacks you?" Didn't he know better since he'd been living on his own until now?

He pulled up short before he could dive in the bushes. "Most of the animals only want to play, but I can outrun the ones that don't." He grinned back at her, making her shake her head.

"What if it's a bear or something though?" Tak asked quietly, watching the kitsune with that concerned look he seemed to favor.

Kyvo abandoned the bushes and all but dove behind Redrinna and her stump. "I saw a bear once. It was big."

"And they might be able to catch you."

Without warning, a buck with an impressive rack of antlers raced through the clearing without so much as a sideways glance before vanishing amongst the brush. Strange.

Kyvo's ears tilted in the direction the buck had come from. "Do you hear that?"

There was a moment of nothing before a distant rumbling filled the air, deep and mournful. Trees groaned as birds launched from their branches in flocks so thick, they were like dark clouds.

Tak backpedaled. "Run."

"What is it?" Kyvo asked, ears back.

Before Tak could say a word, a wave of mud sprayed into the air in the near distance, bowling a young tree over. Redrinna's heart leapt into her throat. A mudslide. They couldn't outrun that.

"Come on!" Tak shouted, sprinting for a nearby oak towering over the aspens and hazels. Kyvo was hot on his heels, and as another spray of mud shot high in the air, Redrinna followed. The rumbling turned into a roar, filling Redrinna's ears so completely, she couldn't hear her own heartbeat. Tak and Kyvo scurried up the sides of the tree like squirrels, and Redrinna stared after them, hands on the oak's rough bark, mouth dry.

She'd grown up in a palace and had almost never left it. She didn't know how to climb.

"Redrinna!" Kyvo cried.

The next second, a wave of mud hit her shins, nearly sweeping her feet out from under her. Her fingers dug into the tree, desperate to find some sort of grip. She scrambled for balance, everything beneath her feet slick with mud.

"Redrinna, I'll help you up," Tak called, legs wrapped around a branch as he reached for her.

If she stretched, she'd be able to take his hand, but all at once, her chest seized with the terrifying possibility that if she accepted his help, she might pull him into the mud too. If she did, they'd probably both drown. She couldn't risk that, but—

The mud surged, rising from her shins to her waist in mere seconds. It almost felt like water, but the muck was stronger than water. It rammed into her like a bull. Her fingers burned, shaking in desperation, struggling to hold on as the tree's bark bit her skin.

"Redrinna!" Tak cried, panic in his voice.

Before she could even glance up at him, something hard slammed into her knee, sweeping her leg out from under her. Immediately, she was yanked from the tree, seized by the roaring mud.

Her gem flared with heat, and somehow, no mud got in her nose or her mouth. She rolled and somersaulted, tossed like a leaf in the wind. Seconds later, she slammed into something hard enough it nearly knocked the wind out of her. Whatever it was, she scrambled to grab onto it.

Moments later, she managed to rip her head free of the mud, gulping in a deep, frantic breath. Tak and Kyvo called to her, but she could barely see anything above the waves of mud, let alone them.

A shadow fell over her. Glancing up, Redrinna stared, heart going still, as a massive, decaying tree trunk flipped up before falling straight at her.

Without warning, Xandrin slapped the tree away, making it crash to the side and shatter, spraying mud high in the air. Moments later, he landed, scooping her onto his snout and lifting her free.

He stared at her, almost cross-eyed. "This is not what I thought would happen if I left."

She pulled her mud-slicked hair out of her face, too shaky to say anything.

He glanced towards the surprisingly distant tree where Tak and Kyvo huddled in its branches and made his way towards them. Despite the fact the mud was high on his legs, he walked through it with ease and carefully set her amongst the branches with the other two.

Kyvo stared at her with big eyes. "That was so scary."

"Sorry," she said, trying to wipe the mud off her head before it could run into her mouth.

"How are we ever going to get you clean again?"

That made her pause and glance down at herself. Even though she hadn't been submerged in the muck for long, she was slimed with it from head to toe. How was she going to get clean? It wasn't like she could just find some water to clean herself off in and then put on clean clothes. These were all she had.

Despite herself, she scowled. She should've tried to climb the tree or done something other than stupidly try to hold on.

"Hey," Xandrin began, getting her to look up. "Are you okay?"

Fighting to keep her scowl off her face, she nodded.

He glanced upwards, towards the mountains, the mud beginning to slow around his legs. "Still, where in the world did this all come from?"

"Mudslides aren't uncommon this close to the mountains," Tak said, voice hushed and gaze on the mud below.

"It has been raining a lot," Redrinna said, studying the mountains too. The peaks were still covered in snow, so while there was a chance of mudslides because of the runoff and the rain, it was more common for mudslides of this scale in summer. Not spring. Given the weather though, maybe this wasn't odd, just a result of the overabundance of rain.

However, the strangeness of the weather turned her thoughts back to Osiris, and his weather-altering magic. There was a good chance this was because of him.

The anxious fear that was never far away crept closer, squeezing tighter around her chest.

Silence fell over their group as they watched the mud slow before it eventually stalled, the rain making rivulets in the mud as it settled. Her gem stayed quiet too, something about its silence leaving her feeling strange, almost empty.

Tak's heart was still pounding when they settled down for breakfast, the mudslide far behind them. The incident replayed in his mind in an endless loop, still bringing unease with it even though it was in the past. Redrinna hadn't been able to climb the tree; he'd seen it in her eyes right before the mud had swept her away. She could've drowned or been seriously hurt. Fortunately, her gem seemed to have helped, and Xandrin had arrived in the nick of time.

Even still, she could've used his help—and he'd offered it. But not fast enough. If only he'd realized sooner or something, maybe he could've helped her out of the way of the slide.

Dejectedly, he shook those thoughts away as Xandrin handed him a piece of meat. Xandrin then turned to Redrinna, momentarily eyeing the wing he was fanning her off with. It was still raining, so Tak wasn't sure how much it would help. Redrinna had dunked herself in a shallow river, leaving her soaked but mud-free. Kyvo was fanning her with a tree branch he'd found nearby, though Tak was pretty sure it wasn't helping much either. He wasn't going to be the one to point that out though.

Redrinna winced as Xandrin fanned a little harder, holding out her hand expectantly for her breakfast.

To his surprise, Xandrin didn't give her anything. "Why'd you run off yesterday?"

She eyed the dragon for a long moment before replying. "You're asking about it now?"

"We got busy, so I kind of forgot."

A scowl settled on her face.

"I won't give you anything until you tell me."

Her scowl deepened. "I thought I saw someone."

Xandrin dropped a meager portion of deer meat into her waiting palm. "Who?"

She paused with the meat almost in her mouth. For a long minute, Tak thought she wasn't going to say anything.

"I saw her."

"Her?" Kyvo asked around his tree branch as he tilted his head to the side.

A dark look crossed Redrinna's face. All at once, it occurred to Tak that she might've seen the dragon. Almost immediately, he dismissed that thought. It made no sense. After all, finding a dragon was what they were here for, so she had no reason to hide it.

"Well?" Xandrin asked, handing out more meat to Tak and Kyvo (who immediately dropped his tree branch at the sight), but withholding it from her again.

A sigh escaped her. "Reyna."

Xandrin's vivid red scales turned a visible shade paler. "The lady from the Imperial City?"

She nodded.

Tak's stomach clenched, almost making him lose what little of his breakfast he'd eaten. Reyna...was the woman who'd chased Redrinna and Xandrin with the Dragon Slayer. Timothon had also said she was the one who'd killed his dragon companion. If that was true, then the dragon-killing lady was *here*?!

"You said she died," Xandrin breathed, his tail curling closer to his side. "She fell off the cliff, didn't she?"

A shadow fell over Redrinna's face, accentuating the dark circles beneath her eyes. "That's what I thought, but I think she's like the Dragon Slayer. They're both working with Osiris, after all. Even if we do manage to kill her, she'll come back."

Tak suddenly found it difficult to breathe. Even Kyvo paused in his eating.

Tak had been sure it would be better if at least one of the people who could kill a dragon was gone, but if Reyna wasn't dead— His breath caught in his throat.

If what Redrinna saw was true, then it was only going to get worse and harder, not better and easier. Nauseating terror twisted through his gut.

Xandrin remained silent for nearly an age before abruptly baring his fangs and hissing, "So you went after her alone?!"

Tak flinched back, heart squeezing on his throat at the fury engraved on the dragon's face.

"Don't get mad," Redrinna said, seemingly unfazed, putting the last bit of her meat in her mouth. "She won't try and kill me like she would you."

"And that makes it okay to run off on your own?! She doesn't have to kill you to hurt you, Redrinna! What would you do then? What would we do, especially if we didn't even know?!" Xandrin's ear frills stood straight out on either side of his head, making him seem almost double his size.

Redrinna didn't answer his questions.

The tension in the air made a shiver run down Tak's spine. Situations like this always made him feel like the sun was targeting him, burning down on the back of his neck in an attempt to melt him into a puddle. The fractures between all of them seemed to spread more, the cracks digging just a bit deeper.

All at once, a realization struck him, making him go cold like the sun had fallen out of the sky, cold enough he couldn't speak for a minute.

"Why is she here?" he managed to say, his voice barely audible, even to himself, but he had everyone's attention anyway. "There's no way Osiris knows we're out here, is there? A-and even if he does, he said he was letting you go, right? So why in the world would she be out here?"

Redrinna and Xandrin paled at the same second. "The dragon," they said in unison.

Immediately, Tak felt downright ill, like he was going to puke. If he'd said something yesterday, maybe they'd be out of danger and back at the Mount, and the dragon wouldn't be in trouble. Now, though, what if the dragon got hurt or killed because he'd told her to go away? But with how long he'd been sitting on this information, how could he tell anyone without making them mad?

They finished breakfast as fast as possible and headed out, moving through the woods at a brisk pace, ignoring the rain. Tak kept an eye out for the dragon, and maybe it was because of the weather, but he didn't see a trace of her.

He appreciated her respecting his request, but this was at such a bad time! For all he knew, Reyna could've already gotten to the dragon, and they were never going to find her again. What were they supposed to do then?

And, even though being around her was difficult for him, he didn't want her to die. That was the last thing he wanted.

The rain was unrelenting, wholly hindering their ability to search. Around what they guessed was midday, they stopped to let Xandrin rest and to get out of the rain for a while. Tak was cold and miserable, but since Kyvo resembled a half-drowned rat, he kept quiet.

Time seemed to crawl by as they sat there, and the longer they waited the more antsy he became. If something happened to that dragon... He stared hard at the surrounding clusters of trees, willing the dragon to appear.

After several minutes, her draconic face materialized beside a tree, almost scaring him out of his skin. He blinked. So did she. With a guilty expression, she began to withdraw.

"Wait!" He leapt to his feet, rushing towards her.

The dragon kept stepping backwards.

"Tak, not you too!" Xandrin called as he raced off through the trees.

"Wait!" Tak cried as he dodged a low-hanging branch, pulling up short when the dragon whirled, staring at him with a hard glare. "Don't go. Please."

Pausing, the green dragon considered him with her dark eyes. "The other day, you told me to leave you alone and now you want me to stay? Which is it?"

He glanced away for a second. "I meant what I said, but you're in danger."

She raised a set of eyespikes.

"It's not safe for you out here alone, so that's why I..." He took a deep breath. "I just...don't want you to die, okay?"

"You think I'm going to die?" The dragon scoffed, flicking her wings.

"That's the goal," said a voice he didn't recognize.

He and the dragon spun. A lady stood nearby, leaning against a slender beech tree. The gleam in her dark eyes unnerved him, and the way she stood made him feel like she was sizing him up like a piece of meat; she was searching for the right place to cut. Was this Reyna?

"So why wait any longer?" She pushed off the tree, an easy smile twisting her mouth.

"Redrinna?" Tak called, taking a shaky step backwards. Would she even hear him?

Annoyance flicked across the woman's face. Then she drew two swords, taking a step closer.

The dragon stepped back, half-standing in front of him. She bared her fangs, a low growl rumbling in her chest.

"Oh, I'm not here for him, you beast," the dragon-killing lady said, taking a step forward for every step they took back. "Your pathetic kind desperately need to learn to be more selfish." One of her swords caught the light of the sun, but instead of reflecting it, it seemed to suck it in, making the air around the sword even darker. Without warning, she charged.

Chapter Eight

Tak's breath froze in his chest. He didn't have a weapon or any-thing, no way to keep Reyna away from him or the dragon.

Without warning, the dragon shoveled him onto her snout, rac-ing back to the others. The moment she burst through the trees, she yelped and lurched forward, dislodging him from her snout. He hit the ground hard, and she narrowly avoided stepping on him.

Fire ripped between them and the crazy, dragon-killing lady with a ferocious snarl. Then, Redrinna was there, planting herself between the woman and them.

"I won't let you kill this dragon, Reyna."

It was her then. The dragon-killing lady. Tak had never felt so sick.

Reyna smirked, but it was frigid. "So, that pathetic lizard of yours is still alive. What a pain." She flicked a wrist and shadowy chains shot out of the ground, pinning the dragons to the forest floor.

Then she turned her frosty smirk on him and Redrinna. "Now, to get you two brats out of the way."

Before Reyna could move, Kyvo launched forward, clamping down on her wrist. A flicker of pain flashed across her face before she stabbed a sword into the earth. Grabbing the little creature by the scruff of his neck, she tossed him to the side like he was a stuffed animal.

As Redrinna took a step forward, fire crackling on her hands, Tak pushed himself to his feet. His heart thudded a thousand miles per hour, but somehow, he managed to stay upright. He planted himself between Reyna and the dragon, hoping he wouldn't have to try and fight.

They couldn't let this dragon die, but if Reyna couldn't be killed, how were they ever going to win?

Tak's attention was redirected to the fight by a harsh scraping sound as one of Reyna's swords ricocheted off Redrinna's scale shirt. Sparks sputtered out as they hit the ground. His throat became so dry, it hurt.

Redrinna jumped back and shot flame at Reyna's face. The woman dodged, rolling forward. She nailed Redrinna right in the gut with the hilt of one of her swords. As Redrinna went down, nausea dumped into Tak's gut. The only thing standing between Reyna and her prey was him.

He knew it.

So did she.

Smirking, she idly twirled her sword before stepping his way.

The dragons thrashed against their restraints to little avail. Kyvo was fighting to get to his feet while Redrinna was struggling to just draw a breath.

Tak didn't have a weapon, but if he got swept aside, the dragon behind him would be as good as dead. He wasn't sure if he'd be able to do much. But if he didn't try to hold his ground, then he definitely had no right to be here.

"So who are you, boy? You joining this ragtag group too?"

His throat hedged itself shut, and he didn't even try to speak. Instead, he started familiarizing himself with the way she moved. Timothon had been drilling that into him, telling him to learn all he could about an opponent before they made their first swing.

Redrinna had once told him Reyna was fast and no one could best her in swordplay. The only reason she'd been able to get away from Reyna before was because she'd had the element of surprise with her magic and Reyna hadn't been trying to kill her.

Tak didn't have magic like Redrinna's or a weapon. But Timothon had said he was fast.

"Or, perhaps," Reyna continued, halting a short distance away. "You're expendable."

"No!" Redrinna cried, on her hands and knees now, but she didn't seem to have her breath back. "He's one of us. If you kill him, you'll be sorry!"

There was the briefest hesitation in her step before Reyna lunged, both her swords swinging for him. He sidestepped one and managed to grab her wrist, stopping the other. As the first sword swung back, he managed to catch her other wrist in time, barely holding both swords away from himself. Well this wasn't good.

Reyna kicked at him, but he managed to evade her. The first time. The second kick caught him in the knee. His leg nearly buckled, but he managed to stay upright. Reyna's dark eyes narrowed.

Out of nowhere, Kyvo pounced on Reyna's back, sinking his teeth into the woman's shoulder. She flinched, bearing her teeth in a near snarl. She twisted and jerked one of her arms free, sword flying out of her grasp. With terrible force, she ripped Kyvo off, tearing her shoulder more. Then she chucked him into Redrinna, keeping them both at bay.

Before his eyes, Reyna's shoulder magically stitched itself back together. The blood drained from his face. They were really going up against people like this?

Without warning, Reyna swept his feet out from under him, sending him crashing to the ground. She tried to step past him, but he grabbed for her ankles. He managed to snag one, catching her off guard and sending her to the ground too. Her second sword spun out of her hand. The green dragon managed to flick it into the bushes with her tail.

"Oh you're all so annoying," the woman hissed right before a blinding pain flared right above Tak's right eye.

He flinched and the woman got out of his grasp. Fighting to blink away the pain, he did his best to ignore the uncomfortable sensation of blood slipping down his face.

Reyna got to her feet, brushing herself off before striding towards the green dragon again. No! He wasn't going to get there in time!

All at once, Redrinna was there, standing between the woman and the dragon.

Use your sword, he thought. She had a weapon. She could stop the woman, possibly long enough for them to get away. Except, for some reason, Redrinna didn't draw it. She stood her ground, but her eyes were different.

It was hard for him to tell, but it almost...looked like she was in pain.

One of her hands twitched like she was going to reach for her sword, but before it could move, Reyna caught it.

Leisurely, she lifted Redrinna's hand, staring at it like she was studying it. "Oh, you poor, poor little princess." Without warning, she twisted it and a loud crack rang out.

Tak flinched.

Redrinna jerked forward, a tiny cry escaping her. Reyna threw her back, and Redrinna landed hard, smacking her injured hand.

"Stay down where you belong," Reyna hissed. "You dog."

Then she moved forward, reaching the green dragon. She pulled a gleaming knife from her belt. Before Tak even realized it, he was up and running. Reyna pulled back, ready to swing her knife. As she stabbed forward, he reached her, lunging between her and the dragon.

Fire erupted in his side for a split second before a terrifying numbness rushed in, the entire world going kind of fuzzy. Reyna's eyes widened before the most irritated scowl twisted her features. She yanked her knife away. Tak couldn't feel his legs, and he fell back. Dimly, he heard voices saying his name, but his mind was a confusing mix of pain and numbness.

He felt more than he saw the green dragon ripping her head free of her bonds. There was a racking hiss and then a loud sizzling. Someone cried out, but he didn't know who. Black bled into his vision, spilling across his sight like ink soaking into paper, and then he knew nothing else.

◦◦◦

Redrinna was pretty sure her heart gave out as Tak went down. The green dragon reared her head, snapping the shadowy chains holding her, unadulterated fury twisting her features. Reyna's gaze flicked to her but she didn't move, knife still in her hand, a strange expression on her face.

The dragon bared her fangs, a strange hissing noise beginning deep in her throat as her chest glowed with a poisonous green color. The next second, green liquid gushed out of her mouth, hitting Reyna square in the face. Recoiling, the woman backed away, steam curling off her skin as an awful stench clogged the air.

Was that acid?!

Redrinna didn't have time to think on it now. "Kyvo, go to Xandrin," she said, relieved that with Reyna distracted, both dragons' bonds vanished.

Then she rushed to Tak, stomach clenching at the red slowly staining his tunic. Working fast, she wadded up the end of his tunic, pressing it against his wound hard enough to shoot fiery pain up the wrist Reyna had snapped. She was sure it was broken, but that was the least of her concerns.

Grimacing, she pressed her uninjured hand harder against his wound. Tak whined a little, but there was a distance in his eyes.

Fear seized her lungs.

"Xandrin!" she shouted, glancing over her shoulder.

The dragon was already on his feet, but at her cry, he leapt forward. Swinging his tail in a wide arc, he flung Reyna into the nearby trees.

"Grab them and let's go," he said to the green dragon, spreading his wings and launching upwards with Kyvo clinging to his horns.

Redrinna wrapped her free arm around Tak's head as the green dragon scooped them up and launched into the sky. Then she tried to stay focused on slowing the bleeding from his side. Fortunately, it didn't seem the blade had gone deep enough to pierce all the way through, but there was still a lot of blood. She didn't have the knowledge to know or be comfortable investigating the extent of his injury.

"Hey," she called to the dragon carrying them, whose green scales seemed to have lost their luster. "You know this place, don't you? Can you take us to someone who can help?"

"Can't you do something?" the dragon asked, her gaze repeatedly flicking to Tak.

"No, I'm not a doctor. He needs real help," Redrinna snapped, trying to not let the fear pounding in her veins take over. Cuts to the abdomen could bleed for hours before the victim passed, but if you got hit in the right spot, it could only be minutes, and she had no clue which one Tak's wound was.

"Fine," the dragon said. "They might not be willing to help though!"

Redrinna ducked as they picked up speed, skimming over the treetops so fast, their leaves almost became a solid sea of green. The wind rushed in her ears, louder than crashing waves. She barely heard Xandrin's familiar wingbeats close by.

In desperation, she silently begged for Tak to be all right. She was already kicking herself like crazy for not realizing sooner what Reyna had been planning, for letting Tak run off and get caught, for being too scared of her sword to use it, and for letting the familiarity of Reyna's face make her hesitate. It was stupid. Redrinna had been stupid. However, if Tak died because of it?

A shudder shook her body. Not again. The last thing she'd wanted was something like this. Why couldn't she just get through something calmly for once, instead of it feeling like she was trying to cook a seven-course meal all at once, all on her own? Without the stupid recipe?!

Minutes later, the green dragon dipped back under the cover of the trees, landing so gracefully Redrinna hardly felt it. Then they rocketed through the trees, the dragon's gait only somewhat awkward despite the fact her front claws were carrying the two of them.

A horn blared in the trees ahead, making Redrinna glance up. She didn't see anyone, but that didn't mean a thing. Hopefully, this dragon knew what she was doing.

Seemingly seconds after the horn blared, they burst from the trees, skidding to a stop in a massive clearing that was almost a meadow. Wait. This wasn't just a clearing. Redrinna's gaze was attracted upwards where, strung like beaded necklaces between the surrounding trees, was a massive network of bridges and treehouses.

However, what truly grabbed her attention wasn't that; it was the people. The few people she saw were brown skinned and dark haired, but unlike her and Tak, each of them bore enormous, feathery wings. Their massive wings were held upright on their backs, accentuating how much taller than them they seemed.

A large, broad-shouldered man with silvery gray feathers landed in front of them, the ends of his feathers brushing over the grass as he rose to his full, imposing height. He held his wings out wide, making him seem even taller and broader than he was. His golden eyes narrowed as he studied them, watching them in silence.

Redrinna's heart stuttered in her chest, unsure whether to sit quietly or run in panic. These were the Torijin people. To be honest, she'd never expected to meet them in her lifetime.

"Astra," the Torijin man said in a deep, rich voice. "What are you doing here?"

The green dragon—Astra, she guessed?—extended her front claws—extended Redrinna and Tak. "Please, my friends are hurt. You have to do something for them, please!"

Astra lowered her claws to the ground and Redrinna hopped out of the way as a couple men came forward. One went straight to Tak, but the other—the tall man with silvery gray feathers—turned to her.

After a minute, she realized her hands were covered in blood—wet blood. "It's not mine," she said quickly. "I'm fine. Please, just help him."

He hesitated for a moment before joining his fellow. Her wrist throbbed, the pain intense enough to make her hands tremble, but she kept quiet, her fear for Tak outweighing the discomfort of the pain. The two men only examined him for a minute before picking him up.

One of them called out: "Mika, go tell Shappa."

A young boy on one of the bridges above them turned and raced off, his small, reddish-brown wings slightly spread. The two men then spread their wings and lifted off in sync, taking Tak out of sight.

Redrinna's worry didn't lessen, but all at once, the pain in her wrist spiked, making her close her eyes. She gripped her forearm in a vain attempt to quell the pain and accompanying nausea and light-headedness it brought with it.

More importantly, now that the shock of Reyna's assault was wearing off, acute discomfort was creeping in to replace it. If any of these people recognized her, she doubted they'd let her stay. Not after the history between their people and her father.

"Hey, didn't you get hurt too?" Astra said, staring right at her.

She fixed her gaze on the ground. What could she say? She didn't know, and the pain was making it hard to think clearly.

All at once, someone approached her, feathers rustling, but she refused to lift her head. "Are you hurt as well? Can you tell me where?" The voice was sweet and quiet, but Redrinna kept her head down.

Her tongue latched itself to the roof of her mouth as her knees quivered, whether from the pain or fear, she wasn't sure. However, slowly, she managed to extend her hand. She winced when the woman touched it. Even though she was gentle, the light brush of the woman's slender fingers made pain lance up her arm like fire.

She risked a glance up. The rest of the people behind her turned back to what they'd been doing before, but she spied an older man glaring at her. Immediately, she lowered her gaze again.

The woman who'd approached her carefully tugged off her gauntlet, clicking her tongue a few times at the deep purple bruise already spreading over her wrist. "We definitely need to have Shappa or Takota examine this. I think it's broken, but they have more experience than I do, and we should make sure. Come along."

Redrinna glanced at Xandrin, panic racing in her chest like wildfire.

Concern marked his face, but he nodded, trying to encourage her to go. Kyvo nodded in an encouraging way too, but Redrinna's knees threatened to buckle. How could she let these people do this? How could any of them be willing to help her? How fast would their generosity end once more of them realized who she was?

"I can't," she whispered, trying to pull her hand out of the woman's grasp.

The woman didn't let her go. "You have a serious injury. If it isn't treated properly, it could become infected, and you'll either be crippled or die. So come on. At least let us make sure you're okay."

Redrinna bit her lip. Xandrin nudged her with his nose, making her take a step forward.

She glanced back, meeting his gaze.

"Go make sure it's okay," he whispered. "Please?"

It'll be okay, Redrinna, her gem whispered.

Against her better judgement, she allowed herself to be pulled forward.

93

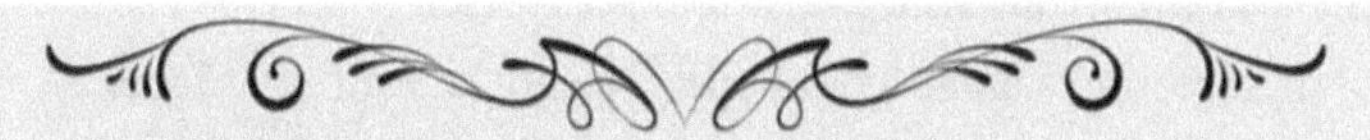

Chapter Nine

The woman pulled Redrinna along by her good wrist, towards a staircase leading up to the tree houses above, leaving her little choice but to follow. She wasn't sure what force made her legs move, but somehow, she made it all the way to the top level where they'd taken Tak. They were high enough she could feel the platforms and bridges swaying beneath their feet as they walked, the sensation making her nerves tense even more. The woman, her shoulder-length hair swaying slightly, led Redrinna past a few houses before they arrived at the largest building—a circular, wooden structure built around the trunk of a massive oak tree.

Her escort led her into the building, where the pungent scent of herbs struck her nose. There was a calm air about the place, a quiet that hadn't been in the rest of the village.

They walked through a short hallway before the space opened into a circular room. The trunk of the tree stood exactly in the center, and there was a small gap between the tree and the building where they didn't quite meet, allowing sunlight to trickle into the space. Doors ringed the room, some open, but most were closed down.

"Hmm," Redrinna's guide said after a glance around. "They're probably both helping your friend since he seemed hurt pretty bad. It might be a bit of a wait."

Redrinna still couldn't bring herself to look up or say a word. She felt so...awful, like she was going to be sick.

"Oh, my name's Chumani, by the way. What's yours?"

Redrinna shook her head. If they knew, would they chase them out? Tak was already hurt because of a mistake she'd made today, and if she said the wrong thing, it would get worse.

Before the woman could speak again, one of the doors to the left opened, and a tall Torijin man strode out, his feathers so brown, they almost blended in with the wood of the building. His hair was short like Chumani's too except it was tied back.

"Takota!" Her guide hurried over to him, and he stopped, turning towards her.

"Chumani? I thought you were checking on your mom?"

"I was, but Astra came with the boy, so I wanted to see if I could help. How is he, by the way?"

"He's doing okay. The cut wasn't as deep as we feared, so Mom could handle it on her own. However," he paused for a minute, and Redrinna was sure he'd noticed her, "is this...another patient?"

"Yes. I think her wrist is broken, but I want you to make sure."

"Oh sure. I have a free second."

Chumani practically bounced back to her. "Come, this way. My love will make sure you're healing good and proper."

Trying to swallow past the dry lump in her throat, Redrinna allowed herself to be led into a nearby room. They sat her in a chair, and Takota took hold of her wrist with his big hands. Honestly, Redrinna's hands were child-like compared to his.

"What happened?" he asked as he checked it over.

It may have been because they weren't outside anymore, but the bruising appeared even worse, now a deep reddish-purple curling around her wrist and hand like a snake.

The reality of what Reyna had done hit her, almost bringing her thoughts to a halt. Then, all at once, Takota's question sunk in, and

Redrinna realized she had to answer.

"We got attacked in the woods," she began, her voice dry and raspy like she hadn't had a drink of water for a whole day.

"Attacked?" He glanced up, brow furrowed, and for the first time, she met his eyes. They were golden, the color almost like sunlit coins. "By what?"

Reyna's dark eyes flashed in her mind, making her drop her gaze for a moment. "A woman. She was after Astra."

She couldn't help noting both Takota and Chumani relaxed.

"And she's the one who did this to your wrist?"

She hesitated before nodding. Then she mentally scolded herself. Why had she considered lying to protect Reyna? They weren't... They couldn't be what they used to be, so there was no reason to protect her or her honor. There was no point in trying to make it seem like what'd happened hadn't.

"She grabbed it and turned it hard," Redrinna said, miming the action, shivering at the memory of Reyna's face as she'd done it—the cold eyes and the hint of a smirk—almost like she'd enjoyed it.

Takota smiled sympathetically. "I doubt that was pleasant. Now, I'm just going to feel your arm, to check if the bones are out of place. Let me know if I touch anywhere sensitive, all right?"

He began close to her elbow, fingering along the bone. It didn't hurt until he got to the bruise, but when he touched her wrist, she cried out. He lifted his hand.

"Will you try bending it for me? Don't force it if it's painful, but if you can..."

She tried, managing to bend it slightly forward and back before it would hurt.

Takota watched with narrowed eyes, checking her wrist over once more. "Well, good news: the break doesn't appear too severe. At the very least, it seems it was only one of your bones, not both, but it is safe to say it's broken." He gently pushed her hand down a fraction, sending an ache up her arm. "See here?"

A part of her wrist bumped out to the side, making Redrinna stare. It was kind of gross but also fascinating. In a disturbing kind of way.

He righted her hand, feeling along her wrist for another minute before he spoke. "Now, I'm going to have to set this for you, and it's going to be several weeks before it's healed, but if you're careful and do your best to let it rest, it should heal well and shouldn't cause you too much grief in the future."

He turned to Chumani. "Will you fetch me some bandages and splints please?"

Turning, she left the room for a few minutes. Takota stayed silent, seeming to scrutinize Redrinna's wrist with an increased intensity while they waited. Chumani returned shortly with the requested items.

"Thank you," he said, beaming as she set them on the table next to him. Then, with a gentle, "This is not going to be pleasant," he dug into Redrinna's wrist with his thumbs. Fire flared in her arm as black gathered on the edges of her vision. Her mind told her he was only realigning the bone, but her body was convinced he was trying to kill her.

After the most agonizing minute (or maybe it was a year) of her life, he carefully wrapped her wrist and most of her palm with a soft bandage. Chumani then held out a small bowl of honey Redrinna hadn't noticed. Takota dabbed a bit of the honey onto the end of the bandage before tucking it under the rest and lightly pressing it down.

Despite the pain and nausea still hunkering in her gut, she was instantly fascinated. Back home, bandages like this had been tucked under, but to keep them from falling off or coming undone, they'd had to be a bit too tight. So using honey was a completely foreign concept to her.

Almost without Redrinna noticing, Takota and Chumani splinted her wrist and wrapped bandages around it again—though these were much heavier and stiffer than the first—before sealing them with honey like before.

"There you go," Takota said. "That should help it heal right. Keep that bandage as clean as possible though, and try not to get it wet, all right?"

She nodded and managed a quiet 'thank you.'

All at once, a voice echoed in from the main room. "Takota? Takota, where are you?"

"Here," he called, checking Redrinna's bandage over one last time before getting to his feet.

A moment later, an elderly woman with streaks of gray overtaking most of her feathers opened the door. "There you are. I wanted to let you know the boy is finished, and he's going to be fine. However, I wanted to go over his care with..." She trailed off, and after a minute, Redrinna plucked up what little courage she had and lifted her head.

The woman's gaze was fixed right on her, the frigidity of her glare making the nausea sink deeper into Redrinna's gut. This was it. What she'd been expecting from the second they'd arrived.

"Why did you bring her here? How dare you let her in?"

Takota put a fist on his hip, staying silent for a few moments. His massive wings unfurled, shielding Redrinna behind them, catching her by surprise. Then, in a hushed voice, he said, "Mom, she's just a kid. You can't blame her for what happened when she wasn't even alive."

The woman's voice remained as hard and cold as steel. "Get out. Get out of my clinic right now."

"Shappa," Chumani said, taking a defensive step forward, her wings fanning out a tad as well. "She's a patient who needs our care. You can't turn her out."

Redrinna's gaze fell for a second before she was able to get herself together. This was okay. In fact, it was probably as it should be.

Redrinna? her gem asked as she rose from her seat.

Forcing a small smile, she said, "It's okay." Silence avalanched into the room as she spoke. "I'll go."

"You'd better," the woman hissed before turning and storming out of the room.

With a small bow to Takota and Chumani, she said, "Thank you for what you've done for my friend and I." Then she stepped past them and left the building.

The sun seemed harsher than usual when she stepped outside, making her wince. She supposed the rain was gone now, and after three days of constant storms, perhaps she'd simply forgotten how intense the sun could be.

Her wrist throbbed, and she found herself holding it to her chest, like she was trying to protect it or something. If nothing else, keeping it up like that made it seem as though it didn't hurt as much.

As she made her way back across the canopy of bridges, most of the handful of people she passed gave her quizzical stares, but there were a few—all of them elderly—who gave her hard glares. She'd been used to getting those at the palace, but she guessed she'd been away from that long enough it got to her more than she remembered. Maybe she'd forgotten what it felt like, or perhaps it was different when it felt like she deserved them.

Regardless, she kept her head lowered as she made her way down the staircase and back to the dragons. It took her a minute to find them, since they were now curled at the base of the tree that housed the clinic she'd been kicked out of.

Xandrin's head shot off the ground when she arrived, and Kyvo practically bounded into her knees. Astra was also there, but she was sitting a ways apart from the others, her head upturned, staring at the clinic above like she could will Tak to come out of it.

"How is he?" Xandrin asked, getting Astra's attention.

"They said he's going to be fine. It wasn't as bad as it looked," Redrinna said.

Both of the dragons relaxed.

Kyvo leaned a little more against her leg. "And you?"

She glanced at the arm she was still holding across her chest. "It's fine. It's just broken."

"Just broken?" Xandrin repeated before letting out an exasperated sigh.

In spite of herself, she found her gaze dropping again. What did he want her to say? Did he want her to freak out?

Astra crept closer. "Are you going to go back to Tak and keep an eye on him?"

She shook her head.

"What? Why?" the dragon said, sounding genuinely annoyed.

She debated not explaining, but at her gem's insistence, she said, "They kicked me out."

"Huh?"

At that moment, she felt someone's gaze on her, she glanced up and behind her. That old man from before was glaring at her as he walked past on the nearest bridge, and she turned away. For the first time in quite a while, she was reminded of yet another reason why she didn't want to be the Imperial Princess. This feeling wasn't one she'd missed.

Stifling a sigh, she walked over and sat in front of Xandrin's elbow. Kyvo curled by her side as Xandrin lowered his head next to her.

"What do you mean they kicked you out?" he asked in a whisper.

"These people, the Torijin people, hate me because of something that happened a long time ago," she said, hoping they'd stop asking her questions. "So they don't want me here."

He cocked his head. "What? That doesn't make sense."

"Yeah," Astra said, scooting closer. "What are you talking about?"

Not even I know what you're talking about, her gem chipped in.

Redrinna didn't want to explain this, but she had a feeling they weren't going to let her be until she at least attempted an explanation. So, she shoved aside all the emotions dragging on her like children clinging to their parent's legs.

"You guys know about the war with the Dragon Kin and all that, don't you?"

Xandrin nodded, but Astra shook her head. So did Kyvo.

In as few words as possible, she caught the two of them up to speed, and when she was finished, both of them remained silent.

"So, this thing you're talking about," Xandrin began, his dark gaze fixed on her, "happened after?"

"It was shortly afterwards. After Osiris was weakened and forced to retreat and the Dragon Kin was destroyed, my father took over as King of Eridia."

"Wait, your dad? Just how old are you?" Astra asked, her forehead bunching up.

"It's not like that. It's one of the side effects of Osiris's power. I don't get how it works, but they can't die and they don't age. He was the king for a long time before he had me."

Astra scowled. "So, that lady you said was out to kill me, even though I spat in her face and this big tough guy slammed her into a tree, she's...still coming after me?"

"Most likely," Xandrin said. "Welcome to the crew, I guess."

She sat back, closing her dark eyes. After a minute though, she opened them again. "Back to the history lesson."

Redrinna sighed. "So, after he took the throne, he invaded the neighboring kingdom of Manon, conquering the entire nation in a single night, creating the beginnings of the Eridian Empire. Afterwards, a proclamation was sent out to the rest of the countries on the continent that they could either surrender to the Empire of their own free will or be taken by force."

The silence hanging over the group was so thick it made her nauseous again. The history of her country wasn't one she was all that proud of.

"The next nation targeted wasn't a 'nation' per se, but it was land many Torijin tribes considered sacred and their homelands. They refused to submit to the Empire, so as a show of force to other unwilling countries, the tribes were rounded up and slaughtered like cattle."

Astra hissed but stayed quiet otherwise.

"There were some people who managed to flee the continent while the ones that didn't get away, but survived the genocide, were forced to leave their lands and herded across the country, ending up in places like this, where those who hadn't perished on the journey were left to die. The remnant of one of those tribes are these people here. They're probably all that's left of their original tribe."

Xandrin dipped his head, staring at the ground.

"So, it's because of that these guys don't like you?" Astra asked, drawing her head back an inch.

She nodded.

"That's stupid."

Redrinna slowly met the dragon's gaze. "What makes you say that?"

"You didn't do it. Plus, this happened nearly a century ago, right? So what's stupid to me is that they're mad at you and kicked you out when you have a broken arm. Especially since I know these people, and this is strange behavior. I've never seen them treat anyone this way."

Redrinna couldn't figure out how to tell the dragon things were different because it was her. In this case, she wasn't just any person to them. She was a descendent of the people who were responsible for horrendous things done to them. Of course they would view her differently.

"Why shouldn't they be mad? Even if they don't realize my father was the one who did that to their people, at the very least, in their minds, my ancestors took everything from them. Because of my family, they've lost everything: their culture, their language, their beliefs. It's all gone."

"Yeah, I get that," Astra said. "But it's not your fault."

Redrinna didn't respond as the rain from the past few days resumed. For the first time in quite a while, her mind turned to the blood pounding through her veins. The blood she shared with her father, and perhaps played some role in why Osiris wanted her. The blood of people willing to kill and destroy was inside her.

The memory of her shoving Reyna off the cliff side in the rain ran through her mind again. Their blood was irrefutably inside her.

She hated it. Lots of people hated her because of it, so why shouldn't these people hate her too?

Chapter Ten

Tak kept his eyes closed as his mind struggled to defog, everything seeming distant and far away. He was acutely aware of a sharp pain in his left side and a terrible pounding in his skull, but as he lay wherever he was, not moving and keeping his eyes closed, the pain ebbed like the tide. It wasn't completely gone, and it definitely didn't recede all at once, but gradually, it became less consuming. Or maybe, he'd been in pain long enough he was getting used to having it there, so instead of going away, it was just bothering him less. Regardless, everything still ached.

A restlessness coiled inside him, making it impossible for him to stay asleep for long. He seemed to keep waking up, though he wasn't sure why. He thought he heard voices, but all his memories were lost in a haze, like a heavy fog had settled in his mind.

Tak wasn't sure how long he stayed out of it, but when he was finally awake enough to crack his eyes open, the world lay blurred and out of focus. He had no idea where he was or what was going on, so he just shut his eyes again. Maybe this was because of the pain. Or maybe he'd died. Though, if he had, would he still be in pain? He wasn't sure, but he had a strong suspicion death was very unlikely.

Wherever he was, it was dim and quiet, and there was a soft cloth against his skin, so...could he be inside somewhere? If he was, where on earth could he be? He doubted Redrinna and the others had had time to build some kind of shelter. Unless they'd left him behind somewhere?

A door unlatched, and his eyes shot open. He wasn't sure why, but everything remained blurry and impossible to pick apart, like dirt trapped in wool. If he concentrated, he could make some things out, but there was two of everything. The harder he concentrated, the worse the headache became.

"You've come to," said a male voice he didn't recognize. "Your friends will be thrilled."

Tak glanced in the direction of the voice, but his sight didn't cooperate. He rubbed at his eyes but to no avail. His vision remained fuzzy, and all he could see was a weird, hazy, double image of an enormous man. Panic bloomed in his chest.

"Oh, I always forget my manners. Good morning is what I should've said," the man continued.

Tak tried to focus on him, but it was extremely difficult when his eyes were refusing to function like normal eyes.

"How are you feeling?"

Swallowing, Tak shrunk back into his sheets as subtly as he could. Desperately, he wished for somebody he knew to appear and tell him what was wrong with him.

"I see," the mystery man said. "Now that you're awake, can I ask you a few questions? Oh, and if it helps put you at ease, my mother and I are the ones who treated your injuries. Your red-haired friend is around here too, but she can't come see you yet."

That did help him relax a little, he supposed. Assuming this person was trustworthy and not trying to play some kind of trick on him.

"How's your head?" the man continued, sounding like he took a step closer. "You took a nasty hit and I want to make sure you're all right."

After a long minute of silence, Tak managed to pluck up his

courage and say, "It...hurts. A-and I can't..."

"Can't what?"

He pushed himself up into a sitting position, almost losing his balance a couple times. He stared at his hands, studying them and their mirror image for a minute. "My eyes...are funny."

"Funny?" The man took another step closer. "Funny how?"

Tak stammered through a poor explanation, but he did his best.

After he finished, the man didn't speak right away. "Well...I know it's weird and distressing, but you probably don't need to freak out too much. You took a nasty hit to the head, though I'm not sure how well you remember it."

Tak closed his eyes in an effort to focus. It was easier to think without the distraction of his wonky vision, but his head still ached. In truth, he didn't remember getting hit in the head. Actually, most of what had happened after Reyna had found them were patchy memories, and in truth, he didn't remember much.

"Yeah, the expression on your face says as much," the man said. "Don't worry. With head injuries, it's pretty common to forget the details of the event surrounding your injury. That's the nature of a concussion. And since the wound on your head wasn't close enough to your eye to injure it or cause any strain, it's probably just the result of the concussion too. In time, it should resolve on its own, but we'll keep an eye on it anyway. In the meantime..."

The man's voice faded out, being replaced by some rustling and shuffling.

"Oh, all that talking and I didn't introduce myself, did I? I'm Takota. And you are?"

Tak hesitated before introducing himself.

"Nice to meet you, Tak," Takota said, a smile in his voice. "I'm going to go fetch something, then I'll be right back."

Tak nodded, and a few moments later, the door shut. He touched his fingers to his eyelids before moving them higher, finding a thick bandage above his right eye. So his eyes were messed up because he'd been hit in the head? A sigh rushed out of him. How in the world was he not supposed to be a burden to the others if he'd gotten hit hard enough in the head it'd knocked his vision askew plus who knew what else? They didn't even know whether or not his sight would ever come back the way it was supposed to. So much for not causing trouble. Instead, he'd taken a couple steps closer to getting kicked out of the Dragon Kin entirely.

A few minutes later, Takota returned. Out of habit, Tak glanced up at the sound of the door opening, but he still couldn't quite make out the guy's features.

"Here's what we're going to do for the time being," Takota said, sounding happier than Tak was ready for. "To take off some of the strain on your head as it heals, I'm going to put a bandage over your eyes, all right? It's not going to help you heal any faster, but it'll help you for the first little bit with the vision problem. Even if they weren't wonky, your eyes are going to be more sensitive to light, so this will mostly just help your head hurt less."

"O-okay," Tak said, a bit nervous about the whole thing anyway.

Within a few minutes, Takota finished wrapping an almost velvety feeling bandage over his eyes. Tak couldn't open them anymore, but his head did hurt a little less, he supposed.

"Now then," Takota continued once he was finished, "if you only had the stab wound, I'd take you to your friends. That wasn't as serious as we'd first feared. The knife didn't hit any vital organs or go in very deep, so it'll probably heal quickly. But because of the concussion, I'm going to have to keep you in bed for a couple days. The last thing any of us want is for you to lose your balance and trip or something like that and add another injury to your list."

Tak nodded, which was not pleasant in any way.

"I have some other things I have to do, but I'll be by to check in on you periodically, all right?"

"B-but..."

"Yes?"

"Where...am I?"

"You're in our village," Takota said. "Astra brought you and your friends here."

Astra? Was that the green dragon's name? She'd...saved him?

"I'm going to go now, all right?"

Tak didn't respond, and after a minute, the door clicked shut and the man was gone. Sighing, Tak settled into the soft pillows behind him.

Astra had saved him. Without his permission, his mind forced that blood-drenched memory to the forefront of his thoughts again. Even when he shoved it away, it lingered like a ghost, lurking in the shadows of his mind like it was waiting for the right moment to spring out again. He didn't want to think about it.

Despite his wishes—perhaps it was because having the bandage over his eyes made it hard to get out of his head—his mind kept hunting for it, drudging it up over and over again, no matter how hard he fought to keep it locked out.

That night, all those years ago, had been the first and last time Tak had ever used his magic, the magic that had run in his mother's veins, and now, for some reason, ran in his. The magic that had killed her and nearly killed him too.

For one instant, he debated reaching for it again to try and heal the wound in his side, but even if it would've worked, he wouldn't have tried. His power didn't work on himself. The only thing he could've done was heal Redrinna's wrist, but he couldn't risk it. If he did, then he would have to explain why he hadn't used his power to help Xandrin, why, when he could've done something to prevent Redrinna from being cooped up for so long—knowing full well he was more than capable of doing so—he hadn't.

To top it off, despite how much he was holding back and keeping to himself, when Reyna had attacked, he had a vague recollection of Redrinna insisting he was part of the Dragon Kin too. And from what Redrinna had told him about Reyna, there was no way he could've come out in one piece unless the woman had wanted him to. More than likely, Redrinna had saved his life.

Swallowing past the lump in his throat, Tak shifted so he was more on his non-injured side than his injured one.

He wanted to feel like he was a part of their group; he wanted it so bad he could barely stand it. However, if he truly was part of this group, then why did everything that was happening make him feel like being here was a mistake?

◦◦◦

As the sun began dipping beneath the trees, a chill crept into the breeze, pushing Redrinna deeper into the protection afforded by the frill running down Xandrin's back. As she did, he shifted his wings slightly, lessening the effect of the wind.

As for Astra, the dragon had moved to the other side of the tree now, a clear sign she wanted to be alone.

As the sun's light faded, Redrinna noted the entire village had vanished into their homes. The only people in sight were guards, who wore leather armor and were armed with weapons whose gleaming edges made her nervous. The emptiness pervading the village carried a sharpness with it, like someone stood behind her with a blade against her back. In a way, the atmosphere here was haunting, eerily similar to how the Imperial City had been the last time she'd been there.

On the other hand though, there was some relief that when she looked up, there was no one glaring or gawking at her like she was an animal on display.

Kyvo shifted in her lap then, calling her from her thoughts. He smiled in his sleep, and for some reason, that eased the tension inside her a bit.

"It feels like it's been ages since we've done this," Xandrin said, his voice quiet, snout angled towards the western sky. The evening sky was rapidly being stained a dark blue, almost an inky purple on the edges as the sun vanished from sight.

"Done what?"

"Watch the sunlight fade," he said, still gazing skyward.

Redrinna lowered her gaze. It hadn't been that long since they'd spent their days in the cave, watching the light recede like a crocus closing its petals, leaving them in darkness, but now, it seemed like it'd been an entire lifetime ago. In truth, she couldn't quite remember what it was like to be calm and enjoy such a simple pleasure.

Not for the first time, it made her wonder how long it would be before she forgot other things that had mattered so much to her. Like having Captain Brion almost always at her elbow, both helpful and annoying. Or the quiet evenings she and Reyna used to spend together. Or her mother's face. Her voice.

Her wrist panged, and she made a small noise of complaint she barely registered. She wished it would stop hurting.

Xandrin shifted, and after a moment, she realized he was staring at her, specifically her injury. She couldn't hide it from his sight, so she tried to bear it.

After what seemed like an eternity, he said, "That's my fault."

She disagreed, but since she didn't want to fight with him again, she stayed quiet.

"There wasn't anything I could do. No matter what I did or how hard I fought, I couldn't break free in time to stop you or Tak from getting hurt."

"You don't need to be sorry. I'm the one who put myself in danger. You didn't have anything to do with it."

"I couldn't keep my promise."

That made her pause. "Your promise?"

"While you were taking your test, Timothon explained the Dragon Kin to me, specifically what the dragon members did. So, I promised myself I would do everything I could to protect you and everybody else who joined the Dragon Kin. That's why I made you that shirt."

Redrinna fingered her sleeve, the scales cool to the touch without the sun to warm them. She'd originally tried wearing them without anything between her and her skin, but they'd been quite cold and sometimes pinched, so she'd taken to wearing the long-sleeved shirt her parents had given her when they'd traveled to Xandrin's cave. It covered her arms, torso, and neck completely, keeping her a little warmer, but it mostly kept the scales from biting her skin.

At the time Timothon had given it to her, she'd been afraid Xandrin would succumb to his wounds and that he, too, would be taken from her life. Even now, the shirt—his scales—sometimes multiplied in weight, threatening to drag her down.

"I know..." Xandrin began before pausing, turning his head slightly away before continuing, "I know I can't always be with you to protect you, but I believed that if you were wearing my scales, then in a way, I still could. But they couldn't protect you much today. And they can't save Tak at all either."

There wasn't anything she could think to say for some time. Redrinna couldn't seem to muster any of that false positivity she'd been trying to maintain, but eventually, she managed, "You know I don't blame you, don't you?"

There was no response.

Leaning her head back, Redrinna watched the sky as it dimmed, a weak dusting of stars poking their heads out of the dark expanse. There was no blame towards him in her heart for how today had played out; he'd done the best he could. The person who did deserve blame, however, was herself. She'd stupidly frozen up when the others had needed her to act. If she hadn't, her wrist probably wouldn't be broken now, Tak wouldn't have been stabbed, and this tribe wouldn't have had to be burdened with her. Maybe they would've been able to convince Astra to come with them, gotten Tak's gem, and be home instead.

However, yet again, her irritating, unavoidable incompetence had nipped any chance of that in the bud. Why was she always so stupid, even now?

All of the sudden, a quiet flapping reached her ears, almost bird-like but a bit too loud. Glancing up, she was surprised to find Chumani winging towards her. As the woman landed, Redrinna gently moved Kyvo off her lap and slid down Xandrin's side.

"Hey, how's your wrist doing?"

Redrinna shrugged. "It's mostly the same."

"I figured as much. So I brought you this." She produced something wrapped in a thin, almost waxy-looking cloth. It was a small, dull green ball of something, the pungent, earthy smell biting at Redrinna's nose and making her recoil a little. "I know it's not appealing, but it's medicine. Don't eat it, mind you. Just put it under your tongue for a few minutes until the pain begins to lessen, then spit it out. Even if Shappa won't permit you to stay in the clinic, Takota and I will still take care of you."

"Oh, you don't have to, but thank you," Redrinna said, accepting the medicine ball. Under Chumani's watchful eye, she put the medicine in her mouth. It was not pleasant to the taste, and the flavor worsened when she pushed it under her tongue. The bitterness reminded her an awful lot of the poisonous berries she'd eaten while taking her test in the forest.

Chumani laughed, making her wings rustle. "I know it's gross, but that's how medicine is. Anyway, I wanted to tell you a couple things before we all go to sleep, Your Highness."

Redrinna inwardly cringed at the title. It'd been a long time since someone had used it, and she hadn't missed it in the slightest.

"What are they?" she said around the medicine ball.

"First of all, your friend woke up, and Takota deduced that he has a concussion."

Astra's head shot off the ground.

"It's affected his vision a bit, but it should return to normal as he recovers. In the meantime, he'll be on bed rest for a few days before Takota is going to let him get up and wander around. Also—it's just to help ease any discomfort from his injury—there's a bandage over his eyes. It's nothing to panic over."

Redrinna took in a slow, deep breath before she nodded. "Okay. Thank you for telling me."

"And, the last thing I wanted to say," the woman began before pausing. She stared at the ground for a moment before meeting Redrinna's gaze. "I wanted you to know that the majority of our tribe doesn't hate you. They're just...uneasy right now, especially with strangers. Yes, we're still angry and frustrated about what happened, and even though most of us here didn't live through those days, the pain of what our ancestors endured was passed to us. It feels like our own. Even still, I can say with certainty that Takota and I don't hold you responsible for what happened. None of us get to choose where we're born or who we're born to. It'll just take the tribe time to relax around someone from...you know."

Redrinna couldn't quite hold the woman's gaze. "I don't mind. I'm used to it anyway."

A concerned, almost wary expression settled on Chumani's face, but Redrinna kept quiet. Whether or not the woman liked it didn't change the fact she was used to people being angry and blaming her for things like this.

The woman sighed. "However, there are people here who do hate you. At the very least, they're more than willing to hold you responsible for their pain. So...be careful."

"I know."

"Yes, I'm sure you saw." Chumani folded her arms as she stared at the village strung through the trees above. "Some of us are the children of those who suffered directly under the Empire's hand—or, in Shappa's case, some of us were children at the time. Infants, mind you, but they were there all the same. I'm not making excuses for them, but...I hope you'll understand."

Nodding, Redrinna kept quiet. They didn't need to apologize to her, but if it put Chumani more at ease, then she would keep her mouth shut.

"You can spit it out now," the woman said, handing her the waxy cloth she'd brought the medicine in.

Redrinna did so as discreetly as possible, hesitating when the woman reached for it.

"This is part of my job too. It doesn't bug me that it was in your mouth."

She relented, letting Chumani take the medicine.

Chumani stepped back, but then she stopped, almost hesitantly. "One last thing," she said, her voice much quieter now. "You should all be careful while you're here, but if you stick with your dragons, you'll be fine."

"Why?" Xandrin asked, sitting up a little straighter.

She glanced down. "There's something dangerous in these woods, and lately, it's been making appearances here. It would be best for you to stay as far away from it as you can." After a moment more, she spread her enormous wings, the black sheen of her feathers reflecting fragments of the dying sunlight. "Well, good night."

Redrinna returned her parting words, staring after her for a long minute before returning to Xandrin's warm back. Then, shifting Kyvo out of the way, she settled down and closed her eyes. Hopefully, now that it was dark, she'd be able to rest. In truth, after everything, she wanted to forget this entire day had even happened, and with any luck, she was tired enough she'd get some decent sleep.

Kyvo got up and stretched, turning in a couple circles before curling right next to her side. She stroked his soft fur a few times, drowsiness creeping in. Please lead to sleep, she kept thinking, over and over.

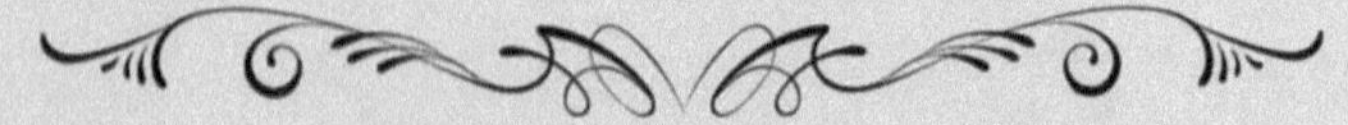

Chapter Eleven

Tak's mind hovered in a gray area somewhere between being awake and asleep, but all at once, he became aware of a presence nearby. He shifted, habitually straining to open his eyes before remembering the bandage keeping them shut.

"Good morning," Takota said from nearby. "Now it's time for you to get out of bed and try walking around a bit."

Tak was just asleep enough to not really understand. "What?"

"You've been resting for two days, and since you've been pretty alert and able to stay balanced, today, I'm taking you outside to sit with your friends."

Before Tak could even think about protesting, he was all but pulled from the bed, his side and head throbbing accordingly. Fortunately, they didn't ache as much as they had for the past couple days, which hopefully meant he was getting better.

With a good deal of assistance from Takota, Tak made his way outside, the wind striking his skin the moment they left the clinic, neither cold nor warm. He could tell there were a few people nearby from the sound, but their voices were hushed, almost subdued, like they were at a wake or something.

After a minute of walking across smooth wood planks, Takota said, "And here are the stairs. Take them slowly."

Tak did, almost tripping a couple times until he figured out their width, and soon, the wood beneath his feet changed to grass. Mere seconds later, something large came at them, something that made a lot of noise as it moved. Takota tugged him to a halt right before whatever it was stopped in front of them. A foresty smell washed over him, and the only thing he could imagine this creature being was Astra.

"How is he?" It sounded like her. "Oh, I guess I could just ask you, huh, Tak?"

"I-I'm fine," he managed.

"There you have it," Takota said. "Now if you'll move to the side, I can finish escorting him and get him something to eat. Then you can talk to him all you want."

"Oh right," Astra said.

Her wings rustled, and then Takota pulled Tak forward. A shadow fell over him, and after another minute, Takota stopped him again. The next second, something soft bumped into his shins. Out of habit, Tak glanced down even though he couldn't see anything through the bandage.

"You're not dead!" someone squeaked, and he was fairly certain it was Kyvo.

"N-no, I'm not."

"Redrinna!" Kyvo squealed, turning so fast, he whipped Tak's calf with his tail. "Wake up! Tak isn't dead!"

Wake up? That was out of the ordinary for her, but perhaps her wrist had kept her awake during the night which was why she was still asleep. At the very least, she probably needed the rest, so maybe it was a good thing.

A moment later, someone yawned, and then Redrinna said, "Good morning." He heard her slide off Xandrin and land on the ground with a quiet thump. "You should go find yourself some breakfast, okay?"

Xandrin shifted, sounding like he got to his feet. "Okay."

"Be careful."

The dragon laughed quietly, almost under his breath. "I know."

"I'll go too," Astra began from his other side.

"Are you sure that's a good idea?" Redrinna said. "It's dangerous for either one of you out there right now."

"All the more reason I should go," the dragon insisted. "Then we can watch each other's backs or whatever."

There was a second of quiet before the dragons turned and romped off, hissing something at each other Tak couldn't quite catch.

"They'll probably be fine," Takota said. "Astra did grow up in these woods, so she'll know where to go to find food."

"Right," Redrinna said, a note of hesitation in her voice.

"And I brought your friend out for a bit of fresh air. He's not recovered enough to do much, but he's staying pretty steady, so he should spend his time out here with all of you instead of being cooped up inside." Takota let go of his arm, making Tak's heart stutter. "Anyway, I'm going to get your breakfasts, so stay here. I'll be back in a couple minutes."

Tak remained where he was as the man left with a strange rustling noise. Even though he was pretty sure there wasn't anything to run into where Takota had left him, he was hesitant to move or try and sit. What if he lost his balance or fell in a hole or ditch he couldn't see? The world was surprisingly formidable without his eyesight.

"Do you want to sit down?" Redrinna asked after a minute.

"Where should I..." he began before trailing off. He wasn't sure why sitting seemed like such a daunting task, but it did.

Redrinna came and took his arm, guiding him a couple steps further before helping him sit on the ground. As soon as Tak was settled, Kyvo crawled into his lap, his soft fur brushing against his hands.

Takota soon returned with food for them, which today was apparently some kind of stew. Until now, Takota had only brought him fry bread, so Tak wasn't entirely sure how he was going to eat this without making a mess down himself and on Kyvo. However, he gave it his best shot. And only had a few casualties.

The food tasted good, full of different flavors and textures, and it was nice to have Redrinna and Kyvo's talking (mostly Kyvo) to drown out the same few thoughts that had been circling over and over in his head. The dragons returned a short while later, adding more life to the conversation. At least most of them seemed to be in high spirits, aside from Redrinna, who was quieter than usual.

Not being able to pick up on any visual cues was surprisingly frustrating, but Tak supposed he'd always navigated the world through sight more than any of his other senses. A shiver of fear trickled down his spine like cold rain. How much would he have to change if his world stayed this way, foreign and imperceptible to his eyes?

Sometime later, Takota returned. "Sorry to put a damper on things, but my mom wants to check you over, Tak, so I've gotta take you back already."

"O-okay," he said, slowly putting his palms to the ground to help push himself to his feet. He managed to stand on his own with only a couple wobbles.

"Bye," Redrinna said, a hollowness in her voice.

He waved vaguely before allowing Takota to lead him back up the stairs and to his room.

Once he was seated on the bed and the door shut, he sensed a change in Takota's mood. He wasn't sure how he picked up on it, but he did. However, he didn't speak, just in case he was wrong.

"Tak...is Her Highness okay?"

Staying quiet, Tak fingered the soft quilt decorating the mattress. A part of him hoped the tiny stitches would give him some sort of answer, but they didn't. So he shrugged.

"So her suddenly not eating sometimes is normal?"

"Kind of...a-at least it is now," Tak said, his voice soft. "Ever since..." Shutting his mouth, he finished with a little shake of his head. It wasn't for him to share. The last thing he needed to do was go around sharing everyone's secrets and anxieties. Not only would that have made him extremely uncomfortable if the situation were reversed, but it was a sure way to put himself into the Dragon Kin's bad graces.

"Ever since?"

He shook his head again, hard enough it made his skull twinge with discomfort. "I-I don't think that's for me to..." Spreading Redrinna's pain around definitely wasn't any of his business.

As he trailed off, Takota released a little, quiet sigh. "I understand. It's clear to me the knowledge of it pains you as well."

It was? Were Tak's emotions so obvious?

"Thank you though, for easing my mind. My mom will be here shortly, so try to relax until then, okay?"

The man left, shutting the door softly behind him.

Tak distracted himself by fingering the stitches in the quilt still, trying to figure out the pattern with his fingertips. He'd been hoping Redrinna would start getting better if they left the Mount, but maybe that wouldn't happen. Maybe she wouldn't ever get better.

He frowned. That was the last thing he needed to be fretting over when he had enough of his own problems. It also occurred to him he needed to thank Astra for protecting him and saving his life. Even still, he didn't want to see or be near her. Not yet. Maybe not ever.

৵৹ও ৩৻৹

Redrinna let out a sigh as she stared at her breakfast, at the vegetables floating in the thick brown gravy staring innocently up at her. She knew she needed to eat, but she had no desire to. Even though she was sure the food was good, the idea of eating made her sick to her stomach.

Are you not hungry? her gem asked. *You need your strength.*

She closed her eyes, pushing the food back and forth with her spoon. It bothered her when this happened, but forcing herself to eat hadn't ever made it better. And, of course, it had to happen now, when she was someone's guest, and they were feeding her out of the kindness of their hearts.

"Redrinna? Do you not feel good?" Kyvo asked, touching his nose to her knee.

Opening her eyes, she studied her food again, vainly trying to convince herself to eat or at least be hungry. Her gem stayed quiet now, but she could feel it trying to give her comfort. Even still, its warmth was dull. Muted, like light shining on metal, no more than a reflection off an empty shell.

"Does it taste that bad?" asked a new voice, making her jump.

She glanced to the side, catching sight of moccasin-clad feet. Was that...Chumani? It sounded like her, at least. Gradually, Redrinna lifted her gaze, meeting the woman's warm brown eyes.

"Hmm, it doesn't look like you've eaten anything. Are you feeling okay?" Chumani knelt in front of her, touching a hand to her forehead. "Well, you don't seem feverish, but maybe we should check your arm to make sure an infection isn't setting in."

The woman gently picked up her hand, but Redrinna pulled it away, hugging it tight to herself. It wasn't her arm. She didn't need to be a doctor to know that.

"Redrinna?" Xandrin asked, concern thick in his voice.

"Your Highness," Chumani said, concern in her voice too. "Please, just let me check your wrist—"

Forcing a smile, Redrinna lifted her head. "I'm fine, I'm just not hungry. Sorry."

Kyvo's ears tilted back. "But—"

"I am fine," she insisted.

"Your Highness," Chumani began. "I need to check it anyway to make sure it's healing okay—"

"I already said I'm fine. Shut up and leave me alone!" Redrinna snapped, anger roaring in her ears.

It got very, very quiet.

Not again. Why couldn't she keep a handle on herself? "I...I'm sorry. I didn't mean it like that... Sorry."

The woman didn't answer right away. "Is there...something you want to talk about, Your Highness?"

Redrinna shook her head.

"If you're sure..." the woman began, but she didn't finish the thought. Instead, she let out a sigh. "I have to go for now, but I'll be by to check on you later, all right?" After hesitating a moment longer, she left.

Redrinna kept her head lowered, doing her best to ignore the concern she could practically feel coming off her friends. She glanced at her breakfast again, but she still had no desire to eat it. So she didn't.

Kyvo touched a paw to her knee. "Are you okay?"

"I'm fine," she said. Then something occurred to her. "Hey...would you mind going and sitting with Tak so he doesn't get too lonely?"

He stared at her for a long minute with his intelligent brown eyes. "Are you sure you're fine?"

She nodded.

His ears dropped a couple inches as he turned and trotted off, tail low to the ground.

While she was concerned about Tak getting bored or lonely, especially after his brief freedom, more than anything right now, she wanted to be alone. She didn't want to talk about anything, particularly not the last few minutes.

Xandrin was eyeing her when she risked a glance at him. "If you feel sick, you should probably rest."

Not wanting to argue or snap at him like she had with Chumani, she quickly climbed onto his back. He laid his head down, and she wished he would go to sleep and not try talking to her. Fortunately, he didn't say a word.

Unfortunately, Astra did.

"Hey, um, it's...Redrinna, isn't it?" the dragon asked, approaching her in a sheepish manner.

She glanced over. "Yes, it is."

"Okay...so that Dragon Kin thing you guys keep mentioning," Astra said, not quite meeting her gaze. "Is it just the three of you?"

"Tak, Xandrin, and me?"

Astra nodded.

"For now. Our group will grow in time."

The green dragon remained quiet for a moment. "You weren't out here looking for me, were you?"

Redrinna's brain couldn't come up with anything for her to say. Maybe? Did Astra live near a waterfall in the forests north of here?

"I'm only asking because I think I was supposed to find you."

That gave her a turn. "What?"

Astra sat, tail curling over her front claws in cat-like fashion. "A long time ago, when I was teeny tiny—and I mean *teeny tiny*—" she held a claw close to the ground, "there was someone who took care of me for a while. The first human I'd ever met."

Both her and Xandrin sat up at that (well, in Xandrin's case, his head shot off the ground).

"Someone took care of you?" Redrinna asked, her voice a bit strained as a person came to mind. "Do you remember who they were?"

Astra shook her head. "It was a long time ago, so I doubt they're alive now. I mean, us dragons seem to have quite a few years on you guys. Anyway, he told me about the Dragon Kin, though not about any of the war and stuff that you told me. He said that if someone ever came asking about the Dragon Kin, I should join."

Redrinna's stomach twisted. That person had been her father; she was sure. At the thought of him, her hand found its way to her mother's necklace, fingering the tiny stones. The instant she realized what she was doing, she dropped her hand.

"What are you trying to say?"

"I'm saying that if you guys are the Dragon Kin, then I'm sticking with you, whether you like it or not." Astra lifted her chin a fraction of an inch, the setness of her jaw giving her a regal appearance. In a way, her demeanor reminded Redrinna of her mother.

Her heart wilted at the thought.

"Are you sure that's what you want?" she asked, her voice quiet as she traced one of Xandrin's scars with her gaze. "It's dangerous. You could die."

"Well, the people you're going up against have already marked me as a target, so logically, I stand to gain more than lose by joining up with you."

The dragon had a point, she supposed, but, at the same time, it meant someone else for her to keep her eye on. She didn't know if she could do it, but she supposed she was going to have to find a way.

"Then I won't stop you," Redrinna said, forcing a smile. "Welcome."

"Yay, I'm not the only dragon anymore," Xandrin said as he lowered his head back to the ground. A couple seconds later, she was pretty sure he was out.

Despite how lackluster she felt, that nearly brought a real smile to her face.

"Is he always like this?" Astra asked, giving him a side eye.

Redrinna nodded. "He sleeps quite often. But when he's awake, he's pretty reliable."

The green dragon eyed Xandrin warily, giving Redrinna the distinct impression Astra didn't believe her. However, she didn't think pushing the issue would do any good, and she was too tired anyway.

"Can I ask you one more thing?" Astra said, halting Redrinna's thoughts. When she nodded, the dragon continued, "That shirt you're wearing. Did Xandrin make it for you?"

"He did."

"Do you think Tak would like it if I made him one?"

Pausing, Redrinna studied the dragon a little more closely. There was an earnest gleam in her eye, something about it reminding her of Xandrin.

"He might," she said slowly. "But I don't know how to make the shirt."

"That's not a problem. The real problem is...well...I don't think he likes me."

"You don't think Tak likes you?" Redrinna repeated, unsure if she'd heard her right.

Astra nodded.

Honestly, she couldn't imagine Tak hating anyone. At least, he was nice enough around her and Xandrin, and he seemed to have a decent relationship with Timothon, but she supposed none of that meant she knew him. He did tend to keep to himself most of the time and was pretty quiet.

However, truthfully, what she genuinely thought was, "I think he's just really shy. It takes him a while to get used to someone before he's willing to open up."

The dragon didn't seem satisfied with that answer, but she didn't say anything more.

Truth be told, Redrinna wished she could go see how he was doing. This morning, before her body had been annoying, he'd seemed like he was doing okay beyond the fact he hadn't said a word. Hopefully he wasn't angry at her for freezing up—which had resulted in him getting stabbed—and was just being his usual, quiet self. At least neither of his wounds had been extremely serious, a fact that made relief fill her chest, though it was weak.

If Astra was joining them, then as soon as Tak was better—provided he recovered like they all hoped—they could get his gem and go back home. Then, these people wouldn't have to put up with her any longer, and he might eventually be okay.

As the thought crossed her mind, Redrinna glanced up, happening to catch the gaze of that old man again. He had dark feathers like Chumani, except the color was beginning to leech out, leaving them a stunning white at the tips and silvering up the shaft. Despite how stunning his feathers were, he shot her a hard glare, one she knew far better than she liked.

A child scampered past him, propping his arms on the railing and waving. "Hi, Princess!"

She instantly recognized him as Mika, the little boy who'd been sent to tell Shappa about Tak when they'd first arrived. However, she was too startled by his greeting to respond to it.

The older man jerked him off the railing, a fierce mien deepening his wrinkles. Confusion crossed little Mika's face.

Redrinna sighed. He'd understand soon enough, she was sure, and realize it was best if they weren't friends.

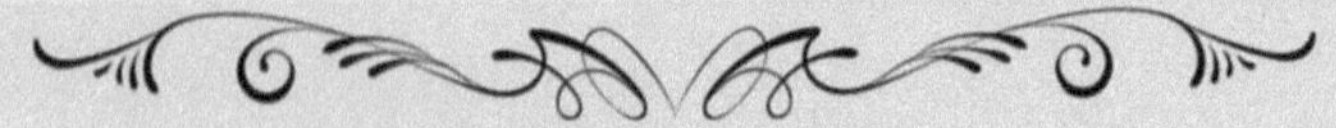

Chapter Twelve

Redrinna paused in her wanderings, gazing up at the ancient, massive oak tree she found herself under. It stretched high into the sky, towering over many of the nearby trees like a fortress, and she was pretty sure it spread a bit farther than Xandrin was long. Green leaves cloaked its hundreds of branches, forming a canopy so thick the sun above filtered down in thin, golden rays.

As she stared at it, the wind rustling the leaves above, something Captain Brion had once said returned to her mind. They'd been taking a break from research when she'd noticed his gaze on an oak tree in the palace gardens.

'Where I come from, oak trees were always special,' he'd said as he stared at it. 'Catching a falling oak leaf was even considered good luck, and in the olden days, oak trees were known as the kings of the forest and were seen as a symbol of courage and wisdom.'

She also suddenly remembered him mentioning a fondness for oak syrup and acorn pancakes, which felt a little random. Even still, the memory was a thorny burr, hurting if she left it alone but also hurting if she tried to remove it.

On a whim, she approached the tree, brushing her fingers over the rough, gray bark. "I wish you were here," she murmured, the captain's face in her mind. Her gaze flicked back to the tree's spindly branches and its light-struck leaves. This was a beautiful spot. Her mind registered that assessment. Regardless, staring at it made her feel nothing. Her heart stayed empty and cold, like an abandoned nest.

"Princess!" someone cried, nearly jarring Redrinna out of her skin.

Turning, she was startled to see both Mika and that enormous, silver-feathered man she hadn't seen since the day they'd arrived striding towards her, their feathered wings scattering the light from the sunbeams. Mika raced ahead of the intimidating man, wings fanned out, bouncing on his toes when he reached her.

"We came to take you back to the village, Princess," he chirped, eyes practically sparkling. "It's not safe out here, you know."

The man stopped a few feet away, looking askance at the boy. "Which is exactly why you weren't supposed to leave the village either. If your grandpa gets mad at me, I'm holding you responsible."

"Grandpa's always mad," Mika said, catching hold of Redrinna's uninjured hand. He tugged, and she let him pull her away from the tree. "Besides, you shouldn't be out here alone either, Chatan."

The enormous guy appeared like he was trying hard not to smile as he said, "You think that demon can get a piece of me?"

"Demon?" Redrinna asked, glancing at Chatan.

His gaze flicked to her, and he shook his head in a clear signal not to talk about it.

Mika didn't seem to notice as he led them back through the forest. "Grandpa's the one who keeps saying we have to watch out for everyone and take care of each other. I don't understand why that would be any different just 'cuz the princess is here. So of course I'm going to take care of you." Mika glanced back at her with an enormous grin.

A few minutes later, they returned to the village and Mika finally released his vice-like grip on her hand.

Pointing a finger at her in an almost scolding way, he said,

"Don't leave the village again, Princess. If you need to, you've gotta take someone with you, understand?" Without waiting for her answer, he turned and launched into the air, skipping as he landed on the platforms above.

Chatan put a fist on his hip. "He's a good kid, don't you think?"

Mutely, Redrinna nodded.

"Plus, he's right. If you wander off on your own, there's no telling what might happen. If you were to get hurt or attacked, we'd have no way of knowing. We might not find you until it was too late, if we found you at all, and your friends would be awfully worried if that happened."

Pursing her lips, Redrinna lowered her gaze. She knew that. However, it was hard to want to comply when she wanted to be alone instead of being smothered by her constant company.

"Oh there you are!" came Chumani's voice, making Redrinna wish she could shrivel into a tiny ball of grass. "I was getting so worried about you."

"I'm fine, really," Redrinna said, regretting her decision to go for a walk now.

"How's your arm?"

"It's fine." It didn't ache as much as it had a couple days ago.

"Good." Chumani smiled, seeming genuinely pleased. "Then I won't bug you anymore today." The woman turned and took off, her black wings shining like obsidian in the sunlight.

"You should go back to your friends now," Chatan said, his gaze searching the sky. "And don't wander off again. I'm not your babysitter and I have better things to do than go hunting for you."

"I can take care of myself," she said with a waspish tone. Immediately, she cringed inside. Not again.

To her surprise, he laughed. "So you do have some attitude in there. I was starting to wonder what kind of future the country would have with a mopey princess."

Her scowl deepened. She wasn't sure she liked him.

"Okay, but for real, go on." He shooed her towards her friends. "Take it easy so your wrist heals right."

Begrudgingly, Redrinna went. As she did, she recalled Chumani's warning from the other day about how a beast prowled the woods and sometimes came to the village. Was that why Mika and Chatan had come after her? It hadn't seemed like she'd been in any danger, but she supposed that didn't mean a thing.

Since she had nothing else to occupy her mind, she poked at the idea of the mysterious beast in the woods. What was it? Why did the village seem so scared of it, whatever it was? What would it have done if it'd found her alone in the woods?

ଶେ ୨ର

Redrinna flexed her fingers, desperately wishing she could scratch her wrist. The itching wasn't painful, but it was grating and incessant, almost buzzing like an entire hive of bees had gotten themselves trapped under her skin. At the current second, she wasn't sure what was worse: the pain from the last few days or this.

As the sun slipped behind the trees for the evening, she watched the village settle in for the night, nearly everyone disappearing into their houses the moment the sun's light waned. Whatever was out in those woods must terrify them.

Even though Redrinna had the dragons to sit with, a part of her felt forgotten. If it was so dangerous no one wanted her to roam through the woods, why were they content to leave her out here in the dark? It wasn't any different. Then again, this was probably fair. It wasn't exactly like she deserved their protection or done anything worth earning it.

She'd been used to loneliness her entire life but being with Xandrin and the others had spoiled her, making her forget the sting. Regardless, loneliness was her lot. She'd get used to it again if she gave herself enough time.

Is your wrist bugging you? her gem asked, its voice as soft as a spring breeze.

She shrugged. "A bit."

I'm sorry. Chumani will probably give you some more medicine for it soon.

Redrinna didn't say anything, her gaze falling to her wrist as a sudden thought entered her mind. The gears in her head whirled as she stewed on it, unease slithering through her chest. All the cuts on her fingers had healed quickly during her and Tak's experiment. Was there a chance the same thing would happen here with her wrist? Her stomach clenched. For the first time, it occurred to her that maybe this was part of what Osiris had been talking about, about how there was something in her veins that made her special, made her different. Was this potentially supernatural healing part of that?

In truth, Redrinna no longer wanted to know.

Shaking those dark thoughts away, she turned her attention back to the forest. As she did, a chill crept across her skin like frost on grass. The sun hadn't completely set, so why had it gone quiet so abruptly? There'd been a few birds and crickets just a couple minutes ago.

Xandrin must've sensed her tension because he sat up, warily eyeing the forest around them before turning to her. "What is it?"

There was no way she could hide it now, she supposed. "Why is it so quiet?"

Astra sat up too, ear frills lifting and tilting from side to side. In a harsh whisper, she hissed, "There's something coming this way. It's close."

Distinctly, Redrinna remembered hearing a horn when Astra had brought them here, a sign there were guards on watch. Which meant whatever was coming—if Astra was right—was sneaking in.

She leaned forward, tensing, ready to leap off Xandrin's back at a moment's notice. Was it what the others had warned her about? Was it Reyna? Her heart squeezed hard against her throat.

All at once, in the brush a short distance from them, a shadowy, hard-to-make-out face appeared amongst the leaves. For a long second, it didn't move and neither did they. Then its eyes opened—two lifeless, milky slits stark amongst the dark green of the forest.

Redrinna recoiled, attracting its attention.

Astra leapt to her feet, wings flaring open as a bone-chilling hiss rattled out of her chest.

The thing in the bushes stared at Redrinna a minute more before vanishing like a shadow into mist.

Chatan and someone else Redrinna didn't recognize thudded down nearby. Her heart hammered against her ribcage. What had that thing even been?

After briefly speaking with Astra, Chatan turned to her. "What was it?"

Doing her best to hide how shaky she was, Redrinna explained. Her chest constricted as the man's countenance became grim.

"That's the thing I was warning you about."

"Is it dangerous?" Xandrin asked, a stern expression on his face too.

"Maybe not to a dragon, but for the rest of us?" He rested his hand on the big knife hanging from his belt, a dark glare overtaking his features. "Very."

"What does it want?" Redrinna asked, struggling to keep shivers of fear at bay. She hated this fear so much, especially right now.

A grim smile twisted Chatan's mouth. "Dinner, actually."

For a minute, Redrinna didn't get it. Then she did, and it was like she'd been plunged into dark, icy waters. "It comes here...searching for food?"

"That's right. And it's not the kind of beast to go after table scraps."

Astra frowned. "You don't mean...it wants to eat you guys?"

"Exactly right," Chatan said, sweeping his wings to the side as he turned to face the forest. "If we've chased it off tonight, it probably won't come back for a couple days. But be on your guard anyway—especially you, Redrinna. The longer it's forced to go without the meal it wants, the more desperate it'll get, and it's mean."

"Chatan," Astra said, brow knit with worry. "You have to take her inside with you guys. It doesn't matter if it isn't the clinic."

"I can't, Astra." His face twisted with frustration. "The chief said Her Highness isn't permitted in any of our buildings. There's nothing I can do."

Even though Redrinna wasn't surprised, it felt like she'd been punched in the gut anyway. They didn't want her here this badly? It shouldn't have stung, but it did. It hurt. Even still, she couldn't be mad at them for it. Maybe they were right, and this was best for everyone.

"This again?" Astra snapped. "Chatan—"

He held up a hand. "I know. But I don't have any say."

"What if something happens to her?"

"Like people would miss her?" said whoever had come with Chatan, their voice notably hushed like they hadn't meant for anyone else to hear.

Even still, Redrinna flinched.

"Wicasa," Chatan snapped with enough venom, his companion shrunk a couple inches.

Astra lunged at the man, who hastily backed off. "I would miss her!"

Redrinna blinked in surprise before Xandrin abruptly shifted, pitching her off his side. She stumbled as she hit the ground, throat clenching at the sight of his face. His eyes smoldered like embers, nearly frightening her heart out of her chest.

"Don't you ever," the dragon hissed, face inches away from the man's, "say something like that about my friend again."

This was getting out of hand. Hurrying forward, she rested a hand on his snout, getting him to look at her. "Xandrin, don't. It's fine."

"It is not fine," he snarled back, eyes sparking with anger.

"It is," she insisted. "So don't fight. Please?"

His snout wrinkled. She knew he disagreed; it was written all over his face. However, he withdrew from the man and stayed quiet.

A tense silence followed, and Redrinna's gaze dove to the ground. What did she do now?

"Wicasa, go back to your post," Chatan said, the authority in his voice giving Redrinna chills. "Let the others know we had a sighting and to double the watch."

"Right," the man said before taking off.

"Don't worry about your friend, Astra," Chatan continued, turning to the green dragon. "There's going to be someone on guard right above you all night."

Xandrin snorted. "Like anyone is going to be willing to guard her."

"Of course there is," Chatan said with a laugh. "It'll be me." He launched upwards with a whoosh of his wings, the air stirring some of the loose strands of hair around Redrinna's face. She blinked as she watched him go.

That was the second time today he'd done something arguably nice for her, and she couldn't understand why. She hadn't done anything to deserve kindness from him. Was he trying to get something from her or play an angle or something?

⚬ℓℓ ℓℓ⚬

Being blind when Kyvo was around left Tak at a severe disadvantage. One moment, he was sitting innocently in his bed, and the next, the kitsune was barreling into his gut, making his side burst with pain.

"Ow!" he gasped. "What did you do that for?"

"Oh, that's your hurt side, isn't it? Sorry, sorry," Kyvo said, tenderly putting a paw on Tak's injury. It didn't help any, but a part of him appreciated the gesture, he supposed. "I got so excited, I forgot."

Tak rubbed his side. It was better now than it'd been a couple days ago, but it was still healing. "I thought you were going to go sit with Redrinna."

Redrinna had been consistently sending Kyvo to spend time with him, which he appreciated, but he was more worried about her. Takota was letting him stay with the others during the day still, but Redrinna wasn't any more talkative now than she'd been when they'd left the Mount. He was sure being here wasn't helping; the few times she spoke, she barely put two words together.

That wasn't the Redrinna he remembered meeting.

Guilt nestled deeper in his chest, making itself even more at home. If he hadn't been so stupid and selfish, they wouldn't have gotten stuck here.

"I was," Kyvo chirped, startling Tak from his thoughts. "But then this thing almost came out of the woods and the warriors outside told me to stay in here."

A thing came out of the woods? That sounded ominous. Not like he could do anything to help.

All at once, Kyvo sniffled, his weight shifting slightly. "They still won't let Redrinna come inside. She seems so sad sitting out there all the time."

Guilt resounded through Tak's chest again.

"I don't like it here."

"I...I'm sorry," he offered.

The kitsune snuggled into his leg then and stayed quiet.

Hesitantly, Tak reached out and stroked his fur, hoping he was doing a decent job. So far, their little Dragon Kin either had the worst luck or they were turning out to be a lousy bunch. He honestly couldn't decide which one. Maybe the gems had chosen the wrong people.

Well, he was sure Redrinna was the right person, but he still couldn't picture himself the same way. Since they'd left the Mount, he hadn't even had the gem dream despite how persistent it'd been before. Had it changed his mind after watching him get had in a fight?

It wasn't like that would've been the worst thing in the world. On the contrary, it probably would've been for the best. He wasn't sure he was cut out for this kind of stuff anymore than he was cut out for being a knight.

Gradually, despite the fact he was sitting up, Tak nodded off. Snippets of dreams intertwined with flashes of reality, enough so he didn't quite know when he was awake and when he wasn't.

For a moment, in his mind's eye, Redrinna appeared. Alone, in the woods. She stared off somewhere, stared at something he couldn't see. He approached cautiously, almost like he was afraid she'd notice him. Hesitantly, he reached out to her, hand shaking as he fought against some invisible force, trying to get close. It was so strong, almost overwhelming, but no matter how hard he fought, he didn't seem to get any closer. He couldn't call out to her; he couldn't make a sound. Slowly, she turned her head, staring him straight in the eye. Without warning, she shattered into tiny, glittering pieces of dust and vanished, leaving him completely alone.

Shuddering, Tak jerked awake, finding himself staring at a blurred, wide-eyed someone.

The man stared a couple seconds longer before relaxing. "Sorry. I wasn't trying to wake you. I was just changing the bandages on your eyes. Have a bad dream or something?" He sounded like Takota.

Disoriented like someone had used his head as a top, Tak glanced around the room for a long minute, unable to make out a thing between his wacked vision and the darkness. Had that just been a dream? What kind of dream had that even been, and why had it made his heart pound like he'd been running?

"Yeah," he began slowly, slightly out of breath. "I-I think so."

"Ah, that's probably because of the medicine we're giving you. Sometimes you get really weird dreams. Don't worry; starting tomorrow we don't have to give you as much."

Tak nodded and then held still as the man rebandaged his eyes. He didn't know if he believed the dream could be explained away by something as simple as medicine, but even still, something about it left him unsettled and uneasy. Had that been some kind of freaky dream or a haunting premonition?

Chapter Thirteen

After two, soggy days that had crawled by with agonizing slowness, Redrinna was bored to tears. At least the itching in her wrist was subsiding, and it only hurt if she bumped it now. Then again, after two, blissful nights of almost normal sleep, last night, she'd returned to long, restless hours spent staring at the night sky. It'd been fun for the first couple hours, but she was sick of searching for the same constellations and planets and things. It was only entertaining for so many nights in a row.

Unfortunately, it seemed tonight was going to be the same. Once again, long after the village had settled into its deathly quiet slumber, she remained awake, staring at the night sky. Above, when the wind wasn't stirring the trees, there came the faint tap-tap of the guards' feet as they walked across the platforms above. There weren't many guards here, and they didn't wear heavy, noisy armor or weapons like the knights she'd known back home. They also could see well in the dark, a common trait amongst the Torijin from what she understood. They were one of the few human tribes that did, but because of their vision, they had no need for torches or anything of the like.

Which made it all the easier to end up staring at the night sky all night long. Redrinna had debated training when she couldn't sleep, but she was concerned they would worry she was plotting something, especially since Chatan had been true to his word about keeping an eye out for her, annoyingly so. If she so much as sighed too loudly, he'd call out to her. Accordingly, she kept herself confined to Xandrin's shoulders all night, sleep or no, doing her best to remain as quiet as possible.

An owl hooted somewhere nearby, and she swiveled her head to try catching a glimpse of it. She didn't, but it'd been worth a try.

Her thoughts wandered aimlessly as she lay there, as wide awake as ever. After a while, she realized the forest had gone quiet sooner than usual. She glanced at the position of the moon to double check. Frowning, she did her best to resist the urge to sit up and look around. Chumani and Chatan's warnings from the other day were still fresh in her mind, as was that glimpse she'd gotten of whatever that beast had been.

Since she'd had to spend so much time sitting and doing nothing, Redrinna had noticed something: everyone in the village was nervous. It was in the way they moved, the way they talked to each other, the way they stuck together in groups. There was a subtle air of dread hanging over the place like a shroud. Some people took flowers to the clinic, remaining inside for hours before leaving, seemingly sadder than when they'd left. Many didn't leave their houses at all. It was rare when the children—especially the girls—were let outside. Mika was an exception, but Redrinna was convinced that was more because the old man who was with him all the time was having a hard time keeping the energetic little boy inside.

Whatever that thing was, it'd clearly crawled straight out of a nightmare.

All at once, a chill raced up Redrinna's spine, making her shudder despite her best effort. Then, out of the corner of her eye, she spied movement.

It appeared human-like aside from the fact it was practically skin and bones, and it wasn't wearing much—just rags. An alarm bell clamored in her mind, but she kept still. It stole across the grass without a sound, moving with the shadows. Then, it vanished from sight.

She bolted upright, frantically searching for a glimpse of it.

Redrinna, her gem hissed. *Whatever it is you're thinking, stop thinking it. They told you not to go near that thing.*

She didn't respond, not wanting to make a sound. Her gaze flicked back and forth across the clearing as she hunted for a glimpse of what that thing had been. Carefully, she hopped down from Xandrin's side, inaudibly landing on her feet.

At least wake Xandrin up, or call Chatan, her gem pressed, but she shook her head.

Redrinna had gotten enough people hurt, and she wasn't risking it again. It was better if she dealt with this threat on her own unless the guards got it first. At the very least, she'd be able to pay these people back for their generosity and for not running her out even though they probably wanted to.

Up! Look up!

She looked, heart stuttering. In the shadow of one of the only houses she could see was crouched whatever it was, beneath one of the windows. Creeping closer, Redrinna stopped at the bottom of the stairs, heart in her throat. Now that she was nearer, she finally got a good look at this thing.

Its skin was a gray, almost blue color, and it had long, claw-like spikes coming off both elbows. Mangled, patchy, black hair covered its scalp, hanging almost to its waist. Peeking out from beneath the matted hair on the back of its head, almost looking like some freaky deformity or something, appeared to be another nose and mouth. The moon wasn't particularly bright tonight, which made it hard for her to be sure.

All the warnings she'd been given about whatever this thing was made her hesitant to go much further, but Redrinna couldn't just close her eyes and leave. If she did, she—

Her heart shuddered in her chest, fear making her mouth go dry. Somehow, the thing had opened a window without a sound and was pulling something out. Almost immediately, she realized what it was: the thing it was grabbing was a *child*. All the doubts in her mind vanished.

"Hey!" she snapped, doing her best to keep her voice level and stern, like her parents had always—

It was better not to think about things like that right now.

The thing paused, hesitating.

One of the guards let out a shout above.

Without warning, the thing leapt, clearing the stairs in one bound and landing with a thud right in front of Redrinna. She recoiled back a step. A rotten, iron-like smell radiated from it, making her nose burn. It peered at her from beneath thatches of matted hair with those disturbing, pupilless eyes. Slowly, it cocked its head from side to side.

Her heart latched on to her throat as she realized the child it'd snatched was Mika. It cradled the sleeping boy in its arms almost like he was... Her first thought was a baby, but that was shoved aside by a more accurate one: food.

"Frezsh meats?" the creature said in a thin voice, creaky from disuse. It blinked, eyelids rasping over its dry eyes like sandpaper on wood.

She took a step back, stomach shriveling almost to nothing.

"Needz more meats," it said, taking a step forward. It flung Mika over its shoulder like he was a sack, making the kid stir. Then, it raised its free arm, elbow up so its bony, spear-like addition was level with her chest. "Childz is bestest, but she-beasts are yums too. Much betterz than he-beasts."

Mika squirmed, letting out a cry of pain as the creature tightened its grip on him. Without warning, Mika let out a blood-curdling screech, the sound ringing off the mountains towering overhead. There was a flurry of noise above.

The creature charged.

She dodged its elbow with barely an inch to spare, mind whirling. She had to get Mika out. That was priority number one.

An arrow from above flashed past, but the creature paid it no mind as it charged again. Redrinna ducked beneath its elbow spear but left her leg in the creature's path, sending it sprawling. Mika tumbled free from its grasp. She vaulted over the flailing creature, narrowly avoiding one of those spears before landing squarely between the creature and Mika.

Priority number two: don't die.

Someone landed nearby, but she kept her focus on the beast as it scurried to its feet.

"P-Princess!" Mika gasped out behind her.

She almost glanced back at him, but Reyna's voice rang out in her mind: 'never take your eyes off your opponent. That's when they'll get you.' Irritation flooded her at the sound of the woman's voice, but she kept her eyes fixed on the beast.

"It'll be fine. Just stay behind me."

The beast glanced around as a couple more Torijin warriors landed nearby, the hungry gleam in its eyes sharpening. It charged. She punched, bright fire roaring out between them in an arc. It flinched back, letting out a hiss. The Torijin warriors behind it moved in.

The beast whirled to face them.

Good. Now if she could get Mika out of here—

"NO!" Mika screeched. "Close your eyes!"

"What?" Redrinna glanced back at him.

As she did, he launched onto her back, clamping his hands over her eyes. He buried his head against her back the next second. The creature let out an ear-splitting screech, so loud it rattled her teeth.

Move! her gem thundered.

Wrapping an arm around Mika, she rolled to the side. As she did, a fiery pain ripped through her cheek.

It's coming at you again!

She tried to back up but slipped on the grass. Frantic, hoping she didn't hit anybody, she threw out her arm. There was a rush, then a boom of heat. A screech and flapping. Stumbling. But only the smell of smoke lingered in the air.

The next second, there was a grunt and a nasty crunch.

Redrinna grabbed at Mika's little hands, but the kid was a lot stronger than he appeared.

Another loud screech rang out.

"There it goes!" someone shouted.

A moment of nothing followed by a thud in the distance. Then silence.

Redrinna finally yanked Mika's hands down so she could see again. A couple of the Torijin warriors flanked them, and so did Chatan. All three of them were staring into the darkness of the forest, grim expressions on their faces.

"And it's gone yet again," Chatan said in a tone darker than she'd ever heard from him.

Redrinna tried to take a steadying breath as she fought to hide her fear. Her hands were shaking like leaves in a windstorm. All at once, she spied Xandrin a little way away in a cat-like pose, just starting to relax. Their gazes met, and almost immediately, his eyes narrowed.

He was probably mad and would chew her out later, but she didn't care. He wasn't hurt, and Mika was still with them instead of becoming some beast's next meal.

Right as she thought that, Mika slumped against her, arms tight around her neck. Her eyes widened as he nearly yanked her off balance, but she managed to keep them from going down.

"I told grandpa you were a good person," he whispered.

Tears stung her eyes, but she managed to keep them in check.

"That may be true," Chatan said, making her heart stutter, "but she's not going to last long if you strangle her. Come on, on your feet now, you two."

The man pulled Mika off and helped Redrinna get to her feet as well. Guilt burbled up in her chest and she avoided his gaze. There was a good chance he was mad at her too; however, when she risked a glance at him, he didn't seem angry. Rather, he seemed calm—just intimidating. In the faint light of the moon, his feathers shone like polished silver, something about it making him seem like a warrior from an ancient legend. His dark, shoulder-length hair was bound back, only a couple strands hanging loose around his face, causing his mien to be all the more intimidating.

Chatan leaned forward, raising her chin and tilting her head to the side. Pain sang through her cheek and down her jaw. Now that the rush from the fight was ebbing, the pain in her cheek was making itself known, and it was loud.

"They're not going to like waking up at this hour," he mused.

"It's fine," she said despite the pain.

Withdrawing his hand, he held out his fingers, Redrinna's eyes going wide at the amount of blood smeared across them. Was the bleeding that heavy? Once he'd pointed it out though, she was aware of it clinging to her skin like a leech and running down her neck. It felt like it was smeared all over.

"Mika!" All at once, the old man was standing at the top of the stairs, a frantic look on his face. "What are you doing out here?" He rushed down the stairs, wings spreading to help him stay balanced, practically swallowing Mika in his arms when he reached the bottom. His massive wings curled around him like he could shield the little boy from the rest of the world. In the weak moonlight, the man seemed older than usual, the thin light seeming to deepen the weathered lines of his face.

"You're crushing me," Mika protested from somewhere beneath those wings.

The old man released him but kept a firm hand on his arm. "What are you doing out here? I know you like watching the warriors at work but—"

"Ohanzi," Chatan interrupted with one fist on his hip. "Mika didn't come out to watch us. The demon came for him tonight."

The old man's face went ashen. "Why can't it leave my family alone? It's taken enough already!"

"I know. Luckily, thanks to our princess, we were able to send the fiend packing empty-handed this time."

Ohanzi's gaze gradually moved from the warrior to her. Redrinna wilted under his gaze, but for once, his expression didn't harden. It didn't do anything, really. He just stared at her like he'd just realized she was there, and she honestly didn't know how to take that.

"Oh," he said after a minute, almost sounding like he was in a daze. "You're bleeding."

"Talutah," Chatan said, turning towards one of the other three guards standing nearby.

A tall, almost equally as imposing woman with dark-ish feathers stepped forward. "Yeah?"

"Please escort the princess to the clinic. Drag Takota out of bed if you have to. You two," he pointed at the two other guards. "Go get the others and bring them back here."

As he turned to Ohanzi and Mika, the tall lady, Talutah, gave Redrinna a gentle push towards the clinic.

She stumbled as she turned and started up the stairs, more than a little stunned by the way Ohanzi had stared at her, though she couldn't figure out why.

"Princess!" Mika called as she and Talutah crested the landing.

She glanced back, too startled to speak.

He grinned from ear to ear. "Thank you for helping me."

All her life, no one had ever said that to her; at least, not in a circumstance like this. Redrinna didn't know what she was supposed to say. A moment later, she realized her mouth had fallen open and hastily closed it.

After a couple seconds more, she lifted a hand. "I didn't do anything. You don't have to thank me."

Then, before anyone could respond, she hurried towards the clinic with Talutah walking only a step behind her. A hot blush burned on her face as Redrinna's mind reeled from Mika's words. They'd been so simple—so ordinary—but even still, it was...she didn't know the word. However, it was almost like the moment when she'd learned Xandrin would be okay.

They made it to the clinic a couple minutes later and were heading through the entranceway before Redrinna stopped, remembering something that made her heart skip a beat. She'd totally forgotten but—

"Is something wrong?" Talutah asked.

"Well, no, but," she began, unsure how to say it. "Shappa and the others...don't want me in here. I'm not supposed to be inside any of the buildings, right?"

The warrior stared at her for a long minute before putting a hand on her back and giving her a strong push forward. "I don't care. You're a patient in need of treatment, whether anyone likes it or not. Plus, I brought you here under Chatan's orders, so if anyone gets mad, we can blame him."

That almost got Redrinna to smile, but it made her cheek sting too much. Then, they entered the main part of the clinic and her ghost of a smile vanished. Sitting on a wooden chair was none other than Shappa herself, working on something almost like embroidery, but instead of using needle and thread, it looked like she was working with long, flat spines dyed different colors.

"Shappa," Talutah murmured, a reverence in her tone. "We have a patient for you despite the late hour."

Shappa didn't even glance up. "It would seem we are fortunate to have a patient at all."

Talutah almost smiled, losing some of her stern demeanor. "I can't argue with that."

"Leave her with me," the elder said, setting her project aside as she stood. "I'm sure you're needed back outside."

With a nod, the warrior turned and left, leaving the two of them alone.

Shappa headed to an empty room towards the back, and Redrinna guessed she was supposed to follow. As she entered the room—it was a supplies closet of sorts, with bandages neatly wrapped on a table and dried herbs hanging from the ceiling, filling the room with their sharp, distinct scent—Shappa was sorting through a small chest on the table, but she pointed towards a wooden pitcher and basin on a second, smaller table.

"Clean up."

Doing as she was told, Redrinna winced when the water touched the cut, making it burn. It was a tad difficult since she could only use one hand, but she did her best.

After a minute, Shappa came and set some things on the table near the pitcher and basin. "Have a seat."

Redrinna glanced around, found a stool, pulled it over, and sat quietly.

Shappa picked up a cloth and began cleaning the rest of the blood from her face. Redrinna fully expected the elder to remain quiet while she worked and planned on doing the same.

To her surprise, however, Shappa spoke. "It would seem I owe you a thank you."

Redrinna had to fight hard to keep her head still and not look at the woman. "Why?"

With a sigh Shappa said, "I was doing my nightly rounds when I heard the commotion. I know what happened. The reason why I owe you a thank you is because Mika is my grandson."

Grandson? "Oh, are you and Ohanzi—"

"No," the elder said curtly. "We're not married. Our children were the ones who married."

Oh. Why hadn't that crossed her mind?

Shappa set the cloth she'd been using aside before lifting Redrinna's chin and turning her head. "Well, the bleeding looks like it's slowing down, but it's still a bit heavier than I'd like, so unless you strongly object to it, I'd prefer to stitch it shut once it's clean. It'll minimize the scarring and ensure it doesn't become infected."

The elder was, seemingly, asking her opinion, rendering Redrinna speechless. This wasn't at all who she'd thought Shappa was.

"I-if you think it's best."

"Wonderful." The woman quickly set to work cleaning the wound, flushing it a couple times, the sting making Redrinna's eyes water. When Shappa finished, she picked up a long, thin needle and some thread.

Redrinna swallowed. She'd never had stitches before, but she'd heard the process wasn't pleasant.

The woman's expression softened. "You can close your eyes, and I can give you something to bite on if you want."

Shaking her head, Redrinna said, "I'm fine."

The woman lifted her chin, and as she eyed the wound, said, "However, if you kick me, I'll make sure it doesn't feel good. Please try to keep your face as relaxed as possible."

She definitely did not like the way that sounded. As the woman threaded the needle, Redrinna's grip on the seat of the stool tightened. Shappa leaned in, holding up the needle. A moment later, there was a sharp prick in Redrinna's cheek. She fought to ignore it and keep herself as still as possible. It didn't hurt as much as her wrist had, so in reality, it wasn't that bad. However, she didn't want to have to do it again.

Within a few minutes, it was over.

As Shappa wiped at her face again, the woman said, "You pity us, don't you?"

Redrinna stared at her in alarm. "What?"

"I've seen the way you look at us." Shappa picked up a small jar, its smell stinging Redrinna's nose as it opened. "I'm not stupid."

"I don't look down on you," Redrinna said quietly, though she had no idea whether or not the woman would believe her. "I'm sorry it seemed that way."

With a frown, Shappa carefully applied whatever was in her jar on Redrinna's cheek as she said, "We're used to people looking down on us and pitying us. They see us as weak and defenseless ever since the genocide, and I suppose in their eyes, they're right. To them, we've lost it all: our homeland, our ancestral way of life, our mother tongue—but they don't understand. Regardless of what happened before, it couldn't strip us of who we truly are. The past didn't take everything because we still had each other, at least. We still have wotitakuye."

"Wo...tita..." Redrinna tried to repeat the word, but her mouth didn't quite cooperate. She blamed it on her swollen cheek.

Shappa repeated the word again, slower this time, and she said it back.

"Close."

"What does it mean?"

"In your language, kinship is the closest word. In my tribe, our families are our most treasured possession. To me, even if you're swimming in a sea of riches, without someone to call family, you're the poorest person on earth."

Redrinna's gaze fell. By those standards, she was very poor indeed.

"We've lost a lot, but we didn't lose everything—we didn't even lose what matters the most, and that's what's important. We're not going to disappear." Shappa took a step back, eyeing her handiwork. "That's the most I can do for you. Spend the night in the next room over if you'd like, or anywhere; I don't care. If the door's open, the room is free."

Quickly, Shappa put the last of her things away and left the room, leaving Redrinna to herself. Biting her lip, Redrinna stayed on her stool for a little longer before leaving the small room. There were a couple open doors nearby, and she debated letting herself relax and spend the night in one of them, but in the end, she couldn't bring herself to do it. They were already imposing on these people enough—she was imposing so much. She couldn't ask for more.

Staying as quiet as possible, Redrinna left the clinic and went back outside. As she neared the stairs, Mika appeared in the doorway of Ohanzi's house, something large in his arms.

"Princess," he said with an enormous grin. "Take this with you, okay?"

She paused, unsure if she should be accepting gifts. It wasn't like she'd done something so spectacular. However, the little boy dumped his gift in her arms, leaving her no choice.

Redrinna's heart skipped a beat as she realized what it was. A quilt?

"It's still a bit cold out here at night, since it's not quite summer yet," he explained. Then, with a giggle, he said, "My grandpa was really the one who wanted to give this to you, but he was too embarrassed. Anyway, use it to keep warm."

Her vision misted over, and she lowered her head slightly in hopes he wouldn't notice. "Thank you," she managed before turning and hurrying back to the dragons.

Despite Mika's kind gesture, she couldn't bring herself to use the quilt, though Kyvo enjoyed it immensely. After all the excitement, she didn't get a wink of sleep anyway. Neither her gem nor Xandrin spoke to her either, but she didn't mind. She knew why they were upset, but no one had gotten hurt. Everyone was safe, even if she'd had to sacrifice her cheek to do it. Why didn't they understand it was better this way?

Chapter Fourteen

Tak shrugged his shoulders, trying to resist the urge to rip the bandages off his head and scratch his scalp like crazy. At least everything was starting to feel better and less painful—except for his headaches, but Takota had said his head would take longer to heal than his side. He was able to go outside now, at least—provided he had somebody's help to make sure he didn't step off one of the many edges and plummet to his death.

As Takota guided him from the clinic to his friends down below, he sensed something different about the village today. Takota was more talkative—hardly even pausing to breathe—and it wasn't as quiet as usual outside. Everyone seemed to be talking, and a couple people even laughed, almost making him stumble in surprise. It was like he'd woken up in a completely different village than the one he'd fallen asleep in.

What startled him the most though, was that despite the sudden enthusiasm abounding in the village above, his friends seemed quieter than before, particularly Redrinna and Xandrin. Something was going on, but from what little clues he could pick up on, he didn't have the faintest idea what it might be.

Takota brought them breakfast and then made himself scarce.

Their breakfast consisted of the usual fry bread and soup, and

Tak wondered once again what the soup looked like. At least, after his struggles over the last few days, he only spilled on himself once this time. However, his success didn't seem to lighten the mood. Not even Kyvo, who sat right next to him, said a word.

There was a weird thud from nearby, almost like someone had dropped something from the sky, but then footsteps, getting a bewildered Tak to glance over despite the fact he couldn't see anything.

A voice he didn't recognize said, "Redrinna?"

"Chatan?" Redrinna asked, sounding polite enough, but Tak detected the usual exhaustion hiding in her voice.

"I need to talk to you about something. Will you come with me?" Whoever this guy was, he sounded so serious, it was unnerving, making Tak even surer something had happened last night.

The only problem was he wasn't sure whether it was something good or bad given he had such contrasting responses.

"Of course," Redrinna said. Without a word to the rest of them, she left.

Once she was gone, an even thicker silence descended over their group for a while, which Tak wouldn't have thought possible.

"Tak," Astra said abruptly from close beside him, making him jump. "How...how are you feeling?"

He turned his head partially towards her before stopping. Even if he'd wanted to, he couldn't see her. However, the fact she'd saved his life the other day popped into his head, making him acutely uncomfortable and unable to physically face her.

Despite his reservations, he should at least say thank you. His aunt would've scolded him like crazy for not doing at least that.

For a moment, Tak's heart panged at the thought of his aunt and desperately wished she were still here.

"Thank you," he said quickly, practically tossing the words at the dragon.

"Thank you?"

"For...for, you know," he began, hoping she would catch on so he didn't have to explain, especially since Kyvo and Xandrin were most likely listening, and he didn't want to say more than he had to. "For saving me. So that makes us even."

"Even?" the dragon asked, sounding sincerely confused. "What are we keeping score for?"

"I saved your life once, and now you've saved mine, so we're even, right?" he said hurriedly, heat creeping up his neck. That wasn't too difficult to understand, was it? Silently, he hoped he wasn't going to have to explain.

"Oh, you mean *that*," she said, her voice softening. "I didn't save you because of that, you know. I did it because I wanted to."

Not knowing what to say, Tak remained quiet. Why would she want to save him for no reason?

"Oh...and I'm sorry," Astra continued, shifting slightly.

"W-why?"

"I make you uncomfortable, don't I?"

He didn't answer.

"But I'm going with you guys. We'll end up seeing a lot of each other from now on. That's why I'm sorry."

Tak had been wondering what he'd do if this ended up happening, but now that it had... His feelings were all sorts of jumbled, like someone had taken different puzzles and thrown all the pieces together.

If Astra came with them, then she would be in less danger from Osiris and Reyna. Plus, the Dragon Kin needed all the help they could get, so having her around would be useful.

The problem then, was him. He didn't fit in, and what if he never did? Well, he supposed if his vision didn't return to normal, then maybe he wouldn't have to worry about it anymore. A part of him almost wanted that, but, at the same time, he didn't have anywhere else to go if the Dragon Kin turned him out.

"Tak, if I—" Astra began.

"Could you stop being so loud?" Xandrin said with a snort,

making Tak jump. "I'm trying to sleep."

"Oh, I'm so sorry, you big, red beast," Astra snapped, venom practically dripping from every word. "You don't have to be so rude. We're just talking. You know? Having a conversation?"

Why were the two of them fighting?

"Well, unlike you, *I* had a busy night. You know, protecting people?" Xandrin snapped back with just as much venom.

"Knock it off, already," Kyvo said before crawling into Tak's lap and settling down. "Give it a rest until after my naptime."

The dragons went quiet, but a near palpable tension lingered in the air. It was almost enough to make Tak wish he was stuck in the clinic still.

"Did something happen?" he said before he could stop himself. Oops. He hadn't intended to do that.

"The village was attacked last night," the dragons said at the same time. Then they hissed at each other, and he could imagine them glaring too, which was not a happy image.

"Attacked?" Tak breathed. That didn't explain the sour mood between the others, nor did it explain why the rest of the village seemed so strangely happy. "By what?"

"I don't know," Xandrin said. "I've never seen anything like it before. It almost seems human but it's definitely not."

"Redrinna probably knows," Astra butted in. "I mean, she tried to fight it."

Tak fought to repress a shudder. It still didn't explain why the village seemed so much happier, but it did somewhat explain the foul air between the others. Unfortunately, there wasn't a thing he could do.

⋯⊙℃ ℂ⊙⋯

Redrinna glanced around the clearing Chatan had brought her to, doing her best to ignore the stares from the couple people who were already here. Her heart shivered at the sight of that Wicasa guy from the other day. Blocking him out as much as she could, she turned her attention back to the clearing.

The place was ringed with oaks and aspens, with a good-sized patch of grass in the center. It looked a lot like a training area, but she wasn't completely sure.

"First of all, I would be remiss if I didn't, very strictly, scold you for attempting to fight the beast that stole into the village last night," Chatan said, stopping in front of her and putting his fists on his hips. "I didn't even know you were there until you were there."

Biting her lip to keep any rude retorts in check, Redrinna turned her head away.

"That said, I had no idea you'd moved until you were fighting that thing." He turned around to face her, his expression resting somewhere between determined and excited. "Therefore, I want you to help us take it out."

Redrinna blinked. He wanted her to do what?

"I saw what you can do. You've been taught how to fight and you have magic, and we need everyone we can get. What do you say?"

"What even is that thing?"

He paused. "I suppose we didn't finish explaining, did we? It has several names, depending on who you ask. I've heard it called the Double-Faced Demon, Two Face, and even Sharp Elbows."

"Does it do anything beyond eating people?"

"Yeah... I'm sure you noticed its second face."

"Yes," she breathed. So it actually had been another face on the back of its head, not some deformity. Her stomach knotted itself.

"If it opens the eyes on its second face and you meet its gaze, it'll paralyze you. It essentially turns you to stone, leaving you trapped until it returns to eat you alive."

The image made her shudder. "Is there more than one of them?"

"Not anymore." Pride sparked in Chatan's eyes. "There were two, but we finally managed to peg one of them and bring it down."

"The one that's left is injured now though, so you don't really need my help, do you?"

Wicasa laughed from off to the side. "It's not like that could kill it."

Chatan silenced him with a stony glare. "What he means to say is the Two Face only has one weakness. You have to hit it right between the eyes on the back of its head, otherwise injuries hardly faze it. Which, there's no way you would've known that." He glared daggers at Wicasa until the guy looked away. Then he turned back to her. "Point being, it'll be fine within a couple days and make its way back here, and we'll need more help if we're going to stop it. So?"

Lowering her gaze, Redrinna couldn't think of anything to say for a long minute. She was flattered they trusted her to some degree—or at least, Chatan did—but what if she messed up again? She'd managed to pull off a miracle before, but she wasn't so sure she could do it again. It wasn't like she'd been able to so far.

"I don't know. I'm not much of a fighter."

Remaining quiet, Chatan tilted his head to the side, an expectant look on his face.

"But I suppose...if you really want me to, I can try."

He grinned. "Good enough for me. In that case, these two over here will train with you. Two Face is no joke, and I'm not going to risk letting you have another go at it without preparing you for it."

Internally, Redrinna cringed. She'd be working with at least one person who didn't like her, and the other guy with him had been watching everything with a blank expression the entire time.

"You've already met Wicasa," Chatan continued, turning to the other two fellows. "His bark is much worse than his bite. He's just loud—so if he yaps too much, you can ignore him."

"Chatan," Wicasa said with a bit of a whine.

"And the quiet one is Kangee. His bite is worse than his bark, but fortunately, I've almost never seen him angry, so you'll be fine."

Kangee nodded but remained silent still.

"I expect the two of you to treat her like anyone else, understood?"

"Fine," Wicasa huffed, flaring his feathers.

Again, Kangee nodded, not saying a word.

Chatan seemed satisfied. "Perfect. I have to go take care of a few things for now, so I'll stop by to check in later." With a spring in his step, he left the clearing with nothing more than a wave.

"Does he ever sleep?" Redrinna muttered, mostly to herself.

"Probably not," Wicasa said.

"Not since the demons got his sister," Kangee added in a near whisper.

That made her pause. Chatan's sister had been taken? If she was gone, then why did he seem so happy?

"Not our business," Wicasa said. "Our business is this." He jerked a knife from his belt, making Redrinna jump. He smirked.

Quiet again, Kangee spread his wings, forcing his companion to take a step back.

"What? It's not like I'm going to attack anybody." Rolling his eyes, Wicasa turned his gaze to her. "So you've got a knife and a sword. You know how to use either of 'em?"

"Sort of."

"Only sort of?"

"I didn't have to start learning how to fight until a couple months ago."

Kangee drew a knife of his own. "Show me."

Begrudgingly, Redrinna drew her own knife, doing her best not to stare too closely. The last thing she needed were some bad memories tripping her up here, especially with Kangee waiting.

She stared at him.

He stared back.

He relaxed his stance.

Wicasa put a hand on his hip, an exasperated look on his face. "You don't know how to use it at all, do you?"

Her gaze wandered to the knife as she tilted the blade, managing to catch a thin ray of sunlight. "The person who gave it to me didn't get a chance to show me how to use it."

The longer she stared at it, the more a glare twisted her face. She'd never wanted this knife, but she'd taken it because she'd thought it'd keep her safe. The only time she'd used it was in the Imperial City. Now, she despised looking at it almost as much as she hated how she couldn't seem to leave it behind. There was no reason she had to keep hooking it on her belt, and yet...

"Let's do something else for now." Kangee slipped his knife back into his belt and turned to Wicasa, remaining expressionless still. "There's a lot more we can work on. Like your lazy form."

Eyes going wide, Wicasa slowly turned to his companion. "Lazy? You think my form is lazy?!"

"Why else do you think you pulled a muscle? You're too lazy to practice your form."

"No, no, no, I did *not* pull a muscle." Wicasa corrected him with a wag of his finger. "The muscle in question isn't pulled; it's tired, okay? That's what happens when Chatan runs us ragged *and* we end up having to fight that stupid Two Face."

"And because you don't work on your form."

"There's nothing wrong with my form!" Wicasa snapped back, face flushed.

Redrinna stared at the two of them, unsure what to make of them. Should she laugh or not?

♦ ♦

Tak had to fight down a wave of nausea as Redrinna finished filling them in on what was going on in the Torijin village later that evening. After disappearing for a few hours, she'd come back with nothing short of a horror story. There was some kind of monster running around in the woods actively trying to eat people, and it was the thing that had attacked the village.

It was also the reason everybody in their little group seemed upset. Honestly, it sounded worse than the Dragon Slayer thing Redrinna and Xandrin had mentioned before.

"The tribe wants us to help them get rid of it?" Astra asked.

"That's right," Redrinna said, exhaustion dragging on her voice. "Since we're still waiting for Tak to recover, they'd like all the help they can get since the Two Face is going to be getting desperate. It failed last night, so it's going to come back soon and be more likely to go for anything it can get, Torijin or otherwise. They don't want to put us in danger or throw all their problems at our feet, but I want to help if I can. None of you have to if you don't want to, but—"

"Of course we're helping!" Xandrin and Astra burst out at the same time, making Kyvo jerk awake with a snort.

"Are we doing something?" the kitsune muttered, sounding very much still asleep. His head dropped against Tak's knee a couple seconds later.

"If there's a demon on the loose, especially one that wants to eat you, you'd better believe I'm not walking away," Xandrin said, a hint of a growl in his voice.

"Right. Red beast is dead on," Astra said. "If people need help, then we, as the Dragon Kin, should help them as much as we can. That's our job, right?"

"Right," Redrinna said slowly. Softly—almost as if to herself.

Tak's throat tightened, but the reality of the situation was that he couldn't be of any help. Without his vision, there was little he could do in a situation like this. If anything, he would most likely get eaten in his current state.

"Fine," she said, but there was something off about her voice, an emotion Tak couldn't quite place. "Fine. I'll let Chatan know."

"Wait," Xandrin said, sitting up straight. "I've been wanting to ask for a while, but there wasn't ever a good time. Why do you keep calling these guys Torijin?"

Redrinna didn't speak, but Tak had a feeling she'd made a face at the dragon.

"What I mean is," the dragon continued, "I thought all humans were like you guys, but everyone here has wings."

Wait, they were with people who had wings? Tak's mind raced, like he finally had all the pieces he needed to put a puzzle together. That explained so many of the weird sounds he'd been hearing. Well, maybe it would.

"For the most part yes," Redrinna explained, a calm tone appearing in her voice for the first time in a while, "but the human race is broken into different tribes which are also sometimes called races. There are twelve altogether, I think, but I know very little about most of them, so I'm not the best person to ask."

"I might be!" Takota cut in abruptly seconds before there came a loud whoosh and thud, making Tak and Kyvo both jump. "Sorry, sorry. I didn't mean to scare any of you. I just came to check on my patient, but I overheard your conversation and got a little excited."

"It's fine," Redrinna said, sounding remarkably calm. Had she not been startled at all? Tak supposed she might've been able to see Takota coming. "So you know more about the tribes?"

"Sure do," Takota said, moving in a way that made his feathers rustle a bit (yep, feathers definitely explained a lot). "Well, for the most part. In our tribe, we have a legend that's been passed down since the ancient days. Admittedly, I'm not that great of a storyteller, but I can summarize it for you. Of course, if you want me to tell you, then you have to let me check your injuries first. Fair is fair, after all."

Tak suddenly wished his eyes were working properly. He'd never heard of human tribes before, but he'd also never left his village until a few months ago, and it'd been a simple, humble fishing village. They'd rarely had visitors, and it wasn't like he'd ever tried talking to anyone anyway, if he'd even left the house.

There was a pause before Takota said, "We'll have to change your bandages soon. After that fight you got in last night, we're lucky they aren't more scuffed. As for this one—" He broke off, something about it making Tak uneasy. It was only for a second, such a brief instant, but it convinced him something wasn't right.

"E-everything seems fine, and there's no sign of infection," Takota continued, hurriedly shaking away the unease in his tone. "So, would you all like to hear the creation legend?"

"Creation legend?" Redrinna repeated.

"Oh, I forgot you wouldn't know what that means since religion and that kind of thing are technically forbidden in the Empire," he said, those wings of his rustling again. "A creation legend was how a religion explained how our world and the people came to be and such."

Tak nodded. He didn't really know what Takota meant by religion, and he'd never heard of a creation legend either, but he was keen to learn. So, he stayed quiet.

"Don't get your hopes up too high, but I'll give it my best shot."

Chapter Fifteen

Takota paused, closing his eyes as he gathered his wings close to himself. Something about the way he stood got Redrinna's undivided attention.

"At the dawn of time, the Divine created the world, carving it from the cold hollow of the universe and crafting it into a home for his children. His children were divided into eleven tribes, each with their own different strengths.

"The first tribe, the Hikarijin, were the overseers and wielders of light. Their ability to harness light and shadow gave them the responsibility of being the guardians of all life on earth. They were to be beacons of hope to all.

"The next tribe, the Sorajin, were the people of the sky. They were given charge of the heavens and power of the skies. Their distinct, long ears were signs of their gift to hear all, and their task to act as mediators—judges of the Divine's children.

"The third tribe were the Umijin, the most robust humans of all the tribes. They were given charge of the vast and deep oceans and became guardians of the seas and protectors of all its life. Along with their endurance and strength, they were imbued with the gentlest of natures.

"The fourth to grace this earth were the Shinrinjin tribe, a quiet and gentle people who are in tune with the elements of the land, the counterpart to the Umijin of the sea. Their quiet strength and long lives aided them in their task to protect the natural beauty blanketing the earth.

"The fifth were the Hamajin, people who were to act as a bridge between the land and sea. To them was given the ability to govern the balance of the land and water, and the skills to thrive in either terrain, to be both fierce and calm.

"The sixth tribe were the Dohbutsujin, the people over all the creatures who inhabit this world with us. Theirs was the gift of life and growth. They were given the ability to speak to all and understand even the littlest of creatures.

"The Sunajin were the seventh tribe to be given a place on the earth. They were given unparalleled strength, making them the strongest of all the races that walked the land. Their fortitude and determination gave them the ability to survive in any situation and the strength to help the weak."

Redrinna's head was spinning. They were on the seventh one, and she'd only heard of the Sunajin before.

"The eighth tribe," Takota continued, strength creeping into his voice now, "were the people of ice, the Korijin. To them were given patience and fortitude. No matter the circumstance, they would stand as the compass of all the tribes, never faltering. Along with the ice in their veins and their natural affinity as hunters, they were gifted with the will to stand strong, no matter how bleak things seemed."

She may not have known most of the tribes so far, but she was very familiar with that one since people from that tribe had nearly captured her as a child. A shiver trickled down her spine at the memory.

"The ninth were the tough but wise Kaenjin, guardians of life-giving fire. Their passion and conviction lent them the ability to make difficult decisions and lead through metaphorical darkness. No matter how desperate the crisis, theirs was a flame that could never be diminished or extinguished.

"The tenth tribe were the small but clever Kinzokujin tribe, crafters by blood. Despite their small statures, they were given the ability to see through darkness and the gift to discover the potential of things cast out and forgotten. Their skill with their hands and willpower aided them in their task to see something's true value.

"The final tribe was mine, the Torijin, the people of flight. We were given powerful wings and the strength to act as guardians, steadfast and strong. Our task was to protect all who needed it— human, animal, or nature—and to be steady, no matter how the wind howled."

And that was the second to last tribe Redrinna knew. Three out of twelve didn't bolster her confidence.

"With his children given a place to learn and grow, the Divine withdrew from their presence, electing to guide them from afar. However, from the chaos of the universe crept a shadow—a beast— its heart set on claiming the power and majesty of the Divine, but it failed. Now, desperate to escape its shackles, its heart became bent on revenge. It vowed to destroy as many of the Divine's children as it could. It could not descend on the home of the Divine's children physically—it was too weak—but its influence leached through, tainting all it touched.

"In time, the Hikarijin hoarded their light rather than share it, plunging the other tribes into darkness. The Sorajin placed them- selves on thrones set high above the earth, proclaiming themselves rulers of the sky's might. The Dohbutsujin's hearts waxed cold, and they scorned all outsiders. The Torijin and Shinrinjin withdrew, preferring to keep to themselves and their own kind rather than min- gle with the other tribes. The Kaenjin delved deep into their moun- tains and refused any and all admittance into their lands, using any means necessary to keep outsiders out. The Sunajin used their great strength to conquer other tribes and reap bounty off their backs. The Kinzokujin, shunted aside and forgotten, also withdrew, taking their wonders and technologies with them. Hurt by the arrogance of the other tribes, the Umijin submerged themselves deep in the oceans and left the other tribes at the mercy of the waters' wrath. The Hamajin hoarded the ocean's bounty while the Korijin were content to watch the other tribes drown in their pride and arrogance. The entire world was dark and cold as stone, friends turning to enemies, family to foes.

"The Divine's heart sorrowed for the weakness of His children, so He graced the earth with the twelfth and final tribe: the Kokorojin, the people of heart.

"To them, no gifts of physical strength or prowess were given. They received no wings nor skin as hard as stone. Instead, they were gifted with unbreakable hearts and unwavering faith in humankind; their potential and deep love of others couldn't be matched by any other tribe. With their strength despite such disadvantages, they managed to heal and restore the peace between the tribes."

Takota fell silent, and no one said a word. After a minute, he lifted his head, his wings fanning open. "So, what did you think?"

Xandrin crept a couple inches closer. "Did that really happen?"

Takota shrugged. "Who knows? It's a story that's been passed down by my people for centuries, so I'm not sure if that was how it actually happened. But I like to think it did."

Lowering her gaze, Redrinna stared at the ground, her mind racing. None of the books in the palace or the Mount had contained anything like it, though there'd been hints of it here and there. She also couldn't help wondering if other tribes had other variations to explain how they'd all come to be.

All at once, Tak whispered, "What tribe am I?"

She turned to him, still startled by the bandage over his eyes. Hopefully he recovered enough to do without it soon. "You and I are part of the Kokorojin tribe."

He jumped, catching her off guard. Had he not meant for anyone to hear him?

Takota nodded. "That's right. You two are a part of that tribe." He glanced up at the village. "Unfortunately, as fun as this is, I have a few things I have to go and take care of now, so I'll check back in on you later, okay?" Flaring open his wings, he launched back upwards and vanished.

Redrinna's thoughts returned to Takota's story, the details calling a different story to mind, a legend she hadn't thought about in a while.

After a moment, Kyvo lifted his head and met her gaze before crawling out of Tak's lap and padding up to her. "What are you thinking about?"

"Oh, I remembered something."

"Remembered what?"

"The priestess legend."

"Oh, the story you told us the other day?" Kyvo stared at her intently, ears angled towards her and head tilted to the side.

She nodded, a smile almost touching her mouth. "But Takota's story reminded me of something, a part towards the end. The legend says she managed to recruit people from all over the continent."

"Yeah, I remember."

"I hadn't thought about it before, but I think that's the only record we have of people from all twelve tribes fighting side by side." She considered it some more. Yes, she was nearly one hundred percent certain that if the priestess' legend was right, the human tribes had only managed to stand together and fight that one time. Afterwards, they'd gone their separate ways, and lived in relative harmony until Osiris. That had changed everything, flipping the entire world on its head, it seemed.

Her ancestor may have had the strength to unite warring tribes, but Redrinna doubted she did. That was one of the many things she hadn't gotten from her ancestor.

As the heat of the sun faded from overhead and the air cooled, Tak returned to the clinic at Xandrin's insistence, heavily relying on Kyvo to make it without dying or getting lost. Part of him had wanted to stay and find a way to be helpful, but with his obscured vision and side limiting his mobility, there wasn't anything he could do.

Once he was safely returned to his room and seated on the edge of the bed to wait for Takota, the kitsune left. So, Tak waited for Takota in silence. The man came by every evening with medicine for him, but he didn't always come at the same time. So until he arrived, there was no point in doing anything else.

His thoughts folded themselves over again and again while he sat, listening as the birds hushed, almost as though they were giving the sun a moment of silence as it vanished beneath the horizon. A light breeze blew, and since he could feel it, he guessed someone had opened a window he hadn't known about. He turned his face towards it, the cool air helping calm his mind.

Redrinna had been busy today. For the first time since they'd arrived, she'd barely been able to spend any time with them, and the few times she had been with them, she'd sounded so drained. Worn out, like a rag on the verge of falling apart. Her mannerisms now were eerily similar to how she'd been while struggling to wake the gem.

Desperately, Tak ached to help her somehow, but he felt utterly lost, like he was stuck in some giant maze.

All over again, he felt like a helpless kid. It was like when he'd been younger and had come across an injured bird. Helping it had been beyond him, and even when he'd rushed it to his aunt, there'd been nothing she could do either. In the end, it'd passed away.

Despite that, his aunt had held him close and told him he was a 'kind person,' but being kind hadn't been enough to save the bird, and ever since he'd been taken in by Redrinna and the others, his so-called kindness hadn't done any of them any good. He wasn't helping. On the contrary, he seemed to be causing more pain for everyone.

As a heavy sigh rushed out of him, Takota arrived.

"Well, that was a big one."

Heat rushed to Tak's cheeks.

"Here," the man set a bowl brimming with a funny, almost earthy smell in his hands. "Maybe this will help."

He accepted it, but it wasn't going to ease this anxiety nettling him like a pebble in his shoe. Carefully, doing his best not to spill, he took a couple sips before his worries pricked at him hard enough he couldn't drink.

"Are you okay?" the man asked, touching the back of his hand to Tak's forehead.

"How do..." Tak began before pausing. Another sigh slipped out of him, but he wanted to ask the question anyway. "How do you help someone...even if there's nothing you can do?"

Takota didn't respond right away. He stood quietly for what felt like an eternity before pulling a seat over (at least, that was what Tak imagined from the brief grating sound of wood against wood) and sitting down, the wood creaking in response. "Do you want to talk?"

Keeping his head down, Tak shrugged. "I...I don't know."

"We can talk if you want, but we don't have to. It can wait if you'd prefer."

"Well...I...Redrinna is..."

Takota stayed quiet.

What was it he wanted to talk about anyway? Tak couldn't seem to think clearly, but he wanted to have someone with him, someone to listen to him. Maybe he just missed his aunt.

He started again. "Redrinna...she's...I don't know. I just want..."

"Hmm, how about we pause here and I'll answer your question instead, and if you figure out how to say what's on your mind, we can talk about it then? So, how do you help someone even if you know you can't?" Pausing, Takota let out a sigh of his own. "I suppose the first thing you should do is decide if the reason you can't help is because the problem is beyond your expertise or because the person in question doesn't want to get better."

Tak lifted his head.

"When you're working in medicine, you see all kinds of people with all kinds of different problems, and every now and then, you come across something you can't solve. Sometimes, it's because you don't have the answers or because nature takes its course regardless of your efforts. Other times, there are patients who don't get better, no matter what you do, because they don't want to.

"So, Tak, if I may, can I ask you this? What happened with Redrinna and why don't you think you can help her? If you don't think you can do something, why do you want to?"

Tak considered the second question for a minute. "I want to help her because...she's a good person. Except..." He paused. He and Takota had had a similar conversation before, and he still didn't want to go around spreading Redrinna's business everywhere. "She...she went through something bad—I mean something awful. A-and it's only been a couple months since then, but she's so...so different now."

"I can't say for sure," the man said, his voice soft, "But she'll probably never be quite the same person she was then. Difficult things do that to you."

"I know, but," he lowered his head again, "I wish...she could be happy again." He wished she could sleep. He wished she could smile, a genuine smile instead of the one she kept trying to paint on her face. He wished they could talk again, like they had the night after Xandrin had woken up. For that moment, that tiny, fragment of time, they'd felt like friends. It hadn't mattered that they'd barely known each other, but for an instant, it was like they'd been best friends their entire lives. He wanted to belong like that again instead of feeling like everything he did made things worse, but maybe it was simply too much to ask for.

"Have you tried talking to her about it?"

His heart stuttered at the thought. How could Tak, of all people, do something like that?

"I mean, does she even realize you guys are worried about her? Or are you all just standing by and watching?"

"I-I couldn't talk to her like that," he protested with a shake of his head.

"Why not?"

"She's a princess. I'm...I'm just me." A peasant—no, an orphan—from a tiny fishing village without a home to call his own. Someone like him had no right to lecture someone like her; they were from two completely different worlds.

"So what? If you're her friend, then your status doesn't matter. I mean, my mom's just a village medicine woman, but she cusses everyone out, child and elder alike."

"That's not...the same..." Tak began, falling silent when Takota shifted, making the wood of his chair creak.

"Okay, then what would you tell her if you could? Do you know?"

Tak wracked his brain for a long time. There were several things he wanted to say, but... "H-how could I say anything? I can't scold her about stuff I don't understand. I don't know what she's going through."

Takota didn't say anything.

"What would...what would you say? What can you say to someone whose mother was murdered?"

The man inhaled sharply. After a long pause, he spoke. "It...probably depends on the person, but perhaps—coming from someone who's also lost a parent—you should just try to help her remember she isn't alone."

Tak's fingers tightened on the bowl in his hands. Being alone was something he knew well, yet it'd never crossed his mind that maybe she was lonely too. After all, while he'd never known his mother, she had. She'd grown up all her life with her mother by her side, but in an instant, that had changed.

Though, knowing someone and losing them, that was a pain he knew. He knew the raw, gut-punched feeling that followed. He knew it like the back of his hand, even if his pain hadn't been caused by the loss of his mom.

"That's the best advice I can give you right now," Takota said, getting to his feet. "Finish your medicine, and get some rest, okay?"

Doing as he was told, Tak drained the bowl and handed it back. Once the man was gone, he laid down, watching his thoughts go around in circles like dogs chasing their tails. The faint light that managed to brush against his eyelids gradually faded until the world around him became completely dark.

Chapter Sixteen

Redrinna paused in her self-imposed drills as the moon drifted out from behind a cloud, faintly illuminating the sleeping forest around her. She lowered her sword after a moment, deciding she could use a brief respite. After all, she was supposed to be guarding against the demon, and she wouldn't be able to confront it if she'd already exhausted herself. Slipping her sword back into its sheath, she scanned the village a few times, hunting for anything out of place.

The demon hadn't gotten the meal it'd wanted, so it was going to come back sooner rather than later. So far, since the demons had first appeared, Chatan said that eight people—all women and children—had been snatched a couple weeks apart, and none of them had been seen since.

As Redrinna studied the village from the midst of the trees, her gaze settled on the shadowy outline of the clinic. It was darker than the massive oak framing it, but there were a couple candles flickering in the pitch-black windows. Somewhere in there were the victims of the demon's paralysis powers, ten men in all. They had to be fed in order to stay alive, but they were like vegetables once ripped from the soil: lifeless and unresponsive.

Redrinna hadn't seen them for herself. She was sure the families of the victims wouldn't appreciate her barging in on them to satisfy her curiosity, so she'd stayed away.

Despite some people's sudden friendliness to her, most of the village now stared at her like she was a stray they didn't know what to make of. Only Mika and Chatan kept seeking her out—which was weird—but even Ohanzi, the grumpy old man who'd shot her the most glares out of everyone, wasn't being grumpy anymore. He wasn't exactly being nice either, but he let Mika wave to her now.

Briefly, for just a minute, she wondered what it would've been like if the genocide of the Torijin people had never happened at all. If the Empire itself had never been brought into existence, maybe then she and these people would've been friends without a second's hesitation. Perhaps they could have met without the need to hold each other at knife point. Then again, perhaps not. If it hadn't been for the past, maybe they never would have met at all. In truth, she was still wondering whether or not the fact they'd ended up meeting was good for either of them yet.

Then she shook her head. Thoughts like those were unproductive.

Right as Redrinna was about to start on a walk around the village's perimeter, a familiar, calming presence touched her subconscious, making her freeze. It was then she realized everything had gone quiet—not the kind of quiet when the demon had appeared, but a soothing kind of quiet. Was this...another spirit?

Turning, she nearly jumped out of her skin. An enormous bison stood a short distance away, its massive head framed by some scraggly, low-hanging aspens. A fuzzy, golden glow emanated from its light brown coat, giving it a similar appearance to Matte. Golden eyes peered at her from beneath its two short but wickedly sharp horns.

The sight of it startled her enough she almost forgot how to speak. "A-are you a spirit?"

Its velvety nose twitched. "I am. An astute observation on your part."

"I've met a couple before." Granted, neither Matte nor the spirit guarding the gems had approached her for seemingly no reason. "Do you need something?"

The spirit tilted its head, almost like it was sizing her up, making a couple butterflies waltz through her stomach. "I have a request. Since you can see me, I think you might be able to oblige me."

A few more butterflies flitted through Redrinna's stomach.

"It was once my duty to watch over these people and their homeland, but when they were ravaged, I lost much of my power. Now, I can't protect these people as I once did. So with that in mind, I want you to help them exterminate the beast."

"What?"

"Consider it a step towards repairing the rift your father tore between your peoples. Help my people rid themselves of this vermin and take one step closer to regaining their strength, which will enable me to grow stronger as well. And someday, they may even help you in return."

A grimace twisted her face before she could stop it. Chatan had already asked her for her help, though she couldn't figure out why. Training with Wicasa and Kangee had done little more than show her how inexperienced she was.

"I'm...flattered by your request, really, but they don't need me. They managed to kill one of them already, so they'll get this one too before much longer—"

The spirit shook its head like it was chasing off an errant fly. "They've already asked for your help, have they not? I also trust they'd solve the problem on their own given enough time, but I want to tip the scales more in their favor, sooner rather than later. After all, to those who are given more, much is required. Is that not so?"

A pang shot through Redrinna's heart. Her mother used to say the same thing. "Okay. I'll...I'll do what I can."

The spirit dipped its head before vanishing in the blink of an eye.

A long sigh escaped her. She'd already been struggling to mentally prepare herself to help the village get rid of its pest, but now, with the spirit's expectations bearing down on her, a monstrous weight settled on her shoulders. If she failed here, if she failed again, she didn't know if she'd be able to find the strength to keep fighting.

"Redrinna," Xandrin said abruptly from behind her. "It was my turn to take over the watch a while ago."

"I know, I know. I'm sorry. I just...got distracted." In truth, she wanted him to rest as much as possible, even if all she could give him was only a few extra minutes.

He stared for a long, tense moment. "You need to sleep. You know that, right?"

"I don't want to talk about it right now."

"Did you think I wouldn't notice you're not sleeping? Do you seriously think I'm that clueless?"

"No, I don't," Redrinna snapped. Then she bit her lip and wrestled her anger into submission before she could say something she'd regret. When she was more sure of her emotions, she turned to face him. However, she couldn't bring herself to look up. "I'm fine. I'm having a hard time sleeping because my wrist has been bugging me, and now that demon thing is showing up. I'm sorry I forgot you. I didn't mean to. So don't worry about me, okay?"

"How am I not supposed to worry about you?" he demanded, wings flaring open slightly. "You keep saying you're fine, but you don't look it. I'm just...concerned."

"I know, but I am fine. Honest." Redrinna forced herself to lift her head and give him a small smile. "So...be careful tonight, all right?"

He stared at her for a long minute before nodding, and she left, heading to the clinic. Takota had insisted she sleep in the clinic now, and she hadn't had the heart to fight him. Plus, with Xandrin out on watch, she couldn't hang out on his back. However, as she made her way to the building, the wood platforms beneath her feet gently creaking in the wind, anxiety pounded through her veins with every beat of her heart. What if something happened to one of the dragons when she wasn't there? What if resting meant she couldn't protect them? What if she couldn't keep Xandrin safe?

Redrinna let herself in the dark clinic without a sound, recoiling at the bite of the sharp, herbal smell before heading to the room Chumani had said was hers for now. As softly as possible, Redrinna shut the door behind her. The second it clicked shut, the full weight of everything on her mind crashed onto her shoulders like the mountainside had given way, trapping her beneath its weight. Her knees threatened to buckle, nearly causing her to fall. She caught herself against the door, banging her head a little.

Grimacing, she pushed herself back up and removed her belt, boots, and the dragon scale shirt before crawling into the achingly soft bed, but instead of falling asleep, an uneasiness roosted in her chest, ceaselessly gnawing and pecking at her.

She knew Xandrin didn't understand, but it'd be better if only one of them had to be in danger.

Resting an arm on her forehead, Redrinna squeezed her eyes shut, fighting to subdue the army of thoughts trampling her mind. There was a soft breeze blowing outside, rustling the trees just enough to make them sound like flowing water. Occasionally, the soft, reedy hoot of an owl broke the stillness, so low and quiet, she almost didn't catch it.

It occurred to her then that her gem hadn't said a word to her all day. That was odd, but she wasn't up to doing anything about it.

⁂

Tak woke the next morning more than a little surprised by a weight at the end of his bed. Hesitantly, he nudged it with his foot, jumping when it let out a drawn-out squeak. What in the world was—

"Kyvo?" he asked uncertainly.

"Good morning," came the mumbled reply. It sure sounded like Kyvo. Except why was the little kitsune in here this morning? He'd never spent the night with him before.

"Wh-what are you...doing?" Tak stammered, not sure whether this was something he should be concerned over.

Kyvo shifted, almost violently, making a flapping sound like he did when he shook his head. "You're the only person who gets to sleep during the night, and since I don't want to be alone, I came to hang out with you. The others are all helping guard the village, so they're always getting up and moving around and stuff."

Tak frowned. If his eyes were cooperating, then he would've been out there too. A part of him was relieved he didn't have to, but at the same time, he would've at least felt useful if he could've done something. Anything, really.

Kyvo sighed, got up, stretched so hard it shook the bed, then flopped back down, resting his head on Tak's foot. "It's not just me, right?"

"What?"

"Redrinna seems different lately, doesn't she?"

Tak's thoughts went back to the girl he'd met on the outskirts of the village, the one who'd seen him as a human being instead of trash, the one who'd stood up for him, the one who'd offered him a home out of fear for his safety. The Redrinna with them now... She was still nice, but something wasn't the same. Something was different, but he didn't know what.

"Yeah," he whispered. He didn't want to say this side of Redrinna was terrible, but she wasn't the girl he'd met back then. He missed the girl he'd seen in that moment, that one time he'd seen her truly happy. It'd been such a fleeting instant, like a dream, and maybe that was all it would be.

Even still, when he'd first realized a gem was asking him to be a part of the Dragon Kin, in the few, passing fantasies in his mind, he'd never imagined their group this...broken. Disjointed. Like a pastry missing its gooey, fruit center. However, that was undoubtedly because those fantasies had been a byproduct of his imagination, and this was real life.

The door to the room unexpectedly opened, but whoever had come in didn't speak right away, so he wasn't sure who it was. It could be Shappa. Probably not Takota though. The guy would've said something the second he'd entered the room.

"Morning," the person said as they shut the door, and he instantly recognized Redrinna's voice. She sounded tired, making him wonder how much sleep she'd gotten last night, if she'd gotten any.

"Hey," he said at the same time as Kyvo. "I-I can't see, so how are you feeling?"

"Fine," she said, a bit too fast for him to believe it. "Mika wanted to show me something today, so I dropped by for a minute to check how you're doing. I didn't get to be with you guys yesterday."

"You have been busy," Kyvo said with a quiet huff. "But not too busy, right?"

"It's fine," she said.

Just like yesterday, Tak couldn't help noting the worn-out tone of her voice, like she was being stretched thin. He wasn't entirely sure, but it seemed more prominent today than it had been yesterday. His and Takota's latest conversation came back to him, but his heart deflated at the reminder. What could he say? What if something he said made it worse, whether he meant to or not? If it got even worse because of him, how could he possibly stay?

"So...how are your injuries?" Redrinna asked after a minute, calling him back to the present.

"My side is doing much better. Takota said if it weren't for my head, I'd be okay to travel in a couple days."

Silence filtered between them like stray leaves drifting in the wind, and he was intensely aware of an awkwardness permeating every inch of the space. This wasn't right either. It'd never been like this between them before, not even when they'd first met. Was he the only one who felt it?

"I'm glad," Redrinna said at length. "Also...I have to ask: did something happen between you and Astra?"

His heart stuttered. How had she caught on to that?

"I'm sorry for prying, it's just that she said you didn't seem to like her. So I wanted to know if things...were okay."

Redrinna was certainly one to talk.

Tak hastily scrubbed that thought from his mind. He hadn't meant to think it, it'd just barged in. At least he hadn't said it out loud. He would've been mortified, and Redrinna probably would've yelled at him too.

"Everything is fine," he said.

A pause. Then she said, "Okay. Oh...I should also tell you she's joining us. She asked me if she could, so..."

Another awkward pause stifled the air, making unease settle deeper in his chest.

"I should get going now. See you both later."

The door opened and closed. She was gone. A sigh rushed out of him and Kyvo at the same time.

"You two make such a pair, you know that?" the kitsune said, his tail (Tak's best guess) thumping against the bed.

"Huh?"

Kyvo didn't reply for a long minute, each second of silence digging into Tak like sharp needles. "You're always so quiet, it's like you're walking barefoot on glass or something. Both of you. All the time."

Tak didn't have a clue how he was supposed to respond.

Kyvo huffed.

"Well it's—I just—" Tak broke off, frustration rising in his chest. Why was he trying to explain? If they knew, if anyone knew, they wouldn't like him anymore. They wouldn't want him around and would ditch him like he was a malformed puppy.

Kyvo didn't speak for a while, but Tak got the distinct impression the kitsune was staring, making him uncomfortable. "The lady who attacked us is still out there somewhere. If she finds us again, she might be able to kill Astra. I can't exactly fight, and even if I could, I'm not strong like you guys."

A chill raced down Tak's spine at the serious tone in the kitsune's voice. The memory of Reyna and her cold, dark eyes flashed through his mind like a lightning bolt. It would be nothing short of a nightmare if she came back, especially since Tak lacked the aid of his sight. Kyvo was right: their group was in worse shape now than it had been when she'd attacked them before. They'd barely escaped the first time, and unless something changed, there was a good chance she'd be able to kill Astra or Xandrin if there was a next time. A shudder shook him.

"Kyvo," he began before stopping, unsure what he was trying to say. "It's just...I...there's something wrong with me."

"I know!" the kitsune chirped. "Your eyes aren't working."

That almost made him smile. "That's...not what I mean. It's something that can't be fixed. I've been this way..." He paused, his fingers searching for the stitching in the quilt again. "It's been this way since I was born. It's just the way it is. So don't...don't worry about it, okay?"

It was almost like, ever since Tak had taken his first breath, there'd been some demon of ill luck that had attached itself to him, shadowing his every move, lashing out at everyone and everything around him.

"You can tell me, right?" The kitsune's voice was hushed, but there was something calming about it. It was different, but it almost made Tak believe he could say anything.

However, he shook his head. Nobody could help him, and anyone who knew shunned him. No one had ever been able to help him. If he said anything, Kyvo wouldn't want to help him; he'd leave.

"Please?" Kyvo rose and crawled into Tak's lap, gently headbutting his jaw. "I want to help you."

All at once, Takota's voice rang through Tak's mind: 'I suppose the first thing you should decide is if the reason you can't is because the problem is beyond your expertise or because the patient in question doesn't want to get better.'

Once the thought entered his mind, it persisted, refusing to leave. He did want to get better. At least, he thought he did. He wanted to feel normal, to have friends and people around him who loved him and needed him. He wanted to feel like he wasn't just a burden. He wanted to belong; he wanted it so badly he could almost taste it.

Never, in all his memories, had he fit in anywhere, though, if he forced himself to be honest, he'd never tried to either. No matter how many times his aunt had tried to get him to leave the house or to just smile at anyone, he'd shut himself away instead. He believed with every fiber of his being that he was nothing more than a loathsome beast who was irreversibly broken, but there was still a small part of him locked away somewhere that wanted to believe it wasn't true.

Right as he considered opening his mouth, his jaw wired itself shut as his stomach clenched with a sudden, paralyzing nervousness. If he told Kyvo, there'd be nowhere to hide. It wouldn't be Tak's secret any longer, and what would happen if the kitsune told someone else? He couldn't risk it.

Yet, right as he thought that, a fuzzy memory of his aunt surfaced in his mind. The only thing he remembered clearly was her face, one of the rare times when she'd smiled. He missed her smile. He missed her. He hadn't felt this alone when he'd been with her, and she'd known all his dark secrets. She'd accepted him for what he was, and maybe if Kyvo knew, if Tak took a chance and shared part of it, then perhaps the kitsune would accept him too. Maybe there'd even be a glimpse of what his life had been like with his aunt.

Slowly, Tak took a deep, shaky breath. "I-it started when I was born. I don't know what was wrong, but something was the matter with me. My aunt said the chance of me making it through the night had been slim, so...my mom used her magic to save me."

"Magic? What kind of magic?" Kyvo asked, sitting back away from his face now.

"It was healing magic."

"Oh."

"Do you...know how it works?"

"Sort of. I have some kind of healing magic, but it's not very strong. The most I've ever been able to do is heal little cuts and scrapes." The kitsune paused. "Healing magic...takes energy to use, right?"

Tak nodded.

"Oh. Your mom...had just given birth to you, but she still...?"

Tak couldn't utter a sound.

The kitsune remained quiet.

Eventually, Tak managed to find his voice. "It might've been fine, her trying to save me, but...but the birth hadn't gone well either. Her being pregnant in general had been difficult, so when she used her magic to help me...it took her life."

The room was hushed, and for a minute, Tak struggled to keep going.

"S-so her sister and her husband—my aunt and uncle—took me in. Shortly afterward, they became pregnant with their own child, but, just like with my mom, something went wrong and she went into labor too soon, months too soon. In the end, the baby didn't make it, and complications with the surgery left my aunt unable to have any more children."

Lightly, Kyvo rested his head against Tak's shoulder but remained quiet still.

"And that was when people began saying it was because of me," Tak managed, struggling to speak, his throat so tight it hurt. It felt like he was trying to speak while trapped in a nightmare. "Th-they said I was cursed, and death would go everywhere I went."

Kyvo hissed.

Tak fought to swallow, trying to clear his throat, anything to get rid of the pressure squeezing his chest like a vice. "A few years later, my uncle was drafted in the Esunian War, and he was killed there. Shortly after, my aunt fell ill, and after years of fighting it, she finally succumbed a few months ago."

"And I bet that made the rumors worse," Kyvo whispered, his head still against Tak's shoulder.

"And then when I came here, Xandrin almost died, Redrinna nearly got abducted, Reyna almost killed Astra, she hurt you, she hurt Redrinna—" Tak jerked back from Kyvo's touch, his skin burning. The people he was around were always getting hurt. They died.

"But Tak," Kyvo scooted closer, making him lean away, "you saved Astra, didn't you? That has to count for something."

Even though he knew it wasn't how Kyvo had meant it, that blood-soaked memory blossomed in his mind's eye. A chill seeped across his skin. Astra lying on the ground, barely conscious, and the blood—there'd been so much blood. There'd been even more blood than when Xandrin had nearly been killed. Tak had stumbled up to her, legs weak as a newborn kitten's. He hadn't known what to do, but he'd wanted to make the bleeding stop. Then— He forced the rest of the memory to stop, fighting to keep it from playing out as a shudder wracked him.

All at once, Kyvo moved, pressing himself to Tak's side. "You...have the magic too, don't you?"

"H-how do you—" Tak stopped, wishing he could hide somewhere.

"I'm not sure how, but I can tell. I'm almost positive you inherited your mother's powers."

He cringed, not wanting to hear it out loud.

Kyvo stayed quiet for a minute. "Is that why you get uncomfortable whenever Astra brings up what happened? That...was how you found out about your powers, wasn't it?"

The memory resumed in Tak's mind. Vividly, he remembered reaching out for Astra, desperate to make the blood stop. As he'd touched her slick scales, white light had sprung from his palms, curling around the dragon's body like a soft cocoon. That was where the memory ended. The next one he had was from nearly a week later, when he'd woken up, and the only thing he remembered was his aunt's pale, drawn face hovering above him.

"You've never told anyone? About the magic, I mean?" Kyvo asked, his voice so quiet, barely a murmur.

Tak shook his head, immediately regretting it as pain lanced through his skull. "My aunt...she asked me never to use it or let people know I had it. It killed her sister...and almost me too."

The power lurking inside Tak terrified him; he hated it. Magic like this was supposed to help people—it was supposed to heal them, not require such a steep sacrifice and cause so much grief and pain.

Kyvo abruptly shot into his arms, nearly knocking him over. "I don't think there's anything wrong with you. Healing magic is scary, but if you knew more about it, then maybe it wouldn't be so scary."

The kitsune refused to leave his arms, leaving Tak utterly speechless. How was he supposed to respond to this? Even still, despite what the kitsune had said, it didn't make him hate himself any less. The kitsune accepting him didn't change who Tak was. It didn't change the power inside him or magically make him better like he'd hoped.

He leaned back, resting his head against the wall. This was who he was, and there wasn't anything that could change it.

All at once, Timothon's words echoed in his mind: 'if you don't like the face staring back at you in the mirror, you still have two choices. One, you can change the face you see, or two, shatter the mirror and get a better one.'

What did that even mean? How was Tak supposed to do either of those things anyway?

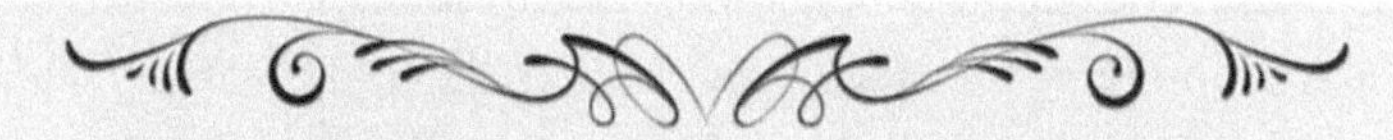

Chapter Seventeen

Redrinna leaned against the door frame as Tak and Kyvo fell silent. So that was what was up with Tak, why he seemed to want to be with them but also kept himself separate like he had an infectious disease he was trying to spare them from.

Despite herself, she smiled a little. At least Kyvo was with him so he didn't have to be alone. A part of her wanted to run back in and tell him she wasn't going to abandon him—vision restored or no—as many times as it took to get him to believe it, but it felt too hypocritical. Redrinna, of all people, was the least suited to help him, even if she understood his hatred for his powers. If it hadn't been for Matte's willingness to teach her how to use them and her need to protect herself and her friends, she wouldn't touch them at all.

This is a strange place to spend your time.

She jumped. This was the first time her gem had spoken to her since Two Face had appeared in the village. Then she shook her head, not wanting to explain when she was close enough Tak and Kyvo would realize she was right outside the door.

Since she'd overheard them by accident, it would be best to pretend she didn't know. That seemed to be what he wanted anyway. This just meant she'd have to try harder to protect everyone and keep them safe so Tak wouldn't have to risk using a power he hated or feel guilty if he didn't use it.

With a shake of her head, Redrinna pushed off the door jam and headed for the entrance, doing her best to remain as silent and unobtrusive as possible. Mika was probably waiting for her by now.

As she stepped into the overly bright outside world, she glanced around, spotting Mika and Ohanzi almost instantly. They were a couple bridges over, in the shadow of their little house.

A bit meekly, she walked over to meet them, the warm smell of flaky fry bread wafting through the air almost making her hungry. However, as she watched the villagers talking and laughing over their meals, the words from the spirit rang through her mind again, making her stomach shrivel to nothing. Chumani caught her eye and held up a golden-brown piece of fry bread, but Redrinna shook her head and hurried away before the woman could guilt trip her into taking it.

"Good morning, Princess!" Mika chirped, sliding to a stop in front of her before she'd been able to make it halfway across the platforms. "You ready?"

"Slow down, Mika, or you'll wear her out," his grandpa said. In his thin, weathered hands, he clutched a meager bouquet of irises, their petals a soft blue with fuzzy, deep purple hearts. When he noticed her gaze, he smiled with a surprising tenderness and said, "My son's favorite. They're from my garden."

So Mika was taking her to visit his dad? Her stomach clenched with nerves. She wasn't sure if she was ready for that.

"Come on," Mika said, taking hold of her hand before she could refuse. "I want you to meet my dad, so he'll know you were the one who saved me. He's pretty curious."

Without giving Redrinna a choice, he led her back into the clinic and through a closed door standing across the hall from Tak's room. She paused on the threshold.

While Tak was the only one in his room, there were three people in this one, all men, one on the bed, and two on cots on the floor. All of them lay motionless, stiff and rigid as though they were dead.

Mika trotted in, going to the man lying on a cot under a window. They both bore the same, reddish-brown feathers on their wings.

Ohanzi stepped past Redrinna, his gaze drifting around the room before settling on her. "Victims of the demon's paralysis powers," he said. Then he ventured in, tugging crumbling, brown flowers from a vase on a table near the bed and placing the fresh ones he'd brought from his garden inside.

She crept in a bit further so she could close the door back down.

Ohanzi leaned down to the man lying on the bed. "Hanska, your wife delivered the baby. Both of them are safe and healthy, and you're the proud father of an adorable baby girl. Her name is Ehawee, after your sister, now that she's no longer with us."

The man didn't move aside from the slow, barely perceptible rise and fall of his chest. After a moment, Redrinna spied a tear running down Hanska's cheek. She found herself putting a hand over her mouth, whether to hold back a sob or what she didn't know.

"Princess," Mika called, getting her attention. "Come meet my dad."

Dipping her head, she crossed the room, crouching next to him. She noticed this man's eyes were open, unlike Hanska's.

"Dad," Mika said softly, "this is the princess. I know you didn't like her before, but she's the one who saved my life. She made sure the demon couldn't take me. I told you she was a good person."

Redrinna had to bite her lip to keep herself from begging Mika to stop.

"You see, Princess," Mika said, picking a stray string off his dad's cot and twisting it between his fingers, "the demon attacked my mom and dad while they were out in the woods, leaving my dad like this."

"And your mom?" she asked, afraid she already knew the answer.

He twisted the string a little faster. "The demon took her and my baby sibling away."

"Baby sibling?"

"My momma was going to have a baby," he said, his voice softer than the beat of an owl's wings. "But they're both gone now. It's just me and Grandpa and Dad."

Her heartbeat was faint in her chest, almost like it was fading away.

However, Mika's smile returned. "But it'll be okay. One day, Daddy will get better, and we'll be okay again." He turned back to his dad, chattering about the things he'd done yesterday and the food they'd eaten for breakfast.

Mutely, Redrinna stared at him, at his smile. It seemed genuine, lighting his face up like the sun. How did he do that? How could he be happy? How?

Why couldn't she do the same?

Remaining still and quiet like stone being eaten by moss, she sat beside Mika, listening as he visited with his father. Eventually, he said goodbye, leaning forward and shutting his father's eyes before getting to his feet. She followed suit, and they left the clinic.

The boy stopped, staring out at the sea of trees for a long minute before meeting Redrinna's gaze. "Thanks for coming with me today. I have to go now, but maybe we can talk again at dinner."

She nodded, and once Ohanzi joined them, the two of them left. The weight of the spirit's request resettled on her shoulders, no longer just one mountain of weight but two. She wanted to help here, but she couldn't shake off the inadequacy digging its sharp fingers into her bones. If she fought and failed... A shudder swept over her, making her hair fall across her face.

Shaking those thoughts away, she turned towards the stairs. Before she could take a step, Takota appeared next to her, surprisingly quiet despite his size.

"My mom wants to see you real quick, okay?" He flashed her a grin. "Come with me?"

Too tired to object or resist, she followed him back into the clinic yet again. They ducked into one of the empty rooms towards the back, and Shappa entered a few moments later.

"Takota told me the cut on your cheek was healing quicker than we expected, so I want to take a look at it."

Wordlessly, Redrinna nodded. She'd forgotten about the injury already. Her wrist hardly bothered her anymore either.

"Have a seat," Takota said, pulling a chair over to her before heading to the cabinet in the corner.

She did as she was told. Shappa gently gripped her chin between her forefinger and thumb, tilting her head back. Almost immediately the woman's eyes went wide.

"How is this even possible?" she breathed.

Takota came back, his face going an ashy color as he looked too. "That's more healed than it was yesterday. See? I'm not crazy."

Redrinna's heart shuddered as she caught on. "Is it healed?"

"Not completely," Shappa said. "But if we don't get the stitches out today, the wound is going to heal over them. I thought we weren't going to need to do this until next week, at the earliest. It was such a deep cut..."

Heart squeezing on her throat, Redrinna didn't protest, allowing them to turn her head. With fast, silent precision, they snipped and tugged the stitches free. It hurt a little, but it didn't bother her. In her mind, she couldn't stop thinking about Mika's father and Hanska, lying motionless in that room. The ache pulsing in her chest stung far worse than the soreness of her cheek could. How many rooms in the clinic cradled people in that same, helpless state?

They finished with her cheek after a few minutes, and Shappa made to turn away but paused.

"Princess," she began carefully. "How's your wrist?"

Redrinna's gaze dropped to it. She wriggled her fingers. That had made it ache a couple days ago. "It doesn't hurt."

Shappa and Takota shared alarmed looks.

"We need to check your arm too." Takota was unraveling the bandage before he finished speaking. As the cloth began to fall away, Redrinna's pulse quickened.

Her father had said her blood was special; Osiris had said the same. During her and Tak's experiment, her cuts had always healed so much faster. She'd started thinking maybe Tak was the weird one, and he'd been taking longer to heal because of where he'd grown up, but maybe that wasn't the case after all.

Takota tugged the last of the bandage away. Redrinna's heart froze, ice crackling in her veins.

The bruising was almost gone. And the bone that had jutted out before? Perfectly set now. Her wrist looked nearly healed.

"There's no way this should be possible," Takota hissed, turning her hand over and over. Lightly, he felt along the bone, only sending a couple dull twinges up her arm. "Does that hurt at all?"

"A little," Redrinna said, an awful dread flooding her chest, "but not really."

She'd never thought about it before, but in Xandrin's cave, she'd recovered from a massive fall so quickly—probably too quickly. The cuts on her fingers had healed with alarming speed. Her cheek was already nearly healed, and her wrist was far too close. Broken bones normally took at least a month to be this close to being healed, not a week.

All at once, she was out of breath like she'd been running for too long, leaving her gasping for air.

"Are you sure it was actually broken?" Shappa asked, but her voice was dimmed like she was standing far away.

"I'm positive, mother. It was a displaced fracture. The break was obvious." Takota stared at her wrist for a minute longer before meeting Redrinna's gaze, something different in his eyes. "Your Highness, is this...normal for you?"

Her throat was so dry it felt like it was sticking to itself, but she managed to choke out, "I think so. I...I didn't notice until recently, not until—" Why was it so hard to breathe? It felt like Xandrin was standing on her chest. "My parents threw me into a cave. At the time, I thought they wanted to kill me, but I met my father later, and he said it was impossible for something like that to do so. Tak and I also tried to do an experiment. We'd make little cuts on our fingertips and compare how long it took them to heal. Mine were always faster."

"How fast are we talking exactly?" Shappa asked, her skin ashen now too.

"Just over a day," Redrinna said, fighting to keep her breathing even. "That's not—it's not normal, right?"

Takota and Shappa both hesitated long enough to make her nerves spark with fear.

Shaking her head, Shappa finally said, "No. This isn't normal, not even for young children who tend to heal faster than adults. This is very strange."

Black ink drops blotted the edges of Redrinna's vision, nauseating dizziness nearly pitching her from her chair. She felt someone grab her, holding her up maybe? Without warning, the room around her melted away, and all at once, she was staring at *him*.

In her mind—she knew it was only in her mind, but that didn't make the terror flooding her any less real—she stood at the foot of the throne, the throne he'd stolen from her parents. Osiris leered at her with his vivid blue eyes and that wide, maniacal grin.

"You are different from anyone else who walks this earth," his voice echoed in her head, every bone in her body quaking at the memory. "Because of your father's...let us say power, you hold in your flesh something special that is vital to my plans to rebuild this continent. That is why I need you and hope you will come of your own free will."

The memory faded, but his eyes and sneer remained, searing themselves deeper in her memory. Weight pressed down, crushing her beneath the burden of the memory. Somewhere in her mind she was aware of being on her knees, no longer in her chair, digging her fingers into her chest. Takota was right in front of her, calling to her; she heard him speaking but couldn't understand the words.

She wanted to scream, run, anything.

She couldn't breathe.

"Redrinna," Takota said, putting his hands on her shoulders.

Slowly, she managed to find his face.

"It's okay," he said, carefully, softly. "Nothing's going to get you here."

She trembled like she'd been given a death sentence. "This is why he wants me. He did this to me; he'll kill all my friends to get me. He wants to kill all my friends."

"Who does?"

"Osiris." She whispered his name like he was right outside the room and would hear her. "He's going to get me, and he's going to kill everybody again. He'll kill Xandrin and Astra and Tak and—" Her throat burned like she was on the verge of tears, but her eyes were painfully dry.

Takota said something. Redrinna couldn't hear him over the ringing in her ears.

Every inch of her body bled fear, terror ripping at her legs, haunting her shadow, squeezing her throat. All she could see was Osiris's face, regardless of whether her eyes were open or closed. He was everywhere. He was there, watching her, reaching for her, grinning from ear to ear. Her lungs burned for air.

She fought against it, hard. But he was strong, stronger than her—just like he'd been before.

All at once, Shappa's face forced Osiris's aside. The woman's warm hands cupped her cheeks, keeping Redrinna's gaze on her. "Look at me, Redrinna, and breathe. In and out, okay?"

Redrinna tried, her breaths halting and stilted.

"That's it, keep at it."

It seemed like an eternity of sitting there, staring into Shappa's golden eyes and fighting to take a complete breath, but little by little, like a sunrise, Osiris faded; the fear ebbed; and the room, Takota, and Shappa all came back into focus.

For a long while, Redrinna stayed where she was with her eyes closed, afraid it would happen again. Eventually, she became aware of the fact she was clinging to Shappa's bony wrists like her life depended on it. Slowly, she managed to relax her iron grip and finally let go. Her hands were stiff and disjointed, almost like they'd frozen solid.

"How are you feeling now?" Shappa asked softly, voice like a gentle breeze.

"I-I'm fine," she managed, opening her eyes.

The woman lowered her hands, wrists bright red.

Redrinna's gaze fell to the floor, and her head dropped into her hands, heavy like it was stuffed with lead. "I'm so sorry."

"For what?" Takota asked, voice hushed.

She curled up tighter, unable to answer his question. Desperately, she wished she could crawl under a rock and never come back out.

"Redrinna, you don't need to apologize," he said, bending down so he was in her line of sight. "That's not something you need to apologize for. The important thing is that you're doing okay now."

"You should rest," Shappa said, pulling her to her feet. "You must be exhausted."

Protests sprang to the tip of Redrinna's tongue, but the stern look on the woman's face made her objections retreat. Meekly, she nodded, and the woman escorted her from the room and into the one she'd spent the night in.

"Do you want some company?" the woman asked, catching her off guard. "Or would you rather be alone?"

"I want to be alone."

Shappa left without a word.

The second the woman was gone and the door shut, Redrinna's knees gave way, dropping her on the floor. She lacked the energy to try and get back up. Shame surged through her chest like a wave, threatening to swallow her, and she wished she could erase everything that had just happened.

A flicker of warmth from her gem passed through her, but it didn't ease the tightness of her chest. Some member of the Dragon Kin she was turning out to be; even the memory of Osiris left her weak and helpless with fear. How on earth was she ever going to fight him and win?

Claws scratched the door. Blinking, Redrinna managed to push herself in a sitting position and open the door. Kyvo slipped in, a concerned expression appearing on his face when he saw her.

"What happened? Are you okay?"

"I'm fine," she said, exhaustion almost making her dizzy. "Weren't you with Tak?"

"Yeah, but I saw them bringing you here and I wanted to make sure you were okay."

She didn't want to repeat herself, so she didn't say anything.

"Everything...is okay, right?"

"Yes," she said, wishing he would leave. "Everything's fine."

"Really?"

"Kyvo," she began, annoyance awakening inside her. No, not again. She didn't want to get angry and lash out at anyone. "Go stay with the others for now. I'm just really tired."

"But I want to—"

"Get out!" Her annoyance bared its fangs. The moment the words were out of her mouth, she wished she could ram them back in.

Kyvo's eyes went wide, his ears drooping. Without a word, he practically ran out the door.

She pushed it shut, digging the heel of her hand into her forehead. Why did this keep happening? Why was her grip on her emotions so tedious, like she was holding onto the blade of a knife and trying not to get cut?

On a strange urge, Redrinna slid her knife out of its sheath, studying the metal blade and the reflections caught inside. Would it hurt? Slowly, she lowered the blade, letting it rest on her fingertips. How long would the pain last? Would she feel any at all?

Shuddering, she lifted the knife from her skin, making to put it away. As she did, she caught sight of herself in the metal. Her red eyes watched her, a worn, haunted look lurking there.

A glare twisted her features. "I hate you."

Her reflection didn't respond, and she shoved her knife away, burying her face in her hands.

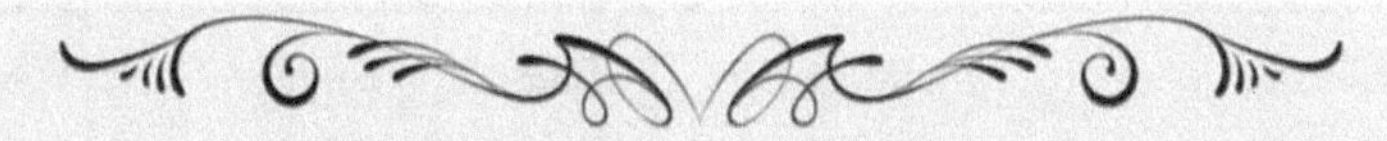

Chapter Eighteen

Tak glanced up as a knock echoed on his door even though he couldn't see whoever it was.

"Hey," Takota began, something in his tone making Tak uneasy, like bugs were crawling up his back. "I think we need your help. Will you come with me?"

"You need me? I-is something wrong?"

"No...well, yes, technically, but this isn't about that. It's something else. The council deemed it important enough they've decided to convene, and they asked for you to come." There was a pause before Takota spoke again. "It's at the Heart—oh, you wouldn't know what that means, would you? Okay, I'll show you."

Uneasiness gnawed at Tak as he let Takota help him out of the clinic. The man stayed strangely quiet as they went.

The wood beneath Tak's feet seemed to move and shift— Maybe they were crossing a bridge? His heart beat anxiously in his chest as the sound of voices—frantic voices—met his ears.

"Here are your friends," Takota said distractedly before letting go of him.

Tak remained still, afraid to move. Kyvo bumped into his leg a second later, nearly making him jump out of his skin.

"Hi," Astra hissed from somewhere behind him, making him

jump yet again. The dragons were here too?

With Astra and Kyvo's help, he settled in a place that seemed out of the way.

After a couple more minutes, the crowd abruptly went quiet. The ensuing silence was so thick, he was pretty sure he would've been able to hear a feather fall.

"Thank you all for coming, despite the suddenness of the meeting," said someone whose voice Tak didn't recognize. The voice sounded aged and weary, like old wood. "I apologize for not holding council in the council house, but some of our guests simply wouldn't fit." He must've been referring to the dragons. "I trust everyone is here now?"

"Yes, chief." That sounded like that guy who'd come and taken Redrinna yesterday. What had she called him again? Chatan?

"Then let us begin with haste," the elder said. "It has been brought to my attention that we have a dangerous enemy looming on our borders, an ancient and powerful one many of us believed to have passed to the realm of legend and myth."

There was a brief spat of intense whispering.

"While Two Face is our foremost concern, we must also prepare for an even greater threat: the heretic Osiris is on the rise."

Tak's blood ran cold. How had they found out about him? Had Redrinna said something? Actually, where was she?

He leaned closer to Kyvo, who was huddled next to him and practically glued to his side. "Where's Redrinna?"

"Not here," the kitsune whispered back, his voice quivering.

Before he could think on that, the chief said, "Macha. I see a few clueless faces. Please share with us the legend of Mato."

Macha, whoever that was, began speaking a moment later. Her voice sounded young, like she wasn't much older than him and Redrinna.

"Nearing a century past now, Mato was born into the warrior clan of our tribe, graced with amazing feathers bearing the blueness of the sky. He grew strong and fleet, able to fly nearly as fast as the wind. While he was young, he and his father set forth on a hunting expedition, venturing deep into the woods. While they tailed their prey, they were being hunted in turn. Unbeknownst to either of them, a desperate cougar stalked their trail. It attacked, grievously wounding his father. Undaunted, Mato fought to protect his father without a moment of hesitation, slaying the beast with his own two hands and saving their lives.

"The next morning, his feathers and eyes were the color of pure gold. This was his call to join the Dragon Kin, and it was a call he bravely answered. Together with the Dragon Kin, he put an end to the vicious war between the Eridian and Manon peoples."

Tak sat up straighter. Mato had been one of the members of the original Dragon Kin? Timothon had probably run with him before, and Tak couldn't help wondering if they'd been friends.

"But that was not the end of his tale. A second war erupted only a few years later, sucking the Dragon Kin inside it. At the head of this war stood the heretic, Osiris, a man who sold his soul to a demon to gain unbelievable and forbidden power. Eridia was steeped in chaos, ripped apart by the beast of war. The Dragon Kin were surrounded by enemies on all sides, but Mato did not shirk from his duty. Never once did he waver.

"At Queen Ioana's execution, a trap lay in wait for the Dragon Kin, a snare laid to catch them all and end their lives. However, Mato, alongside his dragon companion, Mistra, ensured their friends' escape with their own lives. Those two warriors destroyed half of Osiris's army before their lives were able to be stolen from them."

Macha didn't say anything else, which Tak guessed meant the story was over. Silence settled over the group for a minute before anyone spoke again.

Chatan spoke first. "So you're saying the Osiris from Mato's legend is coming back?"

"According to the princess, this is so," the chief said.

"The princess?" Tak didn't recognize this person's voice, but they didn't sound like a pleasant person. "Our people have never bowed our heads to foreign royalty. Please don't tell me we're doing so now."

"We're not bowing our heads," Takota snapped, his voice hard as flint. "But she protected one of our own, and *most* of us wish to show her respect for that, Wicasa."

The chief cleared his throat, ending the conversation. "Yes, the princess has helped us, and the news she brings isn't something we should take lightly. It is precisely for this reason I wish to invite her friends, other members of the new Dragon Kin, to share more with us. Before we decide how to act, we need information."

Tak's heart skipped a beat. So that was why they'd been invited to this. Why wasn't Redrinna here? She was way better at this than any of them.

"Please," the chief said. "Share with us all you can."

"Take it away, red beast," Astra hissed.

With a resigned sigh, Xandrin began. "Er, well, after Mato's sacrifice, the Dragon Kin was chased and hunted down by the people of the land, and they hid their gems before going to battle against Osiris. They gave their lives in the fight, but even then, they weren't able to kill him. The most they could do was reduce him to a fraction of his power."

"Wait," Chatan said, scaring Tak yet again. "How do you know that?"

"Oh, er...Tak?" Xandrin asked.

Tak could feel at least a dozen gazes turn to him, and he had to fight back a shudder. "I-I think Redrinna said it was because when a Dragon Gem chooses a partner, it binds itself to that person's soul until its mission is completed. Since Osiris wasn't killed, the gems don't believe their task is done. So, we learned all of this because of the old Dragon Kin."

"The old Dragon Kin is still here?" Chatan asked, his voice filled with wonder.

A few murmurs passed through the group like wind through the rushes.

"N-not...not exactly. They were killed all those years ago, but because of the gems, their souls are stuck here. They can't move on until Osiris is defeated. T-Timothon told us all this."

More murmuring.

"The King," the chief said in a hushed tone. "Our ancestors were honored to fight alongside him in the Dragon War and passed down many tales of his bravery to us."

Chatan made an appreciative noise. "You guys have spoken with the King? Have you met Mato then? Is he as cool as the stories say?"

"Sorry, but Timothon's the only member we've met." Xandrin cleared his throat in an embarrassed way. "Sorry."

Even though Tak couldn't see anyone's faces, he could sense the disappointment bleeding through the council. Though, he wondered for the first time whether they would get the chance to meet the rest of the old Dragon Kin. Well...maybe he wouldn't get to. If his sight was irreversibly damaged, there was no way he'd be allowed to join.

"Forgive the intrusion," the chief said, getting the group to fall silent again. "Please, continue."

Xandrin resumed a couple moments later. "There are certain individuals who were working with Osiris who weren't killed back then either. Reyna," there was a collective hiss from the group, "a beast known as the Dragon Slayer, and Renoan."

"The traitor prince," a woman spat, her tone inky black. "The one who stole our homeland from us."

Tak's heart skipped a beat, and a tiny squeak escaped him. He hoped no one noticed, but Takota said:

"You all right, Tak?"

"Oh," he gasped, convinced everyone was staring at him now. "It's...I...R-Renoan," it was weird to say the emperor's name without some sort of title, but he didn't think it was the best move here, "he's still the emperor and he's also...he's Redrinna's dad."

A heavy silence fell on the group like someone had tossed a rug over a fire, making him flush with discomfort.

"H-he, Reyna, and the Dragon Slayer still live. We know for sure Reyna and the Dragon Slayer are still working for Osiris," Xandrin said cautiously.

Takota cut in, "Wait. Redrinna said a woman attacked all of you in the woods. That wasn't... It couldn't have been...?"

After a long pause, Xandrin whispered, "Yeah, that was her."

The lady named Macha then said, "Who is this Dragon Slayer? Our legends do not speak of it."

There was another long, uncomfortable pause before Xandrin spoke. "The Dragon Slayer looks somewhat human, but it's too big. It's about half my size, height-wise. It's stronger than a dragon, and meeting its gaze leaves you unable to move or breathe. No matter what you do, it doesn't die. It was what they used to kill the dragons before."

Someone tried to muffle a gasp, making a funny hissing noise.

"Wait, if Renoan is Redrinna's father," Chatan interrupted, "and she's the Imperial Princess and he became the Eridian King, and later the emperor, then Renoan has been ruling the nation the entire time since the Dragon War. Arguably, Osiris has been at the helm of the Empire this whole time?"

"Yeah." Xandrin's voice sounded pained.

"Poor princess," he murmured.

"What does Osiris want? How have he and the others survived this long?" the chief asked.

Nobody answered his questions.

"Tak," Takota interjected, urgency in his voice. "Earlier, Redrinna said Osiris wanted her for something. Do you know what she meant?"

Tak's nerves almost got the best of him, but he managed to shake his head. "I'm...sorry. We don't know."

"I'm sure it's something awful," Xandrin's voice was a low growl, "That man murdered everyone in the Imperial City—not just the people, but every horse, cat, bird—everything. I don't even know how he did it. There wasn't a mark on any of them, but they were dead all the same."

The dragon stopped there, heightening Tak's nerves.

After a long pause of stifling silence, he found himself explaining in the dragon's stead. "Redrinna met her dad again while they were there, but Reyna came too. Reyna caught her and took her to Osiris." Redrinna's pale face from the night she'd come back materialized in his mind. "She...she saw him. Face to face. He tried to make her stay, and she refused."

"Osiris," Takota began before hesitating, "is the one who killed Redrinna's mother, right?"

Tak dipped his head. Maybe he shouldn't have said anything.

"The Empress is dead?" the chief breathed. "But there's been no word, not even of the destruction of the Imperial City. How can this be?"

"Maybe that's what Osiris wants," that rude Wicasa guy said.

"He doesn't want anyone to know what's going on until it happens," Chatan continued, his voice surprisingly calm.

Tak frowned. That hadn't occurred to him before. Granted, he hadn't known no one beyond their small group didn't know what had happened, yet the realization filled him with sharp terror. So many people and animals had died, but if Redrinna and Xandrin hadn't risked going back, no one would know.

"That would be effective," said another woman Tak didn't know. "And impressive it's been kept so secret. The Empire has continued on as though nothing happened."

Several people began talking all at once, but they quickly went quiet. Then the chief spoke. "What happened after Her Highness met the heretic?"

Tak stayed quiet, the knowledge of what had happened enough

to make a chill rush across his skin.

Xandrin mercifully found his voice. "He let her go, but he chased after us. He called it a game. If she could get away, he'd leave her be, but if not..." As he broke off, it sounded like a shudder shook him, making his wings flap. "The Dragon Slayer and Reyna both came after us. We fought, and I...I was going to die." The dragon's voice was so soft, Tak barely heard it. "I knew it, and they did too." He went quiet.

The entire council was quiet.

"And Redrinna saved you," Tak whispered, head still lowered. "She managed to fight them both off, and then brought you back safe." The thought of the Dragon Kin without Xandrin made his heart ache, almost more than he could bear.

"If he wants her so badly, why'd he let her go? That doesn't make sense," someone asked.

"It—" Tak began before clamping his mouth shut. Why couldn't he stay quiet today?

"Please continue," the chief said.

Internally wincing, Tak did so. "I-I think...it's because he wants a new Dragon Kin, and at the time, Redrinna was the only person in it and the only one who knew where the Dragon Gems were hidden. We could be gathered anyway, but it's faster with her here. I think...that's why."

"What makes you think that?" Astra asked, making him jump. "We're supposed to break their plan, not make it work."

"I know, but Redrinna said Reyna is an excellent fighter. When she attacked us in the woods and it was between me and her, she was planning on killing me. I saw it in her eyes. But then Redrinna told her I was a member of the Dragon Kin, remember?"

Someone hmmed, making Tak glance up even though he couldn't see. "According to the legends, Reyna had the strength of a thousand men, able to fell entire armies and trample nations to dust beneath her heel. Whether or not that is completely factual, the point is she was more than capable of killing you but did not."

Tak nodded. "E-exactly."

"She only stabbed you because you jumped in front of Astra," Kyvo said, jumping on Tak's knee. "I noticed she tried to dodge you but missed. I thought it was weird, but I completely forgot until now."

"Which means Osiris doesn't need just Redrinna, but he wants all of you for something," Astra said, her tone thoughtful. "Even still, she seems to be the most important one."

"We can't stop building the Dragon Kin," Xandrin said with a hint of a whine, "but if it's helping him—"

"Even if that's the case, quitting isn't going to help," Chatan cut in, his voice firm but there was a gentleness to it too. "I only know what the old stories say, but if they're even remotely right, then we need a new Dragon Kin. If that ends up being a double-edged sword, so be it. There are few things in war that aren't."

"This is all well and good," said the rude Wicasa guy, "but why isn't the princess the one telling us this? I mean, it's her story, isn't it? If you want me to believe—"

"Redrinna, unfortunately, cannot join us right now," Takota interjected. "And it's none of your business why."

Another complaint burst out of Wicasa, which egged Takota into snapping back. A few others joined in.

A thrill of fear raced through Tak's chest. Had something happened to Redrinna? Hopefully it wasn't anything serious, but given the recent state of things, he wasn't able to convince himself that it wasn't.

"Thank you all," the chief snapped, loudly, quieting the council instantly. "We appreciate your openness with us."

There were a few murmurs of ascent.

"We are not here to argue politics. There are now two threats at our door, and we need to discuss how we're going to address them. So unless you have something to add, I ask that you keep quiet."

Chatan went first. "I'm not sure we can do anything about Osiris; at least, not at the present time. I'm more inclined to focus our efforts on putting Two Face down, as that problem is going to put us in serious danger if we can't do something about it soon."

"I agree," Macha said. "Our way of life is hanging on a thread. On top of that, in the event the Princess requires our assistance in the coming war, we won't be able to help at all if half our tribe is still bound by the demon's powers."

"Why would we help?" Wicasa said.

"We don't know what Osiris is planning, so he might very well try and kill us too. You want to sit around and wait?" Chatan said dryly.

"I agree. Our focus should be on the demon for the time being," the chief said, culling the argument. "With any luck, the next time we convene, we can discuss Osiris in more detail."

Tak's mind wandered as they discussed what to do, why this would be more effective than that, etc. He briefly entertained the idea of joining the watch before remembering his blindness.

Despite his handicap, he had an irrepressible urge to do something, to find some way to be useful. If he could prove himself in even a small way then they definitely wouldn't make him leave, at the very least. The only thing he could think of was finding some way to help Redrinna since she seemed to be key to most of the ideas being tossed around. The thought made his stomach tie itself in knots, but he wanted to try acting on Takota's advice. If everything went okay, then maybe he'd finally feel like he truly belonged. He did his best not to imagine what might happen if it backfired.

Eventually, the meeting ended, and both Xandrin and Kyvo trotted off, claiming they were in desperate need of sleep. Astra started to say something that seemed to be directed at Tak, but before she could, Takota snagged him.

"Tak, given the state of things right now, my mother and I both feel it's best if you stay in the clinic as much as possible until your sight returns to normal. As soon as it does, you can roam, but until then, this is the best way to protect you. Try to understand."

Tak nodded and allowed himself to be led back to his room. He leaned against the door after Takota was gone, his head thunking against the smooth wood. His mind raced as he tried to think of something, anything he could do to help Redrinna get back on her feet.

"I don't know how to help her," he admitted to himself in a whisper. There wasn't much, if anything, he could do. Part of him was afraid if he tried something, the misfortune clinging to him like a ball and chain would make things even worse for everyone.

'I don't think there's anything wrong with you.' Kyvo's voice echoed through his mind.

Tak wanted to believe that. He wanted it so bad he could barely stand it. His aunt had believed it too even though he'd never found a way to accept it. Maybe here, maybe now, he could. If there was a way, for the first time in his life, Tak wanted to find it. He didn't want to live like this, with these feelings inside him anymore, and if he left things as they were, they wouldn't ever change.

Steeling himself, Tak lifted his head and took a deep breath. He had to find something here, some kind of answer, or else he never would.

Chapter Nineteen

Even after having the night off at Chatan's insistence, Redrinna was as drained as she'd been yesterday. She'd somehow fallen asleep for a while before jerking awake drenched in a cold sweat, heart racing, and completely out of breath. It was early morning now, with the sun just starting to poke its head above the mountains. Since she wasn't expecting to get another wink of sleep, she left the room and went outside, the chill morning air the most refreshing thing she'd felt in nearly an entire day.

Her gaze drifted over the forest, the tops of the trees rippling like the waves of the ocean in the dim morning light. In the distance, far past the trees in front of her, she caught a glimpse of the ocean, its waters a pale grey. A few stars still hung in the sky above it, not yet swallowed by the dawn.

Turning away from it, Redrinna almost jumped out of her skin when she found Wicasa standing there, staring at her blankly.

"Oh," he said after a minute, glancing to the side. "It's a bit early for you, isn't it?"

She looked away too. "Not really. You're...on watch still?"

"Just finished."

Nodding, she kept her gaze away. She should get going before he thought up something nasty to say. "Excuse me."

Wicasa moved to the side as she made to walk past him, but as she did, he hesitantly said, "Where...are you going?"

Stopping, she risked a glance back. What did he want?

He only held her gaze for a couple seconds before hurriedly looking away, scratching at his neck.

"I was just...going to go train some." Maybe she'd wear herself out enough she'd pass out and get some rest that way.

"Oh," he said before shrugging a couple times. "I guess...I'm not tired either. We could go together...or something."

"Why?" She edged away from him.

He scratched at his neck again, muttering something she didn't catch.

Redrinna glanced towards the stairs, wondering if she could make it before he noticed.

"I said," he began, the irritation in his voice fading the more he spoke, "Chatan will flay my backside if I let you go alone, so... A-and staying on watch always riles me up, so I'll go whack a few things until I'm ready to pass out. It just so happens you're going to the same place."

She stared at him for a minute longer before heading for the training grounds, acutely aware of Wicasa staying on her heels. A frown twisted her mouth, but she stayed quiet. She supposed, worst-case scenario, if he tried something, she could...do...something.

She'd think about it some more.

They arrived at the training grounds a few minutes later, and for a while, Redrinna stayed where she was, staring at the trees with the sunlight trickling through their leaves like water.

This wasn't helping. Shaking her head, she entered the clearing fully. She didn't have a clue what to practice. Training with her sword or her dagger would be most effective if she had someone to do it with, but she didn't want to spar with Wicasa, so that left only her magic.

It'd been some time since she'd practiced that stance she hadn't been able to master. She wasn't sure if she was comfortable using it here, but if she started in the right spot, she wouldn't hit anything when she was ready to use her magic.

Putting some space between her and her uninvited guest, Redrinna ran through the stances in her mind before crouching into the first stance. Her thighs protested as she sank into the deep squat, but she supposed that was what happened when you took a break.

Keeping her magic tucked away, Redrinna shifted to the next stance, making sure her form was correct before going to the next. She stayed on each stance until they felt right, hoping she was remembering them.

When she finished, she frowned. She couldn't shake the feeling she'd forgotten a step, but she couldn't think of what it might have been.

As she mentally ran through it again in her head, Wicasa barged into her thoughts. "Are you doing some kind of dance?" He blinked at her in an almost innocent manner from the edge of the training clearing as he notched another arrow on his bow.

"No," she said before taking a few steps back and getting back into the first stance.

"You should warm up first," he called. "You don't want to injure a muscle or something."

Closing her eyes, Redrinna tuned him out, picturing the book as best she could. Moving faster this time, she worked through the stances again. She didn't know what she'd done different, but that time had seemed more right.

As she turned to take a couple steps back, she slipped a little on the dewy grass but quickly righted herself. She returned to her resting stance. If she was careful, she could try it with the fire. Her stomach twinged in discomfort, but she ignored it. It would be impossible to master this if she avoided it.

She took a deep breath and then another before allowing her magic to enter her mind. Closing her eyes, she waited for the briefest of moments before sliding into the first stance. Fire roared around her, and she had to fight to keep herself from flinching. She moved to the next stance and the next. All at once, her foot slid out from underneath her, squeaking against the grass.

Redrinna stumbled, falling on one knee. The comet of fire she'd been spinning around herself shot at her. Without thinking, she slapped it upwards, narrowly managing to avoid a tree branch. The fire sputtered and went out.

Not again. Why couldn't she get this move down? It wasn't even that hard!

"A-are you—"

"I'm fine," she snapped. Then she squeezed her eyes shut. She had to keep her emotions under control before they rampaged like a bull in a porcelain shop again. "I'm fine."

Wicasa didn't say anything, fingering his bow while staring off elsewhere.

Redrinna glared at her clenched fists. This was stupid. There was no way she was going to get that move down, especially not here. Pushing herself to her feet, she tried to take a deep breath, but it was a bit stuttery.

"Princess..." Wicasa began warily, taking a teeny step closer.

"This was stupid," she whispered before marching out of the clearing. Seconds later, hurried footsteps rushed after her. The annoyance building inside her burst through the weak dam she'd built to stop it. Rounding on him, she snarled, "Quit following me!"

Staggering back a couple steps, Wicasa snorted. "Aren't you all high and mighty? I'm not following you. If you're not going to train, then I'm going to go to bed, you brat!"

A rude comeback burst on her tongue, but she kept her mouth shut. Silently, she turned and marched back to the village, not stopping until she'd returned to the privacy of her room.

Once there, once Redrinna was alone, all her anger melted like snow. Thunking the palm of her heel against her head, she closed her eyes, already wishing she could erase everything that had just happened. "What's the matter with me?"

The empty room didn't answer her. Unfortunately, she only got a couple minutes of peace before there came a knock on her door.

"Your Highness, are you awake now?"

Slowly, Redrinna turned to face the door, staring at it for a minute before opening it. To her surprise, Chumani stood there, a small smile on her face. Redrinna attempted to smile back, but hers felt awkward and stiff.

"Good morning! I'm supposed to put your cast back on for you," Chumani explained as she entered the room, the bandages and honey in her hands. "Takota was so distracted he forgot." She giggled as she set the materials down.

"But they said it was almost healed."

"Almost is not the same as completely. If you want it to heal properly, then you have to take care of it until it is completely better, not just until it feels better."

Redrinna relented as she glanced at her wrist, eyeing the faint bruising still lingering on her skin. When she twisted it from side to side, it barely hurt at all, only aching a little. A shiver raced down her spine.

Chumani set to work wrapping her wrist. Staying quiet while the woman worked, Redrinna watched, once again mildly fascinated by the whole process.

Once the woman finished, she looked at Redrinna and grinned, her short hair swaying as she dipped her head to the side. "Now, do you want to go for a walk with me?"

Mutely, she stared at the woman.

"I heard you had a rough day yesterday, and while it is good to rest, it's also good to get outside. Staying here in this little room won't help you enough."

"Even still, that's not a good idea."

Chumani laughed. "Kangee will escort us, plus we're not going far from the village, and we'll be in sight of the warriors and dragons the entire time. Also, they already know. So, are you coming or not?"

Slowly, Redrinna relented and got to her feet. As she did so, Chumani clucked her tongue like a mother hen.

"We can't have you wandering about looking like your hair was caught in a windstorm." Chumani's smile vanished, replaced with a frown. "Your Highness, may I do your hair?"

Redrinna wasn't sure if it was because she was exhausted or what, but she was bewildered as to why Chumani had to ask. "If you want to?"

The woman's smile returned, bright as the sun. Gesturing to the lone, wooden chair in the room, she said, "Have a seat, please."

Redrinna did so, and the woman pulled a brush from somewhere and began combing her errant hair into place. There were a few minutes of silence, filled only by the sound of the comb working through her snarls. It'd been a while since anyone had taken care of her this way. Distinctly, Redrinna recalled sitting and watching the outside world through a window as Captain Brion had worked her locks into his simple yet beautiful creations. On rare occasions, her mother had even come and done her hair for her.

The memory of those days struck hollowly against the deep ache inside her, making her close her eyes. She was sick and tired of hurting.

"Did you know that to me—to most of my tribe, actually—hair is special?" Chumani suddenly said.

"It is?" Redrinna asked, almost turning her head back.

Chumani made a 'mhm' of ascent. "For us, your hair is a part of who you are, and we only let those who are close to us touch or work with it."

Redrinna frowned. For her people, hair was just a thing on your head, and how you wore it expressed your rank. Well, she supposed it was more what you put in your hair than how it was worn. She'd heard of some places where the length of your hair was an indicator of your rank too.

Chumani sighed. "I miss my long hair."

"Why did you cut it?" Most everyone in the village had short hair, she'd noticed, but she hadn't thought anything of it.

"We cut it when...we're in mourning."

That gave her a gut punch.

"In truth, I miss Takota's long hair. He has nice hair." She laughed, but it faded out after a couple seconds.

Redrinna didn't say anything.

"Anyway, how should we do your hair?" Chumani ran her fingers through it a couple times. "I'm quite good at braiding if you want one of those."

Reyna with her long, braided hair flashed through Redrinna's mind, and she shook her head. "Not a braid, please."

"All right, then how about we do a horsetail?"

"A what?"

Chumani rummaged through something before handing her a petite mirror. "Watch and I'll show you when I'm done."

The woman didn't talk as she worked with her hair, tugging and pulling it all back into a loose ponytail before tugging it a couple more times and flipping the ponytail. The end of Redrinna's hair whapped her nose as it swung around.

"There."

Redrinna glanced at the back of her head with Chumani's help. It was a ponytail but twisted to hide the string. It was beautiful. Redrinna wished she was better at doing her hair if only to be able to replicate this.

"Thank you."

"Of course," the woman said, grinning from ear to ear. "Now, let's get going before the day wastes away and we don't have time to go anymore."

Redrinna followed the woman from the room and out of the clinic, where they were joined by Kangee, who nodded and didn't say a word. A few of the other warriors waved as they passed, and Redrinna returned their waves, albeit half-heartedly. She noticed Wicasa was still awake, though when their gazes met, he looked away, scratching at his neck.

As they reached the bottom of the stairs, Redrinna noticed the curled forms of Xandrin and Kyvo beneath the clinic tree. She missed them, but she forced the pang in her chest away. Briefly, she wondered where Astra was before spotting the dragon crouched, talking to someone, near the base of the stairs. For a moment, Redrinna wondered what she was doing, but dismissed it. It wasn't her business.

They walked into the woods with Kangee on their heels, just far enough away to feel alone but close enough they could still see the village through the trees.

Chumani scanned the undergrowth, hands on her hips. "We've got to find some herbs today though our luck isn't good. We still can't go to our usual places to hunt and the stores are running low."

Redrinna studied the nearby plants, trying to ignore the way her heart sank. Their medicine stores were dwindling, and yet they'd still gone out of their way to treat a complete stranger and an enemy. Closing her eyes, she pressed her hands to her chest in an attempt to will the guilt away.

Unconsciously, she caught herself searching for the gem's calm reassurance, but its warmth was weak and dim. Oh. She supposed the gem must still be annoyed with her. That was okay. When she opened her eyes again, she noticed Kangee was staring at her, expressionless except for the slight narrowing of his eyes, so she dropped her hands and looked away.

They walked in a circle around the village, moving at a leisurely pace since Chumani kept stopping to shove aside bushes and vines, plucking leaves from various plants and tucking them into pouches on her belt. The woman chatted happily as they went, though Redrinna stayed quiet, that familiar exhaustion creeping through her bones and wearing her down like kernels of wheat that had been ground for too long.

All at once, a chill slithered up her spine.

She glanced over her shoulder, getting Kangee to do the same. There was nothing behind them, but she sensed a presence all the same. For a brief moment, Redrinna wondered if it was Kyvo creeping up on them, but then, she realized the forest had gone silent as the grave.

Kangee bolted forward, grabbing Chumani's wrist as the woman bent to inspect another plant. "We need to go."

"Go?"

Redrinna glanced around again, unable to shake the feeling something was out there. Something out for blood. "I think it's the—"

Two Face dropped barely a foot from her, eyes gleaming like knives, its gray skin taking on a sickly white tint in the light of the sun. It didn't grin or sneer, but hunger simmered in its eyes. It licked its lips.

"Princess!" Kangee shouted.

The next second, an awful, sharp pain burst in Redrinna's skull and the world went dark.

⚜

Tak was pretty sure he left his skin behind as a shrill scream rang out, followed by excruciating silence. His heart thudded against his ribcage, making him too afraid to leave the safety of his bed. Who'd screamed and why? It didn't have something to do with the demon, did it? Except that couldn't be. The demon only came to the village at night; that was what the others had said. So, would it really have come to try and take someone? It didn't seem likely, but it was the only explanation he could think of. Unless it was Reyna... He shuddered at the thought.

Years seemed to pass while Tak sat there in an eerie, unnerving quiet, but then his door abruptly opened, and he turned in its direction. Who was there? Was it someone he knew? Was it Reyna?

"Tak," Takota said, his voice quiet, subdued.

"What's wrong?" he asked, his senses on high alert. Something wasn't right, but he didn't want to consider what the possibilities could be.

The man came closer, slowly, his feet scuffing against the floor like they were the heaviest things in the world. He didn't speak again until he gripped Tak's hands. "The demon came back today."

His heart thrummed harder in his chest.

"It took Chumani, and it took Her Highness too."

Tak's ears went numb. That was—it couldn't be—

"I'm sorry."

The demon had taken Redrinna. Nausea made his head swim. It'd taken her to eat. The idea of her dying—by being eaten, of all things—made him want to puke. What were they going to do? They couldn't build the Dragon Kin without Redrinna.

Panic dug deeper into his chest as he grabbed at Takota, managing to snag his wrists. "We have to save them. Please."

"Tak, I understand, but we can't," Takota said. "We've never been able to find the nest, and the one time someone tried, they vanished. Those it takes are gone."

"No," Tak said, shaking his head. "No!" His chest constricted like a snake had him in its coils, intent on squeezing the life from him.

"Listen to me—"

Tak shook his head harder, making the man stop. Redrinna couldn't be gone. He refused to accept it. After everything, it couldn't end like this.

Leaping from his bed, he tore at the bandage around his head, desperate to get it off. Threads snapped as he shredded the fabric. He had to go, and he needed his eyes right now.

"Tak stop! You can't go out—" Takota grabbed at his hands,

but Tak fought him off.

With one, final jerk that ripped out some hair, Tak yanked the bandage free. He blinked his eyes open, wincing at how bright the world was. There was still a blurriness to his vision, but it was better than it'd been when they'd first arrived, which was good enough for him.

He ducked under the man's arms and shot to the door, needing two attempts to get his hand on the doorknob. Then he yanked it open and ran out of the clinic, Takota shouting after him. The sun burned his eyes, but he didn't care. He raced past people he didn't recognize, all of their faces blurred and hazy.

Tak skid to a stop at the top of the long staircase, hesitating for a second before plunging down it. He stumbled a few times, barely able to keep his balance. When he was almost at the bottom, he tumbled and tripped, falling down the last bit of the stairs and landing in a heap at the bottom.

Instantly, he shot back to his feet, ignoring the flurry of noise behind him. The forest was a distorted mix of fuzzy green and brown trees a short way ahead. Redrinna was out there somewhere, and Tak had to find her. Dashing forward, he made it almost halfway before Astra's claws clamped around him. He tried to stop but skidded into her.

"Let me go," he said, turning and trying to focus on her face.

She shook her head. "You can't go, especially with your eyes the way they are."

"Let me go!" He pushed against her clawed feet, but she didn't budge.

"We'll look for her, Tak," Astra said, voice shaking. "But you can't. You're going to have to trust us, okay?"

"No!" He clawed at her feet to no avail. "Please, let me go!"

"I won't," Astra snapped, but he didn't care. "Stop fighting me, Tak. You're making your hands bleed!"

He didn't care. He didn't even look.

Astra released him unexpectedly. For a second, he thought he was free. Then, Takota grabbed him, lifting him off his feet.

"I get it, Tak," the man hissed in his ear. "Trust me, I do. But getting yourself killed isn't going to help her."

Tak stared hard at the forest's edge, desperate to escape. However, Takota was stronger than he appeared, and Tak didn't get anywhere. He went limp as a void opened inside him, deep and endless. Here it was again, his curse. It'd taken Redrinna from him too. If he just sat here, then she was going to disappear, and it'd be all his fault.

⚶⚶

An hour later, Tak was back in his room, seated on the edge of his bed. There was a new bandage over his eyes and thick bandages on his throbbing hands. Takota was sitting outside of his room to keep him inside; he'd already checked.

Listless, he wilted, falling on his side and lying still. All hope he'd had of being able to defy his curse shriveled like old, dead flowers, so frail they'd dissolve into dust at the slightest touch. If the dragons couldn't find her, then it was all over. His time here was through. He didn't have the faintest clue where he would go, but if Redrinna was gone, then anywhere was better than here.

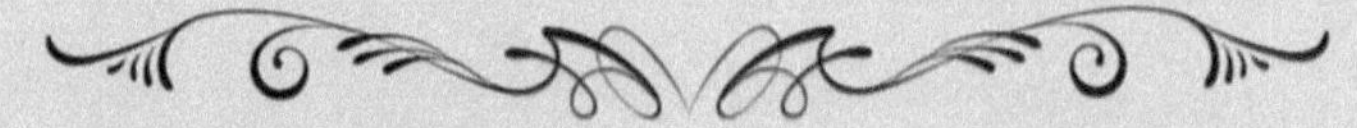

Chapter Twenty

A massive migraine slammed against Redrinna's skull, forcing her awake. It made her nauseous, the urge to vomit seeming only seconds from becoming more than just an urge. Her thoughts were scattered like broken glass strewn haphazardly across the ground. Gradually, she opened her eyes. The night sky, generously dusted with stars, stretched high above her, framed by a ring of tall, dark pines. Her vision blurred in and out, making her head throb.

Faintly, she caught the scent of pine and the bite of iron but couldn't piece together what they meant.

Where was she? Was she back at the Mount? Why would she have been there? There was still...still something she needed to do...wasn't there?

All at once, a loud crack rang out, and slowly, oh so slowly, she managed to turn her head to the right, following the sound. Two figures were there, one standing, one sprawled on the ground.

"I told you: you can't have that one! You worthless beast!" That...that was Reyna. She'd recognize her voice anywhere. "If she dies, I'll kill you in the most excruciating way possible. You will beg for death before I'm through with you, understand?!"

The figure on the ground scuttled back in an insect-like manner. "Waz a mistake. Won't eats it, I swearz!"

Reyna took a step forward, head high in an obvious threat.

The demon scrambled to its feet, rushing over to Redrinna, blocking the woman from her view. It yanked at the cords she hadn't noticed binding her wrists and ankles, all the while muttering that she surely didn't need her fingers and toes.

Despite her sudden freedom, Redrinna's body struggled to respond, almost like she was trapped in a shell, watching the world go by from inside it. Something was wrong with her; she was convinced. But what? She couldn't remember how she'd come here or anything much beyond that morning. The last thing she remembered was going for a walk with Chumani.

Where was Chumani now?

The demon finished untying her, still grumbling, but she could hardly get her body to move in any way, every limb heavy as stone.

Stepping away, the demon hissed, "All donez. Take it."

Reyna glared daggers at it as she approached. She stared down at Redrinna with cold, impassive eyes before grabbing her by the chin and tilting her head. The world careened, almost making her retch, before Reyna made a quiet, almost growl-like sound. The next moment, Redrinna felt like she'd been sucked up by a whirlwind.

It was a few minutes before she figured out the woman had slung her over her shoulder like a sack of potatoes.

"Don't you dare do a thing until I return, or else," Reyna hissed at the demon, who sat on the floor and crossed its arms like a spoiled child who'd been told no.

Then the woman began walking, making intense nausea sweep through Redrinna's stomach. The pounding in her head sharpened with every step. Darkness pressed in on her, crouching on the fringes of her mind with all the heaviness of the dark ocean, gradually creeping closer, growing sharper. The temptation to surrender was powerful, alluring like the call of a siren, but Redrinna would've sworn someone was whispering in her ear, urging her to stay awake.

The smell of pine faded, the powerful, salty tang of the ocean sweeping into its place. Dimly, she heard the wind sighing through the trees, but it wasn't the gentle hum of pine trees as their needles stirred any longer. She didn't recognize the sound of the wind in these trees.

All at once, the ache in her head stabbed deeper, and she managed to put a hand to it, pressing on it in an attempt to make it stop.

Reyna tugged her hand away. "Don't mess with it."

The woman didn't speak again as they continued on. Redrinna's eyes slid shut as she fought to keep the darkness away. She couldn't sleep. Not yet.

❧ ☙

Tak leaned against the railing, his side only twinging with a dull ache as he did so. It'd nearly been an entire day since Redrinna and Chumani had been abducted. Takota and Chatan refused to let him escape or be alone, leaving him stuck waiting every time the dragons went scouting. So far, their searches had yielded nothing. The panic living in Tak's gut gnawed deeper each time they came back empty handed, hollowing him out more and more.

What would they do without Redrinna? Even though their time together had been brief, she was important to him. She'd done so much for him, and to repay her kindness by letting her life end this way...

And what would they do if they couldn't find her gem if she was, in reality, gone? Wouldn't Osiris win? Though, without her, maybe his plans would be ruined for good. Tak shuddered at the thought of that. Neither of those were things he wanted to consider.

Chatan, his appointed escort (surely this man had better things to do than play babysitter though), shifted against the railing beside him. Ever since yesterday, the guy had been more solemn than usual, a dour, brooding air hanging over him like a thundercloud.

"Aren't you getting hungry?" the man asked, every word clipped. "You haven't eaten since yesterday."

Tak was sure his stomach had shriveled to nothing. He didn't feel hungry; he didn't feel anything. Just numbness. Before he could form some kind of response, a chill raced up his spine. Someone was watching him.

"Hey, kid with the green hair," a voice called, cutting through the subdued hush over the village.

His blood ran cold. Reyna. Her voice came from somewhere below him, sounding kind of far, but he wasn't entirely sure.

Chatan turned, wings ruffling. "That's—Redrinna!"

What?

"Come down here, green boy," Reyna called. "I can tell you're blind, so I'll spell it out: I have something for you, so come get it."

Tak hesitated.

"I'll help you," Chatan hissed, his voice frighteningly harsh.

Tak allowed the man to guide him to and down the stairs. Every step felt like it was taking him closer and closer to doom, like he was walking into the cave of a bear. A heavy silence draped over the village behind him.

Chatan pulled him to a stop. Something scaly nudged his arm, almost startling him.

"A-Astra?" he asked, voice faltering.

"Tak," was all she whispered, her voice tight and high.

"I'm sure she won't attack me," he said, voice barely audible. "It'll be okay." He hoped.

He resumed walking, Chatan tugging him to a stop after a few more steps. How close were they right now? Was Reyna just standing there, staring at them with her cold eyes?

After a moment of nail-biting anticipation, Reyna shifted and dropped something on the ground with a hard thud.

"Here's your royal dog," she said, loud enough he was sure everyone heard. "You ought to keep it on a leash. Strays live short lives."

Tak scowled.

"Until next time," the woman said. The grass squeaked beneath her feet as she turned, and then she was gone.

Chatan flashed past a second later, stirring the air next to him.

"I-is she okay?" Tak asked. Something knocked into him from behind, nearly throwing him to the ground. He was almost one hundred percent sure it was Xandrin.

"Your Highness, are you okay?" Chatan asked, voice tight. "Give her some room, Xandrin, or you'll make her suffocate."

"R-really?" the dragon cried.

After an excruciatingly long pause—during which Tak registered a considerable amount of noise from the village—Redrinna spoke, her voice heart-breakingly weak. "My head hurts."

"I bet," Chatan said, a hint of a smile in his voice.

Relief flooded Tak. It was her.

"Let me see her," Takota said abruptly.

"She said her head hurt," Chatan said in a near-whisper.

"Yeah, that's a nasty wound." Takota paused for a minute. "Can you stand, Your Highness?"

There was nothing but silence.

"I'm going to take that as a no." There was some rustling, and then Takota said, "I'll let you all know what's what when we're done, okay?" With a loud whoosh, the man left.

Tak's knees nearly gave way. Redrinna was safe. His ill luck hadn't devoured her too.

Yet, Reyna hadn't brought Chumani back, only Redrinna. If she'd known where to go to find her, then that had to be proof the demon was here because of Osiris, didn't it?

Tak tried to shake the thought away, but it kept popping back in. He couldn't deny it was such an odd coincidence that it wasn't until after Osiris had made his first, bold move in the Imperial City that human-eating demons had appeared here. Tak was well-acquainted with ill luck, but that was too convenient for him to overlook.

If that was the case, if the demon was connected to Osiris in any way, then wasn't it their duty as the Dragon Kin to make sure it was put to rest? After all, Chumani was still out there; they still might be able to save her if they were fast. The problem was finding its...

The world around Tak stopped, everything going still and silent. Redrinna had most likely been taken to its nest. After all, where else would it have wanted to take its prey?

If she could remember something—anything—then they might have a chance. Another chance to save Chumani and prove he wasn't cursed.

Tak took a step forward, but Astra cut into his thoughts.

"Tak?"

"Let's not wander off on our own, all right?" Chatan said, stepping up beside him and taking hold of his arm.

He'd been caught up in his thoughts enough he wasn't sure what they meant. "Huh?"

"Redrinna will be fine," Astra said, her voice firm. "You don't have to worry."

"I'm not," he said. Then he shook his head. "I-I mean, I am worried, but that wasn't what I was thinking about."

"What were you thinking about then?"

"I think...I'm sure there's still time to save Chumani. Redrinna might know something that can help us now."

Xandrin let out a whine. "I don't think we should bug her right now though."

Tak shook his head, his thoughts too jumbled for him to sort through. Turning, he hurried back onto the platforms, tripping a couple times in his haste (Chatan was the only reason he didn't tumble into oblivion) and returned to the clinic. After so long without his sight, he was beginning to memorize the path to his room.

As Tak waited, he distracted himself by listening to the wind brushing through the oaks outside. It was funny how, once he'd been deprived of his sight, sounds had become more vivid to him. They painted the world for him in a way he'd never been able to observe with his eyes, and if his sight returned, he'd miss this side of the injury.

Regardless, once Redrinna was in a better state of mind, they could ask her. Tak wouldn't be able to go, but if he could get the information to the others, then that would put them one step closer to finding Chumani. However, he had to remember, regardless of what happened, he had to ask carefully. Redrinna's mood during the last month had been wild and erratic, and he was wary of her attempting to go after the demon alone. After what she'd done to wake the gem before, he knew there was a chance she would try it if they gave her the opportunity or pushed her wrong.

Worry nagged at him, but Tak set it aside as best he could. Kyvo believed he wasn't cursed, and Redrinna hadn't died. If they could save Chumani and keep Redrinna from getting herself into more trouble, Tak might just believe him.

∽❧ ❧∽

Tak wasn't allowed to visit Redrinna until the next morning, and the tension in his chest had lingered all night long. Takota had assured him she was fine, but she had a concussion too now, just like him. He needed to be careful for both of their sakes.

Takota led Tak into her room, seating him on a stool. Redrinna didn't speak, and he wondered if she was even looking at him. Maybe she was staring at the window instead, with one of those faraway looks in her eyes.

Once Takota had left, he asked, "How are you?"

"I'm fine." Then she muttered, "Why does everybody always ask me that?"

Even though she probably hadn't meant for him to hear, he responded anyway. "You were hit in the head really hard, and Chatan said your face was covered in blood. That's...why I asked."

"Wait, are you serious?"

He nodded. "Plus...I can't see you, so..."

"Oh, right. Sorry." She was quiet for a minute. "You already know concussions are nasty, but it hurts."

He nodded again, trying to work up the courage to do what he'd come here to.

"Hey, where's Chumani? And Kangee?" she asked abruptly, making his heart stutter. "Have you seen them?"

Unease nestled deeper in his stomach. "Y-you don't remember what happened?"

"The last thing I remember is walking through the forest with them...and then being somewhere else. But they were both with me."

Tak almost told her the truth, but Takota's warning from earlier rang through his mind: 'Don't do anything to make her upset. You can't tell her what happened, at least not yet. Her injury isn't letting her think clearly and telling her now will make things even worse.'

"They're busy right now," he said, telling her what Takota had told him to. "But they said they'll stop by when they can. I-in the meantime, can I ask you something? Do you...do you remember anything about where you were taken?"

There was a long pause, and for a tense second, he thought maybe she wasn't going to answer or was glaring at him. Then she said, "I could see the stars and smell pine trees."

That caught him by surprise. The Torijin and the dragons had been searching in caves for the demon, but if Redrinna was remembering correctly, it sounded like it might not have been in a cave at all. Nodding, mostly to himself, Tak tried to think of something else they could talk about. He nearly jumped out of his skin when Takota reentered the room.

"That's about as long as you guys can have right now."

"Already?" Redrinna asked as Tak got to his feet.

"You need to take it slow right now, Your Highness," Takota said, his voice quieter than usual. "A few other people want to visit you, so this is as long as they all get."

"It's okay," Tak said, trying to smile even though he wasn't sure if he was even facing anyone. "The others want to know how you're doing, especially Xandrin."

"I'm sure," she said, her voice startlingly empty.

Quickly, he left, mind racing. He wasn't any good at thinking up plans or strategies, but he had to try.

Once he was back outside, he accepted steaming hot fry bread from Mika, who seemed to be in slightly better spirits today than he had been for the past couple. Tak descended the stairs, almost jumping a mile into the sky when Astra nudged his elbow.

"How is she?"

"She's fine." At least, in regard to her injury. He didn't know enough to say a thing about anything else. Physically, she seemed as well as she could be, but beyond that, he wasn't so sure. That said, the concussion might've been dragging her down too.

"Okay," the dragon said, taking over for Takota and guiding him to the others.

When they reached Xandrin, the dragon immediately said, "How is she?"

After catching him up to speed, Tak paused and said, "When you guys went looking for the demon, you looked for caves and stuff, didn't you?"

"Yeah," Xandrin said. "The Torijin said that according to the old stories, Two Face would hunker underground in massive caves and places like that."

Just like he'd thought. "Redrinna said she could see the stars."

Kyvo let out a squeak of surprise. "She could see the stars? Then she must've been outside."

"It could've been an open cave of some kind," Xandrin said. "There are several of those."

"She could also smell pine trees."

"Pine?" Astra paused, almost a full minute passing before she breathed, "They only grow up there..."

He figured she meant the mountains towering over them.

"The demon's in the mountains," Xandrin whispered.

"But not far," Astra said. "They made it there in less than a day if she woke up at night. And Reyna brought her back yesterday, late in the morning. So it can't be super far, right?"

"We need to find it," Tak said. "I believe Chumani's still alive, for now."

"Tak, it's nearly been two days," Xandrin began.

Tak refused to believe what the dragon implied. "I know, but if we don't at least try..." He trailed off. The village might not recover from another blow like this. As for him... "If we give up, that's the same as leaving her to die."

"Don't be making plans like that without me," cut in a new voice. It sounded like Chatan. The next second, whoever it was landed nearby with a thud, wings rustling. "Chumani is my family, after all."

Tak turned, wondering if he'd turned too far or not far enough. "Chatan?"

"The one and only," the man replied. "But let's focus on planning. I'm more than tired of this half-wit fiend taking my family, and Redrinna's information puts us so much closer to being able to exterminate it."

"Y-you heard?"

"I asked her myself, before you woke up. More importantly, we need to form a plan of attack. Let's get started."

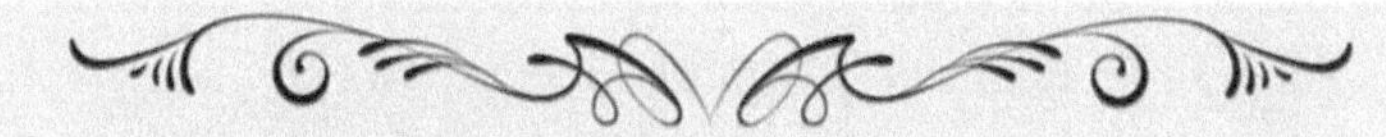

Chapter Twenty-One

Redrinna curled her fists, bunching the star-patterned quilt draped over her. She'd asked everyone who'd come to visit her where Chumani and Kangee were, but all of them had given her evasive answers. Even Tak had dodged her question.

She needed to think, which would've been easier if her head would stop pounding like Xandrin had given her a solid kick, but if she closed her eyes, it got a bit better.

Her memories were still clouded and patchy between when she'd gone for that walk and now, and she'd begun to wonder if they were going to stay that way. Regardless, a paralyzing chill froze her lungs at what she did remember. Two Face had been waiting for them. It'd never attacked in broad daylight before, but it had and it'd gone for her first before presumably going after the other two. Reyna had then saved her life. Her heart wanted to say it was because they were friends, but she knew better.

More importantly, she was certain the demon had snatched Chumani, and she had a horrifying idea of what had happened to Kangee. Because of Redrinna, Chumani had been snatched. Anything that had happened to Kangee was her fault too. It was all her fault. Again. Neither of them would be in whatever situations they were in if she hadn't agreed to go for that walk.

Her chest constricted like it was being crushed beneath a boulder, and for a long while, it was so hard to breathe. The walls of the room seemed to press in on her, threatening to box her in until she drew her final breath. Why did she keep messing up like this? First the people of the Imperial City and her mother, then Xandrin, now Chumani and Kangee. So many people. So much blood on her hands. Why couldn't she do things right the first time?

All at once, Redrinna became aware of the fact her hair was still mostly pulled back. She reached up, fingering the horsetail Chumani had given her.

'Did you know that to me—to most of my tribe, actually—hair is special, almost sacred?' Chumani's voice flowed through her mind, carving a deep, endless ache in its wake. 'For us, your hair is a part of who you are, and we only let those who are close to us touch or work with it.'

A part of who she was? Redrinna jerked her hair free, the vivid red strands tumbling down around her face. She was nothing more than a failure—a wretch—who couldn't protect anything she cared about. She ruined everything. Maybe people had been right: she was doomed to do nothing more than fail, whether she was on the throne or not.

Chumani never should've had to touch her.

The door to her room unexpectedly opened, and Mika peeked around it moments later. When he spotted her, he crept into the room grasping a plate with steaming fry bread resting on top.

"You missed breakfast," he said as he approached, "but Shappa said I could bring you some." He extended the plate.

Redrinna didn't want it, but the sorrow in his eyes made it impossible to say no. So she forced herself to take it.

After she'd spent a long moment watching the steam curl off the bread, Mika whispered, "Your Highness?"

She stared at his feet, unable to meet his gaze.

"I'm glad you're okay and that you came back to us."

Her throat clenched.

He stepped forward and hugged her—mostly just her arm—before turning and leaving the room.

She stared after him for a while before dropping her gaze to the fry bread. Steam still rose in erratic curls, filling the room with its warm, homey scent. It wasn't as round or as evenly baked as Chumani's had been. The thought alone made her gag.

Hurriedly, Redrinna shoved the plate onto the table next to her bed, desperate to get it away from her. A second later, there was a shattering sound. Turning, it took her a moment to figure out what had made the noise.

Shoving the plate of fry bread onto the table had knocked off the little mirror Chumani had used to help her see her hair. The plain frame lay on the ground, jagged pieces of glass scattered around it. Redrinna's heart plummeted faster than a bird shot from the sky.

"Why are you like this?" she hissed at herself as she crawled from the bed to the mirror. Her fractured reflection watched as she gingerly picked up the pieces and set them in a pile on the frame. Tears burned her throat, but she refused to let them fall.

As she stared at the broken mirror, anger sparked to life in her chest, roaring loud. Then, a hollow echo of sorrow swept in, snuffing it out. After it came nothing, a drought of emptiness. Exhaustion crammed itself into the vacancies left behind, but as Redrinna debated whether or not to give in, one, clear thought unfolded itself in her mind: in order to escape this guilt, she had to undo the mistake. She couldn't bring back the dead or turn back the hands of time, and she couldn't make it so Chumani had never been taken at all. However, if she could tear the woman from the demon's clutches, alive and unharmed, she wouldn't have to. That would be nearly as good as it never having happened at all.

Redrinna's body cried for sleep, but there were only thin, waning strands of sunlight spilling through the window. The day was nearly gone, and so long as Chumani was out there, in danger, there wasn't time for her to sleep. That could wait.

She had to go, find the demon, and bring Chumani back. It was the only way to take these feelings away, but Redrinna wouldn't make the same mistake she'd made last time. This time, she would go alone. No one else would get hurt.

Quietly, she got to her feet, ignoring the pain that lanced through her head with every movement.

Redrinna, what are you doing? her gem asked, but its voice was so quiet she could barely make out the words.

She didn't respond. Instead, she scooped up her belt and weapons, grabbed her boots, and left the room. She was about to leave the clinic when she spied someone she knew through a cracked open door. Pausing, she peeked inside the room.

Her heart plummeted at the sight of Kangee on a bed, lying completely motionless. So, the demon had gotten him too. All the more reason she had to go. She refused to repay Kangee and Chumani's kindness by leaving them to drown in their current circumstances.

Clenching her fists, Redrinna turned and left the clinic. As she'd hoped, the majority of the village had already vanished into their houses for the night. All she had to do now was get out of the village without anyone seeing.

It was a straight shot from the clinic to the stairs, which were the only way to get back to the ground. However, there were a couple warriors patrolling on the platforms already. She hoped when they saw her they wouldn't try stopping her because there was no way she'd be able to get past them unnoticed.

While she stood there thinking, she slipped her boots on and fastened her belt around her waist. As she was about to step forward, she heard a voice.

"Chief, we can't stay here. At this rate, it's going to eat the entire tribe." It sounded like Ohanzi.

"Where would you have us go?" returned someone whose voice

Redrinna didn't recognize. "We've already been chased from one home, and we've barely been able to re-establish ourselves here."

The voices were coming closer. Redrinna slunk to the side, stepping away from the door and into the protective shadow of the clinic and its tree.

"So you would have us die?"

"Do you not remember the ordeals of our people, Ohanzi? This is our homeland. This is where our ancestors were born and died—this is our legacy. Would you have us throw that all away now, and force our children through what we've already had to endure?"

"Of course I don't want that, but we're dying."

Ohanzi and an elder Redrinna had never seen before stepped into view, the edges of their wings glowing in the orange light of the dying sun.

"Yes, but the princess was able to bring us valuable information, and with it we might be able to eliminate this threat altogether. We're going to seize this chance before it disappears forever."

The two of them walked past her hiding place, neither looking her way. She held her breath just in case.

"Chatan and the Dragon Kin are forming a plan as we speak," the man she didn't know continued, his voice growing fainter as they moved away. "If all goes well, we will be able to put the demon to rest and bring Chumani back home, if it's not too late. That's the attitude we must hold on to—not the attitude of defeat."

Redrinna's heart thrummed in her chest like a hummingbird's wings. If she didn't act fast, the others would get involved and potentially hurt. She had to go now and quickly, hoping no one stopped her.

All at once, Reyna entered her mind, an old memory on her heels.

When she'd been much younger, Redrinna had been trying to sneak off somewhere (probably the library) when the woman had appeared seemingly from nowhere, catching hold of her arm. She didn't remember most of the event, or what had happened after, but something the woman had said still stuck in her mind: 'If you're going somewhere when you're not supposed to, don't scurry around like a scared mouse trying to escape a cat. Act confident and with purpose. Act like you're supposed to be doing whatever it is.'

Thinking back on it, the advice wasn't stellar, but it still rang through her mind. Then Redrinna shook her head. Even here, after everything that had happened between them, she still thought of Reyna. She still listened to her advice. Maybe there wasn't a way to chase the woman from her mind.

Trying to appear as calm as possible, Redrinna left the platform, taking the stairs slower than she liked. Her headache worsened when she went fast. Her gem weakly warmed its chain, but she ignored it and turned left at the base of the stairs. The forest was dead ahead, and the shadows welcomed her into their arms.

No one stopped her. A chill ran down Redrinna's spine. For some reason, a part of her had hoped someone would notice and stop her, but that was silly—childish, almost. Once again, she reminded herself it was better this way. As her father had sometimes said, there were times when she, as a leader, would have to act completely alone. If protecting her friends meant she had to fight alone, then it was okay. There were worse things than that.

"Wh-where are you going?" a voice said suddenly, but it didn't startle her.

Slowly, Redrinna turned back, surprised but also somehow not to find Tak and Xandrin standing there, just inside the shadow of the trees. For a moment, she stared before looking away. There was no point explaining, and she didn't want to lie to them anyway, so she held her tongue.

Both of them remained quiet for a long time before Tak said, "You're...going to try and find the demon, aren't you?"

"Yes," she breathed. "If it hadn't been for me, then Chumani and Kangee..." She huffed, chiding herself for explaining. "This is something I need to do, but I want you guys to stay here."

"But your injury—"

"Is fine."

"Do you think we're stupid?" Xandrin demanded, a bite in his voice. "Do you think I'm blind and clueless? Did you seriously believe nobody would notice you trying to leave the village after what happened?"

"I'm fine," she insisted. "Stop worrying."

The dragon's brow lowered, a low growl rumbling through his chest. "Quit telling me you're fine. I know you're not."

"Leave me alone," Redrinna snapped back, clenching her fists. "Stop worrying about me and worry more about yourself instead!"

"How am I not supposed to worry?" he demanded, wings flaring open. "Have you seen yourself lately? You look dead, and I'm not okay with that!"

"I. Am. Fine." What did he want from her? Did he want her to curl up on his back and pretend none of this was happening? Did he want her to sit and wait for him to take care of everything for her like she was some helpless child? "And it's not up to you to decide otherwise, got it?"

Redrinna turned to go, but all at once, Tak snapped, "Stop it!"

She blinked. He'd never spoken to any of them like that before. Half-turning, she was surprised to see him facing her head-on, his brow lowered. She couldn't see his eyes because of the bandage, but a part of her was glad she couldn't. This new side of him made her uneasy.

"At least let us go with you. Please."

"So you can get hurt again? Or Xandrin or Astra or Kyvo can?" Even though Redrinna hated it, she couldn't get the bite out of her voice. "That thing won't kill me, so none of you need to worry about me. I'll be back soon—"

"I'm not worried you're going to die," Tak spat, making both her and Xandrin jump. "But...but you keep getting hurt, and I...we just want to help you. Xandrin's so worried he's hardly eating, but you don't even seem to care. Have you even noticed? You're our friend; why wouldn't we worry about you? Do you think just because you're not bleeding, you're not hurt? Do you think you're not going to hurt us when you do this?"

For the first time since Redrinna had met him, anger churned in her chest, her fury directed straight at him. Every second she stayed—every second he kept her here—was another second Chumani lost.

"It doesn't matter," Redrinna said, voice firm as she turned away. "I will take care of this on my own." She began walking, fighting to keep her back straight. Before she'd even taken two steps, Tak rushed into her path, close enough he made her take a step back. He was turned completely in her direction, facing her head on. His ability to hear where she'd been freaked her out more than a little.

"You don't have to. Let us help you, please. This is what the Dragon Kin is for, isn't it? It's why there's more than one member!"

Her throat constricted hard enough Redrinna thought she would choke if she even tried to breathe.

"So what if that thing can't kill you? That doesn't mean it can't or won't hurt you."

She squeezed her eyes shut, the angry fire in her being stoked higher with every word out of his mouth.

"You don't have to go alone," Tak said, desperation oozing from his voice. "Please, just—"

"Enough!" Redrinna snapped, making him take a step back. "I don't need your help and I don't want it! Just leave me alone!"

"But," he began, starting to glance in Xandrin's direction before dropping his head. "We...we're the Dragon Kin. All of us. Together. Aren't we?"

"No." She stepped past him, preparing herself to leave. No matter how much it made her head ache, she'd have to move fast if she wanted to find Chumani before it was too late.

"But—"

"If you don't like it," she began, the words deepening the ache in her chest as she said them, "then leave."

Desperate to escape whatever else they might say, Redrinna raced forward, running beneath the looming shadows of the trees and leaving them behind.

Neither of them followed her this time.

Redrinna glanced at the sky, adjusting her course accordingly based off the couple stars peeking their heads through the twilight sky. As she did, the ache in her chest crumbled into a pain as vast as the ocean. It didn't hurt enough to make her slow or stop, but she pressed a hand to her heart like it would soothe the ache away.

"Ow," she gasped as she tried to ignore the sting. It persisted, relentless as the waves pounding against the shore. An image of Tak standing there, maybe still waiting, flashed through her mind, stabbing the pain even deeper. Then the hurt on Xandrin's face too. "Ow."

No matter how fast Redrinna ran, the pain didn't leave. It clung to her like a shadow. The sun dimmed as it was dragged beneath the trees, inevitably sinking into the maw of the horizon. Night's darkness pressed in, silent and still.

Redrinna glanced up again, the stars brighter and more abundant than they'd been when she'd left the village. This wasn't the sky she'd seen from the lair. The stars weren't in the right spots yet, but they weren't far off.

Chapter Twenty-Two

'If you don't like it, then leave.' Tak's heart skipped a beat as Redrinna's voice echoed through his mind again. She'd left, not just him, but Xandrin too.

The wind rattled through the trees, the chill biting him as it raced by.

Takota had said things wouldn't get better unless they talked to her, so Tak had tried. But Redrinna didn't want to talk. She didn't want their help—especially his. She wanted them to leave.

An ache spread through his chest like fire, searing him to his core.

For the first time in his life, Tak didn't want to leave or hide himself away. Yet this was always the inevitable truth: a person like him, one who could only bring pain, couldn't be with people who were trying to take it away. It didn't work. It didn't make sense.

Even still, he couldn't bring himself to move, almost as though he believed Redrinna would come back if he stood there long enough, just waiting.

"Tak," Xandrin began slowly, voice hushed. "Redrinna says a lot of stuff she doesn't mean when she's angry. Don't...don't take it to heart, okay?" The dragon nudged him with his nose, making him take a step back. "We need to get the others and head out as soon as possible—oh, right. You can't go. I'll get you back to the clinic then."

Xandrin shepherded him back, depositing him at the clinic door. Numb, Tak went inside, running his fingers along the smooth wood walls until he reached the room that had temporarily been his. For a long while he stood near the bed, thoughts almost frozen like an autumn leaf still clinging to the branch even as frost painted its surface.

He knew what he had to do, but for the first time in his life, he didn't want to. However, maybe this was the only way to truly help the others. Staying here—staying with them—wasn't going to make it better; so far, it'd just made it worse. The sooner he got it over with, the sooner the memories of his time here would fade.

Lifting his hands, Tak hesitated for a second before undoing the bandage wrapped around his head. As it fell away, he opened his eyes. There was still some slight, barely noticeable doubling of his vision, but things were much sharper and clearer than they'd been before, and since the sun was gone now, the light wouldn't give him a headache.

He arranged the bandage in as neat a pile as he could and placed it on the bedside table. As he finished doing so, the door behind him opened briefly before closing.

Slowly, Tak turned, freezing at the sight of Takota and Kyvo standing there.

"The dragons and a couple of the warriors left, so Kyvo wanted to sit with you," Takota explained, speaking warily, almost like he didn't want to. "How...are your eyes?"

Lowering his gaze, Tak said, "They're fine."

No one spoke for a moment that seemed to stretch into an eternity. Then, Kyvo did. "You're leaving, aren't you?"

Tak didn't have any lie or excuse to give, so he said nothing.

"Do you really think that is going to help?" Takota asked.

"I...I don't know." Unable to look at either of them, Tak kept his head down. "But it might."

"But this isn't your fault," Kyvo said, padding closer.

A flicker of annoyance flared in Tak's chest. "It's not my fault? How haven't I been making things worse for everyone, Kyvo? Redrinna and Xandrin were fine until I showed up, and it's been disaster after disaster ever since. Now she's run off who knows where, a-and I just—" His voice broke and he stepped back, needing space.

"So when something bad happens, you run from it?" Kyvo's tail lashed behind him. "How are any of the bad things that have happened your fault? Did you make them happen? How do you know they wouldn't have happened if you hadn't been there?"

Tak grimaced, that flicker of anger catching on something and starting to grow.

"Kyvo," Takota hissed. "This isn't going to help."

Kyvo took another step forward, ears back and lips curling in a snarl. "Did you ever think things might've been worse without you? What would've happened if you hadn't been there to protect Astra in the woods? Redrinna and Xandrin might not have found her at all, which means Reyna probably would've killed her. And if you hadn't been around all those years ago, she would've died then."

"What would you know, Kyvo?" Tak snapped. "None of those things matter because any good I've done gets drowned out by all the screw-ups I'm causing! Ever since I showed up, it's been one thing after another. I wanted to believe you. I want to believe there's nothing wrong with me, but there is, and staying isn't going to make that go away!"

Kyvo barked, stamping his front paws. "Stop it! I don't care about any of that stuff because I want you here with the rest of us. I don't care if you're cursed or whatever—I just want you to stay." All at once, Kyvo's tail wilted, his ears drooped, and his head sank towards the ground. "I don't remember my family. I don't know anyone in this whole wide world except for you guys. You and the others are the only family I've ever had. Please, don't leave me."

All the anger and annoyance festering inside Tak dissipated. Hesitantly, unsure what to say, he crouched, gently laying a hand on Kyvo's head. The kitsune rushed to him, nearly bowling him over.

"I wanted everything to be like how it was when I first met Redrinna," the kitsune whimpered, eyes scrunched up tight. "I wanted things to be okay. But when I found you guys, she wasn't the same and nothing feels okay. I'm scared."

"I know," Tak managed.

Redrinna wasn't the same person he'd met that day on the beach. She wasn't the same person who'd saved him from the clutches of that village and from himself. Maybe that person was still in her somewhere, but now that Kyvo had said it, he realized once again how deeply he missed her too. He missed what she was, who she'd been. The way things were now left him helpless and terrified.

After a pause, Takota approached, crouching beside the two of them. "I'm not sure what's going on precisely, but if it's okay, I have something I want to say." He stared at Tak with his golden eyes, unrelenting as the sun. "It's okay if there are sides to yourself you don't like. I think that's part of being human. We can't be perfect, and we can't always do things the way we want to or be who we wish we could. If you believe you'll escape that by leaving, I won't stop you but...Tak, if you do, you will spend the rest of your life on the run from yourself."

Tak's gaze fell. Somewhere inside him, he knew this, but he didn't want to accept it. Accepting that meant he had to, at least in part, accept himself. What he was, and what he simply was not. "But I'm...I just..."

"If there's something you don't like about yourself, you can change it, you know," Takota said, his voice soft like the night wind sighing through the oak trees. "That's the beauty of being human, I think. Change is difficult; it's hard. It's uncomfortable. It might take you several years, or it might even take you your entire life, but if you want to change this part of you, you can."

Closing his eyes, Tak stayed quiet, a wedge in his throat. How could he change this part of him, the part that, regardless of whether it was practical or not, always blamed himself? How could he change something that'd been a part of him for so long, it felt like it was inscribed in his blood—on his heart? How was it possible to be more than he'd always been?

All at once, something Timothon had said reverberated in his mind like an echo: 'There are things about ourselves we cannot change. That's true. However, if you don't like the face staring back at you in the mirror, you still have two choices. One, you can change the face you see, or two, shatter the mirror and get a better one.'

Had he been trying to tell Tak what Takota was telling him now?

"Takota," Tak began, not looking at the man, afraid that if he did, he wouldn't be able to speak, "what do you think is better? Is it better to get rid of the things you hate about yourself or to find a way to accept them? What...what do I do?"

The man sat back on his heels. "That's a good question." Takota stayed quiet for a while. "I think, for me at least, it would depend on what the thing was. Is the thing you hate something that can be changed, or is it something that is a part of who you are, like the way you look or something? There are some things, like a bad habit, that we can change. Even if it's hard, it's possible, and if it bothers you, you can fight it. But there are other things that are a part of who you are, things you may not like, that can't be changed. In that case, maybe the thing you need to change is how you see it."

How he saw it? Tak's frown deepened. He stared at his hands, his frown shifting to a glare. "But this magic killed my mom. If she hadn't used it on me, then she never would've died."

Takota was quiet for a minute. "Perhaps, but if she hadn't used it, then I'm guessing you would've died instead. Like it or not, this magic saved your life."

Tak had nothing to say. He'd tried to see it that way before, but it hadn't changed anything.

"Let me put it this way then: you don't have to use the magic inside you. You don't have to acknowledge it even exists, but so long as you do, then it will always be a part of you that you hate. Your mother may not be with you anymore, but the magic inside of you was hers; it's something the both of you share. That part of you is a part of her that you have with you always, and, in a way, hating it means you hate that part of her too."

His heart stuttered. Tak didn't hate his mom, nor did he hate what she'd done for him. He hated what it'd cost her to save him; he hated that it'd taken her in exchange for him.

Although... His gaze drifted back over his hands, lingering on the bandages still wrapped around his palms. The power inside him, the power he'd spent his life hiding from, was the only thing he had left from his mom. It was the only part of her that hadn't vanished that day. When she'd been alive, she'd used it often—according to his aunt—before that final time for him.

All at once, it occurred to Tak there was a good chance she'd known what it would cost to save his life—she'd known she would die, but she'd chosen to save him anyway.

For the first time, as he recalled Xandrin and his willingness to defend Redrinna with his life, it struck him that the dragon had also probably known exactly what it might cost him when he'd hidden her and gone to face the Dragon Slayer alone.

The knight from the priestess legend, too, had also most likely known what was going to happen to him when he'd left the priestess and faced their enemies by himself.

And Mato, from the previous Dragon Kin, had done the same.

Each of them had made a hard choice—almost an impossible one—and had stuck with it to its inevitable end. Yet, they'd all chosen to see their choice through because there'd been someone they'd wanted to protect, someone whose safety had mattered more than their own.

If Tak was honest, he hated it—he hated that they'd had to die or be so hurt, they'd been on the brink of death. That hadn't changed. However, all at once, he could respect the strength and conviction a choice like that required, and the idea of shunning the part of himself that reminded him of his mother's strength made him feel ashamed.

The power to protect, the power to save, ran in his veins, just as it had run in his mother's. And all these years, he'd been so ashamed of it and himself.

"I do want to accept it," he breathed, making Kyvo snuggle harder into his side. "But I don't know how."

"That's something that only comes with time," Takota said. "You might spend your entire life searching for that answer."

Even if Tak never did find a way to accept the magic in his veins, he wanted to search until he could. This power had been his mom's, after all, and maybe if he could find an answer someday, then he'd find a way to connect with the woman he'd never had the chance to meet. The woman who'd chosen to pass from this world in order to give him a chance to live in it.

He clenched his fists. "That's fine. I don't mind."

Kyvo's ears perked up as the kitsune rose and licked Tak's face. He recoiled as Takota laughed, though it was subdued.

"So what do we do now?" the kitsune asked, tail wagging slowly. "Now?"

"Redrinna's out there somewhere, and I'm tired of having to sit around and do nothing. I mean, I can probably track her with my nose; I am pretty good at it."

Tak hadn't seen his skills in that regard, so he'd have to take Kyvo's word for it. Regardless of whether or not Redrinna had meant what she'd said, it didn't matter to him anymore. Doing something wrong and then leaving the mess for someone else wasn't right. If his cornering her and pushing her to stay had been what'd made her run off like that, then he had to do what he could to make amends. Even if he ended up not joining the Dragon Kin, he wasn't going to leave it like this.

Tak got to his feet, taking a deep breath before remembering Takota was there.

Rising too, the man smiled. "Don't look at me like that. That thing has the person I love more than anyone in the entire world, so if you want to go, I'm going with you."

⚜

Redrinna staggered to a stop, panting so hard, she was almost wheezing. She studied the sky again, pulse roaring in her ears. She was so close. The sky was almost a perfect match with her memory, and she was at the base of the mountains now. There was a hint of pine in the breeze, but it wasn't strong enough yet.

If only she could remember *when* she'd woken up in the demon's cave. Her gut feeling was early at night, but since she couldn't remember the exact time, she'd have to search a wider area than she'd been planning on.

That was fine; she was willing to do anything to find Chumani.

Redrinna raced off again, barely making any progress before her head was spinning like a top, forcing her to stop once more. She gasped for air like a fish ripped out of water before vomiting. Her nose wrinkled at the taste it left in her mouth, but as soon as her head quit swimming, she ignored it and took off again.

She glanced at the sky. Her heart skipped a beat. This was almost exactly the sky she remembered from that night, which had to mean she was close. She halted, giving herself a minute to breathe. Fragrant pine struck her senses, strong enough it vividly brought back the memory of lying in the demon's cave.

Slowly, fighting to calm her galloping heart, Redrinna studied the forest around her, hunting for any hint or sign that would reveal where she should go next. It was difficult without the light of the moon—the night black as pitch—but after a minute, she noticed a scraggly path heading up the mountainside, disappearing into the dark cliffs above. It was too obvious and wide to be a deer path, so it begged investigation.

Hurrying towards it, Redrinna nearly tripped in her haste. She rushed up the worn stone shaped like steps. This was far too convenient to be natural.

A short distance above her, the stairs vanished into the darkness of a tunnel. Her heart skipped a beat as she raced for it. Right as she reached the top of the path, an all-too-familiar woman with dark hair and eyes materialized in front of her.

Redrinna pulled up short, her hair whipping over her shoulders. "Reyna."

The woman smirked. "Princess."

Eyes narrowing as she stared at the woman, Redrinna fought to shove the rush of emotions that slammed into her as far away as possible.

Reyna laughed, but it was hollow. "Look at you. After all this time, I don't think you've changed one bit."

Sharp pain dug into Redrinna's chest and annoyance followed right behind it. Reyna wasn't her friend; she was the enemy. Why couldn't she see her that way?

"What? Now that we're alone, you've got nothing to say?" Crossing her arms, Reyna leaned against the tunnel's entrance. "That's disappointing."

Redrinna's gaze flicked away from the woman as she wrestled the waves of stupid emotions into submission. "Go away."

"What business could you possibly have in an empty place like this?"

"If there's nothing here then why are you here?"

Reyna didn't respond.

That made Redrinna one hundred percent positive she'd found the demon's nest.

"Fine," the woman sighed. "You win. Regardless, you have no

business in there. All you should be worrying about is those little gems of yours and the people attached to them. Problems like these aren't your concern anymore, right, Princess? Oh, wait, I suppose I should say ex-Princess."

It was Redrinna's turn to remain silent.

With another, almost resigned sigh, Reyna pushed herself off the wall. "Then again, you've always been a bleeding heart, haven't you? Too nice for your own good, even if it means letting people get hurt." There was a bite in the woman's voice.

"Get out of my way," Redrinna said again, clenching her fists.

Without warning, the memory of shoving Reyna off the cliff flashed through her mind, making her breath catch in her throat. If she didn't tread carefully, that could happen again, and she was so sick of the nightmares and memories she couldn't escape and didn't need more.

"No can do," Reyna said.

Turning her head away, Redrinna glared at the darkness.

The next second, the woman's hand clamped on Redrinna's jaw, almost her neck, barely high enough to not choke her. Panic flooded her as her gaze frantically met Reyna's.

Fire raged in those dark eyes. "How many times did I tell you not to look away from an opponent?" The woman shoved her back down the stairs, the tight hold on her jaw forcing her to move. "You little coward. You never listen to anything I say."

Redrinna stumbled back, nearly falling several times, only being saved by Reyna's vice-like grip. Her jaw screamed in protest, feeling like it was a hair's breadth from breaking.

When they hit the bottom, Reyna shoved her into a tree. Pain burst through Redrinna's skull as the bark crunched beneath her. Air rushed out of her lungs, leaving her dizzy.

"You will not interfere here," Reyna snarled, her voice quiet but cold like a blade hissing out of its sheath. "All the tribes will die, but this one will be the first, even if I have to do it by my own hand."

She splayed her free hand and magic so dark it made the night seem bright zipped between her fingers like lightning.

Redrinna flinched as the woman held it over her. Shadow-like bars shot to the ground, stabbing through the earth as panels of grey, window-like shadows grew between the bars like ice.

"Now, you stay out of *my* way." Reyna glared at her for a moment longer before vanishing.

Redrinna pressed her hands against the barrier of her cage, a strange numbness assaulting her senses the instant her skin made contact. Her knees gave out, pitching her to the ground. Heaviness latched on to her like a boulder, dragging her beneath the weight of what felt like the entire ocean. Darkness flooded her mind, a vice clamping around her chest.

No. She couldn't give in. If she stayed here, if she let Reyna win, then Chumani would— It'd be like her mother all over again. Like Xandrin—

Fighting with all her strength, Redrinna managed to push herself onto her knees. Then she couldn't get any further. Her arms shook from the effort. This barrier, whatever it was, seemed to siphon away her strength until she was left empty. She hugged her waist, head pounding as she fought to stay upright as a wave of dizziness assaulted her senses. Tears pricked her eyes, but she held them back, trying to keep them at bay. She didn't want to cry again. She wanted to keep fighting, to stop Chumani's suffering, to stop Osiris, but, as seemed her fate, she'd failed. Again.

A tear slipped past her defenses, and she didn't have the strength or balance to wipe it away. She wanted to scream, but with the weight settling like silt on her back, she could scarcely draw a breath.

Her vision blurred, and another tear slid down her cheek. Finally, she surrendered, letting the tears go. She closed her eyes, shutting out the impassive night sky and trees towering over her.

Redrinna? Her gem's voice was dim, faint like the tail of a distant echo. It seemed like it hadn't spoken to her in ages, and her chest ached to hear its voice again. However, she felt nothing from it, no comfort, no warmth. It was empty.

Chapter Twenty-Three

Tak stumbled and had to snag a nearby tree to keep himself from falling. As he gasped for air, Kyvo and Takota skidded to a stop, both turning to him.

"You're stopping again?" the kitsune asked.

"I can't breathe," he wheezed, waving a hand. "Give me a minute." Never in all his life had he tried to run like this, and he was pretty sure his legs were on the verge of catching fire and being reduced to ash.

"It's okay," Takota said, his gaze searching the trees. "You won't be able to do anything if you kill yourself getting there." Even still, the man kept his gaze focused on the forest rather than them.

As Tak fought to calm his breathing, he listened to the silence of the woods, uneasiness creeping through his gut. The silence was different, unnatural, like something had taken all the sounds and shoved them into a box. There wasn't even any wind, leaving the trees motionless and utterly silent, like they were standing on the rim of a bad storm. He tried to convince himself he was just worried about Redrinna, and that was making him perceive the world this way, but he couldn't quite manage it.

Closing his eyes, Tak fought for composure. Panicking wasn't going to help. It'd already made things bad.

Kyvo stamped his feet, getting his attention. "Come on, Tak, she's close. I'm sure of it."

"Okay, okay." Pushing himself off the tree, he did his best to shake off his exhaustion.

The kitsune dashed off, Takota on his heels, and Tak begrudgingly followed suit. Minutes crawled by as they raced through the darkness, each root and branch that clawed at him tightening the anxiety in his chest.

"Tak!?" Astra's voice broke the curse of silence, nearly scaring him out of his skin.

He risked a glance up—managing to spot something dark and vaguely large overhead—but didn't have the breath to answer.

"There she is!" Kyvo squealed, pelting forward into the darkness at nearly the speed of light.

Tak raced to keep up. After a couple minutes, he spied a faint, red gleam shining in the dark. Was that Redrinna's gem?

They slid to a stop seconds later. A hint of relief shot through Tak: Redrinna!

Then his throat tightened. She was in some sort of shadowy cage, curled into a ball and not moving. The light from her gem faded, returning them to the near complete darkness of the night. Kyvo propped himself against the barrier, but Redrinna didn't move.

Astra abruptly landed nearby as smoothly as if she'd dived through water instead of trees. Xandrin crashed down a second later like a rock dropped into a pond. Branches rained down around him, leaving an opening for three, fierce-looking warriors Tak didn't recognize by sight.

"What are you two doing here?" Astra glanced back and forth between him and Kyvo, eyes wide enough they caught glimmers of starlight. "You weren't supposed to come."

"Kyvo and I are part of the Dragon Kin too," Tak choked out, still panting. "We're not being left behind."

"We left you behind because you're hurt."

"Is she...?" Xandrin began, his voice pitched higher than usual. He took a cautious step in Redrinna's direction.

Tak took a few steps closer too, his heart stuttering. Redrinna hadn't even looked up.

"Stupid—magic—!" Kyvo grunted, pushing against the barrier with his head. All at once, the blue markings on his narrow face began glowing, pulsing brighter and brighter with every second. He pressed harder, squealing from the effort, his markings glowing like a full moon. Cracking rang out. The cracking swelled, almost sounding like glass breaking, but slightly quieter and more subdued.

The barrier vanished, and Kyvo plowed into Redrinna a second later. His markings dimmed and went out. For a moment, no one moved. Then, slowly, almost gingerly, Redrinna sat up.

Hesitantly, Tak ventured a couple steps closer.

With wide, bewildered eyes, Redrinna stared at Kyvo. "What are you doing here?"

Kyvo huffed, blowing a few stray hairs out of her face. "What did you expect me to do? Sit on my tail and do nothing while you run off and try to get yourself killed?"

She turned away, her gaze stopping on Tak's feet before she slowly looked up, meeting his eyes. The tears on her cheeks caught the faint light of the stars. A heartbroken expression blossomed across her face.

After a minute, she glanced around. When her gaze reached Takota and the others, a long sigh escaped her. Pointing towards a difficult-to-see-hole in the mountainside a short distance above, she said in a lackluster voice, "Chumani's up there. I'm sure of it."

After a moment's hesitation, the warrior with silvery feathers nodded. "All right." He and the others left, vanishing into the mountain.

Tak noticed Takota gazing up, though he hadn't left. "You should go too."

The man startled, glancing between him and Redrinna. "But..."

She gestured for him to go. "Chumani needs you more. We're okay."

After hesitating for a couple seconds more, he relented. "Okay. Don't follow us, all right?" Then he left too.

Tak glanced at the dragons, both of whom wore matching, concerned expressions. "You two should go with them."

"But—"

"They're going to fight the demon in its home. They'll need all the help they can get."

The dragons shared a glance.

Astra took a tiny step forward, lowering her head near Tak's. "Promise me," she whispered, gaze fixed on his face, "you'll be careful. Don't do anything crazy."

"We won't."

She opened her mouth, almost as if to say more, but then she only nodded and hurried after Xandrin. They launched into the sky and quickly vanished into the dark mountainside.

Tak watched them for a minute longer before turning back to Redrinna. Hopeless frustration welled in his chest. They'd been in this situation once before, and the things he'd said had made it worse, not better. How did he not repeat that all over again?

Unexpectedly, his aunt's voice came to him, gentle as the evening breeze. 'Sometimes, speaking gets in the way.' He could almost picture her back in her humble kitchen years ago, delicately wrapping a basket of bread in a cloth for the young mother down the lane who'd just found out she'd become a widow. 'At times like this, people need you to simply be there and listen. Use words only if you must.'

Closing his eyes, Tak braved moving a couple steps closer before sitting with the other two.

⚬◖❂◗⚬

Redrinna kept her head down, fighting the urge to glance at either

267

Tak or Kyvo. If she did, all the shame and guilt from her earlier actions would bubble up again. So instead, she kept her gaze on her hands—her useless hands—curled in her lap.

Even still, a sickening realization swept over her: everyone had come for her and to fight the demon, and they'd ended up rescuing her. She hadn't done a thing to help herself or them yet again.

"None of you need me, do you?"

They both stayed quiet.

The longer they sat there, the harder the weight of all Redrinna's anxieties pressed on her. She curled a little tighter to herself, feeling like she was on the verge of capsizing. Kyvo wormed his head into her lap, but she couldn't bring herself to pet him.

"Tak, you and I...we're the Kokorojin," she began in a harsh whisper, fighting against another wave of tears. "The tribe with the strongest hearts—whatever that means—but weak in every other way. We can't fly, can't live in water or fire, can't handle heavy loads. We even have the shortest lifespans out of everyone."

He stayed quiet still.

Once Takota had told them the story, some details she'd heard or read somewhere had flared to life in her mind. "Why does it seem like everything is against us? Why can't we just seem to—" She broke off. She hadn't meant to say 'us' or 'we.'

Tak whispered, "I don't know."

Redrinna shook herself. "It doesn't matter anyway. You two should go with the others. I'm fine."

"I'm fine here," Tak said.

Kyvo nodded. "Me too."

Redrinna's heart squeezed on her throat. A loud cry from the mountain split the quiet, making her shudder. Fervently, she hoped it wasn't something she'd have to worry about.

"I'm not leaving," Tak whispered again, his voice calm.

She kept her mouth shut, trying to outlast him.

"Can't we talk about it?" Kyvo asked, putting a paw on her knee.

"What for? I already yelled at you guys once." The shame filling her like water slithered out in her voice. "I might do it again."

"Then instead...why don't you tell us what happened? You were in some sort of cage when we arrived," Tak said.

"Reyna." She shuddered at the memory, another that would plague her nightmares and haunt her shadow.

"What did she do?"

She explained what had happened in as few words as possible.

"Well...it's gone now." A question lingered in his tone, though he didn't ask it.

Huffing, she said, "It doesn't matter. Nothing I do makes a difference. It never has."

He returned to being quiet.

Hitching her shoulders up, Redrinna glared at the nearest tree.

Not a sound slipped out of Tak's mouth.

"It doesn't," she insisted, bothered by his silence.

"Then why'd you come out here alone?"

She didn't want to say it. Despite her intentions to keep everyone safe, Redrinna had failed to protect anyone.

"So...all this time...all of this running around and refusing to sleep and doing things without us...was pointless?"

"No," she protested. Then confusion filled her, making her doubt what she'd been doing. What had been the point of all this, the lying and pretending? "I don't know."

"Then what?" he pressed, though his voice remained quiet. "Do you not trust us? You really don't want us around?"

She tried to glare at him, but the earnest, concerned expression on his face snuffed out the fire.

Tak was quiet for a long time before inhaling sharply. "No. It's not that. It's...it's because you don't want any of us to get hurt, isn't it?"

Hearing it out loud didn't make it sting any less. Shrinking into herself as much as she could, she whispered, "Xandrin almost died, and it would've been all my fault. If it happens again, or if someone actually died this time—" She squeezed her eyes shut as another cry rang out from the mountain. "I can't. I just can't."

"I understand."

"And I thought," she continued, not sure where all the words were coming from or how he was getting them out of her, "if only I had to get hurt, then none of you would. But I couldn't protect anybody. All I've done is make things so much worse for so many people."

Tak let out a sigh, but something about it made her look at him. A ghost of a smile touched his mouth. "You haven't made things worse for everybody, you know."

This time, she did glare at him.

That seemed to make him smile even more. "What happened to Xandrin was not your fault; it was Osiris's. You *saved* Xandrin."

Fiercely, she shook her head. "That was Timothon and the gem. If it'd been up to me, he would've died."

"Perhaps, but you used the power of the gem to take him to someone who could help him. That's what saved his life, and nobody can take credit for that but you."

"You saved me too," Kyvo butted in, gazing at her with his warm, brown eyes. "Remember? Back in the forest?"

Her mouth opened, but no sound came out. She did remember, but...

"And you saved me," Tak said, his voice barely a murmur as his gaze dropped to the ground.

Redrinna raised an eyebrow. "Are...you sure?" She had no recollection of having saved his life.

"Very." He stared at the ground before taking a deep breath and meeting her gaze again. "Can I tell you something? Something...something I've never told anyone?"

Not sure what to say, she stayed quiet.

"It's about my family...but mostly me."

Guilt made her cheeks flush. "I heard you tell Kyvo about your parents. A-and your powers. I didn't mean to; it just happened that way. I wasn't trying to eavesdrop or anything. It was...an accident."

"That's okay," he said, catching her by surprise. "I accidentally heard you telling Timothon what'd happened in the Imperial City, so it's fair."

He'd heard it all? That explained a few things, like why he'd never asked about it.

"And it relates to that, so it means I don't have to explain as much. But...you remember how everyone believed I was cursed?"

She nodded.

"After my aunt passed, it got worse. And because I was alone, I couldn't seem to get what people said out of my head. It kept gnawing at me." His gaze dropped back to the ground, hands shaking as he yanked on the grass. "So that day we met, in the woods, I was coming back from visiting my aunt and uncle's graves. I was... I was apologizing. A-and...saying my final goodbyes."

Her heart skipped a beat.

"I was ready to...to be done. With everything. I was just so tired." His voice broke, and though no tears fell, she could hear them. "But, for some reason, that day, I met you. I don't know why I stopped, but I did. A-and then you helped me escape that guy, and you offered me a home and food and taught me how to read, and I—I hadn't had that in so long—" His breath hitched, and he took a couple, shuddery breaths. "I don't know if it was chance or if some being or something willed it so, but if I hadn't met you, I can say with absolute certainty that I wouldn't be here."

She tried to swallow, but her throat was too dry.

Finally, Tak met her gaze, his eyes glistening. "So, yes, I know for a fact you saved my life. I've never doubted that for a second."

For some reason, a smile touched her mouth. Just a couple days ago, Redrinna had held her knife to her skin and wondered how much it would hurt, and for some reason, knowing that Tak knew that feeling was like she'd found a little sunbeam in an endless, pitch-black cave. For the first time, it was like there was someone else in that empty space with her, someone who made the darkness retreat just a bit.

"You don't have to do anything special or extraordinary in order to keep us safe. Protecting us...and caring about us, is something you're already doing without thinking about it. It's already a part of who you are. And that means more to me than anything else you could do."

Something inside her chest flickered to life like an ember.

Suddenly, Tak flushed and swiped at his cheeks. "I'm sorry."

She shook her head. "No, don't be. I'm the one who should be sorry. I was so focused on myself and my feelings I never realized for one second that you," she stared at him before pausing and laying a hand on Kyvo's head, and he gazed up with adoring eyes, "or you could be hurting too. I'm so sorry."

Her heart went out to Xandrin most of all. This entire time, she'd assumed he'd be happy so long as he wasn't hurt. She'd assumed that would make all her friends happy without considering for even one second that maybe they felt like she did, and her cold shoulder had been inflicting more pain.

Tak shrugged one shoulder. They both glanced up as another cry rang out from the mountain, though that one sounded different from the others. Then, Tak's gaze returned to her, a quiet strength Redrinna had never seen before flickering in his eyes.

For some reason, that made her want to keep talking.

"I miss my parents, both of them. It'd been the three of us for so long that now I... I can hardly even believe my mom is gone—that I could go anywhere in the world, travel to every part of it, and she wouldn't be anywhere."

Kyvo rested his head against her arm.

"And I don't know how I feel about my dad now. I don't know if he's trying to be a good guy or if he's still a bad guy, but even still,

I...I miss him. I love him so much, and I just hate this. And Reyna," she glanced to the side, annoyed by the strong desire to fix their friendship burning in her chest, "there's a part of me that can't seem to let go of her. I still want to be her friend, except now...now I see her for what she truly is. I know I don't really want to be her friend, but I still feel like I do."

"You miss it," Tak said, his voice kind. "That's normal."

Redrinna grimaced. "It just...makes me feel so...dumb."

"Dumb?" He cocked his head to the side, a thoughtful frown on his face. "I guess, but... There's something my aunt told me once: if there's something that's been a part of your life for a long time, then when it's gone, even if you hated it or it'll be better for it to be gone, for a while, you'll still feel its absence. It's like when you have a splinter stuck under your skin. When you leave it there, your skin will grow over it, and it may not always bug you, but it's still festering and hurting. But once you remove it, while it'll eventually heal, for a time, there'll still be a wound. So it's normal for you to be hurting right now, and you don't have to be ashamed of it, R-Redrinna." Tak paused and blushed. "Th-that's what my aunt said, anyway."

She put a hand to her chest. "It just feels so hollow. That was the only life I've ever known. How do I just...leave it all behind?"

Tak didn't respond, but Kyvo sat up. "It's easy. You have a better life with us now, don't you?" His head was tilted to the side, ears angled towards her. "We can't replace what you had, but if it was just you, your parents, and the crazy lady before—"

"Plus a knight."

"Plus a knight, then here with us, you already have more, don't you?"

The world stopped in its tracks as Kyvo's words sank in. It wasn't easy, but he was right that Redrinna did have more. Before, she'd had a circle of four people around her, and one of them hadn't even truly cared about her. Now, she had a circle of five, and all of them were at least honest with her, if not some of the closest friends she could've imagined.

All at once, something Shappa had said rang through her mind. 'Regardless of what happened before, it couldn't strip us of who we are. The past didn't take everything because we still had each other, at least. We still have wotitakuye.'

Glancing down, Redrinna breathed, "Wotitakuye." Kinship. At first, she'd thought nothing of the fact that kinship was a closer word in the Eridian language than family, but now it made her pause, a different memory coming to mind.

Once, when she'd first begun struggling with her family-gifted duty to rule an entire continent, she'd turned to Captain Brion. She couldn't remember most of what he'd said, but it'd been something along the lines of questioning what she thought defined family. Was it only blood that connected you to people? And what if that blood was rotten? What then? Did she resign herself to a bitter fate or was there something else, something she hadn't understood then?

Perhaps the better question to ask was whether or not the Eridian word for family truly encompassed what family meant? Could family—could kin—only be defined by something as happenstance as blood? Or was it something more?

For the first time in what seemed like ages, a genuine smile tugged on Redrinna's mouth. "You're right. I do have all of you, don't I?"

Kyvo grinned, his pink tongue lolling out of his mouth.

Redrinna laid a hand on her gem, startled by its familiar warmth against her skin. "And you."

Of course.

She looked up, meeting Tak's gaze.

He almost smiled.

The ache in her chest didn't disappear; Redrinna wasn't even sure it lessened. Yet, for some reason, it seemed more manageable than it had before.

Taking a deep breath, Redrinna pushed herself to her feet, Kyvo hopping onto her shoulders as she did. Tak rose a second later, and they all stared at the mountain. It was difficult to make out in the dark, but Redrinna imagined the darker blob above them was the tunnel's entrance.

"Are we going?" Kyvo asked, his nose quivering as he sniffed the air.

She didn't answer right away. Despite what she wanted to believe, a part of her was convinced if she went up there, she'd get in the way and maybe get someone or herself hurt. However, the dragons were there, and they—all of them—were the Dragon Kin, not the people who sat on their haunches while the dragons did the fighting.

"Redrinna?" Tak asked, watching her expectantly.

"Yes. Reyna's still out there somewhere, and so long as she and Osiris are involved in what's going on here, then this is our fight too." She had to take a breath to keep herself calm.

Tak and Kyvo stared at her with determined expressions.

"I don't think I have much right to ask you guys to come with me after how I've treated you, but," Redrinna met both of their gazes, the resolve burning in their eyes strengthening her own, "will you come with me?"

They both nodded, a hint of a smile on their faces.

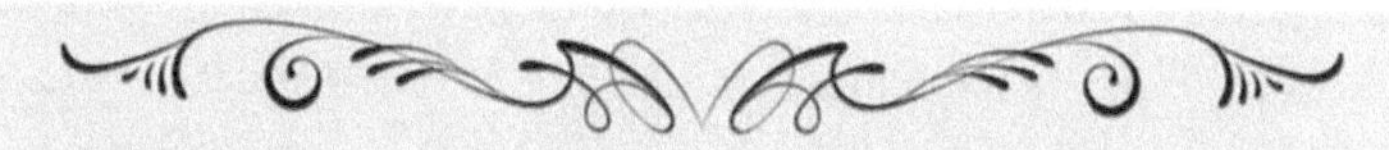

Chapter Twenty-Four

Bracing herself, Redrinna took two steps before stopping and turning back to Tak. "Your bandage is gone."

"You just noticed?" Kyvo said, sounding surprised.

"And you don't have a weapon," she continued.

Looking a bit abashed, Tak said, "I took off the bandage because it was dark and I needed my eyes. My sight is a lot better, just a little wonky still. I can't quite tell in the dark though."

That almost made her smile.

"And yeah, I don't have a weapon."

"Then I want you to take this, okay?" She pulled the sword Timothon had given her from the sheath and held it out to him. Even though it would mean she'd have to use her magic, it was better than sending him into a fight without any way of protecting himself.

He accepted it without hesitation. Her heart stuttered at the sight of him with a sword, but she needed to accept it. Deciding what dangers her friends could or couldn't face to make herself feel better wasn't fair. On the contrary, she should be relieved they cared about her enough to not want her to plunge into danger alone.

Sighing, Redrinna closed her eyes, set those thoughts aside, and focused on what she had to do.

"Sh-should I go first?" Tak asked, catching her by surprise. He held up the sword. "So you don't trip and fall on this or something?"

That was fair. She nodded, allowing him to lead the way up the mountainside. Her heart quivered as they climbed, but she kept going.

As they neared the crevice, Reyna didn't appear, but a garbled shout rang out from inside. Redrinna's heart stuttered. Were they still fighting the demon?

Kyvo leapt off her shoulders, padding after her quietly, both of his ears pointed forward. Silent as the night, the three of them entered the cavern in single file. Darkness blotted Redrinna's vision, but a short way ahead, she caught a glimpse of light.

In barely a minute's time, Tak stopped at the end of the tunnel, just outside the faint light from the night sky. Redrinna peeked out from behind him, taking in a handful of blurred shapes darting back and forth in the small cave. Deep shadows clung to the edges of the cavern, making it hard to see much beyond the center, but she made out the shape of Xandrin near the edge of the light. Pale bones stood out against the earthen floor, mismatched and scattered haphazardly like broken toys.

A blade flashed in the moonlight, and she realized the dark cluster of movement in the center was Chatan and his fellow warriors, the three of them shifting in a circle around the demon.

All at once, the demon lunged for Chatan, making the man hop back. At the last second, it whirled for Wicasa, an elbow spike going for his chest. The man dodged, but his foot hit a bone. He reeled back, wings flaring out to help him find his balance. The spike cut the air inches from his chest. Redrinna's eyes went wide. The demon was drawing its other arm back while Wicasa scrambled for balance.

Before she even realized what she was doing, she burst past Tak.

Chatan's eyes widened as he realized what she had. "Wicasa!" he shouted.

The demon plunged its arm forward. Redrinna leapt the last bit of the distance. The spike slammed into her back, skidding against her scales, making her stagger. She crashed into Wicasa, taking them both down. Pain burst through every inch of her body.

"Redrinna?!" Chatan and Xandrin cried at the same time.

Redrinna glanced at the demon, scrambling to her feet.

It hissed at her, face puckered like a spoiled child's. "Not you! Go away!"

The third warrior, Talutah, swung at it with an axe. It dodged before stopping, panting, glancing between them with wild, frantic eyes. Without warning, it turned and bolted for the exit.

Before she even had a chance to shout, Tak pounced from the shadows. He swung at the demon, narrowly missing its ribs. The demon skidded to a stop, backtracking a couple steps.

In a movement so fluid she almost didn't see it, Chatan flung a knife. It flashed through the air as it spun. In a split second, it struck the demon in the back of the head, right between its eyes.

The demon went rigid, still as stone before collapsing. Its eyes were wide and empty as its gray skin paled to the color of ash.

Redrinna's breath rushed out of her, almost making her knees give out. They'd managed to take out the last demon.

From the ground, Wicasa groaned as he pushed himself to his feet. Scowling at her, he brushed the dirt from his clothes. "Really?"

"Sorry."

"Did you have to save my life?" he demanded, drawing her up short. "Don't make me like you!"

Talutah laughed, so loud it echoed off the walls. Even Chatan cracked a smile.

"More importantly, are you okay?" Chatan asked.

She nodded, patting her scales. "Fit as a fiddle."

"What the heck is a fiddle?" Wicasa grumbled as he stretched his arms over his head.

Rolling his eyes, Chatan said, "I'm glad you had those scales of yours." He glanced over as Tak and Kyvo padded over. "Good job keeping it from leaving. You handle a sword well."

Tak flushed. However, there was a small smile touching his mouth.

Xandrin crept over, making Redrinna glance up. "What are you doing here, jumping in the middle of blades and pokey things? You could've got hurt."

She grinned. "But I had your scales, so I knew I'd be fine."

His ear frills shot straight up in the air. He stared with wide eyes before grinning as well and rubbing the end of his snout.

All at once, Takota's voice split the quiet. "Chatan!"

The man rushed off without a second's hesitation.

Astra staggered out of the dark recesses of the cave a moment later, calling Redrinna's attention to her.

"Where were you?" Tak asked, his voice sounding a bit tight.

"That creep got me with its paralysis power," she said with a scowl. "But once it died, I was free. So, I guess that's that."

Redrinna's heart soared out of her chest. If Astra had been struck by Two Face's power and was freed when it died, then that had to mean— Her vision misted over.

"Um...are you okay?" Astra asked, a worried note in her voice.

"Mika's dad is free," she said, pressing her hands over her mouth in an attempt to keep the tears at bay. "And Kangee— All of them are free."

Tak's eyes widened a fraction before he smiled an actual, real smile. He had a nice smile. Had Redrinna actually ever seen him smile before? She couldn't remember, but, either way, it was nice to see him happy.

She turned her head in the direction Chatan had gone, wondering why Takota had called him over. Had they found Chumani? Was she all right? Had they gotten here in time? Redrinna began walking in the direction they'd gone, her steps slow and uncertain.

There was a movement ahead, making her stop. Chatan stepped out of the darkness followed by Takota, who was carrying—

"Chumani," she breathed, hurrying over.

She only made it a few steps before stopping, heart faltering. Chumani's face was ashen, but there was still life in her cheeks. However, her wings were gone.

Slowly, Redrinna managed to look up into Takota's face before speaking in a hushed voice. "It...took her wings?"

He nodded, not speaking.

"But," Chatan said, squeezing her shoulder, "she is alive."

Without her wings, Chumani seemed half the size she'd been before. She seemed tiny and frail, especially compared to Takota and the others. Would she be okay without her wings?

"It seems the demon enjoyed eating its victims slowly and making them suffer for as long as possible," Chatan continued, a pained expression on his face. "So it took away her ability to escape."

"Torijin wings are powerful," Talutah explained from behind her. "If given the chance, she could've escaped easily, even from chains."

Redrinna closed her eyes, fighting down the nausea stealing into her gut. The important thing was that Chumani was alive. That was more important than anything.

"Let's get back to the village then. Quickly," she said.

Chatan glanced between her and Tak. "I'm sure Shappa is eager to get the two of you back."

Wicasa laughed from behind them. "She's probably going to tie you both to your beds."

For the first time that night, Takota cracked a tiny smile. "Or lock you guys in your rooms."

Redrinna grimaced. Even though she didn't know Shappa well, she could picture the woman doing both of those things.

The warriors and Takota stepped out of the shadows of the cave, spreading their wings once they were under the large opening. Everyone took off but Chatan, who hesitated before turning back.

Wings spread, he faced Redrinna. "Redrinna...no, Your Highness. Even though you were reckless tonight, if it hadn't been for you, I'm not sure we ever would've found Chumani in time. So thank you. I mean that." Then his gaze drifted over the others. "Hurry along. None of you should linger here longer than you have to."

Redrinna stared. Chatan had always been kind to her, despite plenty of reasons not to be, but that was the first time he'd used her title. And for some reason, it was one of the first times she'd ever heard it and it hadn't made her cringe.

❧ ❧

Tak glanced at Redrinna as the man took off, almost smiling at the startled expression on her face. He knew she didn't see it, but he truly believed she'd make an amazing princess—at the very least, she was an incredible person, and to him, he didn't doubt for one second why the Dragon Gem around her neck had chosen her. However, given how much she'd been through that night alone, he held his tongue.

She shook herself. "I guess we should go."

Astra nodded. "This place is creepy."

"Agreed!" Kyvo launched onto Xandrin's head, and the dragon almost went cross-eyed trying to watch him. "Let's go back to the village and finally sleep!"

Redrinna stared at them for a moment before smiling. A real smile. "That does sound nice, doesn't it?"

Tak grinned before turning and approaching Astra. Hesitantly, she stared at him for a minute before lowering herself so he could climb on. He hesitated too.

Before, he'd pushed her away because she reminded him of the incident that had almost cost him his life. However, that moment, that day in the woods, had also been the day he'd found out a part of his mom had survived in him. He couldn't fully accept that as a good thing, but he didn't want to push it away anymore or be angry. He wasn't sure he'd ever be able to bring himself to use it, but making

Astra suffer because of it wasn't fair.

So, carefully, he climbed onto her shoulders.

She glanced back, worry flickering in her eyes.

Tak smiled, which got her to smile too. Then they launched out of the cave and into the cool night air.

❧ ❧

By the time they made it back to the village, the sun was peeking its head over the mountaintops. Redrinna did her best to put the exhaustion dragging on her aside, unable to keep a smile off her face at the sight of the warriors on the platforms above and other villagers excitedly gathering around. At least for them, this part of the story had a happy ending. Chumani was safe, and the demon was dead. What more could Redrinna have asked for?

Xandrin lowered her to the ground, and she carefully climbed down. She held his gaze for a second before glancing at the village again. She needed to apologize to him, but she was going to save it for when she was more awake and her head wasn't pounding.

Astra glanced from her to Tak once the young man was off her shoulders. "Wow. You two look awful."

Tak yawned in response.

Kyvo stretched. "We've only been up all night long."

"Hurry and go to bed already," Xandrin said, sounding tired too.

Redrinna nodded. "You be careful, okay?"

He nodded too, a hint of a smile on his face.

She turned and followed the other two up the stairs, pausing at the top as she watched the villagers who were awake helping Takota take Chumani to the clinic. Her heart brimmed with warmth, so much it almost felt like it was going to leap right out of her chest.

"What is it about you, huh?" hissed a familiar voice, making her blood run cold. "Why in the world are you so stupidly special?"

Redrinna turned, glancing around frantically before she spotted her—Reyna, standing on the railing at the end of the platform, the dark trees almost making her difficult to spot.

Redrinna's heart leapt into her throat, all its warmth dissipating like dust in the wind.

"First, it's we have to have you, but then you escape and suddenly it's you're free to go," the woman spat. "Then it's slaughter everyone in this stupid village, but because you came and made a mess, now I'm supposed to leave it be. Why? Why, why, why?!"

Reyna stomped a foot, making the railing crackle beneath her foot before she leapt onto the platform, landing only a short distance away. Dimly, Redrinna registered that the village behind her had gone quiet, but all her focus was on Reyna as the woman stalked closer. Her heart frantically beat at her ribs. Her throat clenched so tight, she couldn't speak.

All at once, Tak skidded to a stop in front of her, Kyvo hot on his heels.

"What do you want this time?" Kyvo snapped, tail lashing from side to side.

"That," Reyna snarled, pointing a finger straight at Redrinna.

"No," Tak snapped.

Reyna didn't look away from her face. "You're in the way— always in my way. I had to let you go before, but now, you have this little, green-haired brat, don't you? The Dragon Kin doesn't need you anymore, does it?"

Panic flared hot in Redrinna's chest.

All at once, Tak shifted his weight, putting himself between her and Reyna, completely blocking the woman from her vision. She glanced at the back of his head, not sure whether to be grateful or scared for him.

"Everyone who doesn't want to die, stand aside," Reyna demanded, two, shadowy swords appearing in her hands. She pointed towards the Torijin behind them with one sword. "Especially you lot. The royal dog belongs to me."

"She's not a dog," Xandrin snapped as he reared onto his hind legs, neck arched. He lunged for the woman. She vanished in a flash of shadow, and his jaw snapped close seconds later, right where she would've been.

Reyna reappeared to her left. Redrinna backed up, trying to keep as much distance between her and Reyna as possible. She didn't want to fight her—she still didn't know if she could do it again—so she needed to make sure she didn't stupidly get in the others' way or make herself an easy target.

Xandrin snapped at Reyna again, but the woman dodged like she was made of water. Then she slipped past Astra too. Then she dodged Kyvo and Tak in two movements so fast, they almost looked like one.

Frantic, Redrinna pressed back further, almost slipping down the first stair.

Redrinna, you must fight her!

Reyna's dark eyes turned to her, a dangerous light gleaming there. For one instant, Redrinna considered throwing fire her way before a memory of a snowy evening by the glowing hearth with the woman swept through her mind. It was shoved out by the memory of the cliff—

Her hands shook. She couldn't do it again.

The woman took another step forward. Kyvo shot out of nowhere, latching onto the woman's forearm. Reyna's face twisted into a glare. She let go of one of her swords—the weapon vaporizing into nothing—before grabbing Kyvo, yanking him off, and tossing him like a rag doll. He hit the platform hard.

Redrinna winced, heart stuttering as the woman resumed her advance. There had to be something—

In less than a second, the woman had a sword to Redrinna's throat. She stiffened, the blade burning her skin.

Everybody froze.

"As I said," Reyna began, not even breathing hard, her eyes

gleaming like blades. "You are mine this time."

Redrinna shook her head, unable to speak or look away.

"You think you're so brave even though you're shaking like a leaf?" The woman smiled, but it was cold and humorless. "You've always been such a coward."

That stung.

Redrinna, please! She's not your friend!

Without warning, the woman went rigid. The sword at Redrinna's throat flickered before vanishing like a flame at the mercy of the wind.

"You will do no such thing," Tak hissed from behind the woman, "with my friend."

Reyna jerked back as Tak pulled his sword free, and Redrinna finally saw him. A glare twisted his face as he flicked her sword, which she now realized he still had. He nodded when their gazes met, a resolute fire burning bright in his eyes. Her friend...yes. Tak was her friend. He'd protected her from someone who wanted to hurt her, someone who'd proved more than once to not be her friend. Someone who wanted to destroy the things and people she loved and relished in the act of doing so.

She took a step back as Reyna's wound healed over with that disturbing crackling sound.

The woman got to her feet, swords reappearing.

"Watch out!" Redrinna cried.

With a snarl, Reyna swung at Tak, who barely ducked in time. The next second, she kicked him square in the chest. He stumbled before falling on his back, sword leaping out of his hand.

Redrinna's gaze flicked to the dragons, both of whom looked unsure of where to strike. Chatan and his warriors were stalking closer, but there was a hesitancy to their movements. Then her gaze went back to Reyna as the woman stepped closer.

Had they truly been friends, her and Reyna? All those years they'd spent together in the palace, had that been friendship? It'd sure felt like friendship. Or maybe Reyna had been manipulating her, tricking Redrinna into trusting her so she would've later been able to convince her to stay with Osiris?

Redrinna didn't know the answer to that question, and, in truth, she didn't know if she wanted it. However, holding onto their friendship—if it'd even been real—was like gripping the blade of a knife. Reyna would keep twisting it no matter how futile her efforts to endure the pain of holding on.

Not only was she hurting herself, but the longer she held on made it even more likely that the rest of her friends—her real friends, the people who cared for her and were kind, regardless of whether or not she deserved it—were going to suffer too.

"Now," Reyna said as she leveled her blade at Redrinna's throat. "It's time—"

"No." Redrinna stepped away from the sword before twisting forward and grabbing the woman's wrist, forcing the sword away from her neck. Timothon would've been proud since he was the one who'd bullied it into her. "I'm not going anywhere with you."

The woman grimaced, trying to twist out of her grip. "You little—"

Redrinna squeezed harder, refusing to let go. Reyna yanked hard, nearly pitching Redrinna off-balance. All at once, strength surged through her, through every finger and toe, strengthening her grip and allowing her to hold the woman fast.

Her memories with the woman flashed through her mind, but then all her memories with Xandrin, Timothon, Kyvo, Tak, and Astra eclipsed them. It should've been obvious long before now who cared about her and who wanted her for who she was, not what she could potentially give.

"I don't belong to you," Redrinna hissed. "I never have, and I never will. You don't deserve my loyalty—you earn it—and you lost it. You can go back and tell him that."

Reyna jerked her arm. Redrinna let go. The woman reeled back, and Redrinna took a deep breath. Then she kicked, a flash of flame striking the woman in the chest. The woman crashed on her behind, the flames on her clothes disappearing as a crackling rang out.

Reyna stared before her expression shifted to a murderous glare. "You rat!" Rearing an arm back, she threw a shadow orb at her.

Redrinna had a split second to register it flying at her face. Then an arrow rammed into it, sending them both spinning out of the air. She flinched as the arrow zipped by her ear. The orb hit the wood planks, crumbling like dust on impact.

"Okay, Princess, you and I are even now," Wicasa called. "I'm not saving your life anymore."

She glanced in his direction. Despite what he'd said, he still had his bow out and was drawing another arrow. A spark of amusement passed through her, but it died out as Redrinna returned her attention to Reyna.

A livid expression burned on the woman's face as she climbed back on her feet. She took a step forward. Without warning, the space between them erupted with a swirl of black shadow, the force of it making everyone stagger back.

Redrinna's heart stilled as an unsettlingly familiar mammoth of a man emerged from the shadows like he was rising from a lake. When he reached his full, imposing height, the shadows vanished and his weight settled on the planks. They groaned beneath him, making her heart shudder. The Dragon Slayer.

It shook its mangy head, its haphazard collection of furs eerie in the darkness. Xandrin hissed, rising a little taller.

The Dragon Slayer turned to him and waggled a finger. "No. Bad...dragon. Today...is not for...fighting."

Redrinna blinked. What?

The massive creature turned to Reyna. "That's...enough. Let's go."

She glanced back and forth between the two of them. Was this some sort of ruse?

After a minute, Reyna bowed her head, and the Dragon Slayer scooped her up like a broken doll. The swirl of shadows returned, sweeping them both away without a trace. The world seemed to go quiet, and then there was nothing but the wind rushing through the trees.

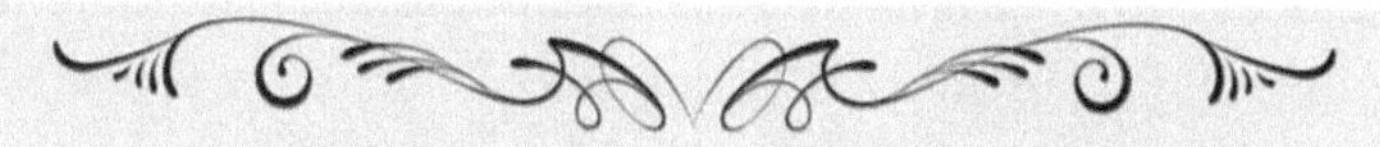

Chapter Twenty-Five

Redrinna remained still. Was it over now? For two seconds more, she just stared around the village, then Xandrin just about bowled her off the platforms. She stumbled before he caught her on his snout, lifting her off the ground.

"Sorry," he said quickly.

Resting her elbow on his snout, she grinned. "You're a big goof, you know that?"

He grinned too—at least, that was what it felt like he did—then set her down. "Now that they're gone, you should go to sleep." A bit sheepishly, he met her gaze. "I-if you can, I guess."

"I'll try."

"Yeah, let's all go to sleep for a change," Astra said, her chin resting on the railings, eyes threatening to close.

Tak stepped up, Redrinna's sword dangling from one hand as he cradled Kyvo in his free arm. He returned the sword, and she tucked it away, wondering who she could ask to teach her how to clean it later.

Xandrin glanced at them before yawning. "Night."

He and Astra disappeared below.

Redrinna smiled a bit. Then she turned, her heart skipping a beat at the sight of Kyvo. His head was up, but his ears were back, and he made no motion to leave Tak's arms. "Are you okay?"

He nodded, a thin smile curling his lips. "I'm fine. Just sore."

Her eyes narrowed, concern dampening the happiness dancing in her chest.

Then, Redrinna happened to glance up in time to see Takota practically sprinting towards them. She had just enough time to step clear of Tak so Kyvo wouldn't be bumped before the man tackled her in a bear hug. It lasted for all of two seconds, but she was tired and startled enough she ended up staring blankly at him.

"You little— I can't even—" Breaking off, he shook his head. "Do you have a habit of running into danger?"

She grimaced.

From down below, Xandrin called a quiet, "Yes."

Takota grinned, and she distinctly heard Wicasa snicker. Talutah smacked him.

"But I believe the better thing to say," Takota lightly—almost tenderly—put a hand on her head, an enormous grin on his face despite the dark circles under his eyes, "is thank you."

She shook her head. "I didn't do anything."

Holding up a finger, he said, "We found its nest because of you. And she's alive." His dark eyes glittered in the waning moonlight. "She's alive."

It was an incredible feeling; Redrinna had to admit it. Her heart seemed lighter than it had in a long time.

"Let's talk later though. You look like you're going to fall asleep on your feet." He gestured towards the clinic. "How 'bout it?"

"Okay," she said.

Nodding, he slipped past her and began herding her and Tak to the clinic. As she passed the warriors, Chatan shot her a smile—even Wicasa did. In response, she yawned so hard tears came to her eyes, which made the two of them laugh.

Soon, they were back in the clinic, and Redrinna was back in the room they were so kindly letting her stay in. She barely had enough energy to take off her boots and belt before collapsing on the bed, immediately falling asleep.

⁂

Tak carefully set Kyvo at the end of the bed as Takota left the room, shutting the door behind him. He had just enough energy to yank off his boots before crawling into the bed, more than ready to shut his eyes and fall asleep.

A minute or so after he settled in and found a comfortable space to lie, Kyvo shifted, letting out a whine as he did.

Tak propped himself up on his elbows, staring down at the little creature for a long minute. Kyvo had played it down in front of Redrinna, but he knew the kitsune was hurt. He should've mentioned something to Takota, but he was so exhausted, it'd slipped his mind. He wanted to do something for him, but...

All at once, something Kyvo had said popped into his mind: 'Healing magic is scary, but if you knew more about it, maybe it wouldn't be so scary.'

Tak didn't move for a minute as he stewed on that. Since that first time, he'd never touched his powers. He'd never even tried; instead, he'd kept them locked as tightly away as he could. Without even realizing it, he'd kept a piece of his mom locked away.

Very slowly, he stretched out a hand and lightly laid it on the kitsune's side. Closing his eyes, he searched inside himself, trying to summon something, to find that piece of himself he'd shut away. For a long moment, there was nothing. Then, all at once, there was. It was almost like a heartbeat or a flower's petals unfurling in the morning sun's first, tender rays. Somewhere deep inside him, it was as though someone had turned a key in a lock, undoing the barricade he'd spent years building around his powers.

A clean, white light flickered to life beneath his hand, a familiar coolness passing through him before vanishing. The light rippled once like water, passing over Kyvo before fading. Tak withdrew his hand. Even though the light had only been there for a few seconds, the room seemed darker than it had before.

He was a little more tired now, but otherwise he was fine. Not dizzy. Not sick and weak.

Maybe the magic wasn't completely bad after all. Smiling just a little, he laid down and closed his eyes.

⁘

Tak blinked awake, feeling like he'd barely closed his eyes. However, since the sun was up, shining its brightness into the room, he assumed he'd at least slept for a little while. Sitting up, he stifled a yawn as he absent-mindedly rubbed Kyvo's head. Kyvo crawled further up the bed, putting his head better within reach.

Nope. He was still tired.

Right as he made up his mind to go back to sleep, there came a knock on his door before Takota entered. The man grinned from ear to ear, though Tak struggled to keep his eyes open long enough to get a good look at him.

"Oh hey, look who's awake!" The man approached his bed, ruffling his hair.

Tak's head dipped under the pressure, and he nearly couldn't open his eyes. Perhaps he was more tired than he'd thought.

"Hmm, maybe that's an overstatement," Takota said, taking his hand away. "But it is noon, so you should get up and move, at least for a little bit."

Kyvo's head dropped back onto the sheets, and almost instantly, the kitsune was snoring again.

"I guess we can leave him there," Takota said before turning back to Tak. "So, Mister Rebel, how are your eyes?"

Tak blinked at him, having to stare for a good minute before his brain figured things out enough for him to speak. "It's...mostly clear."

"What a relief." The man grinned. "We don't need to wrap

them up anymore but be careful. You are still recovering, after all. Anyway, let's go. Someone desperately wants to see you."

"Me?"

With a nod, the man said, "Astra has been bugging me to come and wake you for hours. You can come back to bed afterwards, but since you're awake right now, come and see what she wants."

After a long minute of really not wanting to, Tak relented and followed the man out of the room. He yawned and rubbed his eyes, trying to convince them to stay open. They begrudgingly complied.

"You're too late for breakfast, but I'm sure we can find something for you."

Tak yawned again. "Where's Redrinna?"

"Hmm? Oh, she's still asleep. I thought about waking her too, but given how little she's been sleeping lately, I figured it was better for her to wake up whenever she was ready. And Xandrin's just as asleep, unlike Astra, so..." Takota trailed off as they stepped outside.

Tak winced in the sun, his eyes immediately snapping shut. For a long minute, he couldn't convince them to reopen, but they eventually relented. The first thing he noticed was the amount of people everywhere. The village seemed twice as full as it had when they'd first arrived, but he couldn't be sure since this was his first time really seeing it. It was a good deal noisier, at least.

"What's going on?" he asked as Takota led him through the crowd towards the stairs.

"Oh this?" The man gestured vaguely with one wing. "Since the beast is dead and we were able to explore the cave, we found the remains of everyone it'd taken. Granted, they're...too jumbled to tell whose bones are whose, but at least we'll be able to give them all a proper burial. So, everyone's preparing what we'll need. It looks a bit chaotic, I know, but don't worry. They know what they're doing."

Tak nodded, fighting his eyes still as Takota led him down the stairs.

Astra met them at the bottom, a slight smile on her face.

"Thanks for bringing him to me."

Takota grinned. "Anytime." Then he zipped back up the stairs and disappeared amongst the people there.

"Good morning, sleepy," Astra said. Then she smiled in an apologetic way. "I guess it's actually 'good afternoon' though."

Tak yawned in response.

"Okay, I know you're tired, but I'm going to go help them with their burial tomorrow, so I had to talk to you today."

"About what?"

She beckoned him to follow, grinning from vivid green ear frill to ear frill. He stumbled after her, rubbing his eyes again to try and convince them to stay open for a while longer.

"I made something for you," she said once they were in the shadow of their usual tree.

He noticed Xandrin was sleeping rather soundly in the shade of the village. That made the sleepiness worse. Shaking his head, Tak turned his attention back to Astra.

"I wanted to give it to you before, but it didn't work out. So, I'm going to give it to you now. Are you ready?" She picked up a thin, wrapped bundle from behind the base of the tree and handed it to him.

He tilted his head to the side as he took it. He was too tired to puzzle out what it was wrapped in, but as he pulled it away, his eyes went wide, finally cooperating.

Vibrant green scales rested in his hands. It took him an extra second to realize the scales made a shirt a lot like Redrinna's. Slowly, he held it up, trying to take it in. It seemed close to his size but maybe a little too big. Even still, it took his breath away.

Hesitantly, Tak looked at Astra, who watched him expectantly. "You made this...for me?"

She nodded so fast, her frill shook like a tree in an earthquake. "The red beast over there said dragons used to make these all the time for the humans they cared about, so of course I had to make one for you when I found out. You are, like, my most favorite person in the whole wide world."

Tak didn't know what to say. "But...but after..."

She smiled once again, looking the happiest he'd ever seen her. "What? Is it weird that I made you a shirt?"

"W-well, no..." Studying the shirt in his hands, he fingered the surprisingly smooth scales. "It's just...I'm not used to anyone doing something like this for me."

Her smile softened. "Then I'm happy to be the first."

He didn't know what to say to that either, but he found himself smiling too.

"Okay, that's all I needed to tell you, so you can go back to sleep now," she said. "You look like you didn't get a wink of it."

He waved before heading back to the clinic. With the amount of people around, he thought he might have to dodge a few wings or something, but there weren't any near accidents, and he returned to his room in one piece. Then, because he didn't want to try and crawl in around Kyvo, he settled at the bottom of the bed, and a few minutes later, Tak fell asleep with his new shirt in his arms.

⚬◞◟ ◞◟⚬

The next time Tak woke up, it was early morning again. Had he slept for an entire day?! Shaking his head, he pushed himself up, his gaze falling on the scale shirt Astra had given him. It had him smiling before he even realized it. This really, truly made him feel like he belonged here. That he wasn't just welcome; he was wanted.

He should wear it. As he went to change into it, he paused, frowning. Redrinna wore something underneath hers, and he didn't know the exact reason why, but he figured he ought to do the same. There was probably a good reason why she'd done so.

He could keep the tunic he always wore, but it was getting pretty raggedy, and he wasn't sure how it would hold up. However, it wasn't like he had anything else to wear.

Right as he thought that, Takota knocked and entered the room. "You live yet again," the man said with a hint of a smile.

"When do you sleep?" Tak found himself asking.

Takota laughed. "I sleep more often than you think. Nice shirt, by the way. Astra worked hard on it."

Tak blushed. The shirt was amazing.

"Are you going to wear it?"

"I want to," he began. "But Redrinna wears a shirt under hers."

Frowning, Takota said, "You're right, she does, doesn't she?"

"I would wear it over this," Tak pinched the collar of his tunic, "but...I'm not sure it'll work. A-and I don't have any other clothes, so what should I do?" He supposed he could try and convince Redrinna to go to a village to trade for new clothes or something, though that might be dangerous for her and the dragons.

"Actually, you know what?" Takota's face lit up. "I have an idea. Wait right there, I'll be just a minute." He whipped out of the room, leaving Tak alone.

Tak glanced at Kyvo, who was still fast asleep. Had he ever got up yesterday or had he been out the entire time too?

Shortly, Takota came back with something in his hands. He held it up. "Ta-da!" It was a plain shirt made of some kind of light brown leather. It seemed far too small for Takota to even attempt to fit into. "You can have this."

"What is it?" Tak asked as the man offered it to him.

"It's an old shirt of mine. I was planning on giving it to one of the other kids since I outgrew it, but I was always on the smaller side when I was little, and they're all too big for it already. I was at a loss for what to do with it, so you can have it."

Tak blinked. "A-are you sure?"

The man nodded, grinning from ear to ear. "Definitely."

"Thank you." Tak slowly took it, looking it over. It was similar to any other shirt he'd seen, but there was something quite different. It closed in the back with long threads weaving through the hems, presumably to tie it shut. There were also two openings cut into the back with more threading running to the back seams.

He stuck a hand through one. "Are these for your wings?"

"Yeah, but don't worry about that part. Now that I know you need it, I'll just sew them shut, then you'll just have to learn how to tie it shut."

"O-okay." Tak stared at it for a second longer before a grin touched his mouth. Having a place to belong was nice—so nice, he never wanted it to end. With any luck, it never would.

Takota took the shirt back and set to work pulling out the threading for the wing holes and using it to stitch them shut. They chatted for a while about how his injuries were doing before falling silent. Tak was content to watch Takota's needle flash in and out of the leather, steadily pulling the gaps closed. He and his aunt had used to spend nights in front the hearth fire just like this, and his chest ached at the memories. He longed for those days again, but, even still, this was nice in its own way, even if it wasn't the same.

When Takota was finished, he checked the mostly healed wound on Tak's side before teaching him how to tie the shirt closed on himself. Once it was on, the man checked to make sure he could move freely in it, making some adjustments as needed.

"Well, it's going to sit a bit tighter since I closed the holes, but it should still work fine. Luckily, you are smaller than I used to be." Takota inspected the shirt once before nodding, appearing quite pleased with his handiwork. "What do you think?"

The leather was smooth and cool against Tak's skin, and despite it being a bit tighter on the sides than his other shirt had been, he loved it. It even covered part of his neck.

There was a knock at the door and then Shappa entered. She blinked at the sight of him before a smile broke across her worn features. "I see you finally found a good home for it. Anyway, it's almost time for us to leave for the burials, so when you're finished, I need to see you, Takota."

"Sure," the guy said before turning back to Tak. "Okay, now let's see how it works with your new shirt."

Tak turned and picked up the green scale shirt, the scales clicking against each other like chimes as he did so. He tugged it on, having to fight a little bit to get it over his head. However, once it was on, it fit nicely. It went to his mid-thighs, and the sleeves were long enough they covered some of his palms. Other than that, it was a perfect fit.

"You look so cool!" Kyvo shouted from the bed.

Tak nearly left his skin behind before turning back. "Th-thanks."

The kitsune was sitting up now, tail wagging. Some errant patches of fur behind his ears stuck straight up in the air, reminding Tak of his own hair, which was probably extra wild given he'd only crawled out of bed a short while ago.

"You know what you need?" Shappa said, making him jump again since he thought she'd left. "A belt. Hold on."

Just how much were they going to give him?

A few minutes later, the woman returned with a belt in tow. It was similar to Redrinna's plain leather belt, but there was some quillwork around the buckle in red, yellow, white, and black. It was a small detail, but it was a nice touch.

"I was going to give this to Mika later, when he was a bit older, but I can make him a better one now that I'll hopefully have more time. And since you need one..." She helped him put it on, instructing him to wear it high on his waist to prevent the scale shirt from dragging him down.

She and Takota stepped back, admiring Tak's new attire like he was a work of art or something.

Then, beaming, Takota said, "Now you look like an official member of the Dragon Kin."

Warmth bubbled up in Tak's chest. Belonging was very nice indeed, like a fire on a cold winter's night.

Chapter Twenty-Six

Redrinna blinked awake, feeling alive for the first time in what seemed like months. She must've been utterly exhausted; she hadn't had a single nightmare. She hadn't even dreamt. Pushing herself upright, she stared around at the wood panels of the walls and floor of the room before realizing she was starving.

"Oh, you're finally awake," came a voice she was starting to know well.

Glancing up, she was pleasantly surprised to find Tak in the doorway. Then she did a double take. Instead of his regular clothes, he wore a green scale shirt. It was a bit big with the sleeves hanging low on his hands, but it seemed to fit him almost perfectly otherwise. Under it, he had on a leather shirt, and there was a belt around his waist with what appeared to be some of that quillwork she'd seen Shappa doing from time to time on the buckle.

"You look different," Redrinna began. Hastily, she added, "In a good way."

He blushed. "Astra made me this." He put a hand to his chest. Then he pointed at the leather undershirt and belt. "A-and Takota and Shappa gave me these. It was nice of them."

She couldn't help a small smile. "It makes you look official." Not to mention she was way more comfortable with the thought of him fighting now that he was much better protected.

"Thanks." He glanced away for a second. "So what do we do now?"

A frown touched Redrinna's mouth as she thought. "Well, the village is safe now, so the next thing to do would be to go get your gem and return to the Mount. But we'll need to make sure it's okay for us to travel." A bit self-consciously, she put a hand to her head. The cut was mostly gone, but her head was still sore.

Tak rubbed his own head with a rueful smile. Then he dropped his hand. "Oh, I just remembered something. Takota told me to tell you we're not allowed to leave until after the rest of the tribe comes back."

She raised an eyebrow. "The tribe isn't here?"

"Most of the tribe went to the demon's cave. They said they were giving the ones who didn't make it a proper burial, and the ceremony was going to last all of today and most of tomorrow. Astra went to help."

"Ah," she nodded a couple times before climbing out of the bed. Then, she remembered something else that made her heart stutter. "How's Kyvo? Is he okay?"

Tak glanced to the side, cheeks going pink. "Yeah. He's...doing great, actually."

The way he said that made her pause. Kyvo had been hurt enough the other day (whenever it was) he hadn't even been able to walk to the clinic. "Did you...?"

Blushing harder, Tak stared at the ground. "Just...a little."

Relief washed over her, making her smile.

"T-Takota and Chumani have food waiting for us, if you're hungry," he said hurriedly, stumbling in his haste to back out of the room.

"I'll be there in a minute," she called, smiling a little more as she glanced around for her boots. There was something different about him. So far, that was one of the longest conversations they'd ever had, but she supposed she knew why. If he'd felt completely worthless before, perhaps now he felt like he mattered. Something like that would change you.

Regardless of the true reason, Redrinna was glad that for the first time since they'd met, he seemed happy. Truly happy.

When she was ready, she went out in the hallway, stopping when she found Kyvo waiting there. He stared at her with a strange expression, one she didn't understand.

"What?"

He stared for a moment longer before grinning. "You look happy again." Without another word, he trotted out the door without a trace of injury. Tak's magic had worked wonders.

Even still, the kitsune's words gave her pause. Was she happy? Redrinna wasn't sure if that was the right word to describe her current emotions. Her heart still hung heavy in her chest, and she was terrified of Osiris and the road before them, but the burden on her shoulders wasn't as suffocating as it'd been before. For the first time in months, it felt like she could breathe.

As she thought that, warmth from her gem flickered through her chest, sudden enough it startled her from her thoughts. Subconsciously, she laid a hand on it.

"Why were you so quiet before?" she asked before she could stop herself.

I wasn't. You just couldn't seem to hear anything I said. I didn't know what to do.

She frowned. All this time, Redrinna had thought the gem had been ignoring her, but it had been the other way around. Just like with everyone else, she'd shut it out. What startled her the most, though, was that enclosing herself in a box had been easy. Walling herself off hadn't been hard; it'd been so simple, she hadn't even realized she'd done it.

"I'm...I'm so sorry." She winced. If she wasn't careful, she was going to spend the rest of her life constantly apologizing to someone.

I'm not offended. I'm simply relieved you seem to be doing better now.

Redrinna nodded before lowering her hand and heading towards the exit. She hoped she'd genuinely made a turn towards becoming better. Desperately, she wanted to get better—so she could stop hurting her friends, at least—but a part of her couldn't help but wonder if it was okay. After all that had happened in the Imperial City and to the people there, was it truly okay for her to be happy? Was it okay to move on?

In truth, she didn't know the answer to those questions, but she'd tried giving in to her misery, and it hadn't helped anyone. It'd almost added to the body count of this war.

So maybe, when she thought about it like that, it would be okay to let the pain go. She had the feeling—she wasn't entirely sure why—nobody would honestly be angry with her for making that choice.

Redrinna was so wrapped up in her thoughts she didn't see Takota until she slammed into him, sending herself stumbling back.

He was unmoved, but he glanced over in surprise. "Oh, hey, Your Highness. I didn't expect to see you yet, but it's nice nonetheless."

Blinking a couple times, she could only stare at him and his broad smile for a long minute. Then she noticed he had some sheets bundled in his arms. "What are you doing?"

He glanced down. "Oh this? Since the demon's spell is broken, there's a lot to clean up. But everybody else went to the burials for today and most of tomorrow, and since I'm staying here to keep an eye on Chumani, guess who gets to do all the cleaning?" He huffed, but he was still smiling.

She couldn't help a small smile in return. "I could help, if you'd like."

"I might take you up on that, but for now, you need to go eat. You slept for almost two whole days, you know." He took a step back, clearing the path between her and the door. "Go on. There's someone out there who's anxious to see you."

Her brow furrowed, and she quickly went to the door. Kyvo waited there for her, his tail wagging the second he saw her. Once she opened the door, he zipped out, bee-lining it for Tak who was being given some fry bread by—

Her heart stumbled.

Chumani glanced up, smiling the instant she saw her. "Hurry before they get cold," the woman called.

For a long moment, Redrinna just stared, unable to convince her feet to move. She'd almost forgotten what the woman looked like—the warm brown of her skin, the black of her hair, the way her skin crinkled around her eyes when she smiled.

As she stood there, Chumani said something to Tak before handing him the fry bread in her hands. Then she strode towards her.

Redrinna swallowed, finding herself taking a small step back. A hoard of butterflies unleashed themselves in her gut with such intensity, it took her breath away.

Then the woman was there, standing in front of her. "You look like you're staring at a ghost or something. Am I that scary?"

She shook her head. The woman did seem a little haggard, but definitely not ghostly.

Frowning, Chumani pointed a stern finger at her. "You are a reckless child. Takota told me you ran off after me and put yourself in a great deal of trouble and danger. That was irresponsible and care-less."

Redrinna's gaze fell.

The next second, Chumani gathered her into a hug, startling her. "But thank you for finding me."

Her vision misted over.

The woman pulled back, gently cupping Redrinna's face in her hands before her smile returned. "Now go eat. You won't be able to do a thing for your friends if you don't take care of yourself. As for me, I'm going to help my love." She turned and entered the clinic.

Redrinna stared after her for a second before getting herself back together and heading over to the others.

With a hint of a smile, Tak lifted his stack of fry bread. "Hungry?"

That almost made her laugh.

"I am!" Xandrin's head shot up from down below, making all three of them jump.

Some of the fry breads slipped off the stack in Tak's hands. He caught one and Redrinna snagged another. Kyvo snatched one with his teeth. The fourth one hit the ground with a quiet flop. They all stared at it for a minute before Redrinna looked at the dragon, who stared at her with wide eyes.

"That one's yours," she said, pointing at it.

Meekly, he stretched forward and scooped it up with his tongue before he withdrew. She couldn't help grinning as she headed down the stairs, the other two following after. They sat with Xandrin and immediately tucked into the food.

The food was good—so good, eating it almost made Redrinna want to be even hungrier so she could have more. It'd been so long since she'd felt like this, and for the first time in what seemed like ages, she wanted to sit with others, simply eating and chatting, enjoying the feeling of being almost normal again.

As she sat there, listening to Xandrin and Kyvo's excited conversations, it really sunk in that instead of protecting her friends, she'd been shoving them all away so she couldn't get hurt again.

That hadn't been protecting anybody. She'd only been protecting herself, which had almost cost her more than she'd lost before.

For the first time since she'd gone back to the Imperial City, it occurred to her that losing everything—her home, her family, any sense of normalcy—had taught her something after all: what she had now was arguably next to nothing. She had no money and no possessions beyond what was on her person. However, she was still alive. She had her freedom and her friends. Back in the palace, she'd never had friends, so it was still strange to her, but in a good way. With them by her side, she didn't need anything else. This... They were all she needed.

On that note, there was another apology she needed to give.

Taking a deep breath, Redrinna got to her feet. "Hey Xandrin?"

His ear frills shot up, and he looked so startled and guilty she nearly laughed.

"Can I talk to you for a minute?"

"Oh, sure." Rising to his feet, he followed her to the other side of the village, where she didn't have to worry about the others listening in.

Steeling herself, she met his big, concerned eyes, not at all surprised to find that there instead of anger. Shame planted itself in her gut. "You...aren't upset at all are you?"

"Not right now," he said, tilting his head slightly to the side. "But I was. A few times, actually. At you. Then, I'd get mad at myself for getting mad at you because you were already upset and I didn't want to make it worse, but any time we were together, we ended up arguing and..." Trailing off, he shrugged, making his wings flap a little.

It took her a minute to find what she wanted to say next. "I'm sorry, Xandrin. For just about everything, I think."

He lowered his head. "It's because of what happened when we went back to the city, isn't it? And what happened on the cliff side."

"I didn't want to risk losing you again," she said, unable to look up. "I was so scared, and I thought if only I had to struggle or get hurt, then nobody else would."

He sighed, his breath stirring her hair. "I know. I don't want that either. I never want to risk putting you in a position like that again. I never, ever want to let you down again."

She met his gaze. "You've never let me down." Before she even realized it, she was stretching her hands towards him.

In less than a heartbeat, he pressed his snout against her palms.

"I'm sorry I let you believe that."

His eyes closed for a long moment before he met her gaze again, this time, with a much more serious expression. "Promise me we won't do this again."

"Do what?"

"The avoiding each other and not being honest. And all the fighting. No more. I don't like it."

That almost made her smile. "You could say that again."

"The avoiding each other and not being honest. And all the fighting. No more. I don't like it."

Redrinna paused, staring at him. He stared back with the most earnest, innocent expression on his face. She couldn't help it; she burst out laughing.

"What?" A hint of a smile appeared on his face.

"It's just an expression," she explained. "You're not really supposed to say it again."

"Oh." He stared for a moment longer before shrugging, an actual grin appearing on his face.

A pang shot through her heart. When had she last seen him smile like that? "Xandrin?"

"Hmm?"

"I promise I'm going to do right by you from now on. I'm going to protect you guys for real." She wasn't sure how well she would do, but she was going to do her best. "I just might need some help."

With a grin, he said, "You can count on me."

⁂

The next morning, Redrinna woke before the sun but not enough before it to be annoyed. She was early enough that when she went outside, the sky was still mostly dark, just brushed with light on the horizon, a thin strip of pale sky framing the dark mountain peaks.

For some reason, she found herself watching the light of the morning sun blooming across the sky, content to stay there, drinking in the smell of rain hanging in the air as beads of moisture trickled off the wooden railings and platforms. It felt like it'd been years since Redrinna had been at ease watching the sun rise. It was a simple thing, a sunrise, yet she'd missed it.

She stood there a while longer, watching thin sunbeams of light lance through the heavens as the first bit of the sun crested the mountains. She should go check on the others now. It was unlikely anyone was awake, but she didn't mind waiting.

Right as she turned to do so, someone said, "So here you are."

Chumani stood in the doorway of the clinic, a basket tucked under one arm. She seemed so much smaller without her wings, but she still had a presence. Redrinna blinked in surprise, at a loss for what to say.

"Couldn't sleep?" the woman asked with a slight smile as she approached.

Redrinna shook her head. "I slept okay, but I woke up early, I guess. Are you going to gather herbs again?"

Chumani nodded. "We're still low, but since the demon is gone, I can go wherever I like." She paused for a second before turning her warm gaze to Redrinna. "Do you want to come with me? I'd feel better if you did."

Redrinna had to fight to keep a grimace off her face. "But your injuries."

"They're fine," the woman said. "They'll heal faster if I move around a bit, so long as I'm careful. So, do you want to help me or not?"

Despite her reservations, Redrinna relented, understanding the need to do something, and followed the woman down the stairs and into the woods. Birdsong accompanied them as they walked, the brush and trees rustling faintly in the cool breeze.

Chumani paused for a minute, glancing at the light blue sky.

"It's a lovely morning, isn't it?"

Redrinna nodded, and they walked on. A short time later, they came to a narrow meadow with little white and yellow flowers blooming everywhere. They almost looked like little daisies perched on tall, ferny stalks, but she wasn't sure they were actually daisies.

Chumani's face lit up as she stared at the field, at least an acre of the delicate flowers dipping in the breeze. "Chamomile. Not only great for medicine, but also a sure sign summer is finally here. Help me fill the basket?"

Redrinna hesitated for a minute, watching the woman pull out a knife and slice off a stalk near the ground before crouching and drawing her own knife. She stared at the cool grey metal for a moment. The last time she'd used this, it'd been a weapon. Today, it was merely a gardening tool. It'd never occurred to her a weapon could do anything more than cause pain.

"Don't take every plant," Chumani instructed before she could even begin. "We have to make sure we leave enough for them to keep growing."

With a nod, Redrinna set to work. They worked in silence, quickly filling the basket to nearly overflowing. As she set her final stalk in, Chumani grinned and hefted the basket, making the heads of the flowers bob.

"This is amazing," the woman said with an enormous grin. "We'll be able to replenish the stores so much with this."

That got her to smile too. At least she'd been somewhat helpful. Perhaps this would help pay them back for their kindness, even if only a little.

"I've missed this hobby of mine," Chumani murmured as she gazed across the meadow.

"Hobby?"

"Yep. I've always enjoyed going outside and working with the earth. Now that the forest is safe again, we can garden and do what we used to. Takota said being able to gather herbs might help us all heal faster anyway. Having something to do—a purpose—chases away a lot of pain."

The woman's smile was so bright, Redrinna found herself smiling too. However, a tiny voice in the back of her mind worried whether or not Chumani was putting on an act to convince everyone she was okay. At the same time, the woman did seem to be acting like her usual self, so maybe she really was doing okay.

A short time later, they returned to the village, and everyone was awake except for Kyvo and Xandrin. Redrinna was a little surprised to see Tak and Takota attempting to get the cooking fire started.

"Good morning," Takota called without lifting his head.

Chumani grinned. "Hello you two. Are you going to be able to light the fire today?"

The man waved a hand before straightening, a triumphant light in his eyes. "Perfect. Now we can make breakfast."

Redrinna helped the woman take their basket into the clinic before helping make breakfast. When it was ready, they sat down to a meal of a berry soup she'd never had anything quite like before, and it tasted nicer than she'd expected. Once again, Redrinna found herself marveling at the feeling of being hungry, hungry enough to eat her portion completely.

After they finished eating, they passed the time by sitting and talking. Well, it was mostly Redrinna and Tak listening to Takota and Chumani talk. The rest of the tribe wouldn't be back until the evening, and they were going to relax until it was time to make enough food for everyone once they returned.

After a while, Takota and Chumani left, so she and Tak went to join Xandrin and Kyvo—who were both asleep.

Redrinna couldn't help smiling at her ever-sleepy friends. Then she noticed Tak watching her with those startling green eyes of his that she'd kind of missed. "It was nice here in the end, wasn't it?"

He nodded.

"I wonder where we'll end up next though."

"Or how much more danger we're going to get in?" Tak added, looking deadly serious for two seconds before the corner of his mouth quirked upwards.

She almost laughed, but the mirth of the moment soon faded. Were more people going to get hurt because of her? How many?

All at once, that soldier who'd protected her at the trial all those months ago flashed through her mind. Captain Brion's face came right behind it. Then Xandrin's.

"You know," Redrinna began, her voice soft like the wind stirring the trees, "all my life, there's been someone protecting me. No matter where I've gone, there are other people and creatures willing to get hurt so I don't. Even here, despite the demon and the bad blood between us, the tribe was willing to use precious herbs and resources to help us. Even you were trying to watch out for me."

Tak lowered his gaze, almost like he was embarrassed.

"I was going about it the wrong way before, but I still want to fight with the rest of you and protect you guys like you protect me. If I could keep everybody out of this, I would, though, I think that would make you all mad." Her gaze rose to the bits of sky peeking out from behind the platforms, bridges, and trees above. "I am not weak and helpless, and I don't want to keep hiding and running. So let's make a promise."

"A promise?" Tak tilted his head to the side. "Between you and me?"

"That's right. Both of us have lived through crappy things, and just because we're fine right now doesn't mean those things won't ever bother us again." After all, she'd thought she was fine after losing her mother before being proved very wrong. "When it gets hard, we should have a hobby to do. It doesn't have to be the same one, but we have to promise each other we'll find a hobby. Promise?" She held up her pinky.

He blinked. "I thought you were going to say we had to be honest with each other from now on."

That almost made her laugh. "I thought about it, but...I think there might be some things we shouldn't feel forced to share before we're ready. There might also be things we're never ready to talk about, so I don't want you or me to feel pressured to share things we're not ready to. So, finding hobbies seems like a good place to start."

Tak stared at her hand for a second before nodding and locking his pinky with hers. "I promise."

"That said..." Redrinna began, hesitating for a moment before continuing. "Tak, if there ever is something you need to tell somebody, or if there's ever even...just something you want to complain about, you can come to me. Anything at all. Okay?"

He slowly nodded, a peculiar look on his face that she couldn't quite place.

She made to turn back to the forest, but he abruptly inhaled, making her freeze. Despite that, he didn't speak right away. She stared, watching the debate in his eyes.

"Then I... Regarding things we're not ready to share, there's something else I have." Tak frowned, brow all furrowed.

"You don't have to tell me."

"I won't, not yet. At the same time, if I don't tell you a little bit, then it feels like I'm still lying to you. And I just...I want there to be someone else who knows so it's not just me." After a moment longer, the conflict on his face disappeared and he met her gaze, his green eyes clear like the ocean on a calm day. "I just want you to know that Tak...isn't my real name."

Redrinna's eyes went wide.

"It was a nickname from my uncle. I don't know why he started calling me it, but in a way, it fit easier than my real name. The name my mom gave me...has this legacy and weight to it, and even now— but especially when I was growing up—it seemed to come with a lot of expectations, and I just...couldn't do it. I still can't."

She nodded. That explained why he had such a strange name, and as curious as she was now, she was going to respect his choice and not ask about it.

"But someday," he continued, a hint of a smile on his face, "I want you to know what it is."

"I look forward to it." She couldn't help a smile of her own.

"But hey," Tak said, quieter now. "Can I ask you something?"

"Sure."

"When you were fighting Reyna, for a minute or two, you were glowing."

"Glowing?"

"Yeah, you started glowing red. It was cool, but I don't know what was going on. Do you?"

Redrinna stared at him in disbelief, but he was so earnest she didn't think he was lying. Even still, she'd been glowing and hadn't even noticed?

"Maybe it was something to do with the gem?" she suggested with a shrug. "I'm not sure, but I can ask it later."

They lapsed into a soothing silence, listening to the birds, the wind in the trees, and Xandrin snoring for a while. Even if this ended up being only a brief moment in time, it was wonderful. Redrinna closed her eyes to soak it in.

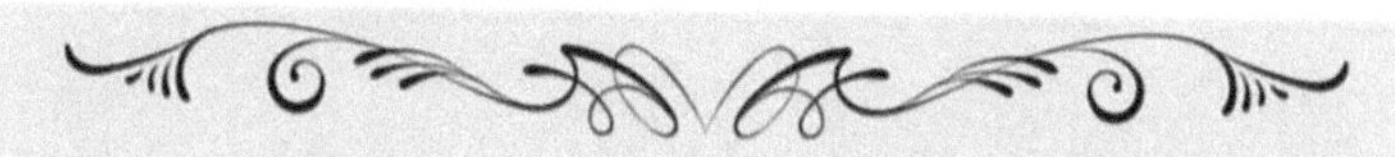

Chapter Twenty-Seven

By the time the sun was starting to set, they almost had dinner completely ready. Redrinna's pants were splattered with flour from her attempt to help Chumani make fry bread, but it'd been a lot more fun than she'd expected despite the mess.

A short time later, the rest of the tribe began returning. Mika was the first one to touch down, and he charged Redrinna at a full sprint when her back was turned. He bowled into her, nearly knocking her and the stack of fry bread in her hands to the ground.

"Mika, don't tackle her! She's still recovering, remember?" Ohanzi quipped before he'd even landed on the platforms.

"Sorry, Your Highness," Mika said, talking fast. "But I'm so happy to see you!"

She smiled. "I'm glad to see you too."

He grinned before letting her go and taking off as more people landed on the platform.

Her heart leapt in her chest as Kangee landed, sweeping his massive wings in without even brushing a feather against the ground. He met her gaze, a small smile touching his normally impassive face.

Before she could move, someone landed with a loud thump next to her, nearly scaring her right off the platform.

To her annoyance, it was Wicasa.

He leaned forward, sniffing the fry breads in her hands with a suspicious air. "Did you make these?"

"With Chumani's help," Redrinna explained, unsure if she should humor him or run away.

He made a noise of surprise, but it almost sounded sarcastic. As she narrowed her eyes at him, he lifted one from her stack and took a bite.

"Hey!"

"Not bad, not bad," he mused, flipping the bread over a couple times. "Not as good as Chumani's though."

"I know," she admitted, her shoulders drooping a couple inches. "Hers are so good."

He laughed.

She scowled in response.

"They are still pretty good though." He took another bite. "Yep. Probably have to have at least two." Without another word, he snatched another one off her stack and left, deftly dodging Chatan's accusing glare.

She rolled her eyes. At least he didn't seem to hate her anymore, she supposed.

As Redrinna turned to continue about her business, she noticed a painfully thin man whose appearance was strikingly like Mika's staring at her, his reddish-brown wings pulled tight to his back. He was Mika's father; she was almost positive. She remembered Mika saying he didn't like her, so she nodded his direction and once again turned to assist Chumani.

All at once, someone cleared their throat behind her. Nearly jumping out of her skin again, she turned, rendered speechless at the sight of Mika's dad right behind her.

"You..." he began, breaking off and rubbing the back of his neck. He lowered his hand and stared at her through narrowed eyes. "Are you really the Imperial Princess?"

She winced. "Well, not technically anymore." She almost explained, but she didn't want to explain that still. "But I was. Once."

He slowly nodded before extending his hand.

After a moment of staring and not knowing what to do, Redrinna shifted the fry bread to one hand so she could take his.

He clasped it briefly, letting go just as fast. "Th-thank you. For saving my son."

She wasn't sure what to say, so she just nodded. He left then, hunting down the rambunctious Mika, but for some reason, she found herself smiling. It was a small smile, but a smile nonetheless.

✿❧ ☙✿

The village settled down for the night quickly, almost as though everyone was simply exhausted. Yet Tak found himself jerking awake, completely alert. For a minute, he lay perfectly still, then a sigh rushed out of him. The dream was back.

He swiped at the tears that always seemed to come with it. "I'm coming, " he whispered. "Can't you give me a break?"

Takota had said his and Redrinna's injuries were nearly healed enough for them to travel, and within a matter of days, they would be continuing on their way. Tak understood they couldn't stay here forever, not even long enough to see these people return to normalcy, but it still left him a tad melancholy. However, there were things they had to do, otherwise things would get a lot worse than a couple demons running loose and wreaking havoc.

His gem was out there, waiting for him, a dreary reminder they had to go, but for the first time, the thought of obtaining the gem didn't scare him. Tak wasn't sure if he was entirely thrilled about getting it—well, more what getting it meant—but there was some part of him that finally felt ready. It was like he'd been trapped in a dingy, run-down house and was taking his first step into fresh air and sunlight. He was alive. Real. Wanted.

Tak doubted he'd be able to fall back asleep, but he settled into his pillow and closed his eyes anyway. Sleep danced on the fringes of his mind, but for the first time in his life, it seemed, he relaxed, not a worry passing through his mind. No guilt from the tragic circumstances that had deprived him of his mother. No despair from watching the suffering of the two people he'd loved most in the entire world. No self-hatred at things people had blamed him for that had been beyond his control. Blissfully, almost like it was a dream, there was nothing but peace.

Right as he was drifting off, he could've sworn he felt someone stroke his hair. He managed to open one eye—for just a moment—but no one was there. Then, for the first time since the gem had begun calling for him, Tak fell back asleep.

⚬⚮⚬ ⚮⚬⚮

Redrinna bolted awake, mind reeling from a vivid nightmare. Terror pounded in her veins, making it hard to take a deep breath, but, almost immediately, her gem pulsed with warmth. She touched a hand to it, closing her eyes and focusing on breathing. As she did, her fingers found their way to her mother's necklace, tracing the familiar pattern and stones, something she hadn't done for a long time.

She'd been hoping the dreams would go away, but it seemed like they were going to stick around for a while yet. Perhaps she'd been imagining it, though, but that nightmare hadn't seemed as intense as usual. So, maybe they would eventually go away and leave her be.

However, for now, Redrinna doubted she'd be able to get back to sleep—and a quick glance out the bedside window told her it was morning anyway—so she got up and left the clinic.

Nobody else had risen yet, but she didn't mind. While she didn't miss the reason she'd scaled the mountainside at horrendously early hours, she did miss the crispness of the cool morning air and the calming, pale blue of the sky as it woke. She'd missed listening to the first, tentative notes of the birds too.

It's a beautiful morning, isn't it? her gem asked, voice gentle.

She nodded, stopping at the railing and gazing out over the ocean of trees that eventually gave way to the sea. As she stared at the distant waves, her mind returned to a couple days ago, to the demon's cave and then to Reyna. Her heart still couldn't seem to decide whether to be depressed or angry, but she knew without a doubt now that those old feelings couldn't be allowed to make her hesitate and let one of her friends—one of her real friends—get hurt. Perhaps someday she would be able to reconcile with these feelings and come to terms with the end of their friendship, but that day wasn't today.

Redrinna didn't want to think about that though, so she pushed the thoughts aside. Instantly, a new one popped into her head: Tak said she'd glowed while fighting Reyna. The only moment she could figure was when she'd grabbed the woman's wrist and, with a strength that hadn't been her own, held on. The only possible explanation she could think of was her gem. Was it one of its abilities?

What's on your mind?

How did it always seem to know when she was thinking about something? Was she that easy to read?

"Tak said while I was fighting Reyna, I started glowing. Was that you?"

Yes, it was. I'm not entirely sure how it happens, per se, but it was my power.

She tilted her head to the side as she considered that. "What do you mean?"

I know how to make it happen, but at the same time I don't, if that makes sense. Basically, during that fight, you and I were completely united in purpose, almost as if we became one soul. My power and yours were inseparable.

"Aren't we already united in purpose though?"

Yes, but... It paused. *Maybe a better way to put it is we were united in very thought and desire. That's why we were able to connect like that.*

United in very thought?

After a moment, she knew what she'd been thinking. "I wanted to protect my friends," she breathed at the same second as her gem.

After a minute, Redrinna nodded. So that was what had happened. For some reason, it made her smile.

A familiar prickle unexpectedly raced up her spine, and after a moment's hesitation, she glanced behind her. The bison spirit stood there, its coat almost radiating a golden hue in the morning light.

"You're back," she said.

It moved a couple steps closer, its hooves soundless against the wood. "I am. I'm here to thank you. You fulfilled my request, and life here will be much easier as a result."

She smiled a bit ruefully. "Thanks, but they did most of the work. I just helped them find it."

"Which was no simple task, otherwise I wouldn't have asked for your aid," the bison said, its words mean but its voice kind. "I already knew they were strong. They simply needed a hand. So you have my thanks for doing something I was unable to."

Redrinna almost reached out to stroke its head or something of the like, but she kept herself in check. "I'm sorry you weren't able to help them, but can I ask you a question?"

It stared at her with its unblinking, golden eyes. "Yes?"

"Why did you come to me? Isn't it strange for you to come to me instead of your own people?"

"Yes. In truth, it wasn't what I wanted. Once, I walked this land with these people. We lived together. But after the destruction visited upon them, not only was I left weak, but many of them lost faith in their beliefs and customs—those who were even allowed to continue to believe—and as a result, they cannot see me now. However, for some reason, it is easy to appear to you. I am not overly concerned with why, but it is strange that it is." It shook its head like it was shooing a bothersome fly. "But it is fine now. As they grow stronger, so shall I. In time, I will be able to return to my duties, and I believe one day, my people and I will walk together again."

She smiled. "I would love to see it."

"Until then, I expect you to continue to do your part to watch out for them. They need you still, for now."

Her smile morphed into a grimace. "Need me? I didn't kill that demon, you know."

It snorted, and she got the distinct impression it was laughing at her. "You underestimate the power of knowledge and hope, young one. Greatly. But at least you are honest and brave."

Did these spirits get a kick out of making fun of her or something?

"I bear a gift for you, something you will need in the days ahead."

A gift? Redrinna shook her head. "I don't need anything."

It shook its head in return. "You may say that, but you did me a favor, and that requires payment. Allow me to bestow this gift upon you."

The spirit lowered its head, stretching forward with its nose. It took her a second to realize it wanted her to offer her hand. She relented and extended her right hand, palm up, unsure if that was what it wanted.

The spirit drew a long, deep breath before exhaling sharply. When its breath struck her skin, a cool burning hit her palm before shooting up her arm. It spread like fire through her entire body—not uncomfortable but not exactly pleasant either—before returning to her palm.

The spirit vanished, startling Redrinna at the suddenness. It'd left abruptly, but perhaps giving her...whatever it had given her had been exhausting for it. Or maybe that was just how it was. Matte was similar, in a sense.

Shaking herself, she pulled down her cast as far as she could and glanced at her palm, one eyebrow lifting. Nestled there, looking completely natural as though she'd been born with it, was a mark in the shape of the sun. It was a perfect circle with eight triangles around it, all pointing outwards like sunbeams. The spirit said it'd given her a gift, but what in the world was this? And what was she supposed to do with it?

Redrinna blinked at her strangely marked palm before pushing her cast back into place and turning to gaze at the world once more. With any luck, she would find out what this mark meant and why the spirit had given it to her soon.

"Oh," Chumani said from the doorway of the clinic, nearly scaring Redrinna witless. "Sorry, Your Highness. I didn't realize anybody else would be awake quite yet."

Redrinna stared for a solid minute before shaking her head. "No, no, it's okay. I was just...distracted. Why are you awake?"

"I expect it's the same reason as you."

Nightmares? Redrinna didn't say it, but the look on Chumani's face confirmed it.

The woman hefted her herb-gathering basket. "Since you're awake, you wanna come with me again?"

She was smiling before she even realized it.

"After all, you guys are leaving soon, aren't you? This might be our last chance to do this...for the rest of our lives."

That smile vanished. "The rest of our lives?"

Chumani nodded as she led the way down the stairs. "Well, after this, we're going to move on to other things, aren't we? I'm going to get married soon, and my responsibilities will change. Eventually, Takota and I will probably have children, and I'll have more duties in the clinic as I learn more. As for you, you'll be out on the frontlines in this war, and once it ends, you'll be off leading the Empire or something, won't you?"

Redrinna blinked. "I...don't know."

She was so caught up in the magnitude of what was happening now and the problems looming on the horizon that she couldn't imagine life beyond it. Not yet. But for just a moment, she could. After everything was over, if they managed to defeat Osiris and put this entire war to rest, what would she be doing? Ruling the Empire? She shuddered at the thought.

Even still, for the first time, she had a twinge of doubt over her decision to turn her back on that part of her life. She hadn't done much here, but this was the first time she could remember somebody who knew who she was—beyond Captain Brion or her parents—treating her with kindness. They'd been understandably wary at first, but now, being here with them, Redrinna felt human.

Being an Empress would also give her the ability to help these people in a way she wouldn't be able to otherwise.

However, it was naïve to think the rest of the continent would react the same as this tribe, regardless of whether she did something amazing or disastrous in the days ahead.

The sun had risen completely by the time they'd filled the basket with today's herb: feverfew leaves. The village was much more awake when they returned, and there was a different air to it now, like the sun had finally returned to the sky after a long, tempestuous night.

Instead of heading back up to the heart of the village, Redrinna went over to the dragons. Astra was awake, but as she'd expected, Xandrin was not.

Astra glanced at him. "Do you want me to wake up the red beast?"

Redrinna shook her head. Why was she calling him the 'red beast' anyway? "No, you can pass on the message when he wakes up since Shappa wanted to see me. I wanted to tell you I'm planning on leaving tomorrow, if that's okay."

A sadness crept over Astra's face. "I guess we can't stay here forever, huh?"

"It'd be nice though, wouldn't it?" Redrinna said with a bit of a smile.

"In some ways," the dragon replied before she smiled too. "You best get going. I'll make sure the red beast knows."

With a nod, Redrinna ascended to the village above. Several people waved to her as she made her way back to the clinic, and she honestly didn't know what to do with that. Being accepted here...was bizarre.

Once inside the clinic, Redrinna spent several minutes hunting for Shappa, weirded out by all the empty rooms, but in a good way. Eventually, she found the woman in the back room, where they stored the bulk of their medicinal herbs and things of that nature, her back to the door.

Even though Redrinna didn't make a sound, the woman said, "You wait right there, young lady. I'm almost finished."

She did so, and a few minutes later, the woman turned, pushing an errant, greying strand of hair off her brow. "Let's check that wrist of yours."

Nodding, Redrinna entered.

A minute or so later, Shappa had the bandage on her wrist unraveled. Carefully, she turned Redrinna's wrist this way and that, feeling along the bone.

"Does it hurt at all?"

"No," she said, relieved and discouraged at the same time.

"Then I see no point in bandaging it any further." Shappa sighed, gathering the discarded bandages. "Well, at least I won't have to worry about you so much anymore."

"Huh?" The sound burst out of Redrinna's mouth before she could stop it.

"I distinctly recall you not liking this healing ability of yours," the woman continued, staring her down with those sharp, golden eyes of hers, "but I'm not going to lie. It's a relief. For me at least. You and your friends are leaving soon, aren't you?"

"Tomorrow," she said. "Most likely."

"I won't be following you around to keep patching you up, but if you get hurt, you're going to recover quickly, and that's a relief."

Redrinna blinked. She'd never thought of it that way, but it almost made it seem like this weird ability of hers could be something good.

"Now scat. I've got work to do." Shappa's words sounded mean, but Redrinna caught the woman hiding a smile.

For some reason, that made her smile too.

Chapter Twenty-Eight

The next day dawned bright and clear. Redrinna was up early again, but, for once, not due to a nightmare. Rather, it was her own free will. She had nothing to gather, so getting ready to depart was a simple process. The thing that was going to take the longest was getting Xandrin awake enough to fly. Fortunately, to her amusement, Astra was already working on that, jabbing him in the side with a sharp claw no matter how much he tried to scoot away.

To her surprise, quite a bit of the village was already awake and seemingly waiting for them. Redrinna, Tak, and Kyvo shared a glance before facing the small crowd.

"Here," Chumani said, approaching them first, holding a small basket filled with fry bread. "So you don't get hungry."

Redrinna accepted it with a small nod. "But how do we give you back your basket?"

"You can return it the next time you come," Takota said with a grin.

The next time they... She dipped her head for a minute. These people. She couldn't resist a tiny smile.

Mika bounced up next, holding something out. "Here! I made this for you."

Redrinna gave the basket to Tak so she could take the thing

from him. After a second, she realized it was a lumpy, bison-shaped pendant made of quills dyed white, red, black, and yellow. "What is this?"

"It's a gift!" Mika said that like it should've been obvious. "I made it with my dad's help. My mom was better at it, but I'm going to keep practicing, and next time we meet, I'll give you a better one. Promise?"

Next time again? She smiled a little more. "Promise."

Beaming, he turned and raced back to his dad and Ohanzi.

The village chief then stepped forward. "We wish you well on your journey."

"Thank you," she said. "And...and if anything happens like that demon again—I don't want you to leave your homes, but you could always...you could come and find me. Find us, I mean."

He smiled, his sun-worn skin crinkling like paper. "Hopefully the next time we meet, it will be under better circumstances than that. And should you need our help, you may call on us. I'm not sure how much help we will be able to offer, but for you, we would do what we could."

"You would?" The question she actually wanted to ask was why, but she thought that might have been rude.

"Our tribe will not bow to foreign royalty, not with fealty, but you," he paused for a moment, and the wind tugged at his feathers. "You are well on your way to becoming a leader I would respect."

Redrinna's mouth popped open a bit. What...had he just said? Had she heard him right?

The last people to step forward were Chatan and the warriors, Kangee, Wicasa, and Talutah. They grinned at each other before Chatan said, "You know, even though we're not supposed to speak our tribe's language, I do know it. Interestingly enough, there isn't a word for goodbye. And even though your language has one, I'm not going to use it. Because when this is over, we should meet again, whether in this life or the next."

"Agreed," she said.

"Until next we meet," he said.

Kangee dipped his head, not smiling, but not looking completely stoic either. Talutah waved with two fingers. Wicasa winked, and then the four of them took a step back.

She nodded, and then they turned to go. A minute later, Redrinna was situated on Xandrin's neck with Kyvo in one arm while Tak perched with the basket between Astra's shoulder blades. They waved to the village one final time—Takota shouted a few last-minute instructions about caring for their injuries—before the dragons lifted into the air. Within a few minutes, the village vanished amongst the green of the trees.

Would they ever see each other again? Redrinna couldn't help wondering, a part of her doubting but the rest of her hoping. Only time would tell, but she would look forward to that day, whether or not it came.

⋘ ❦ ❦ ⋙

In a time that seemed too short, the beach beneath them shifted to the one Tak recognized. He spied his old village a short way off in the distance, almost too close for comfort, but Astra and Xandrin landed far enough from it to put him at ease. Maybe somebody would notice them here, but they were too far away for anybody to realize they were staring at him.

The pale blue of the ocean stretched out for miles in front of him, the white tips of the waves catching the dazzling light of the sun and making them glimmer. He'd missed this. It was one of the few things he missed, but it was one of the ones he missed the most.

The instant his feet touched the beach, Tak knew his gem was nearby. He hadn't doubted Redrinna, but he knew for a fact now.

"Are you ready?" Redrinna asked him, concern scrunching up her face.

He nodded and turned to face the sea. After taking a deep

breath, he stepped into the cold waters. The water was colder than he remembered, but it wasn't as frigid as it could've been.

When the water was up to his waist, Tak noticed something swimming towards him and stopped. It was probably that enormous spirit who had shown up when Redrinna had gotten her gem. Even though he'd had the dream, a hoard of butterflies launched into his stomach. What if the gem had changed its mind and the spirit attacked him?

The spirit broke the water's surface, sending water raining down around him like he'd gotten caught in a wayward thunderstorm. Shaking water off his face, Tak pushed his drenched hair out of his eyes. The spirit stared at him with its enormous eyes, the lack of emotion on its face increasing his nerves.

After a long minute, the spirit extended a claw. "Yes, a gem has requested you. It has been waiting for some time." Its gaze turned to something behind him, and after a second the spirit acquired something that resembled a smile.

Tak followed the spirit's gaze, a part of him not surprised to realize it had looked at Redrinna. Then he faced forward and took hold of the proffered claw with both hands. A second later, he was under the water, being pulled deeper and deeper in mere seconds. The world beneath the waves was completely different than the one he knew. Everything was more muted, more blue, but there was a beauty to it too. He wished he had more time to take it all in and commit it to memory, but all too soon, the spirit stopped in front of an underwater cave.

"It waits inside," the spirit said.

He nodded and then was lowered into the cave by the spirit. It really was just like Redrinna had said in here. Nine gems rested around the space, their myriad of colors reflecting against the rough walls by the sunbeams filtering through the water, but the one that captured his attention was the deep green one. That was the one.

Tak approached, hesitantly kneeling before it. Doubt flooded his mind, making him hesitate. For a long minute, he couldn't get those thoughts to leave, but all at once, the faces of his friends surfaced in his mind. They were waiting for him up there, and they believed in him. They trusted him.

So, slowly, Tak reached out and closed his hands around the gem. A bright light pulsed in front of his eyes and a warmth settled in his chest. When the gem's radiance faded, he glanced down. It hung around his neck like Redrinna's, pulsing with a quiet, clean glow. It was warmer than he'd expected, and it felt like he'd arrived home after a long time away.

Yeah, Tak was pretty sure this was where he belonged.

Unable to stop smiling, he got to his feet and the spirit lifted him from the cave. With a dip of its head, it left, and in what seemed like mere moments, his head broke the surface of the water close to the shore.

Redrinna watched him nervously as he climbed out of the water, completely soaked. Her eyes flicked to his gem, and when she saw it, an enormous grin appeared on her cheeks, lighting up her entire face.

He was grinning so much, his cheeks ached.

"Well, now that it's official," Astra said, trotting up to him, "shall we go to our new home?"

Tak blinked at her in confusion before it dawned on him it was a new home for her, and while he'd been there before, this would be his first time going to the Mount as a member of the Dragon Kin. In a way, it was a new home for him too.

A few minutes later, they took off, flying high. Tak closed his eyes against the wind, still reeling over the light warmth emanating from his gem. It was surreal, but he figured he'd adjust soon. There was still a lot for them to do, after all.

Astra trailed after Xandrin, following his every movement closely, and before long, the familiar peak of the Mount came into sight. It was strange that despite what it housed inside, it appeared completely ordinary from the outside, and in truth, Tak wasn't sure how he knew it was the Mount. He'd sincerely questioned Xandrin and Redrinna's sanities when they'd first brought him here, but fortunately, everything had turned out well for him. At the time though, he hadn't been in the best state of mind, so he supposed he could cut himself some slack.

They landed on the Mount's ledge, though Astra had to stand back to avoid knocking either herself or Xandrin off. The enormous red dragon pried the doors open, and a minute later they were back inside the familiar coolness of the Mount. Soft orange light shone all around, making the bare stone glow faintly.

It was good to be back. It didn't occur to Tak until right then just how much he'd missed being here.

"Well, you all certainly took your sweet time." Timothon's voice cut into his thoughts.

He turned towards the entrance of the main hallway, a rush of excitement bursting through him at the sight of the red-haired man. It felt like it'd been ages since Tak had seen him, and all at once, he felt at home.

Redrinna slowly climbed off Xandrin's back, putting her hand to her head for a moment before turning to him and saying, "Well, a lot of stuff happened."

"Tell me something I hadn't figured out," her uncle replied, a bit of a smile tugging on his mouth. "Oh? Who do we have here?" He crouched as Kyvo hopped off Xandrin's back and padded over.

"I'm Kyvo!" the kitsune burst out, his tail wagging quite hard. "Redrinna's my friend, and since I was lonely, she let me go with her. So now I'm here."

Timothon nodded, one eyebrow lifting. "You're a long way from home, aren't you?"

"I don't know where that is, so maybe?"

"Ah," Timothon's eyes widened. Then he smiled. "Well, welcome to the Mount." He got back on his feet, his gaze flicking to

Astra, who introduced herself. Then he glanced at Tak, smiling a little more when he did.

Tak couldn't help smiling back.

"Well, I imagine you all need some rest and such, but I expect a full summary of what happened while you were gone," Timothon said. "In the meantime, I guess I'd better make some food." He turned and went up the hall.

Redrinna put her hands on her hips as he walked away. "I guess we're going to have to find a room for you on our own, Astra."

"That shouldn't be too hard," Xandrin said, turning towards the hallway with all the rooms. "Just go up the hallway and pick one, but you can't have the first one because it's mine."

Astra sniffed. "Don't tempt me, red beast. In fact, I think I'll go check it out." She turned and trotted up the hall with Xandrin fuming on her tail.

Once they were out of earshot, Redrinna said, "Does anybody know why she calls him that?"

"Oh yeah, I guess you guys weren't there," Kyvo said, sitting on the ground. "Apparently it's because that one time they went hunting together, they both went after the same deer and crashed into each other or something. So she calls him 'red beast' now."

Tak frowned. That hadn't been the reason he'd expected, but there were worse things, he supposed. All he knew was that it was nice to be here. Compared to how he'd lived before, even crazy dragons were nice, and they made him feel even more at home.

❦❧

Stepping softly, Redrinna slowly made her way towards the kitchen, having to fight very hard not to run into the library and stay there for hours. As tempting as that was, there was something she needed to do first. It was good to be back here though; she couldn't deny that. While it was nice to have been able to see more of the world, it was even nicer to be back in a place where she wasn't considered royal, nor did she have to fight for her life. However, her mind returned to what the elder had said that morning, about how someday, she could become a leader he would respect.

His words almost made her want to reconsider her decision, but at the same time, Redrinna knew herself, and her not leading the Empire was for the best—not just for her, but for everyone. After all, she'd put her friends in serious danger more than once because of her careless and rash mistakes, and it was only because of them a true crisis had been averted.

There was no point in agonizing over it though. She couldn't change the mistakes she'd made in the past, and from now on, she didn't want to be so wrapped up in something behind her she lost sight of what was happening right in front of her or got so distracted by her own problems she failed to realize others were struggling too.

Shaking her head, Redrinna left those thoughts behind as she entered the kitchen. Timothon was standing near the oven, the red light of the flames flickering over his face as he stared into its depths. She expected him to realize she was there—since he seemed to have a weird knack for doing so—so she said nothing, but neither did he. He stared into the fire, seeming to be worlds away.

After a minute more, she stepped closer, moving to the other side of the table. He noticed her then, his gaze flicking her way.

"Hey," he said. "It's been a bit since you and I have been in here, huh?"

She dipped her head. It had, not only because they hadn't been here, but before, while Xandrin had been recovering, she'd avoided here, and she'd avoided him. At the time, she hadn't understood why, but now, Redrinna knew it was because her uncle had an unnerving knack for being able to ask the kind of questions that hurt and made her think about things she didn't like. So, instead, she'd hid. She hadn't wanted to feel those things, but her behavior had caused her to shut out more than just those emotions.

"What's up?" Timothon asked, shifting his weight onto one foot as he turned most of the way towards her.

What could she say? She'd originally come to apologize—something she was making an annoying habit of—but as she stood there in that small, cozy kitchen, she suddenly missed him. Her heart ached; she missed him so bad. Even though he was standing right in front of her, she just missed him. She'd avoided him, ignored him, and mistreated him. He hadn't deserved any of it.

As Redrinna met his gaze, her throat started burning. A startled look appeared on his face before her vision blurred and then she couldn't make him out anymore. She stepped forward, but suddenly he was there, wrapping his arms around her. He was warm, but even with her ear pressed against his chest, she couldn't hear a heartbeat. She didn't know why she'd expected one, but she had.

"What is this?" he asked in a hushed voice.

"I'm sorry," she managed to choke out. "Again."

He put a hand on her head, making her feel childish for a moment. "I'm not angry."

Nobody ever was, it seemed. That made her feel even more immature.

"Pain makes you absolutely crazy sometimes, doesn't it?"

She squeezed her eyes shut. "I miss them."

"I know."

"Does it ever get better?"

He was quiet for a minute. "Not really. Eventually, you figure out how to keep going, and time dulls your memories, so the pain fades, but sometimes, you see something or remember something that brings it all back."

She squeezed her eyes shut, trying to keep the tears at bay. "Do you ever miss your friends?"

"All the time. And while I'm devastated they're gone, the memories I have of them make it a little easier."

Maybe one day Redrinna would be able to see it like that, but for now, her hands clenched at his shirt as the tears flowed freely.

Timothon held her the entire time. Eventually the tears stopped, and swiping at her face, she stepped back.

"Better?" he asked with a ghost of a smile.

She shrugged one shoulder, which made him smile even more. "Can I ask you a favor?"

"Sure, provided it's within reason."

That almost got her to smile. "Will you teach me how to cook?"

"How to cook?" His eyebrows shot up, making him look genuinely surprised. "Why do you want to learn that?"

"Because I don't know how," she said immediately. Then she remembered Chumani's herb-gathering hobby. "And I thought it might help me...with this stuff. Plus, it'd be handy, you know?"

Timothon nodded once, slowly. "It would be useful to know how to cook, it's true." He frowned like he was thinking hard, but then she spied a smile tugging at the corners of his mouth. "All right. Why don't you help me make food for everyone starting now?"

She beamed.

Then he paused. "Just as a side thought, what are you all going to do next?"

"Well, we can't leave here yet. Tak and I both got hit in the head while we were out, and a friend we met out there made us swear to stay here and rest until we were better, so we'll be here for a while longer. But we'll have to continue on eventually."

"Okay." Then a genuine smile lit up Timothon's face. "Anyway, shall we get cooking? You won't want to wear your gauntlets for this."

She nodded, taking them off. However, Redrinna found herself grinning, before they'd even gotten started. This time she got to spend with Timothon wouldn't last forever; she knew that. When they had to part ways, that would ache too, but even still, she wanted to enjoy the time they had together, and she wanted memories of him she could hold on to for the rest of her life.

Chapter Twenty-Nine

Tak distracted himself from his hunger by watching Kyvo attempting to pounce on Xandrin and Astra's tails. He was glad the kitsune had energy. After all the traveling they'd done, he was ready to go straight to bed, but Timothon had insisted they all had to eat something before he would let them hit the hay.

As Redrinna came in with a plate full of roughly chopped, sautéed vegetables, Tak glanced her way. Timothon came on her heels with bread, the smell enveloping the room, making him feel even more at home.

Redrinna set the plate down, pursing her lips as she stared at it.

Timothon glanced at her before staring at the plate too. "It looks amazing considering it was your first try."

Kyvo vaulted onto the table, making both of them jump. "Redrinna made these?" With a delicate bite, he nicked a carrot from the plate. His ears shot up. "That was good."

He lunged for another, but Timothon scooped him up with a stern look on his face. The kitsune laid his ears back and grinned.

Astra studied the food from above Tak's head. "So this is what we eat here?"

"Sometimes," Redrinna said.

They tucked into the food, the group falling silent as they ate.

Timothon watched them with a little smile on his face, something about it making a gloom settle in Tak's chest.

The vegetables were delicious, the lightness of the seasoning bringing out the natural flavor in the food. Some of the pieces were a bit too hard or too soft, but Tak didn't complain. Between it and the bread, it was some of the best food he'd ever had.

When they were beginning to slow down (except Kyvo. He was still going strong), Timothon leaned forward.

"So how did it go out there?"

The others filled the man in on what had happened, and Timothon nodded several times while he took it in.

"So Mato was one of the other members of the Dragon Kin with you?" Tak asked, tearing his attention away from the remains of dinner, trying to convince himself that while it had been good, he didn't have any more room.

Timothon nodded, a scowl on his face.

"What's with that face?" Astra asked.

"I'm mad at him," the man explained. "The jerk. Pulls a whole noble act of staying behind so the rest of us could get away, and then he dies." He huffed.

Tak almost wanted to laugh, but there was a pain in Timothon's eyes preventing him from doing so. Even though the man smiled, there was an emptiness to it.

Xandrin stared at the man for a minute before he said, "We found something while we were out."

With a surprised look, Redrinna glanced at him.

Then Tak remembered. "The blood circle."

Redrinna's eyes widened. "Right. You remember how we told you about that blood circle we found in the Imperial City?"

"I remember," Timothon said with a hint of a frown.

"We found another one just like it in a cave."

"That seems kind of random," Astra said, one eyebrow raised.

"Another one?" Timothon frowned.

"You don't know what they're for?" Astra asked, eyes wide.

He shook his head. "Osiris didn't use anything like them before, so I don't know why either one of them exists. It worries me though."

Tak dipped his head. Why did he get the feeling they might find more of these blood circles in the days ahead?

"Oh, we found something else out," Redrinna said, getting her uncle's attention. "Do you remember that experiment Tak and I were doing?"

Timothon nodded. "The questionable one?"

"Right," she said, a bit hesitant. "The people we met had some doctors with them, and since I got hurt, I was able to ask them about it."

That got Tak's attention. She hadn't mentioned asking Takota and Shappa about that.

"What did they say?"

"They said," she paused, lowering her gaze to the table, "they said it was very strange how quickly I got better. It shouldn't be possible."

"How quickly are we talking here?"

She held up her wrist, the one that had been broken. "Would you believe me if I told you that while we were gone, I broke my wrist?"

Timothon's brow furrowed as he stared at it.

"Yeah," Xandrin said. "There was a big cast on it and everything."

"And now it's perfectly fine." She eyed her wrist, almost as if she was suspicious of it.

"You know what it reminds me of?" Astra returned to hovering above Tak's head. "That dragon-killing lady."

"Reyna?" Tak glanced at her.

"Yeah, it's similar to how fast she heals when she's hurt."

Xandrin frowned, tapping his claws against the ground. "It kind of is, I guess."

"Just slower," Timothon murmured. "But I suppose that explains some things. Before, when you first discovered your magic, I thought it was a little odd how quickly you recovered, but this must be why."

"It's supposed to take longer than a day?" Redrinna's eyes went wide.

"It only took you a day?" Tak asked, leaning forward. "Recovering from my first time took me nearly an entire week in bed."

"Wait, really?"

"You have magic?" Timothon cut in.

Astra nodded enthusiastically. "Healing magic. He saved my life with it once."

Timothon blew through his lips. "Well, look at the lot of you." His gaze turned back to Redrinna. "I wonder what they did in order to make you the way you are."

Something about the way he said that made Tak pause. He supposed that was true. In order for Redrinna to be the way she was, that had to mean Osiris had done something to her when she was little, right? Or maybe he'd used her dad or Reyna to do something. After all, she'd been close to both of them most of her life.

"Why would they do something to you?" Xandrin asked, turning big doe eyes on Redrinna.

"If only we knew," Redrinna said, folding her arms on the table and resting her chin on top of them. Her apprehension didn't show on her face, but her fingers gripped her arms so tight, her knuckles were white.

Kyvo curled up next to her arms, resting his chin on top of her head. "We won't let him get you."

Slowly, Redrinna lifted her gaze towards him, but she kept her head still.

"Yeah," Astra said, nudging Xandrin hard enough it nearly knocked him over. "Red beast and I will make sure he can't lay a finger on you."

Xandrin glared at her, and she glared right back.

After a minute, Redrinna ducked out from beneath Kyvo's head and got to her feet. "I'm going to go think for a while," she announced before leaving the room.

"Well, that's new," Timothon said as he watched her go. "Normally she just leaves."

Tak couldn't shake the feeling she was going to go to the Hall of the Dragon Kin, and on a whim, he went too. He caught sight of her heading up the right tunnel and followed, managing to catch up as she reached the entrance of the room.

Surprise lingered in her eyes for a moment, but she seemed to accept it and let him follow her in.

Muted, multi-colored light shone around the statues, and it occurred to Tak that this was his first time here in the evening. He sought out the golden statue—the statue of Mato. He was one of the tallest statues, his golden wings tight to his back with his long, golden hair pulled back into a braid.

"You know," Redrinna said, sudden enough it startled him. "He kind of looks like Chatan."

"Chatan would probably like that."

She almost laughed, but it seemed a little strangled.

He glanced at her.

"Sorry. Even thinking about Osiris still—" She broke off, clenching her fist in front of her throat. "Sorry."

Shaking his head, Tak said, "It's okay. I've never met him, but he scares me too." A shudder shot down his spine. "M-maybe that's not the same though."

Even still, her hand relaxed and caught hold of her mom's necklace. "No, but it does make me feel a bit better. I mean, he's letting you live too, for some reason we don't know."

A chill raced across his skin. "Oh yeah, I forgot about that."

She shrugged in an apologetic way.

Tak glanced back at Mato's statue to distract himself. Osiris didn't want him specifically, at least he didn't think so. Unlike Redrinna, he didn't have any special healing abilities. "Why would he want the rest of us?"

"What do you mean?"

"I mean, you're the special one. He didn't want anyone but you, but Reyna didn't kill me on purpose once she knew I was joining the Dragon Kin."

Frowning, Redrinna stayed quiet for a minute. "I wonder...if it's because of the gems."

He laid a hand on his gem.

"Timothon said they were extremely powerful, but they lost most of their powers when the first Dragon Kin died. It doesn't make sense that if he didn't want the Dragon Kin around, he'd give us room to rebuild it. I'm not sure we as people are special enough to warrant his attention, but maybe it's not us he wants."

Lightning shot down Tak's spine as he got it. "He wants the gems for something, but without new people to bond to, they're powerless. He won't kill us because we're the fastest way to make sure he gets what he wants."

A grim expression settled on Redrinna's face. "I think that's exactly right. He wants the gems for something badly enough he's willing to risk giving us the opportunity to oppose him to get it. I always thought it was kind of weird the last Dragon Kin hid the gems away, but maybe they had a reason for believing they had to do that."

A chill seeped into his veins. Was Osiris really so confident in whatever he was planning he was willing to wait for the full power of the Dragon Kin to be restored? How were they supposed to fight against someone like that?

"Hey now," Redrinna said, putting her fists on her hips, the evening sunlight making her hair blaze like fire. "We're in this together, right?"

She caught Tak off guard, but only for a second. "You bet."

Even though it scared him like crazy, he wasn't going to turn tail and run. Not anymore.

⁂

Redrinna took a deep breath of the cold, crisp morning air as she stepped out of the Mount. The sky was clear, and the birds were already awake, twittering to one another.

"Don't be too long," Timothon called from behind her. "Breakfast isn't going to cook itself."

She waved over her shoulder before ascending the mountain to her old practice spot, her book under her arm. Perhaps today would be the day she executed the move, but she hadn't practiced for a while, so maybe it wouldn't. Either way, Redrinna was going to make sure she had a good practice session regardless of whether or not she was able to fully perform this move.

She opened her book to the correct pages and set it on the ground, placing small stones that weren't overly dirty on the pages to keep the wind from blowing them around. Then she removed her boots and made sure her hair was still securely tied back before stepping into the center of the barren space.

Do your best, her gem said.

She nodded before taking a deep breath and relaxing into the low, resting stance. Redrinna stayed there for a few moments, running through the series in her mind before carefully moving into the first step, not tugging on her magic.

She ran through the series a few times, not using her magic to make sure she still had them in her head, making corrections where she needed to.

All right. She took a deep breath after completing the series almost perfectly. It was time to try it with the magic.

Returning to the center of her practice ring, Redrinna hesitated before dropping into the resting stance yet again. Her thighs protested, but she did her best to hold the form. The earth's spirit pulsed beneath her feet, and she focused on it for a moment. When she was ready, she moved into the first stance, fire crackling to life between her hands. She moved to the next stance before shifting to the third, the fire blazing brighter and snarling with a different kind of intensity than usual around her as she moved. Then there was the fourth stance.

Finally, she prepared for the fifth stance. Reyna's face flashed in front of her eyes yet again, like it always had before, but Redrinna stepped into the final stance, thrusting her fist forward.

A stream of fire shot out in front of her with a loud roar, the heat almost making her wince.

She blinked, staring at the wisps of smoke drifting through the air for a long minute before straightening.

You did it! You did it!

So she could do this after all. Redrinna allowed herself a small smile. "One more time," she said, turning back towards the center.

As she dropped into the resting stance again, Reyna's face still lingered in her mind. Redrinna closed her eyes, shaking her head until the image went away. She hated that after all the memories they'd had together, things had turned out like this. She loathed it. However, for the sake of the future, her friends, and herself, she had to stop holding onto the past and expecting the future to turn out different. She had to keep moving forward without looking back, otherwise they were going to lose.

Epilogue

Reyna pressed her palms against her forehead, scalp protesting as her fingernails dug into her flesh. Redrinna's face lurked in her mind like a reflection in water, always there no matter how much she tried to break up the image. Her pale face going ghostly white in fear. Her smiling face as she talked with those beasts. That light she got in her eyes when she spoke with that glaringly colored reptile.

"Get out of my head!" she snarled into the darkness, but to no avail. That innocent face lingered like a specter.

Reyna, Osiris's voice spoke in her mind. *I wish to speak with you.*

An exasperated sigh slipped out of her before she could stop it. Closing her eyes, she lowered her hands, trying to pick the pieces of herself up and stick them back together.

"Fine," she said. Adjusting the sash around her waist, she waited a minute longer before snapping her fingers. Writhing shadows appeared at her feet, swarming around her before sweeping her up. Seconds later, she arrived in the throne room, faint sunbeams striking the rafters above.

Osiris leaned back in his throne, studying her intently with those vivid blue eyes of his. He didn't say anything.

"What?" Reyna snapped, trying to find a spot to stare other than where he was.

"You acted against my orders. I understand it is annoying to alter our plans, but that does not mean we are sitting on our hands."

She huffed. "She's tripped us up twice. That's not a good thing."

Grinning, Osiris rested his chin in his hand. "You think her successes were accidents on our part?"

Her gaze flicked to him before she could stop it.

"How dull and brainless do you perceive me to be? My plans do not hinge on a set series of events. We attempted that before and look where we are now."

She scowled at the reminder.

"Do you not understand? While it would make me happiest for those feathered rats to be eliminated sooner rather than later, if we had remained in the village, so would she, which very likely might have frustrated our plans, and our struggles would amount to nothing. Therefore, she must be directed back onto the correct path. I will merely have to suffer those beasts for a while longer."

Redrinna's face popped into her mind again, that determined expression she'd had back in the village when she'd attacked Reyna. Even though the wound was gone, Reyna put a hand to the spot the brat had struck. It still burned but she couldn't figure out why. It was healed now. It had been for a while. So why did it still ache?

"That aside," Osiris continued, something different in his voice now. "Something plagues your mind, does it not?"

"I'm fine," she spat.

"No," he sat up straight, dropping his hand. "Redrinna afflicts you."

Wincing, she turned away from him. "I'm fine. I just lost my head for a bit."

"I did not realize she was so dear to you."

"She is not dear to me," she snapped, whirling back on him. Annoying tears burned her eyes, but she refused to let them fall. "I feel nothing for that rat! She means nothing to me!"

"I see."

Closing her eyes, Reyna wished she could take her outburst back.

"I will give you a different task for now, but..." He tilted his head to the side, studying her with his intense eyes. After a minute, he said, "Do you wish to forget?"

She blinked, her anger dissipating. "What?"

He extended a hand, palm up. "I can take away the memories haunting you. She will be eradicated, completely, if you wish it. You will not remember a single thing."

She stared at his hand, the pale skin seeming brighter in the faint bits of sunlight falling around him. Forget? Forgetting...would take these feelings away. She knew that. He'd done this for her once before, taken away something she didn't remember and now, no longer missed. If she could forget Redrinna, then all this frustration, this agitation that didn't ever seem to leave would finally be gone. She'd be able to focus on what truly mattered.

Yes. She wanted that.

Stepping forward, Reyna extended her hand, hesitating for a minute before lowering it into his waiting palm.

Don't miss the next book...

IGNITE

Book Three in the Rise of the Empress Series

Coming Soon

Thanks for Reading!

No, seriously. I mean that!

If you enjoyed this book, then I have a tiny request for you (I promise it's small. It'll take maybe five minutes of your time). You may not be able to tell, but I am an indie author (indie stands for independent). That means I published this book alone, without the help of a publishing house and the team that would go with that. I spent the money from my own pocket in order to put this book in your hands.

Since I chose not to enlist the services of a publishing house (there are several reasons why), then I need your help to keep making books like this one. How? Please, if you liked this book, leave a review wherever you purchased the book (or on Goodreads)! That's it. You don't even have to be on social media or anything like that, nor do you have to think of something to say. Even just giving it a star rating helps too! I know it's intimidating, but just answer this question: what did you like about it?

The point is, please just tell people about it. That helps me so much.

And, of course, if you liked it enough, buying the next book helps too. Once again, thank you! Enjoy some artwork as a treat.

Acknowledgements

In many ways, writing book two was a different struggle than writing book one. Not only does publishing and being published not get much easier after book one, but becoming a published author has ultimately been filled with both the highest of highs and the lowest of lows. The doubts and fears I had when publishing my first novel didn't go away, and I have accepted the reality that they probably never will.

Even still, I'm deeply grateful for the support of my family, friends, and readers who've given me so much encouragement and given my characters so much love. It really means the world to me. I'm also deeply grateful for everyone who helped me bring Chatan, Takota, Mika, Chumani, and all the others to life. Their tribe was inspired by the Lakota tribe in North America, and the two-faced demon came from their legends as well. That said, there were so many variations about the beast depending on who told it, I kind of did my own thing with it.

Thank you to Shaylee, my wonderful critique partner, and my lovely betas, Rachel and Emma. Thanks also goes to Janae for her insights. I'm so grateful for everyone who was willing to edit this book to help me make it the best thing it could be.

I would also be remiss if I failed to express my gratitude to God for helping me on this journey and with this book specifically. Book two was a completely separate beast, and publishing it honestly scares me more than publishing the first. But He was there for me and helped me find the resources and capacity to tell this story.

A huge thanks also goes to Lexi for her amazing work on the cover once again. I'm seriously blown away by how talented she is and how hard she works on every project.

And lastly, I give another round of endless thanks to my readers. Your support and kind words help me keep picking up the pen.

About the Author

C. S. Doraga is the author of the *Rise of the Empress* series. She grew up in the shadows of the Rocky Mountains with her nose stuck in any book within reach and imagination constantly running wild (to her parents' chagrin, at times). Her favorite author is the amazing Mangaka, Hiromu Arakawa, the author of *Fullmetal Alchemist* and *Silver Spoon*. What little free time she has, she spends playing the *Fire Emblem* video game series and a few, choice others. She has a deep love for the fantastic but also loves mystery and those characters that sit with you long after the story is over.

She has a bachelor's degree in creative writing from Weber State University and lives in beautiful Northern Utah with her family and two, crazy cats.

Socials:
Facebook
Goodreads
Instagram: @bookdragons.nest

www.ingramcontent.com/pod-product-compliance
Lightning Source LLC
Chambersburg PA
CBHW030109310726
48970CB00004B/1210